DREAMLAND

ALSO BY M. K. LORENS:

Deception Island
Ropedancer's Fall
Sweet Narcissus

DREAMLAND

M. K. Lorens

A Perfect Crime Book

DOUBLEDAY

NEW YORK   LONDON   TORONTO   SYDNEY   AUCKLAND

A PERFECT CRIME BOOK

PUBLISHED BY DOUBLEDAY

a division of Bantam Doubleday Dell Publishing Group, Inc.

666 Fifth Avenue, New York, New York 10103

DOUBLEDAY is a trademark of Doubleday, a division of
Bantam Doubleday Dell Publishing Group, Inc.

Grateful acknowledgment is made for permission to reprint an excerpt from
W. H. Auden: Collected Poems by W. H. Auden, edited by Edward Mendelson.
Copyright 1940 and renewed 1968 by W. H. Auden. Reprinted by permission of
Random House, Inc. and Faber and Faber Ltd.

BOOK DESIGN BY TASHA HALL

Library of Congress Cataloging-in-Publication Data

Lorens, M. K.
     Dreamland / by M. K. Lorens.
          p.   cm.
     "A Perfect Crime book."
     I. Title.
PS3562.O7525D74   1992
813'.54—dc20   91-43562
                                                        CIP

ISBN 0-385-42237-7
Copyright © 1992 by M. K. Lorens
All Rights Reserved
Printed in the United States of America
May 1992

1   3   5   7   9   10   8   6   4   2

FIRST EDITION

For Susan, who plays for keeps
and
For Edward, who bought the typewriter ribbons

And they said one to another, Behold, this dreamer
cometh.

Come now therefore, and let us slay him, and cast him
into some pit, and we will say, some evil beast hath
devoured him: we shall see what will become of his
dreams.

—Genesis 37: 19, 20

DREAMLAND

1

"Spring always brings out the suicides," the girl said, and laughed as she passed him.

Down Central Park West the sirens screamed. There was a teenage jumper on top of the El Dorado and a man with a gun to his head at the U.N. In the East Village a man with AIDS doused himself with gasoline and struck a match. On Staten Island an old woman dying of emphysema slit her wrists with a sterilized razor blade. In a SoHo loft, the vice president of a Wall Street brokerage, newly divorced, took too many sleeping pills and died of desire.

April is the cruelest month, he thought, drawing deep gulps of the cool, damp air. It tasted of carbon and smoke and the love of death.

Ahead of him the man he was following stopped, looked round to make sure his silent guardian was still watching. Then he turned, as usual, into Central Park.

David paused where the walk sloped toward the beds of rosemary and bergamot, letting the tall, stooped figure in the worn corduroy jacket stay well ahead of him. Those were the rules; they both knew them instinctively and obeyed them. No contact, no acknowledgement. This fictional invisibility was their only protection from one another, now that David had a name to put to the mechanical voice of the anonymous phone calls.

McKelvie. Gilbert McKelvie.

Today David Cromwell had followed him from Eighty-seventh and Amsterdam up to the Russian Orthodox Cathedral on Ninety-seventh Street, where McKelvie made his usual stop. He did not go inside. Nobody was waiting for him there, nobody seemed even vaguely aware of his presence except David, his watcher. McKelvie paused about five feet away and at a forty-five-degree angle from the front entrance and stood there in silence, letting the foot traffic swarm around him. It was, David would've said, a devotional visit, but it had nothing at all to do with the sullen, flat-faced Christs with old men's eyes whose icons hung inside.

This accomplished, McKelvie always turned onto Central Park West, striding all the way down to the Museum of Natural History. Then, at last, he would cross the charging traffic and enter the park itself, with David—as he was now—just far enough behind to keep the lean, rounded shoulders well in sight. Now McKelvie had taken the same curving path as usual into the Shakespeare Garden, where he would wander among the herbs and flowers for exactly ten minutes. David had timed him every morning for a week and it was always precisely ten, no more, no less. When they were over, McKelvie would select a bench at the corner of the lavender bed— always the same bench—check the watch on his left wrist, and begin his wait.

Often the woman who came each day to meet him was late, but today she arrived in less than five minutes, a frail, elegant figure in a belted raincoat of soft gray suede, a wide-brimmed garnet-colored cloche pulled low over thick black hair she wore in a single heavy braid, the way David's own sister, Sarah, wore hers. Other things about the woman reminded him of Sarah, small things, mostly indefinable—the purposeful tilt of the firm jaw, for instance, and the long, measured stride as she approached the bench and sat down beside McKelvie.

Are you the one? thought David, watching her. She sat with her proud head bent slightly, only half-turned toward McKelvie as she murmured a greeting.

Are you the one who is going to die?

She perched tentatively on the bench, her narrow feet in their expensive shoes poised on tiptoe, ready to run. The shoes, like the coat, were a pale gray suede. Even though it was almost the end of April, a chilly, windless mist had hung over the city for days and the nap of the woman's coat was damp across the shoulders and the caped back. But the suede shoes were soaked all the way up the sides and across the instep, the soles caked with mud and grass.

You came across the park, thought David. *You walked a long way, but not on the paths. You live in some white palace on Madison, Park, Fifth. Now I could follow you there, find out your secrets.*

Jenny, he called her. Of course it was not her name. He had not traced her as he had McKelvie, had no idea who she was. But the name drifted into his memory from somewhere and he invested her with it. Jenny.

She seemed almost grateful for the dampness, gulping deep breaths of it, exhaling in painful gasps. Had she run to get here? Was she running away or merely toward McKelvie? *Hardly,* thought David the watcher. *Hardly that.* These meetings of theirs were no love trysts. He could not conceive of her loving anyone.

Jenny carried no umbrella and her hands were broad and stubby, so different from her slim body that they might've been grafted on as an afterthought. They lay flat and useless upon her knees, the fingers spread slightly, bracing her. The short fingers were heavy with expensively set rings; David counted six of them, all amethysts.

You're afraid, he thought, watching her. *Afraid, but not of him, not of McKelvie. Yours is a fear like stage fright, a huge, dark, empty space you walk into alone and find you cannot breathe and cannot ever, ever leave.*

He had himself been caged for some time in such a space, trying to find his way out. He felt he understood the woman, that if they spoke they would know each other instantly and completely. He could give no reason for this belief; his rational mind would have told him it was absurd, no more than the actor in him creating a subtext. But reason was hardly what had led him here, watching as McKelvie, he was certain, watched him, expected him each day.

I love you, he thought suddenly. The idea shocked and excited him. He had had no intention of becoming emotionally involved with her, quite the opposite. But McKelvie, too, had come to matter terribly to him, a long stick of a man, brittle as charcoal, thin and balding, effacing himself with a constant hunch of the shoulders as if he would like the ground to swallow him.

God damn you, thought David, abruptly furious with the pair of them. But he knew they were only partly to blame. The anonymous phone calls had baited a hook, but he had snapped at it, hungry for involvement. He had needed to be used, and now he had broken again the first law of self-preservation: THOU SHALT NOT GIVE A DAMN. He was risking real damage, he knew that, more than merely the distrust of whatever currently found itself in power and liked its subjects passionless and dispensable as mechanical toys. There were other, subtler costs, exacted of memory and imagination. When you presumed upon the delicate membrane separating your life from another, the private losses mounted up. But what was the alternative? A crustacean universe, dying safely in its shell.

When did I begin to love you? he thought, the pulse pounding in his ears. *Which one of you is going to die?*

He had not felt so alive in months.

The woman he thought of as Jenny was talking. David was still too far away to hear the words, but he had an actor's ear for inflections, and the sharp rises and falls of her voice told him she was angry this morning. On her lap the stubby hands clenched and unclenched to some inner rhythm, drawing McKelvie along by the sheer force of her will. He could see little of her face under the hat brim except the thin, tightly set line of her mouth. Whatever brought her here each day, it had reached a climax. There was a new urgency about Jenny; she suddenly grasped McKelvie's hand. David had never seen her touch him before, and the spontaneity of the gesture surprised and pleased him. Until now she had done nothing on impulse, each movement a careful choreography of intent.

You are more than you seem, he thought. *Braver, more reckless. You are not afraid of falling.*

But as soon as she had touched McKelvie, Jenny seemed to regret it. She stood up, swayed a little on her sodden high-heeled shoes, then sat down again, rummaging in her purse. She handed McKelvie a stapled sheaf of cheap yellow pages which she riffled through, looking for something. When she had found it, she folded a page back and, taking a pen from her bag, circled something on it, speaking insistently. Her words became abruptly audible, and David stepped closer.

"It's too late for that," she said. The voice was shrill and commanding. "It was too late long ago. But if you mean what you say, you have to do it now. You understand?"

McKelvie did not answer. He merely sat staring at the flower beds, his thin shoulders slumped. David strode calmly past and settled himself on a bench at the end of the path, pretending to read the morning *Times*.

Although he had become more involved than he at first intended, he had not abandoned all caution. Until this morning he had been careful to stay at a safe distance from them, but not just because of the unspoken rules of his silent game with McKelvie. His face was, after all, famous enough to have attracted a slasher who laid it open to the bone one rainy autumn night a few years back. Obscure destinies attached themselves to him, deceived by the roles he sometimes played on TV and the stage; inevitably they were disappointed to find him no larger than life and no more immune than they to its indignities. Some turned nasty and dangerous, and those he was proof against.

But some clung to their fictions too long and were destroyed, or destroyed themselves. Often they sent him photographs that tumbled from letters labored out by hand on childish wide-lined paper, addressing him always by his first name, as friend and equal: *"Dear David. This is me. You won't laugh, will you?"* He could name them all and call up their faces. The letters came from Des Moines, from Memphis, Albuquerque, Winnipeg, Omaha, beginning after a splash of publicity during some acting project, usually on TV.

And he would answer. He always answered.

With the faintest encouragement, the letters continued, chronicled the dissolution of marriages, careers, the vain hope of escape to some promised land. *"Do you think, if I came to New York—"* they would say, and drift off again into chatter. They wanted to be actors, writers, singers, dancers, designers of costumes, sets. It did not matter how remote their ambitions might be from his own small realm. He had fame, and fame could work all miracles, resolve all doubts. *"Do you think, if I got the right agent—"* the refrain went on. *"Do you think, if I bought a computer, hired a publicist, made the right contacts, joined the right clubs—"*

Help me to be famous, to be rich, to be perfect. The words ran through his mind like the lyrics of a song. *Show me where they hide the keys to dreamland.*

Just before Christmas, an envelope came in the box office mail at the Booth Theatre, where David was then playing T. Lawrence Shannon in Williams's *Night of the Iguana*. There was no letter inside, just a clipping from the Rapid City, South Dakota *Register*. Services, it said, were pending for Mrs. Vernelle Maguire, thirty-eight, found dead in her closed and locked garage on Rosebud Street, the engine of her ten-year-old Toyota still running.

"If I left him," she had written, *"if I locked the door and just took off and came to New York, do you think I could make it? Do you think I might have a chance?"*

Knowing there was none, David had refused to feed her delusion. This once, he had not answered.

That summer he had been forced by circumstance to witness the killing of his own mother, many years estranged from him. But it was only after the suicide of Vernelle Maguire that the dead began to travel constantly with David Cromwell. Looking up from his *Times* on the crosstown bus, he saw them coming toward him down the aisle. In restaurants, they occupied tables by the door, waiting. His mother, Maureen, was joined by others in whose fates he had been involved—Ben Timmons, the slasher, his own wrists slit in a Bellevue prison ward; Sonny Emerson, smashed in the rush of New York traffic; old Luther Morley; Richard Brant; John Falkner.

Though he had barely known some of them, he had participated in their destruction. Something, he felt, should have been done to save them. A monstrous unpayable debt was owed. He had had too much loss; he wanted desperately to care for nothing at all.

But it couldn't be done. He had become personally responsible for the universal dirty trick.

He tried to absorb his doubts in work, as he had always been able to do in the past; but it was no use. He grew more and more restless. On stage each night he dropped simple props, fluffed lines, missed cues; his professional poise had deserted him entirely, but this was ascribed by the critics to the nature of the burnt-out soul he played. He was nominated for a Tony Award, was almost certain to win. This absurd reward disgusted him. Couldn't they see he had become a fraud? He was leaving more important things, he knew, undone, though he couldn't have said what they were. For the first time in his career, he asked to be replaced and left the show before it closed.

That had been eleven weeks ago. He did no work, read no new scripts. At home he paced nervously back and forth from window to window, shut himself in his bedroom all day with his books, waiting. When his sister phoned, or family holidays demanded his presence, he turned in a nearly flawless performance.

But the practical realities of living irritated David out of all proportion, and even his little daughter, Gemma, in whom he had always delighted, got on his nerves. He snapped at her, exploded at his wife, Alex, and stalked out of their apartment, taking long walks through ruinous neighborhoods where boys lounged in gangs on the doorsteps, watching him with cocky, mistrustful squints. They formed up teams, dodging the traffic, and threw forward passes with the bulging trash bags at the curb until the bags split open, spilling soiled Kotex and soggy Pampers onto the cracked concrete steps.

The boys would laugh, then, and crouch against the parked cars smoking crack all night, pitch pennies up and down the steps, make love sometimes among the garbage they had spilt, piss where they felt like it, take what they wanted from anyone who passed. Other people were ordinary, but they were not. They generated and consumed themselves, eternal as phoenixes in their invisible cage. With lithe, energized limbs they jived to their secret dance, long-fingered hands beating out a rhythm on the hoods of cars.

Give us, it pounded in David's ears. *Give us the answer without the test. Give us everything, and right away. You're stupid and dead, and we're alive. Give us the keys to dreamland.*

The morning after one such night, David went to see his doctor. Elevated temperature, slightly rapid pulse, blood pressure a bit too high, but nothing to worry about. The doctor mumbled something about a midlife crisis, lectured him about overwork, and prescribed the latest trendy tranquilizer. On his way through the lobby, David went into the john and flushed the pills out to sea. They were not the answer. He could only wait, gaunt and desolate, for the path of escape, watched by the expectant dead.

And then the calls began.

"Someone is going to die," the voice said. Then came a silence. In the background, a monotonous yet rhythmic humming sound, like some life-support machine that dare not be shut off. Then the voice again. The words came relentlessly, slowly, as if they were being read from a script.

"Someone is going to die. You can stop it."

Then a click as the connection was broken.

That had been two months ago, in February. The calls had come regularly ever since, always late at night and growing gradually more and more frequent. David raced to beat Alexandra to the phone, knowing what he would hear.

"David? Is David there?"

"Who are you?" he would whisper. "What do you want from me?"

"Someone is going to die."

"Where are you? Let me meet you, so we can talk."

"Someone is going to die. You can stop it."

No threats were ever made. There was only the tantalizing promise that offered an end to his long self-accusation:

"You can stop it."

Often he tried to question the caller: Did he know him, was he in trouble, why didn't he call the police? But it was no use. The decisive click came always too soon. There were no clues except the unequivocal statement, the pulsing hum in the background, and the soft, monotonous voice.

But David was determined. He had a lot of friends, and one of them had worked as a telephone lineman between acting jobs. It was only marginally illegal for him to fiddle the phone line in David's flat and trace the source of the anonymous calls. They came from a second-floor apartment in a run-down brownstone on Eighty-seventh Street, just off Amsterdam. David had gone there, waited outside, watched. He was good at it; he had learned from an expert —the spy Zachary Pasco, whose private exile he now felt he understood. At last he had the caller's name.

McKelvie. Gilbert McKelvie.

Across the Shakespeare Garden, the woman in the gray suede raincoat stood up and took a few uncertain steps away from the bench on which McKelvie sat. Then she pulled off the deep red cloche and turned her face to the damp April wind. Her black hair was matted to her forehead with perspiration and her face was flushed under her makeup—a bit too much rouge for a woman her age.

She must, thought David, *be almost sixty.* The realization stunned him for a moment. He had never seen her without the hat before, and her bearing had given him no clue. The slim, high-breasted body was proud and sensual, aware of its own attractions, able to emphasize them subtly. The bones of the face were small and regular, the eyes veiled by heavy false lashes and mascara. The black hair—obviously dyed—was braided as usual, but wound today into a Byzantine maze of braids and knots at the back of her head, a pair of heavy gold earrings set with amethysts dangling against her neck.

A commanding woman, he thought, *but broken. Broken deep like a ship on hidden ice. Jenny.*

She drew a deep breath of the mist, and as she breathed out again a slight sound came from her, animal, deep in the throat.

"I owe her the last move," she said aloud. *"You* owe her."

The proud posture slumped a little, the back curved, the ringed hands clutched the belt of the raincoat. Then she straightened once more, put on the hat, and sat down again on the bench, speaking in an undertone, half to herself.

Through all this, Gilbert McKelvie sat with knees apart, hands gripping the seat of the bench, head bowed and shoulders hunched, like a man sitting out a storm. He was in his late forties, thin and more than six feet tall, clean shaven, with graying brown hair cut raggedly just below his ears. It fell over the worn collar of his brown corduroy jacket in back, and receded from his already high forehead above pouchy gray eyes that darted relentlessly round and round the carefully laid out flower beds. The face was not handsome, though well-modeled; the features were drawn too tight, with a faint flush of broken blood vessels across the wide cheekbones and a glaze of myopia in the eyes.

A patient man, thought David, *used to waiting. Used to being used.*

Just then McKelvie looked up. His eyes met David's for a split second, then looked away again. Certainly he had recognized the face that appeared in every *Times* ad for *Night of the Iguana,* that popped up on TV reruns and talk shows. Certainly he had known all along the face of the man he telephoned to issue his oracle: *"Someone is going to die. You can stop it. You."*

But if he did, McKelvie gave no indication. He stuck to the rules. Instead he turned to the woman beside him, who had unclasped her handbag again. He shook his head as if to clear it of the invasive mist, took the piece of yellow paper she had given him, and crumpled it up. He let it fall to the wet ground, then with characteristic fastidiousness picked it up and shoved it into his pocket, still crumpled.

"I'm sorry," he said simply. "I wasn't any use to her. I'm none to you, either."

And then the woman took the gun from her bag.

It was a tiny weapon, so small it might've been a perverse play-house toy. Such miniatures were in vogue today, when nearly a third of the population of Manhattan carried guns, legal or illegal, in self-defense. They were lightweight, popular with women. Jenny handled the gun as though she were used to it.

But she did not point it at McKelvie. Instead, she took his right hand and pried the clenched fingers open, laying the grip of the gun into them and locking the fingers tight again. McKelvie seemed unconscious of its weight in his hand. He sat pointing it at her as though she had posed him for an incriminating photograph. She got up, began to walk away. Then she changed her mind, turned quickly back to where he sat, put both hands on his shoulders, and bent to kiss his forehead.

When she had gone, McKelvie stared down for a moment at the gun. He made no move to leave, merely shoved the tiny weapon into the same pocket of his jacket as the crumpled yellow paper. Jenny's figure had almost disappeared down the path toward Seventy-ninth Street.

David had to decide quickly, before she was gone. Until today he had always stuck with McKelvie, his anonymous oracle, followed him back to his brownstone uptown or down to some publisher's or agent's office where McKelvie picked up the slush pile manuscripts he read free-lance. But today it was Jenny he was interested in, Jenny who had brought the gun, the mysterious yellow paper. She was almost out of sight when he decided to desert McKelvie and follow her.

He could not have said how many seconds, minutes, it was before he heard the shot. At first he thought it was a backfire from the traffic racing through the park. It was Jenny who told him. She was no more than a hundred yards ahead of him, moving with her usual confident stride, when the shot echoed from the trees, trapped and amplified by the mist. David saw her stop suddenly, hesitate. She turned to look back along the path and saw him following, and her face beneath the mask of makeup was afraid.

David spun round on the wet blacktop of the path and ran back through the thickening drizzle to the Shakespeare Garden.

Gilbert McKelvie was still alone in his corner of the lavender bed. He sat there on the familiar bench, his long body folded almost double, the balding head dangling between the knees, the thin arms limp. The tiny gun lay on the wet grass next to the left shoe, the fingers of the left hand almost touching the butt. Only a little blood stained the tan corduroy trouser leg, and between McKelvie's feet lay the scrunched-up yellow paper.

David knelt on the ground in front of the flaccid figure, put his hands under the shoulders and leaned them squarely against the bench, the head thrown back, mouth gaping open. There was a small, precise hole in the middle of the forehead that might've been drilled in, so little damage had it done. The bullet must have lodged itself in the bone of the skull; there was no exit wound at the back of the head, and very little blood. McKelvie had died instantly.

David got to his feet and stood for a moment, uncertain. He did not pick up the crumpled yellow paper between the dead man's shoes and see that the name circled in marking pen was that of his own foster father and best friend, Yours Truly, Winston Marlowe Sherman, Ph.D. Neither of us knew that I would soon be floundering in the same tangled nightmare into which he had already stumbled. At that moment, David had only one obligation.

He took McKelvie's body in his arms and grieved for all his dead.

2

"What's that in your pocket, Merriman? Looks like a telegram, except they're probably extinct, like honest-to-God record albums and cars I still fit into. It *is* a telegram, isn't it?"

I paused, hoping he'd come clean. But he just sat there looking pale and interesting and gazed out the window of my bedroom. My old friend Eddie was still convalescing from his latest bout with pneumonia, too weak to do anything more strenuous than driving me nuts. I stepped up the pressure, hoping to goad him into shape.

"It's a telegram, all right. I knew I heard you muttering to somebody down in the front hall a while ago. Who's it from?"

Eddie shoved the flimsy blue paper deeper into the recesses of his costume. "If you've been hearing celestial voices, Winnie, perhaps it was my Uncle Horace. According to this cablegram, the old boy's finally turned in his dinner pail and left me the ancestral home, a title and assorted pounds sterling," he said with a grin. "But I am not to be led astray by side issues. Sarah ordered me to stand guard over you, and stand guard I shall. Now, then, Winnie. Pull up your pants."

"Ancestral home, my Nellie! You're enjoying this, blast you!"

I scowled at the gleam in his baby blues and tried for the fifteenth time to conquer the zipper in my fancy dress pants. Merriman curled himself on the window seat, considering me like a pussycat sizing up an overweight canary.

"Of course, Winston, the invitation does read 'dress to kill,' " he said at last. "But if I were you, I'd seriously consider wearing a kilt to the Teddy Bears' Picnic tonight."

"Merriman," I growled as the zipper pull came off in my hand, "I've never biffed a man in your delicate condition, but there's always a first time. This is no laughing matter!"

Well, I mean to say, there I was, scantily clad in a pair of elderly jockey shorts, size 3X, my favorite soup-stained undershirt and my native charm! My trusty old evening duds, made to order for me back in 1961, had unaccountably shrunk to fit a peewee two sizes smaller than me, and possessing, as I do, a silhouette along the lines of Charles Laughton, I could hardly pop over to Mr. Tux and grab something off the rack, now could I? In two hours we had to catch a train for Manhattan, check into our favorite unfashionable hotel, and prepare to be fascinating.

For as Merriman delighted in reminding me, tonight was the night the teddy bears had their picnic.

It was spring, you see, and in every ballroom in New York somebody in a monkey suit was handing out prizes. Teddy bears of all sorts—screenwriters, actors, playwrights, journalists, tinkers, tailors, soldiers, and, for all I knew, beggarmen and thieves—were holding mutual admiration societies all over town, fingernails clean, sequins polished, hats on the sides of their heads. The Edgar Awards, for which I'd trotted out my own soup-and-fish, is the annual Walpurgisnacht when mystery writers of all species gather to get in a bit of elbow-rubbing and convince themselves that the editors who barely had time for them last year haven't *really* been replaced by computers after all.

The Edgar is the Oscar, the Emmy, the Tony of the mystery novel, and its yearly dinner is one rubber-chicken extravaganza I usually avoid the way Job avoided boils. But this year, for one reason and another, I'd sworn to grit my teeth and go. The bash was being held that April Thursday night in the Versailles Ballroom of the Hornsby Empire Hotel on Park Avenue. Yours Truly, Winston Marlowe Sherman, Ph.D., alias Henrietta Slocum, Dowager Empress of Detection, had been nominated for the tenth year in a row. And for the first time it really bothered me that I didn't have a snowball's chance in hell of winning.

"Why can't I just send my editor, like I always do?" I growled, tugging at my zipper. "I mean, it's not as though I'm actually going to *get* that Edgar. Do I serve on executive committees? Do I volunteer to dun the membership for delinquent dues? Do I do penance on panels entitled 'How to Write with Your Socks On'? Do I mail out postcards with my latest book cover on them? Do I lurk in doorways handing out bookmarks bearing an airbrushed glossy of Yours Truly at the age of twelve? Self-promotion and literary politics are Jenny Vail's territory, not mine; she's spent twenty-five years repelling invaders. I ought to know. They've nominated me for Best Novel nine years running, and for nine years they've handed *her* those cheesy little statues of Edgar Allan Poe instead." I sighed and yanked at my pants again. "What has Imogen Montague Vail got that I haven't got, anyway?"

"Nine cheesy little statues of Edgar Allan Poe," said Merriman brightly. "And you can't send your new editor because you haven't met her yet. Now then. Take a nice deep breath, and hold it."

"What business has Cliff Munsen got retiring, confound him? When *I* was a lad of sixty-two, retirement was the farthest thing from my mind. Still is, damn it," I gasped, as Eddie got my zipper within an inch of the top.

"Your beloved editor did not retire, Winnie," he reminded me. "He *was* retired, as you very well know."

He let go of the zipper and stood back. Slowly, like a car in neutral rolling down a steep hill, the blessed thing traveled head-long down my central slopes, taking my dress pants with it.

I sank onto the edge of the bed with a groan. "What's the use, anyway? I don't think the Brave New World of publishing fits me any better than these old pants do. Authors hanging out at fan conventions like a bunch of racetrack touts, standing by the book-store racks like carnival barkers. 'Roll up, roll up, three shies for a nickel, you can win that Kewpie doll!' And look at the other side. Forced retirements. Leveraged buy-outs. Poor old Clifford out to pasture after all these years, and Garner and Sloan bought out by that high-handed pirate of a Dutchman. If he weren't paying for my Edgars ticket, I'd damn well stay home, and a pox on Willem Van Twit."

"Willem Van Twist," said a voice. "And put on your pants."

Sarah Cromwell, love of my life with whom I have shared the joys of un-marriage for more than thirty years, stood glaring at me from the bedroom doorway. Her long dark hair, delicately veiled with gray round the temples, fell loose nearly to the waist; she had on a long cotton robe the color of bronze chrysanthemums and the same look she gets when she catches me munching crackers and liverwurst in bed. Storm warnings seemed to be out for the immediate area, and it was no time to get cocky. I sighed and stood up to face the music.

Then, suddenly, the phone out in the hallway began to ring and I made for the door, figuring I was saved by the bell.

"Don't you dare set foot out of this room!" Sarah dug in her heels and blocked the doorway.

"But it might be David, you know he always calls me before Edgars night!"

Sarah's kid brother, whom we raised from a pup, had us both worried. Lately his phone calls were few and far between, and at the family Easter egg hunt in our backyard a month before, his efforts at sociability had been just that—efforts. Even over our usual late-night Scotch he hadn't dropped the mask of placid good manners he used to keep intruders at bay.

But I was no intruder, damn it! I was the sucker who taught him how to roller-skate when he was six, and the result of my demonstration still smarts in rainy weather! How could he have shut me out? I was hurt, but worse than that, I was feeling guilty. My recent excursions into real-life crime had cost him a lot, maybe too much. David seemed to have had enough of me and my passion for the human puzzle, and I suppose I really couldn't blame him. But it didn't stop me waiting for the phone to ring.

"I'm sure that's Davy," I insisted.

Sarah hesitated, then shook her head. "If it's him," she said, "he'll call again. Anyway, it's probably only Tommy, pestering you about that damn Professor of the Year Award again."

Thomas Van Doren Sheffield, Dean of Arts and Letters at Clinton College, master of the computerized, multiple-choice final exam, was out to corner the award, and I was determined to scuttle him. But he was the last person I wanted to talk to right now, and the phone's frenzied ringing did have that peculiar quality of executive hysteria Sheffield exudes like musk, even over the wire.

Reluctantly I convinced myself Sarah was right. I obeyed orders and didn't answer it—a mistake that landed me in the soup up to my withers before the night was done.

The phone rang four times, five, and Merriman was just getting up to answer it himself, when it stopped.

"Now," said Sarah, with a sigh of exasperation. "Does that ridiculous old suit fit, or doesn't it?"

"Must be something wrong with the zipper," I grumbled. "Look at the jacket. Fits me like a glove."

I struggled into the dinner jacket. The sleeves seemed tighter than usual, but I was heated from the chase. I stuck to the lining a bit, but finally managed to worm my way into the thing and button it.

"Stop holding your breath," commanded Sarah.

Just then, as if it, too, had only been holding its breath, the phone began to ring again. Surprised, I exhaled with a hiss like air from the leaky back tire of my old bike. There was a tearing sound, followed by the machine-gun rattle of every button on my dinner jacket popping off and raining down on the bricks in front of the bedroom fireplace.

"Perhaps a sarong?" suggested Merriman, and I could hear him cackling as he trotted off down the hall to answer the phone.

As Eddie left the room, I could've sworn I heard a car door slam at the back of the house, muffled just a bit by the roof of the portico that spans our drive, once a carriage entrance. I made my way to the window and peered out, but there wasn't a sign of a car. It had been a heavy sound, slightly different than a normal car door—a grating, sliding noise and then the catching of a latch. But I chalked it up as a pre-Edgars hallucination and trudged back to the bed to sit beside Sarah.

"I know when I'm licked," I told her, staring at those buttons on the floor. "I'm not going. They can have Manhattan, the Bronx, and Staten Island, too. I'm staying right here in Ainsley and grading that stack of miserable Mystery Fiction term papers."

"Win," she said, "I know how you feel. Really I do. But you've got to at least meet this new woman who's taken over Cliff's job. Sally, Stephanie, Stacy—"

"Tracy," I said, grinding my teeth. "Tracy Valentine. Sounds like a Bobbsey twin."

"I don't care if she's Andy Hardy, you've got to meet her! Charm her a little."

"Snakes, yes. Birds out of the trees, possibly. But I refuse to charm editors. Especially twenty-five-year-old tootsie editors imposed on me by the Flying Dutchman. Anyway, I hate charm. Gives me gas."

"Oh, hush. You're an old curmudgeon, but you do cut a figure in evening clothes that *fit*. The child may be susceptible. I was. Just try, Win, maybe it'll help. Thanks to those damn multiple-book contracts, it's been over three years since your last real advance, and you haven't seen a royalty statement in months, let alone a check. We simply must have a new furnace in this old barn before next winter. Those rooms of Eddie's are like Alaska when there's an east wind, and I won't be responsible for his getting pneumonia again."

It had, indeed, been a tough winter on good old Eddie, who rents the disused servants' wing off our kitchen. The damp chill of the Hudson Valley seemed to creep into his bones, and he'd been in and out of the respiratory ward of Ainsley Memorial twice since December. I hadn't much liked seeing the old blister with an oxygen tube up his nose, and I certainly didn't want another winter like the last.

On that score, too, I was feeling guilty. Why hadn't I chosen at least *one* reasonable, lucrative profession, like dermatology or plumbing? The two I had were like riding a seesaw. When I made money at writing, I lost it at teaching. Sheffield was determined to force me to retire this year, and since taking away my beloved Shakespeare classes and replacing them with mystery fiction hadn't done the trick, he'd resorted to salary cuts. The money disappeared into something he referred to as the Floating Fund, but none of the stuff ever seemed to float my way. After fifty-odd years of working life, my bank account looked like a sieve. I wanted to do my share with the expenses, and at the moment I couldn't see how. Maybe, I thought, I should be sensible at last, kill off my fictional alter ego, old Winchester Hyde, once and for all, and sell vacuum cleaners door to door. I sighed, and decided to bluff for Sarah's benefit.

"Don't worry, kiddo," I told her. "We'll swing that new furnace, one way or another."

"If it were just one, maybe. But you heard the heating contractor. To do it right, this old white elephant needs two, one for the main house and one for the west wing. Damn Erskine and his delusions of grandeur! Why couldn't he have left me a sensible house that wasn't always falling apart somewhere?"

"Your esteemed father thought he was Czar of all the Russias, and so far as the New York Theater was concerned, he was. That *Times* column gave him more power to bind and loose than any pope since Peter. You'd hardly have expected him to put a down payment on a nice split-level with a double garage, now would you? Besides, you love this old barn as much as he did." I leaned back against the pillows, thinking about the price tags of energy-efficient heating systems. "Maybe the insurance would cover it," I said, defying augury. "Or maybe a short-term loan from The Bank That Cares?"

Or maybe, said a secret voice proceeding from the tiny compartment of my brain labeled 'Dreamland,' just *maybe* I'll win the Edgar this year, and Willem the Pirate will have to sit up and take notice. There'll be juicier contracts, movie deals, maybe even a TV series like the one Jenny Vail's been cashing in on for years. . . .

"God, I hate money," said Sarah, searching the bedside table for one of my favorite Turkish smokes. "Anyway, I don't see why we haven't *got* any. I'd have gone on that summer tour with the Chamber Society, but I thought you'd have the advance from the new contract by now. You agreed to the terms months ago. What's Van Twit doing, having it illuminated by monks?"

"Van Twist," I reminded her. "It's part of the pirate's code, he does it with all his authors, likes to keep us barefoot and pregnant."

"Pirates, of course, have no nationality," said Merriman, whizzing back in to park on the window seat again. "But the Dutch are a very frugal people. He no doubt assumes you'd only squander your substance on food, clothes, and similar forms of riotous living. . . . By the way, Winnie, that was Cliff Munsen on the phone, wanting to wish you luck. He's still holding the line, I expect."

I curled my lip at him, tripped over my pants, and toddled off to the phone.

When I picked it up, I heard my ex-editor's whisky baritone humming something that sounded remotely like "The Road to Mandalay."

"Clifford, old top," I said, "I don't know how to break this to you, but you're not Frank Sinatra."

"Sorry, Winnie," he said, laughing. "It's all these travel guides. I'm going to do it right, now that I'm retired. No more piles of manuscript, no more genuflections to the Lord High Publisher on alternate Thursdays. I'm free, by God, and I'm going to enjoy it. A world tour—Russia, China, Japan, the South Seas, Africa, South America. I've missed too much for too long, and there isn't all that much time left, is there?"

He paused and I heard him knock back a shot of the Irish whisky he favors. I knew exactly how he felt. Since Eddie's illness, that particular shadow had been falling across my own path about once an hour. I was feeling old, sour, underrated and overused, and time's winged chariot was hot on my heels. The last thing I needed was Cliff playing time-and-temperature man over the phone.

"So you're off to see the Wizard, are you?" I growled. "Well, huzzah, huzzah, kiddo, and I hope your banana boat springs a leak. Leaving me to the mercy of the Flying Dutchman and this new tootsie! And on Edgars night, too, my annual exercise in humiliation."

"Oh," he said with a chuckle, "speaking of Jenny Vail. She

phoned me last night, must've been almost midnight. Wanted your agent's name. Naturally I told her you'd never had one. Which reminds me, Winnie, I think you ought to get somebody. There's a woman named Emily Brownson, you'll like her. I told her to button-hole you at the Edgars tonight. I know you like to keep the reins in your own delicate paws, old sport, but types like Van Twist and this Stanway character are in another whole ballpark."

"Stanway?"

"Steven Stanway, the TV producer. He does that Lieutenant Hilliard series of Jenny's. Didn't I tell you? Hell, yes. He phoned just before I left the office for good last Friday. Since Jenny's filed suit to break her contract, he's short one series and the network's on his case. He's here on a fishing expedition, been talking to anybody who's in town for Edgars about buying rights. And he might be interested in a TV version of the Winchester Hyde books."

Visions of furnaces danced in my head! My Hyde novels were period stuff, set in the Newport palaces of America's Gilded Age. The TV boys had come sniffing around them before, but had backed off as soon as they priced the sets and the costumes. Stanway, though, was one of the big guns. The long-running series based on Jenny's novels had made him rich.

"Might be interested?" I said. "What's the catch?"

"Well . . ." Cliff hesitated. "It would clinch the deal if you, um, happened to—"

"Win the Edgar." I sighed and came back to earth with a thud that popped my ears. "Was that why Jenny called, because of the TV brouhaha?"

Imogen Vail's suit against Stanway was front page stuff, good publicity but mostly, I figured, a play for more money, the kind of cagey maneuver Jenny executed with Machiavellian skill. Nobody really took her lawsuit seriously. Whichever Vegas comic happened to be standing in for Johnny Carson routinely used it in his mono-logue of an evening to give America a giggle.

"Warning me off Stanway, was she?" I asked Cliff. "Doesn't want anybody muddying the legal waters before she gets what she wants out of him, probably."

"Funny," he replied. "She wouldn't say much. Just wanted your phone number. I was surprised. Thought you two knew each other."

"We do. Did. Once. Before she turned into a lady with three names and seven figures. Know each other."

There must've been something in the tone of my voice. Cliff gulped and took another slug of Irish. "Christ, Winnie. You and Queen Jenny?"

Imogen Montague Vail and Yours Truly had less than nothing in common, and I'd never been able to wade through even one of the string of kinky pseudo-Freudian thrillers she ground out thirteen to the dozen. But for some reason I liked the woman. One snowy night at a writer's conference in Minneapolis, when Sarah was in Europe on a concert tour and I was crashing down on the far side of fifty, I had even convinced myself that I loved her. The intoxication wore off before the snow melted; still, I suppose the knowledge of it had kept those nine cheesy statues of Poe from rankling as much as they might.

"Did she seem angry? Upset about anything?"

Cliff just laughed. "You know Jenny, she's perfected the telephone voice. Cool, polished, and sweet as honey. She was persistent, though. I thought she'd have called you by this time. Probably just wanted to wish you luck."

"When donkeys fly," I grumbled.

"Just before she hung up," he added, "she asked for your number at WNYT, and the name of that woman who produces *Bookends*. I told her Myra Fish. That's right, isn't it?"

It was, indeed. For the last couple of years, I'd been moderating a weekly interview and book-review show on the Manhattan public TV station, a project I had taken over from my friend John Falkner, who might be said to have given his life for it. I wasn't quite that dedicated; on camera, I'd never stopped feeling like an ichthyosaurus in a technological fishbowl. But the thing paid a small honorarium, and even fossils have to eat.

"Probably just wanted to line up a little publicity for *The Black Palace*. Jenny's a master of the art of juggling contacts," I said. I thought of that insistent ringing phone and was glad I hadn't answered it. Sitting across from Jenny Vail in a TV interview—especially considering my memories of her—wasn't a prospect I relished, but I wasn't too sure I could've refused.

"Oh, well," said Cliff. "You'll see her tonight at the Edgars anyway. And Winnie?"

My former editor spoke in a sort of hushed, confidential whisper, and I thought for a minute he was about to give me the skinny on Willem Van Twist and Tracy the Bobbsey Twin.

"The sun coming up over Nairobi," he crooned. "Moonlight on the Kremlin domes. Sunset across the China Sea. Think about it, Winnie, before it's too late."

"Think about it, hell!" I growled. "Who's going to pay for it?"

But he just hummed a few more bars of "The Road to Mandalay" and hung up.

I crashed the receiver down and made for my Cave, the three gloriously cluttered upstairs rooms in which I go to ground with freshman themes, page proofs, and that great eternal puzzle—who done it, and why. My companions are a trusty manual Remington with a sticky letter M, a secondhand office chair whose springs long ago surrendered to the demands of my portly posterior, and a desk heaped with papers nobody else is allowed to touch. It is my kingdom, my court, and the seat of such unfashionable magic as ancient wizards possess, and except by invitation, nobody enters Prospero's Cave but me.

Which was why, the minute I stumbled through the door with my pants still at half-mast, I screeched to a halt and grabbed for my trusty bottle of Haig & Haig. Somebody had not only been messing about with my desk, he'd left his calling card. Nothing was where I'd put it. Papers, books, and files were strewn around as usual, but they were all in the wrong places; the chapters I'd begun to accumulate in fulfillment of my mythical new contract were completely out of order. The place had been carefully, methodically tossed, but I had to admit that whoever did it was no cheapskate. In the place of honor on top of a stack of term papers lay two dozen of the whitest white roses I'd ever seen, beside them a vintage bottle of Dom Perignon.

"Merriman!" I roared. "Is this your idea of a joke?"

In a minute I heard his opera slippers slapping along the hall, and Sarah's bare feet not far behind. Like me, they froze and stood staring at the flowers and the pricey bubble water.

"Bit flamboyant for our David." Eddie sniffed gingerly at the mass of roses.

"I didn't hear the doorbell," said Sarah. "When did they arrive, Win?"

I parked in my desk chair and lit a Turkish Delight, my mind in a tailspin. Now I was sure I'd been right about hearing that car door out in the drive. Distracted, I picked up the mass of white roses and then put them down again beside the wine bottle. Every face in the room, including mine, was a blank. "You mean neither of you put them here?" I asked, knowing the answer already.

Sarah shook her head and Merriman took another whiff. "Don't know what they do to flowers these days," he said. "No fragrance at all, might as well be plastic. But they've certainly perfected their delivery service. It's too late for the Easter bunny and too early for Saint Nick."

"Look, there's a card!" cried Sarah. "Read it out loud, Win."

I pulled off the small single-fold card tied onto the neck of the bottle with narrow black velvet ribbon. The paper was creamy white, deeply embossed, and I recognized the monogram and the tiny, cramped signature below the typewritten message even before I read the thing. When I finally did, I gasped and choked on my Turkish Delight.

Sarah pounded me on the back. "Here, you old goose, give it to me," she said, grabbing the card. "It says—It says—"

Eddie pushed a chair under her just in time and she sat down with a thud. He looked over at me expectantly. But I didn't need to read the words again. I already knew them by heart.

"It says, 'Someone is going to die. You can stop it.' "

I paused to pour three large glasses of the Haig & Haig.

"And it's signed 'Best wishes, Jenny Vail.' "

3

"New snow on the Kremlin domes. Sunset in Pago Pago . . ." I sighed and closed my eyes. " 'Last night I dreamt I went to Manderley again. . . .' "

"Oh, will you wake up, for pity's sake!" cried Sarah, punching me on the kneecap. "We're almost there!"

Our destination was neither Manderley nor Moscow, but the Edgar Awards, in the posh Park Avenue precincts of the Hornsby Empire, a world away from our usual Manhattan home-from-home, the Battersea, an unassuming relic of a residential hotel downtown where chocolates on the pillow are forbidden by edict and among whose balding carpets and benignly potty permanent guests I always feel entirely at home. Here in midtown, a forest of flashy marquees and towering transient palaces, nothing is in permanent residence except the price tag.

The cab nosed into the turning lane and as the three of us swayed to the left I almost squished Merriman, who was looking his dapper best—blast him—in the evening suit he bought for the Hasty Pudding Awards of 1935. On my right, Sarah glowed like a flame of flowing scarlet silk against the exhaust-stained, gunmetal gray of the misty evening already clamping down upon New York.

As for me, I sat glumly between them, present only in the too, too solid flesh—which, by the way, was now encased in a snappy little number borrowed at the eleventh hour from the costume graveyard of the DeWitt Clinton College Players. It was left from an old production of *The Man Who Came to Dinner*, and though it might've resembled a tux from the front row stalls, it pinched everywhere that mattered and made me look like a black silk bratwurst.

I opened my eyes and caught a glimpse of myself in the cabbie's rearview mirror, squeezed them shut again and tried to call up once more the Cliff-inspired vision of Yours Truly, bronzed as a jolly Buddha, my shaggy mop of chicken-feather hair caressed by tropical zephyrs, my bunions freed from Hush-Puppy bondage, my arthritic neck massaged by smiling native girls.

But it was no use. Everywhere I looked in that inescapable interior landscape I saw the face of Jenny Vail—not the studio publicity portrait, but the Jenny I remembered: a small, high-boned face from a Renaissance portrait indelible even under the Maybelline, heavy blue-black hair crimped from braiding and set free to swirl across her shoulders, huge reproachful brown eyes crinkled with latent laughter at her newest uneasy conquest, my bumbling self. And there had been, I remembered, white roses in her room, far too many for that snowy season. Dozens of heavy, full-blown white roses.

"There! Isn't that Jenny Vail? Getting out of that limo!" Sarah dug me in the ribs with a silken elbow. "Open your eyes, you old toot! How can you be so calm, after the nasty card on that bottle of wine?" She shuddered.

"I told you," I said, as the cab dived in behind a shiny black limo at the curb. "It's just a trick, some kind of self-promotion gag. Everybody in this business who can pick up a knife and fork will be here tonight, and unless it's a pretty dry year, you can count on at least one stunt. Mysterious gunshots during the salad course, a scream or two between Best Paperback Original and Best Children's Book. Don't know how true it is, but Cliff Munsen told me that Rex Stout once showed up with bodyguards. Sometimes people come dressed as their own characters. See that old girl smoking the meerschaum? And look at that jackass Sloan!"

A doll-faced young man in his early thirties was helping Jenny Vail out of her limo. Jed Sloan wore a ratty old trench coat and a belligerent squint; a cigarette dangled precariously from his lower lip, and as Queen Jenny stepped into the crush of celebrants milling around the curb, he pulled a .38 from under the trench coat and waved it around, clearing a path for her.

"Weapons seem to have no effect on the lady," said Merriman, as we slid out of the cab.

I sniffed disdainfully. "That one certainly shouldn't. It's not real."

There was a ripple of applause and some rather forced laughter, as Sloan leveled the gun at the third brass button of the Hornsby doorman and pulled the trigger. Out popped a little flag with a smoking gun on it, Jed Sloan's trademark. "ANOTHER ACHILLES HALE ADVENTURE," it said underneath. "COMING SOON FROM CROCODILE BOOKS."

"Don't you dare say I told you so," said Sarah, paying off the cabbie.

But to tell you the truth, I'd been bluffing. If that bottle of wine and those funereal white roses had arrived in the ordinary way, I might've written off the warning on the card as a practical joke. I didn't want to alarm Sarah, and I'd been making light of the whole business, but somebody professional had gone through my papers in the Cave. That might very well mean hired talent, the boys with the shoulder holsters and the picklocks in their back pockets. The whole thing was carefully orchestrated, flawlessly carried out. And I believed every word of the warning on that expensive little card: *Someone is going to die.*

Jenny Vail believed it, too. The instant Jed Sloan leveled his gun, she dodged out of the line of fire and into the crowd at the doorway. She saw, as I did, that he wasn't really aiming at the doorman in the blue-and-gold Hornsby livery. That fake automatic had originally been pointed straight at Jenny, a slight, graceful figure in a low-cut gown of silver satin encrusted with what looked for all the world like real amethysts—or more precisely at Imogen Montague Vail, a remote public woman I scarcely knew at all. She had seen that gun aimed at her, and I had seen her face, the wide dark eyes fixed, staring at Sloan, the ringed hands clutching her small, beaded silver bag as if she were being mugged. The only thing missing from her expression was surprise. She had expected that gun—or a real one just like it. The fake gun went off, and I lost sight of her as she disappeared through the huge gold revolving doors into the lobby.

"She's really rather lovely. From a distance." Sarah slipped her arm through mine and we followed the crowd inside.

"Must be a Pisces," piped up Merriman. "All those amethysts, bottomless purple depths and all that. Being born in August, I have only the ignoble peridot to show for myself. Greeny, watery sort of thing, not at all interesting. Always rather envied people born in February."

"Jenny Vail was born in June," I said as we navigated through the lobby to the reception room.

"How do you know that?" Sarah snapped to attention.

Eddie came to my aid. "Winnie's right. I'm a bit fuzzy between the ears this evening. June, certainly, it's in all the press releases." He shot me a warning look and forged on. "Well, then. Perhaps she can't hold her liquor. The Greeks, you know, used to make winecups from solid amethyst, legend being one can never get squiffed whilst in the presence of the jewel, no matter what the liquid intake."

"She doesn't drink, either," I mumbled.

"Win," said Sarah, stopping in her tracks. "Just exactly how well do you know Imogen Vail?"

Those storm warnings were out again, and I figured it was time to execute a sneak. "Speaking of drinks," I said, "what'll you have? I'm not prepared to scintillate all night with my gauge on empty."

Then, without waiting for an answer, I began to bulldoze my way through the crowd toward the bar at the other end of the reception room.

And what a room it was. It ran the full width of the Versailles Ballroom beyond, its thirty-foot ceiling supported by columns of pinkish marble. At least, I thought they were marble until somebody shoved me against one of them. It resounded with a hollow thud, and I half expected Ernie Keebler to stick his head out and offer me a chocolate chip cookie.

An ornate plasterwork frieze with a gleam suspiciously like vinyl siding set off huge imitation-Fragonard murals with wallpaper seams in them where rosy-bosomed wenches in powdered wigs sported with a bunch of Elvis impersonators in knee breeches. Huge chandeliers winked overhead, and in the center of the room a gold-and-white dolphin spouted into a three-tiered fountain surrounded by polyester potted palms.

True to my favorite Mack truck principle of social interaction, I was just forging through a roadblock of spangled sweethearts when I heard a voice from behind a nearby column, and I knew at once it wasn't Ernie Keebler.

"I didn't believe it, but by God it's true." The voice was female, adenoidal, the accent flat as the Dakota plains, though the brain, I happened to know, had been forged in the fires of Radcliffe. "They told me you were coming this year, Winnie," she hooted. "I figured it was just a crock of crap. But, by God, here you are!"

"Hazel Hancock!" I yelled. The room had filled up fast and the gabble of six or seven hundred *misteriosos* networking their tails off had begun to rival the Concorde on takeoff.

Hazel scooted out from behind her pillar and gave my stage suit the once over. "Brooks Brothers, right?" she said, and I could hear her hyena cackle above the swelling jibber.

"Wouldn't talk if I were you, Haze," I told her, "not in that outfit."

I swiped a swig of the brown stuff in her plastic Hornsby stemware deluxe and coughed, not so much because it turned out to be rye—by any Scotch-lover's standards the Drāno of hard booze—but because Hazel was dressed as her own star character, Mrs. Mapleton, a grade school principal who keeps finding corpses in the wheatfields. Twin set and pearls, flared skirt, huge leather pocketbook, sensible shoes, tortoise-shell-rimmed specs on a chain around her neck—the image was almost perfect, except for the frustrated energy of her small, sturdy body, longing for the freedom of her usual shirt and jeans.

The specs, it appeared, were Hazel's own. She put them on and peered round like a small, dowdy barn owl looking for mice. And any vermin in her path, I thought fondly, had better head for the hills when old Hazel was flying low. A tough Pulitzer-winning reporter before she turned to crime, she had taken on more high-handed editors, broken more abusive contracts, and led more protest campaigns than Smith Brothers have cough drops. Her books were airport novels, competent little amusements you could toss away before you picked up your luggage, but they sold like crazy, and if you wanted to know anything about anybody in the mystery business, it was Hazel who kept the files.

The crowd parted as a wiry, pop-eyed woman goose-stepped past, glaring to right and left. "Christ, the Thought Police!" muttered Hazel, and ducked behind a pillar. When the crowd had closed again and it seemed safe, she zoomed out, keeping a wary eye on the woman's disappearing back.

"Rita Kovacs," she said. "You know, Winnie, the Dusty Dvorak books? *Dust Cover, Dust Storm, Mortal Dust*. She's nominated this year, Best Novel, just like you and Jenny. Don't let her see me, okay?"

Lovely Rita, known to the membership as the Godmother, had been karate-chopping her way up the committee ladder of mystery-writer politics for ten years, and now she had reached the top—almost. Her books hit the best-seller lists regularly, but they didn't take up residence there the way Jenny Vail's did. Once they tired of the slick, bad-broad language and got wise to the gimmick of each book, the readers went elsewhere. And where they went was back to Queen Jenny. She could still command better covers, better publicity, better distribution than anybody in the business. Nobody had more influence among her peers, more power with publishers and agents.

Hazel grabbed hold of my sleeve and held on as tidal waves of overdressed bodies washed against us. Everybody in the room seemed to be trying to find somebody else, who probably wasn't there anyway. Hazel held on tighter and I breathed a silent prayer for the survival of my phony suit.

"Rita wants to be head honcho next year," she honked at me

over the roar. "She's got Perfidy, Unlimited canvassing for her, and she's dragged everybody on the nominating committee to lunch at least twice. Like spending two hours with a goddamn tape loop. 'Jenny Vail is a tool of male elitism and oppression.' She even drove up to Sioux Falls and bought me steaks and Coors while she did her number on me."

"Did it help?" I asked her, watching as Kovacs buttonholed a distinguished, pear-shaped little man with a full black beard and an eye like the Prophet Elijah. Rabbi Nestor Perlmutter, whose books were an education in everything from the Torah to terrorism, would be more than a match for Lovely Rita.

Hazel's hyena cackle resounded again. "Hell, Winnie, Jenny Vail's the Earth Mother of us all. She was taking an ax to the old-boy networks when Rita was still getting the hots reading Spillane with a flashlight under the bedclothes. Jenny's turned down the nomination six times and this year she finally accepted. Nobody on that committee, including little Hazel, was about to vote against her."

The name of the new president would be announced from the podium that night, and though Rita Kovacs's thin, pinched face didn't look cheery, it was obvious she hadn't stopped campaigning yet. I saw her elbow her way through the crowd, headed for this year's president, Charlie LaCroix. "Doesn't she know the voting's over?" I asked Haze.

Hazel stood on tiptoe to get a better look. "Hell, she doesn't care. There's always next year, and if she gets herself on the right committees, she'll have more power than Jenny anyway. Besides, it's more than a campaign with Rita. It's a goddamn holy war."

I glanced toward the bar, which stood at the far end of the room on a sort of royal dais. A knot of business-suited guests, most likely editors or agents, parted suddenly and there she was, Jenny Vail, her silvery dress a leaden gray against the cheap gilt and plaster of the bar.

"Matter of fact, it's a comedown for Jenny," said Hazel. "Being president. The real power in this bunch is in the executive committees, the nominating committees. She's controlled those for years.

Now she'll have this term as president, but she can only serve once. Then she's finished. Judging from her last book, she's just about finished writing, too. You read it, *The Black Palace?*"

I shook my head. "She sent me a copy, she always does. I haven't read it yet." Rubbing it in a bit, I'd always thought, sending copies to the loser. I frowned. "I don't much like Jenny's stuff, myself, all those seething psychoses. But *finished?* Come on, Haze. The book was on the lists for four months, it's won half a dozen awards."

Hazel stood peering over my shoulder at the figure of Jenny Vail. "I didn't say she was bad, sweetie. Just finished. Over. I think she thinks so, too. Look at her."

Jenny stood poised at the end of the bar, a plastic glass balanced on the palm of her hand, a mild, absent smile on her face, her dark eyes raking the crowd below her.

It was then that she spotted me. She looked steadily at me, as if she could part the crowd like the Red Sea. She took a step down into the crush, coming toward me. Then she was gone, swept away.

"You're going to win this year, you know."

The woman's voice was almost in my ear. I felt a slight pressure on my elbow and endangered my suit by whipping round much too fast. Of course it wasn't Jenny. It was a muscular strawberry blonde in a navy blue blazer and a bow tie, and her eyes, too, were navy blue as she smiled down on me from what must've been a height of six feet two.

"I'm Emily Brownson," she said. "But call me Brownie. Emily's such an extra-virgin, frustrated sort of name. Cliff sent me. I'm your new agent."

I was a bit overwhelmed, but I still didn't want an agent. I could deal with Stanway and Van Twist just as I dealt with Tommy Sheffield and his faculty cadres, straight from the shoulder—not counting the odd bit of blackmail judiciously applied under the table.

"Now look here," I began, "I don't really—"

But my protest was abruptly squelched by a sudden blow to the thorax as a young body hurtled past, arms flailing, charging through the crowd toward the spot where Jenny Vail had disappeared a minute before. He was no more than nineteen or twenty, the remnants of teenage acne still exploding here and there on his fine-boned face. He had one of those trendy designer haircuts, the sides shaved and a thick square cap of brownish-blond hair sitting up top like a furry beret; the color of the Armani suit he wore exactly matched his hair, and the single gold stud in his shell-like ear was worth more than at least three of the royalty checks I hadn't gotten.

"Jenny!" he bellowed, in that grandstand basso peculiar to fraternity boys when nicely lit. "Jenny, goddamn it! Where are you?"

He collided with a rumpled bald-headed little Daddy Warbucks and almost upset Merriman, who seemed to have made it through the human maze to the bar by some magical underground passage only he knew about. He was balancing three glasses of elixir and weaving neatly in and out among the gabbling guests, when Childe Harold on his headlong pilgrimage appeared out of nowhere. Eddie executed a step that would've done Gene Kelly proud and the kid zoomed on by, alone in an irrelevant universe.

"Didn't spill a drop," said Merriman proudly, handing a plastic goblet to Sarah, who had materialized during the rite of passage of the recent kid, and was now paging through several mimeographed sheets of cheap yellow paper.

"Is that the seating chart?" said Hazel. "Where the hell have they put me this year?"

Hazel had had so many publishers in her career that she was never quite sure which one would spring for a ticket until the last minute.

I peered at the sheet. "E.P. Alexander and Sons, Haze," I said, spotting her name. "Table seven, right next to Garner and Sloan."

"Good old Philip." She smiled fondly and knocked back the rest of her Drāno. "He's the last of the old-time gentlemen, Philip Vail," she said softly.

"Vail?" Merriman pricked up his big ears. "As in Imogen Montague Vail?"

"Her husband," said my new agent, Emily Brownson. "At least

that's what she still calls him. He's associate publisher at Alexander and Sons, one of the Inner Sanctum. Philip's probably the only top-of-the-line editor in New York who still reads unsolicited manuscripts."

"Divorced?" said Sarah, glancing at me over the seating chart.

"They never bothered," honked Hazel. "Just like you two never bothered getting hitched!"

"She's seated right in front of us, Winnie," said Merriman, kibitzing over Sarah's shoulder. "Jenny Vail. Crocodile Books, table four."

"Crocodile Books?" Sarah looked up, surprised. "Imogen Vail has the same publisher as that dreadful idiot with the trench coat and the—"

She broke off as the lights went out and a pistol shot echoed in the darkness. Sarah grabbed my arm and held on; the roaring, jabbering crowd fell instantly silent. The grandiloquent trappings, the fake murals, the phony marble, the cheap gilt—everything dissolved with the sound of the shot. We stood in a dark, breathless vacuum.

Then somebody laughed, a little hysterically. Another voice joined in, and the laughter moved through the damp warmth of the pressing crowd like a cool wave passing. The lights went back on.

"What's happened, Win?" Sarah didn't let go of me, even now. "What was it?"

"Nothing much, kiddo," I said, steering her through the moving crowd toward the candlelit tables in the ballroom. "Just some mystery nut ringing the dinner bell."

4

"Hi!" said a weary blonde sort of voice behind me. "I'm Tracy."

"Spencer or Dick?" I said, turning round. Sarah stomped delicately on my instep as I gave my new editor the once-over.

Tracy Valentine wasn't blond after all. Her hair was chestnut brown, thick and shining, and expensively cut to balance her small pointed chin and round gray-green eyes. She had one of those delicate, oval faces that age into perfect cameos, a Lillian Gish, a Helen Hayes of a girl. She would probably, I thought, resent such a word, but what else could I call her? At my age, everything female under sixty is a girl, and Tracy still had a lap or two before she caught up with thirty-five.

We all sat down, letting the crowd flow around us as the tables began to fill. Ours was decked with bunches of tulips and little wooden shoes at each place setting, at the behest, no doubt, of Tracy's mentor, Van Twist, the Flying Dutchman. Under each shoe was a slip of white paper, and I was about to check out mine when Tracy grabbed my hand and trapped it in both of hers. She glanced nervously at the squat, bald, beetle-browed Daddy Warbucks I'd seen earlier, as he stalked in and parked himself at the far end of our table.

"Actually," she said, fiddling with the beaded trim of her dress, "the Tracy is in honor of Katharine Hepburn. You know, Tracy Lord? My mother saw *Philadelphia Story* about fifteen times before I was born." She pasted on a near-perfect imitation of the famous

Hepburn grin, smiling and waving at other Garner and Sloan authors as they took their places. "I'm supposed to be an authority figure at these clambakes," she said between the glittering clenched teeth, "but how can anybody take them seriously?" Tracy suppressed a giggle, coughed, and gave my hand a squeeze. Her own were small and rather chilly, and the fingernails, I noted, had been nibbled to the quick. "I'm so glad to meet you at last, Winston," she said. "May I call you Henrietta?"

She opened her red silk evening bag, took out a square white envelope, and handed it to me. It was addressed to Henrietta Slocum, in care of Garner and Sloan, Inc.

"It's a summons from Perfidy, Unlimited," she said. "I thought I saw Rita Kovacs about to corner you outside. They want you to come to tea tomorrow afternoon, their annual post-Edgars war dance."

As a matter of fact, the partisan politics of mystery writing had hardly escaped me. I'd been masquerading as a woman in print for thirty-five years, and although Sarah didn't seem worried about it, the feminist lobby—represented by Lovely Rita—had recently expressed grave doubts about my sexual identity. Cliff Munsen had sent me her review of my latest Winchester Hyde novel, *Death of a Double Agent,* and it seemed the Godmother had seen fit to devote one of her tape loops to Yours Truly, too. "Cloaking his male supremacism in a female disguise," was the way mine ran, as I recalled.

Now don't get me wrong. I don't mind taking it, provided I get a fighting chance to dish it out. But I might as well have tried squaring off with General Schwarzkopf's tank corps. PU, as the united front of pressure groups called itself, had lately become a power-in-the-land among mystery writers of all sexual persuasions; there were buzz-groups, regional clans with newsletters, secret conclaves, and nationwide self-promotion workshops. Women writers in twos and threes pulled into the shopping mall bookstores, handing out homemade fudge with their business cards and blitzing their books into the windows next to the best-sellers. Tough guys like Jed Sloan organized stag smokers and plied the booksellers with booze and blue jokes. They raided the computer banks for relevant membership lists and mailed out postcards of their latest covers by the thousands; they tied up the phone lines coast to coast, compiling the inside dope on agents, editors, publishing houses, contracts; they badgered unsuspecting writers for cover quotes; they invented awards and gave them to each other.

The accolades of this mystical alliance were bestowed, like corporate promotions and nominations for President of the United States, on team players only; independents of whatever persuasion need not apply. The partisans inhabited a dangerous Manichaean universe of warring dark and light, of insiders and outsiders, and woe betide anyone who traveled without a label. I've spent nearly seventy years as the most fervent of outsiders, and frankly, the whole thing made my back teeth ache.

"The Red-Headed League," I grumbled, and I was about to wad the invitation up when Tracy snatched it and handed it to Sarah.

"You'd better go, Henrietta," said my editor. "Because I think they want to give you an award. We'll talk later. Have to go and mingle now." She pasted on her toothsome grin and went to join a woman in hoop earrings the size of bike tires who was flirting shamelessly with Daddy Warbucks.

"What will you wear to tea, my dear? The ecru lace or the white silk with the high collar?" Eddie was beaming like a lighthouse.

"Merriman, the next crack will be your last," I growled.

"Well, I think it's lovely," pronounced Sarah. "It's the first good thing that's happened all day. Who are all these people? That man over there with Hazel, the one with the thick glasses and the red toupee? You know, I think he made a pass at me during the reception! Rather a remarkable man, he must be. Said he'd just been hired by the State Department and was going to work for the—" She changed to a nervous whisper. "The CIA. He must be over sixty. Isn't that extraordinary?"

"Incredible," I told her. "Especially since he's been telling the same story at every convention and writers' workshop and most of the bars this side of Montana since he was thirty-five. Fred Tilden, writes hard-boileds."

Merriman looked puzzled. "I defy anyone to read more mystery novels per annum than ~~myself~~ F(dp)," he said, "but I confess I've never heard of a Fred Tilden."

"Neither has anybody else," I said. "That's why he has to keep telling that story."

"And who's that little bald-headed man at the end of our table who hasn't spoken a word to anybody? Why don't you introduce us?"

"I'm a stranger here, myself," I said.

And it was true, not so much because I hadn't attended an Edgars dinner for years, but because most of the writers Cliff Munsen had lured onto the Garner and Sloan list had already had enough of the Flying Dutchman and gone elsewhere. Nestor Perlmutter, whose eleven Rabbi Rosenfeld books were minor classics, had jumped ship a month ago and was sitting at the E.P. Alexander table, deep in one of his philosophical ruminations with a tall, grayhaired, rather exquisite fellow who might've been impersonating Peter Wimsey, but wasn't.

Philip Vail would never have dreamed of such a stunt; the delicate manners, like the antique gold spectacles that perched on the end of his long, straight nose and the ivory holder in which he now and then raised a small cigar to his lips, were part of Vail's family heritage, no more an affectation than the intelligent pale blue eyes or the long, nervous fingers that drummed the tablecloth impatiently. In his buttonhole was a single white rose.

"What the hell do you think I am? I'm not your fucking beanbag, man!"

It was the fraternity-brother basso again, our young friend from the cocktail reception. The explosion of angry noise brought Philip Vail to a halt. His fingers clenched into fists and he sat as still as the ice sculpture centerpiece. He didn't turn to see where the shouting came from, though everybody else at our end of the ballroom did. The elegant Vail seemed to know. He shoved the glasses up on his nose and opened his program carefully, leaning hard against the back of his chair.

"You don't know what you're doing, Jenny!"

The crowd around the Crocodile Books table in front of us drew back and I got a look at the kid. He was knotted up inside his fashionably baggy suit, arms cocked, fists tight and swinging at his sides, and opposite him, slender and motionless, her amethysts glittering in the candlelight, stood Imogen Vail.

"Gregory," she said. "If you have to be tiresome, don't do it in public. Wait for me at home."

Jenny didn't seem angry, but the kid was furious and shaking. "I'm not leaving here until you answer me," he yelled. From the sidelines, three men in hotel security uniforms were pushing their way through the crowd toward him. Gregory saw them and his belligerence seemed to crumble. "You use me," he quavered, on the verge of tears. "You fucking use the *world*."

I saw Philip Vail's trim shoulders square, bracing for collision. He laid the cigarette holder carefully beside his plate, and then, in what seemed like one smooth motion, he got up and glided past the onlookers to where the boy was standing.

"He's all right," Vail told the security men. He spoke gently, clearly—not a man to be resisted. "I'll see to him."

But Gregory, whoever he might be, was anything but all right. He seemed only now to realize where he was, what he had done. The clenched fists slammed against his thighs in hammer blows, pounding, pounding, over and over, with punishing regularity; the strange, cropped head bent low, chin against chest, and the wide brown eyes stared at the floor.

Jenny remained motionless and her husband said nothing to her, merely stepped close to the boy and grasped both the pounding fists in his own thin hands. "All right, Gregory," he said softly. "All right."

The boy looked up, stared blankly for a minute at the luminous figure in the silver gown. Then he walked past the security guards and disappeared among the tables.

Philip Vail turned to his wife. I thought for a moment they were about to speak, but they didn't. Jenny reached out a heavily ringed hand and grasped her husband's arm, not so much in affection or gratitude as in the manner of someone keeping a precarious balance in a narrow place.

It lasted only an instant. Vail made no overt response, but the pale blue eyes glanced briefly down at Jenny's fingers, the long-lashed eyelids flickered. For a fraction of a second he met her gaze, a silent compact between them somehow honored. Then she let him go and turned away as though he were invisible. Vail returned to his own table as earnest, scholarly Lydia Hallam—the Crocodile editor —and an anorexic white-faced woman in clinging black silk who might've been painted by El Greco joined Jed Sloan to close in around Jenny Vail. The waiters were beginning to serve the salad and everyone settled down to serious conversation.

"You're dying to go over there and talk to her, aren't you, Win?" said Sarah.

"Aren't *you?*" I brushed a carrot curl off my shoulder as the waiter zoomed past.

"Who was that boy, the one she called Gregory? Do you know him?"

"No. Eat your rabbit food."

"Goopus," said Eddie, chomping delicately on a radish, "anyone would think you were afraid of her, the way you're blinding and stiffing."

Of course, he was right. I *had* always been a bit afraid of Jenny, even on that snowy night in Minneapolis. She was gentle, funny, full of dark places that made the light moments astonishing. She could talk intelligently about nearly anything and teetotal though she was, she was the most intriguing drunk I've ever known, intoxicated at will with whatever subject was at hand. But something about that will—the perfect poise, the guard that never came down, the brown eyes calculating the most vulnerable moment—had made me realize exactly what the kid Gregory had just so publicly decided. Jenny Vail did not equate herself with the rest of us. We were a deck of cards, and she was playing solitaire.

I glanced up from my salad, then, and saw her watching me. She was sitting directly opposite, her back to the podium. When she caught my look, she took a slender gold fountain pen from her bag and began to write something on the back of her copy of the seating chart. The El Greco woman sat next to her, a flat cardboard figure leaning precariously in order to see what she was writing. Jenny shielded the paper carefully, then tore off the single sheet and folded it, speaking angrily to the thin woman, her lips barely parted, her eyes fixed on me. The thin woman strained to hear over the noise of conversation, and she must've succeeded; the lantern jaw set angrily, the almond-shaped black eyes, dead as paint, narrowed further, and the leaning body straightened as though someone had tied her to the chair. Whatever Jenny Vail had said to her, it certainly hadn't been a declaration of undying love.

By that time the main course, some inedible species of fowl specially bred for awards dinners, had arrived, and no one was bothering to eat it. People began to mill around and table-hop again. I saw Lydia Hallam, Jenny's editor, get up from the head of the Crocodile table and go over to where Philip Vail and my friend Hazel were standing, deep in conference. Vail looked up and smiled, then frowned again as the El Greco woman attached herself to them.

Whatever that note had been, all the signals told me it was meant for me. There was an empty chair beside Jenny; I laid down my fork and hoisted myself to my feet. "It's about time," I heard Sarah mutter, as I made my way to the Crocodile Books table.

But I wasn't the only one headed for that empty chair. A man who'd been talking to Rita Kovacs at the Harvest House table got up and began to zero in on Jenny. He was tall and perfectly tanned, the sort of celestial tan you only get by long and devout effort. The man was muscular, but thin for his height, with small, sleepy eyes, a fussy little beard, and streaky brown hair that made him look striped.

"Steven Stanway," I murmured. That famous profile appeared at the end of each episode of his TV series, like Caesar on his coins. But Caesar didn't have a weak chin and little piggy eyes and a forked beard like a musical-comedy Mephistopheles. All of a sudden I had a queasy feeling about selling him the rights to my Winchester Hyde books, furnace or no furnace.

Jenny, too, seemed a bit queasy. When she saw Stanway coming toward her through the maze of tables, she took the folded sheet of paper on which she'd been writing, shoved it inside the glossy program booklet for the awards ceremony, and got up, taking off in the opposite direction from the object of her famous lawsuit. I ducked behind Philip Vail's table and intercepted her, grasping her wrist as she passed.

She froze and stared at me. If she'd been writing that note to me, she certainly hadn't brought it with her. All she was carrying was the stylish evening bag. It dangled from her wrist, gaping open, and inside it, carefully wrapped in a sheer silk scarf, lay a small handgun as patently real as Jed Sloan's was fake.

"Ah, Jenny." I glanced down at the pistol. "Planning a little target practice? Sort of a follow-up to that note you sent with the wine?"

She gave me a blank stare. "I need to talk to you," she said. Her voice was low and hoarse, heavy with some suppressed emotion—fear, anger, or perhaps only the intense energy that made her, even at sixty-one, a stunning woman. "We may need—"

"Jenny!" Steven Stanway was gliding between the tables toward us; I saw Rita Kovacs move her chair to get a better view of them.

"Not now!" said Jenny, and pulled away from me, her bag still dangling open.

"Take your seats, ladies and gentlemen," implored a voice over the mike on the awards platform. "Take your seats for the beginning of the Forty-eighth Annual Edgar Allan Poe Awards!"

Another phony shot rang out. Somebody screamed. Everybody laughed, and the lights went out again. By the time they came back on, Jenny had disappeared. I scanned the crowd for her, but I wasn't wearing my specs, and without them everything more than five feet away was pea-soup fog. I looked around. Stanway, too, was gone, and I couldn't spot the El Greco woman or Philip Vail either. Lydia

Hallam had taken her seat, but Rita Kovacs was missing from the Harvest House table.

"Welcome, everyone, to this year's Edgars," said Harlan Landis, one of the Chicago mob of hard-boiled crime writers and this year's emcee. He was, I happened to know, a corporate lawyer in real life, and this was the biggest damn courtroom he was ever likely to get. If I knew Harlan, he'd go on for at least twenty minutes before he got to the Best Novel award. I ignored Sarah's high-sign and made for a gap in the tables, the same way Jenny had gone.

Despite some searching glances, I ducked and dodged from one table to the other, covering the width of the ballroom, but there was no sign of the gleaming silver dress. Landis was rabbiting on up on the dais, giving them the history of mystery fiction starting with Sophocles, and he'd just gotten to Dickens when another shot rang out, a tinnier, more muffled sound than the others. The audience laughed on cue; I shrugged it off and soldiered on. Champagne corks were popping all over the room as people settled down for the ceremony, and through the doors to the reception area I spotted Hazel Hancock at the end of a long line of women queued up for the ladies' room. It would be one place, at least, where neither Steven Stanway nor the bumptious Gregory could follow Jenny. I could send Hazel in on a reconnaissance mission, I decided, and I headed in the direction of the long, snaking line of impatient faces. I had just bulldozed my way to the back wall of the ballroom, where several last-minute tables had been set up near the swing doors to the kitchen and serving area, when I saw Jenny.

She sat uncomfortably, leaning back against the mural wall-paper, her heavy dark hair wound like a crown around her head, her eyes closed. The proud head leaned slightly sideways, cradled between her shoulder and the wall. The ringed hands lay on the table-cloth; one was open, palm up, the other flat on the table, which was pushed so close to her body that its edge bumped her breasts. A squad of waiters charged by me loaded with dirty dishes and I waited at a little distance until they passed, studying Jenny.

She seemed to be concentrating, and I didn't like to disturb her.

On the platform the tinny voice of Harlan Landis droned on, but she didn't laugh at his jokes or applaud on cue. Suddenly, seeing her at ease and alone, I knew why I had been drawn to Jenny Vail all those years ago. She was very much like Sarah—the heavy dark hair, the proud bearing, the strong, well-formed face. With Sarah an ocean and a continent away, I had been alien and incomplete, stumbling through the book signings and panel groups and pompous luncheons like a visitor from Mars, and Jenny had offered me the comfort of a temporary delusion. I had needed her and let her go and counted myself lucky to wake up in time. If Jenny was a user, so had I been. Whatever she'd become over the years, I still owed her a debt.

I stood beside her table and put my hand on hers and knew at once why the edge was jammed so close to her body. It was keeping her upright against the wall. I slid my fingers to the base of her thumb and lifted the hand to feel for a pulse. The moment its precarious balance was disturbed, her body slumped forward, head dangling, chin smashed against neck.

Jenny Vail was dead.

I could see no wound, at least at first, but the wall behind her was soaked with blood. When I saw it, a wave of nausea rose and crested; I thought I would faint, but I had never fainted in my life before and I was damned if I would do that to her now. Jenny, I thought, would never have flinched, and she expected an equal return.

I pushed the table away so that I could lean her body far enough forward to look for a wound. There was blood on the carpet behind her chair and all down the back of the silvery gown. At last I saw where the bullet had entered; her heavy coils of dark hair concealed it. It was a small wound, and—except for the blood-matted hair—reasonably clean and perfectly round. The bullet had pierced the skull fairly low, around the same level as the base of her ears, traveling upward to exit near the crown of the head—an odd and rather difficult angle from which to fire, and absolutely impossible to construe as suicide. The exit wound was larger, jagged and more evident, but when Jenny's body was bent back toward the wall, as she had been left, it was scarcely visible.

I leaned her gently back again and pushed the table forward to hold her safely. Again the sick disgust washed over me and I took her hand for the strength of it and held on. If she had been hollow, someone had convinced her she must use herself up in a ruinous race to prevail. She had profited, but so had they, those nagging voices. Now she was dead, and they would profit again. New editions of her books would appear, the sales would skyrocket, retrospectives of her career would open the six o'clock news. At table after table around the room sat writers, agents, publicists who would calculate her death to the decimal: a slot open on the best-seller lists, a contract worth megabucks that could now be spent elsewhere, a publicity budget up for grabs. Steven Stanway could use her books, spoil them, exploit them as he liked—flashing on the screen, no doubt, a tasteful memorial message in her honor that would spin the ratings into the stratosphere.

I had spent all my life, in the classroom and at the typewriter, as a man of books. I had believed in their dignity, in what they preserved of integrity and human truth. But in that pretentious room, surrounded by other men and women of books, I saw only monkey tricks and greed, my own among them. I had no urge to be rich; I merely wanted to afford the price of my own survival, and for months now, while Willem Van Twist adjusted his cash flow with the help of my savings account, I had thought only of contracts, royalty checks, my shrinking pension fund—and scarcely at all of words or of what would be lost when they all carried a bargain price tag. How could I blame the partisans for their frenzied passion to prevail, when money and nothing else had drawn me here, money had put me in a silly suit and made me suffer fools and smile and be a fool myself? At that moment I wanted only to take Jenny away, to hide in some lone place and mourn what had been taken from us all as we dozed and dreamed. I sat holding her dead hand, the waiters rushing by us with dishes clattering, the banal drone of the awards ceremony punctuated by conditioned applause, and knew that though I had not always liked her, some part of me had certainly loved Imogen Vail.

But I didn't have much time to think about it. Somebody else was bound to discover her soon, and there would be police, hotel security, crime scene teams, doctors. I couldn't take her away and hide her, but I could certainly see that the thing was done right. I had, after all, a good friend on the New York City police. The thing to do was call Lieutenant Lincoln, before some official idiot came barging in and messed up the evidence.

There was a pay phone in the lobby, but a call meant money. I reached for my pants pocket, then realized my phony stage suit, made for appearances rather than function, didn't have pockets. Hoping for some change, I looked for Jenny's purse, the fancy beaded evening bag in which she'd had that gun of hers. It wasn't on the table. I pushed my chair back and looked on the floor, but it wasn't there, either.

I couldn't make my call, but there was one thing I could do. Up front, on the Crocodile Books table where Jenny had been sitting, lay her program, and—if I was lucky—inside it was the piece of paper she'd hidden as Stanway approached. Up front, Harlan Landis was polishing off his introduction of the most important award of the evening.

"And now, ladies and gentlemen," he said, "the award that traditionally comes last in our ceremony, for the single novel of the year that best exemplifies the finest of mystery fiction . . ."

I tried my legs gingerly, took a step or two. It was like walking across the deck of a ship in a high gale. The floor seemed to give under me, and I made my way toward the front of the ballroom reeling like a drunken sailor.

". . . in the great tradition of Poe, of Agatha Christie, of Rex Stout, Raymond Chandler, Ross Macdonald . . ."

Another shot rang out and Landis ducked, grinned, laughed with the audience. I paused beside the Crocodile Books table, not daring to look over at Sarah and Eddie. Jenny's program was still lying there. I grabbed it and stuffed it inside my jacket without peeking at the paper inside.

"This year's nominees are: George Paul Donovan, *Ghost Dancer;* Margery Beekman-West, *Mr. Bones;* Rita Kovacs, *Dusty Death;* Imogen Vail, *The Black Palace;* Henrietta Slocum, *Death of a Double Agent.* And the winner is . . ."

I stepped up onto the dais, suddenly on solid ground. Landis stared, the envelope half open in his hand. I shooed him away from the mike and usurped the podium.

"Ladies and gentlemen," I said, "I'm sorry to interrupt the awards, but I have an announcement to make."

I caught a glimpse of Sarah's scarlet dress, her face a pale blur beneath the dark hair. In the back of the ballroom, at her lone table, Jenny, too, was waiting. I grabbed hold of the podium and forged on.

"Imogen Vail has been murdered," I said into the mike.

My voice, echoing through the microphone, sounded heavy and short of breath and I knew they could not fail to believe me. Everyone stared, and for a moment there was only silence.

"She's been shot to death," I told them.

I wasn't certain where it began. A nervous, tentative venture of laughter. Then another, and another after that, taking fire from each other, catching, rising, swelling into certainty, filling that immense fraud of a room where mortality was a meal ticket designed with all the ingenuity greed and the hunger for fame could devise.

The audience seemed to be delighted. Jenny's dying was the perfect climax to the evening's charades.

5

It had taken until almost ten-thirty that desolate wet morning before a woman jogger with three greyhounds on leashes discovered the body of Gilbert McKelvie on the bench at the corner of the Shakespeare Garden. Others had passed him, but by then he was stretched out the length of the bench, as though asleep; his clothes were shabby, a copy of the *Times* lay across his legs, insulation from the chill and the mist. The small gun was almost hidden by the wet grass; the crumpled piece of yellow paper, sodden with mist, looked like so much litter. At a distance he seemed no different from a dozen other rootless men sheltered in packing box lean-tos and mattress cartons, rolled up in old clothes and discarded rugs, stealing a night's sleep on benches in the rain. People saw McKelvie, shook their heads, wondered why the Mayor, the Governor, the President didn't do something about this sort of thing, and then moved on.

In the end it was not the woman herself but her three overbred dogs who found McKelvie. The smell of death drew them like food.

David knew he should have waited for the police and told them the whole confused history of the anonymous phone calls and the woman he thought of as Jenny. But police meant a day lost to irrelevant questions; he would inevitably be a suspect himself, and everything he told them would be doubted, checked and double-checked. He couldn't involve the friend who had obliged with the dubious wiretap, and there was no other way to explain how he had known McKelvie's name and address. Besides, every minute he wasted in futile official procedures and explanations was one minute more for McKelvie's killer to escape.

And David did believe there was a killer. McKelvie's automaton voice on the telephone still hummed in his ears and half the message had come true. Somebody had certainly died, but David, the actor caught foolishly inside his role, had once again been powerless to stop it.

It had looked to him at first like suicide, one shot to the head from the tiny gun. McKelvie was alone in the garden when David left it, still alone when he returned, and because of the drizzle not many people had been anywhere in the park that early. After she left McKelvie, Jenny had been in David's view all along, and she had been as stunned by the sound of the shot as he was. Though she had given McKelvie the gun, she had certainly not intended it to be used on him. In his own mind, David had cleared her completely.

But it must've been someone McKelvie knew. Who else could have walked straight up and put a bullet in his forehead? There was no sign that the dead man had struggled, tried to run, even moved from where he had been sitting during the meeting with Jenny. The instinct of anyone threatened by a stranger surely would be to run. But McKelvie hadn't moved. Someone he knew and trusted had simply walked up to him, taken Jenny's foolish little gun, shot him to death, and walked away again.

One other thing made David certain the death had not been suicide. He had found the gun lying on the grass next to McKelvie's left foot, as though it had fallen from his dead left hand when his body slumped over. But Gilbert McKelvie was right-handed. He opened doors, rubbed his eyes, wound his wristwatch not with his left hand but with his right. When Jenny gave him the gun, she had put it into his right hand. If the person who killed McKelvie had been trying to make it look like suicide, he or she had not known him well enough to succeed. A right-handed killer, an impulse killer sickened and stunned by what he had done, might've dropped the gun exactly where David had found it—out of the killer's right hand as he faced the body, onto the grass beside McKelvie's left foot.

Who could it have been? In all the days since David had identified and trailed him, the elegant woman in the gray suede coat was the only person who had seemed even to know McKelvie, much less think him important enough to bother getting rid of. McKelvie was an isolate, bound by ironclad routine. He got up in the morning, raised his bedroom shade halfway, looked out onto the blind doorways and parked cars of Eighty-seventh Street, then pulled the shade down again and disappeared. Forty minutes later, at exactly seven thirty-five, McKelvie came out the basement-level front door of the old brownstone, up the few worn steps past the iron-barred windows of the first-floor flat, dropped a brown paper bag of trash into one of the green garbage cans at the curb, and went on toward the avenue.

On the first morning of watching, David had risked losing his quarry in order to examine the contents of that paper bag. They proved just as disposable and anonymous as their owner: a used plastic safety razor of the cheapest brand; several mass-mail ads for magazines, book clubs, insurance policies, all addressed to Occupant or with the address labels torn into tiny pieces; a few used tissues, white, of the cheapest paper; one foil tray with the remains of a TV dinner—a sodden lump of mashed potato, a few mushy emerald green peas, some slippery gravy.

But there had been one exception to this deliberate anonymity. Under the trash and carefully sealed in a Ziploc bag was a photograph, three by five, color, of a dark-haired young girl in cardinal red cap and gown, posed in front of some flowering bushes. On the back, written in red ink in a woman's handwriting, so carefully drawn it was almost printing, was a message.

Mr. Mac, it read. *This was my Elizabeth, so beautiful. The world is too much with us. Go well.*

It was signed at the bottom with a single word: VANGIE.

David saved the photograph. Next day he checked the bag of discards again. It contained the usual throwaways, and in the bottom was another photo, this time a sawtooth-edged Brownie snapshot, sepia-tinted with age and showing a young couple in Forties swimsuits splashing and laughing on a crowded beach. On the back, as before, was a message:

Mr. Mac, honey. Here is me and my Walt, Miami, 1946. In a real dark night of the soul it is always three o'clock in the morning. Go softly. Your friend, VANGIE.

Each day the photos continued to appear in the trash bag and each day David kept them. They were the only things bearing McKelvie's name in any form: Mr. Mac. He had been able to destroy every other trace of his own existence, but the gentle messages of introduction addressed to him had been written in ink. The only way to destroy them was to tear up the pictures themselves, and that he had not been able to do. Instead he had left them in the bag, carefully packaged for his watcher to find.

That first morning David stopped to investigate the bag of trash, he'd been almost sure he had lost McKelvie by the time he'd finished, but there was just a chance he could spot the tall, thin, stooped figure once he turned onto Amsterdam Avenue—waiting for a bus, perhaps, or trying to hail a cab. David hurried round the corner and stood there scanning the morning traffic on the sidewalk for five minutes or so when he saw the lean, shabby figure of McKelvie across the street, hunched against the plate glass window of a toy shop, watching him. He was waiting for David to catch up, giving him plenty of time to explore that bag of trash and find the photograph.

After that, each morning was the same. Whatever the game was, the leaving and finding of these snapshots was part of it, and both of them continued to play by the unspoken rules.

Now McKelvie was dead, and there was only one person aside from Jenny who seemed to have known him. Had that gunshot not forced David to let her go, he would've followed Jenny home, perhaps even questioned her directly; finding her now would take days, if he could do it at all. Except for laying McKelvie's body carefully on the bench, he had disturbed nothing in that garden; he hadn't even nudged the gun or the crumpled yellow paper accidentally with his foot. But he couldn't be sure he hadn't been seen—by the killer or by some good citizen who could describe him to the police. Even now they might be on his trail. He had to find the woman who called herself Vangie quickly, before they caught up with him.

It was nearly noon and the lunch hour traffic was heavy on Amsterdam Avenue as he sat in a coffee shop pretending to eat a tuna salad on rye. Before him on the chipped Formica tabletop lay the photos—eight of them, one for each day he had trailed McKelvie, including today.

The most recent was a Polaroid, overexposed, of a middle-aged woman in what looked like a fancy-dress costume—a purple, beaded turban and some sort of cloak. *Dearest Mr. Mac, my darling. Here is screwy Elva Ziegler from the third floor front, in her uniform for reading the horoscopes.*

Underneath was a verse David recognized as Housman:

> *The stars have not dealt me the worst they could do:*
> *My pleasures are plenty, my troubles are two.*
> *But oh, my two troubles they reave me of rest.*
> *The brains in my head and the heart in my breast.*

It was signed as before—*Go gently. Your best friend,* VANGIE

The photos were a wordless biography of a woman who had been, from the look of her, in her thirties in 1946. Now she must be in her middle seventies. Aside from the faded old seaside shot, none of the pictures were of Vangie herself. One was labeled *Walt, 1969,* another *Elizabeth's wedding, 1972.* The remaining three were of buildings on what looked like New York streets. One was a narrow storefront squeezed between a deli and a bookstore, the sign over the door reading KRAUS AND GLICKMAN, FINE SHOES; the second was a downtown theatre, people in Forties outfits lined up for tickets to a show called *Slap-Happy;* the third building was a neat brownstone with flower boxes at the windowsills, a spreading elm shading the open windows of the first-floor flat.

It took David more than one look to convince himself that the legend on the back was true: *Mr. Mac, sweetheart. Here is our building, can you believe it, the year my Walt and I moved in, 1952? Bare ruined choirs where late the sweet birds sang. Go well. Your friend,* VANGIE.

And so it was. Forty years had worn the front steps swaybacked, brought Dutch elm disease to kill the precious tree, eaten the brickwork away with grime, exhaust and acid rain, rotted the flower boxes, shut and locked and barred the windows. But it was the same building where McKelvie had lived and where Vangie herself must be living now, reading Shakespeare, Wordsworth, Housman, Scott Fitzgerald, and writing out her messages to "Mr. Mac."

The cracked concrete front steps seesawed a little under his weight as David stepped down onto them from the sidewalk at just past two that afternoon. Someone had smashed a crack pipe and bits of glass glittered in the mist that still fell intermittently. But no mist could wash away the scrawl of white paint above the door. "Fuck off!" it screamed, and nothing contradicted it but Vangie's quiet adjurations. Go gently. Go softly. Go well.

As was usual, the front door opened into a cramped no-man's-land, a vestibule with a second, electrically-locked inner door connected to a buzzer system mounted on the wall. The buzzers were arranged according to apartment numbers, small cards underneath with the tenants' names. David squinted at them dumbly, his head pounding. When he'd found McKelvie's body, he had taken no time for physical reactions, had barely noticed the racing of his pulse. Now the jolt of adrenaline had worn off; he was exhausted, queasy, nerve-ends rising in tidal floods like violent chills along his spine, his arms and legs. He had to fight for control as he stood in the tiny entryway, where the heavy stink of urine battled with cheap disinfectant, bringing tears to his eyes. He wiped them away and looked again.

McKelvie, G. Two-A.

Above that, in Three-A, was Ziegler, E. Beside the name a silver new moon and a tiny gold star in stick-on foil had been added. *Screwy Elva Ziegler,* thought David, *who reads the horo-scopes.*

Below McKelvie's buzzer, in the space for apartment One-A, the card was yellowed with age, dog-eared and slipping out of the holder at one end. David pushed it back in and stared at it in relief. One-A. Glickman, W. *My Walt. Kraus and Glickman, Fine Shoes. Walt and Vangie. Mrs. Walter Glickman.*

David pushed the buzzer of One-A. No answer. He pushed it again.

"What?" demanded a voice from the speaker beside the door.

It was a rich voice with a good register; nothing querulous about her. David felt he had come to the right place.

"Mrs. Glickman? Vangie?" he said.

"How do you know?"

"I've got the photographs you gave McKelvie."

There was a pause, but still the buzzer that opened the door into the building did not sound. A minute or so passed, and David was about to ring again when at last she broke radio silence.

"Mr. Mac gave *you* my pictures? He gave them *away?*"

The ache of betrayal was in her voice. David felt himself losing her. He had to pull her back, but imagination failed him. He hadn't slept more than three or four hours a night for over a week, and last night not at all. His head was reeling, pounding.

"He—he wanted me to hold them for him. He asked me to bring them back to you," he told her thickly. "Please let me in."

"Go to hell," said the voice. But he knew she was still listening.

"Please, Vangie."

As he spoke into the choking stink, the sudden calm of his words surprised him; he heard them at a distance, like a voice on the radio. The old woman's breath was against the open speaker, rooms away. He knew he had to speak a tongue she would under-stand.

"Vangie," he said. "No man is an island, entire of itself. Please."

She said nothing, and in one second more he would have turned away. Then, suddenly, the buzzer sounded. He grabbed the door-knob and pushed his way into the front hall.

The door of apartment One-A was still closed tight, but there was a tiny peephole at eye level. She was checking him out.

Vangie saw a slender, long-legged man with grace and control that showed even through his weariness. The guy looked exhausted, maybe sick. Maybe tapped out of crack and burning dry, like the kids who broke into her mailbox, forced the security door and roamed the halls, banged and kicked on the door of her apartment claiming everything she had. She had called the cops, but when they got there, the kids were gone. As soon as the cops left, they were back, kicking, pounding, yelling filth, lighting pieces of paper and shoving them under her door. Vangie got saucepans of water and drenched the rug, pushed her old buffet against the shivering door, and sat all night with Walter's old tire iron in her hands. She had looked out through the peephole at their faces, desperate faces full of fear, needing to punish her for making them afraid, making them empty.

Vangie got a better grip on the tire iron and squinted again through the peephole at her visitor. He was somewhere past thirty, but how far past it was hard to say. There were, Vangie would've said, complications in his dark blue eyes that didn't depend on age. They depended on the payment of dues, the secret official union card of the human race. Across great spaces you spotted a member, as she had spotted McKelvie in Two-A. You raised a hand and offered welcome.

She considered opening the door, but the tire iron in her hand stopped her. With it came Walt's voice. *"For dreamers like you, my dear, caution is the order of the day. When tempted to trust, count ten and pick up a big stick."* She continued her inventory.

The guy—you had to face it—was a looker. He had dark hair, almost black but not quite, not if you looked close. High, narrow bones, straight brows, a perfect nose. Definitely an upper-class nose, Duke of Windsor stuff. Even the ears, what showed of them under the hair, were pretty good. Good ears were not a common thing; they played most good-looking guys for suckers, flapping around like Dumbo. This guy's were understated, close to the head, and they detracted nothing from the handsome face. But though the two halves of his face were each almost perfect, they didn't exactly match. One eye didn't open as wide as the other, one corner of the mouth lifted a bit higher, at a different angle than the other. This difference intrigued her; without it he might've been too pretty and fallen for himself in a big way. A lot of handsome guys had no insides and didn't miss them; they prowled the world like tomcats on the make, licking and preening and purring like hell.

"What's your name, Mr. Photographs?" said Vangie through the door.

"David."

A nice voice, but he talked funny. From the other side of the moon instead of the door. The wide eyes were red around the edges, he didn't get enough sleep. Or maybe it was nose-candy, after all—that made you red rabbit eyes, too. He needed a shave, also, this David, the sweet curve of the jaw was blue with whiskers.

Vangie opened the door a crack. If you kept the chain on, it was okay, and she still had the tire iron. You were okay, so long as you could swing a tire iron.

"So, David Photographs?" she said, peering around the edge of the door.

She was perhaps seventy-four, small bright eyes behind bifocals with pink plastic frames, a wide, full mouth with false teeth that didn't quite fit.

"So what can I do for you? And where's Mr. Mac, if you don't mind?" said Vangie.

David tried to answer, but couldn't. His head felt as if it would explode and he grabbed the door with both hands to keep from falling.

"I got a tire iron!" she cried. "Don't try a thing! What did you do with Mr. Mac?"

"Dead," breathed David, and crumpled onto the cracked linoleum outside Vangie Glickman's door.

*   *   *

"It's really Evangeline," she told him. "My Papa was an English teacher, Brooklyn Heights, forty-seven years, bless his heart. He loved Longfellow." She made a face. " 'By the shores of Gitche Gumee.' Baloney, but the man was going for the mass markets. The good stuff I read with my Walter. Shakespeare, Yeats, John Donne. It was the Donne that got me, that 'No man is an island' stuff you pulled at the front door."

By now David was propped against the door frame outside Vangie's flat, a cold wet towel across the back of his neck and a glass of straight whiskey in his hand. She had brought them, tried to rouse him and then, the instant he began to respond, had scuttled back inside again. Now she sat on a kitchen chair pulled up to the partly open door, the chain fastened tight, Walt's tire iron laid across the lap of her plaid cotton housecoat as she talked.

"Drink the booze, honey, it'll make you feel better." She was silent for a long moment; somewhere in the room beyond her a clock ticked with ponderous regularity. David caught the scent of her, made of peppermint, flowery talcum, bourbon, and old age. Vangie took a deep breath. "Mr. Mac's really dead, then?" she said softly.

"Yes." David closed his eyes and gulped some of the whiskey.

Vangie studied him. He was jumpy as hell, a sign of guilt, maybe. How else did he know McKelvie was dead? Somehow he was mixed up in it, but you couldn't tell. *"Don't jump to conclusions,"* the voice of Walt grumbled in her ear. *"Fools rush in, but most of them never rush out."* The guy was as white as paper sitting there on the floor. Did killers have such backlash reactions? Guilty, scared, or running on the rims—they could look a lot alike.

"So," she said suddenly. "He had a heart attack? A bus ran over him? A jerk pushed him in front of the IRT?"

"He was shot," David said. His voice sounded loud in the empty hallway, the diction careful from habit. "One shot, in the forehead. I found him."

"Where?"

"In Central Park. I left him for a minute. I heard a shot. When I came back, he was dead."

"Friends?" She meant lovers. The guy was handsome and seemed gentle, and McKelvie had been alone too much. "You and Mac, you were friends?"

"He was—important to me," said David grimly. "But, no. Not friends."

All of a sudden Vangie slammed the door shut. It stayed shut for perhaps two minutes. Then it creaked slowly open again.

"You said friends, before!" she cried. "You lied to me!"

"No. I only said he gave me your photos to keep." He dug clumsily into his pocket, found them, and shoved them through the open space toward her.

Vangie grabbed them, shuffled through them. Then she stood up and slipped the chain off the door. David didn't move, just looked up at her.

She laid down the tire iron. "What the hell," she said, and pushed the door wide.

"Two years, he's been here." Vangie Glickman eased herself up off the balding green plush sofa in the middle of the room and reached for her splay-footed steel cane. She pointed to the ceiling. "Upstairs, Two-A. Unfurnished. When he moved in, not even an easy chair, a couch. They took up a mattress, a table, a hard chair. Like a monk. In two years, he only brings home books, as bad as me. You can find everything in a book."

If she was right, Vangie had certainly given herself every opportunity. The small flat overflowed with books. They stood in toppling heaps on the floor, spilled out of bookcases and onto tables, lay open on the tops of counters and refrigerator, lined up neatly between bookends. They warmed the dim old room and filled it.

"And the stereo," she said. "He had his stereo. He had to play the record, didn't he?"

"What record?"

"A record, music. The same every night. Classical stuff. Me, beyond Bing Crosby, nothing, I'm a musical illiterate. Voices, a choir, Latin maybe, but I don't have the gift of tongues. That record, with Mr. Mac it was a form of worship."

David put a chipped enamel pot of water onto the old gas stove in the kitchenette as Vangie spooned instant Folger's into delicate blue-and-white cups.

"You like them, honey?" she said, beaming. "My wedding dishes. The last two cups I didn't bust. The damn arthritis, I drop a lot of stuff. I was careful to keep two. One for me, one for Mac."

"Did he come for coffee often?"

She laughed, a good laugh, not just from the head but as though her whole body were laughing. "Never! Not once. Only up here." She tapped her temple with a thick forefinger, then grew quiet again. " 'The lunatic, the lover, and the poet/ Are of imagination all compact.' For a lunatic, I qualify. Every day I waited, when he came from work. After the photographs, I hoped he would come. Never once. I waited anyway, what the hell?"

"He didn't work at home, did he?"

Freelance manuscript readers were a sort of cottage industry in Manhattan. Most were publishing hopefuls, would-be editors without connections to a regular job, or they were actors between parts, writers nursing the Great American Novel on the side—the half-failed, dreamy ground-clutter of the arts, with a habit to feed as long and pernicious as De Quincey's opium. Only a few had no other incomes. They were the lost causes, solitaries who seldom left home and worked wherever they lived, in such spiritual ghettos as McKelvie's brownstone, venturing out only to collect their assignments. But during the days David had followed him, McKelvie had scarcely spent enough time at home to read his manuscripts.

"He went out in the morning, at night he came back," said Vangie with a shrug. "What do I know? I assumed." She dumped a packet of sugar into her cup. "What work was it?"

"He read manuscripts for publishers and agents," said David.

"So! I knew it, always books!" It seemed to please her. "Until the last month, six weeks maybe, he was home most of the afternoon. Complete quiet upstairs, no music. Not even the phone would ring. I figured he was reading, maybe he's doing research, a scholar, right? Lately, though, he goes out, he's gone all day, more or less. Only at night, that quiet. And every night, around nine o'clock, his telephone rings. Then he plays the record. After that I went up and put the pictures under his door. Those stairs, with my knees, it wasn't always fun, I'll tell you. One night I heard him talking."

"Was somebody there with him?"

"Just a voice. A man's, something like Mr. Mac's. But not really. Tinny, like over the phone."

"Could you make out any of the words?"

She shrugged. "Not many. It wasn't a loud voice. 'Drop it.' " Vangie thought for a moment. " 'Stop it.' Something like that."

You can stop it, thought David, hearing again the mechanical voice on the phone. *Someone is going to die. You can stop it.*

He followed Vangie back to the sofa with the cups, helped her to sit. She squinted at him over the bifocals.

"You got nice manners, honey, you know that? Somebody taught you what was what." The rich alto voice grated, cracked. Her words came in jerks. "He did, too. Have nice manners. Mr. Mac."

Then suddenly, carefully, she set down the cup and began to cry. Her mourning was as complete as her delight, but she made no sound, just crouched there shaking with grief for a man she had perceived only in haphazard fragments. She had seen him through windows, thought David, heard his music through the floor. From this she had created a life and invested it with her own complexities; needing an equal, she had selected McKelvie and trusted him. Now she was alone again.

David laid his hand on the sofa between them, open for her to take. At first she hesitated, but after a minute or two she touched him, fingertips barely brushing his palm. Then she grasped his hand and held on, held hard for what seemed a long while. At last she let him go and blew her nose, then matter-of-factly picked up her coffee cup again.

"I'm a fruitcake, right?" She smiled and coughed and tried to smile again. "But you gotta hitch on somewhere, don't you, honey?" she said. "Otherwise, at my age, the old gray matter goes sailing out to sea. You go sour. Screwy. The doctor gives you happy pills. You start trying to read the goddamn stars."

"And you hitched onto McKelvie."

She nodded. "I don't go out. Who strolls around in a war zone? Anyway, D'Agostino's delivers, they bring me my pills from Medicine Chest. I belong to seven book clubs. With a touch-tone phone today, you can get anything—Dial-A-Prayer, Joke Line, sex advice, weather reports, movie reviews. I got my books, the phone, the radio." She fell silent, staring into her cup. "I'm a good listener," she said at last, half to herself.

"And," said David, "you can look out your windows."

The two barred windows over Vangie's kitchen sink looked straight up onto the sidewalk. A couple was passing, a man in joggers and a woman in high-heeled pumps.

Vangie glanced up at them. "Sexy Suzy from next door," she said, "and Mr. Big, the pusher from the corner, his regular spot. Every day he walks her home to see she isn't mugged. Big tough guy, right? Look at Suzy."

The shiny patent shoes stopped and so did the expensive leather joggers. The pointed toe of the black pump teased, brushed itself like a cat across the instep of the man's foot, her other foot up on tiptoe.

"Big sloppy kiss," groaned Vangie. "That's old Suzy for you."

"You get to know a lot of people, for a lady who never leaves home."

"Hell, honey, I made the names up, didn't I? Names I only know if they're in the building. Elva Ziegler, Three-A. Freddy Adler, Two-B, he plays the flute all night, Elva says in the altogether but how would she know, a woman who thinks Ed Koch is the reincarnation of Franklin D. Roosevelt?" Vangie set down her cup. "Three-B, next to Elva, that's Mrs. Graybill, she's in Our Mother of Hope. Some hope, an old people's home out on Staten Island. All her stuff sits up in the apartment, furniture and dishes and all. I tell her on the phone, she ought to sublet whether the landlord likes it or not.

She thinks she's coming back some day, she keeps on paying rent."
Suddenly she grabbed his hand again, squeezed it, let it go. "And of
course, Mr. Mac over my ceiling. Otherwise, I just know shoes,
through the window. Forty years my Walter sold fine shoes—not
junk like Sexy Suzy wears, plastic without even a tricot lining. Real
leather, lined, hand-stitched. I know shoes, all right."

"Have you ever seen a pair of gray suede shoes go past?" said
David. "Light gray. Expensive. High heels."

"Oh, *her,*" said Vangie. "The Queen of Spades. She came twice,
once in January. She waited a long time, those shoes back and forth
on the sidewalk. Second time around Valentine's Day. He was expecting her that time, he came down and let her in. Early in the
morning, before he went out."

On the table under the lamp was a book of Russian stories,
among them Pushkin's classic tale of a mad gambler. "Why do you
call her the Queen of Spades?" asked David.

"In her own eyes, there was no mistake about it. A queen. She
indulged herself and she expected to be indulged. Imperious. Is that
the word? And plenty of bucks, believe me. Those shoes cost two
hundred, rock bottom. Italian, handmade. Anyway, all those rings
she wore—would such hands clean the john and scrape ketchup off
the dishes? I figure a maid, maybe a chauffeur."

David knew how it must've been, the old woman watching
through her peephole as McKelvie let his visitor in, led her past the
door and up the stairs. Two grotesque figures between surreal con-
verging walls, seen through the funhouse mirror of that tiny lens.

Vangie studied him over the unnerving pink glasses. "You know
her? You know who she is? She's got something to do with Mr. Mac
getting killed?"

"I don't know her name, no. I saw her with McKelvie. I—think
she was involved in his death, but she couldn't have killed him, not
directly."

David considered telling her about the anonymous phone calls
and his days of trailing the dead man, but decided against it. How
could she understand his involvement when he didn't understand it
himself?

Vangie forced the issue. "You said you weren't friends, but you hung around watching him? You kept track of who he saw, you knew where he lived. You knew what he did for a living. Okay." She reached for the bottle of bourbon and poured herself a coffee cupful, another for him. "You're a cop? A private detective? A spy?"

"I'm—I'm a reporter. Writer. Magazines. Freelance. Investigative reporter." It sounded fishy as hell and he knew it. "McKelvie called me about a story, something he thought I ought to write. I was checking him out, seeing if the guy was genuine. I followed him for about a week."

"Okay, Geraldo. What kind of a story?"

"It was—" He tried to remember the headlines on the latest *Enquirer.* "It was about a rock star, faked tapes, lip-sync on the videos." He inhaled the rest of his own bourbon and took a deep breath. "I figured I'd better get a line on him. It sounded phony."

Vangie studied him. "Phony as hell," she said.

David forged on. "The woman. The Queen of Spades? She knew him. She met him every day, walked across the park to meet him. She was with him this morning, just before he was shot. Or shot himself." Though he didn't believe it, suicide was still a possibility.

Vangie sipped at the whiskey. "I thought if I gave him the pictures," she said softly. "If he had something. Real faces, you know? A piece of life to get you through. Even on loan, it's better than nothing. And I've got plenty of pictures, I could afford it. I was afraid for him. A lone thing." She stared into the cup. "I didn't trust that woman, the gray shoes. You remember Pushkin, 'The Queen of Spades'? The old bitch with the magic secret, for which the soul is the price tag?" She shivered. "Lousy vibes, honey. A man-eater."

She grabbed her cane suddenly and heaved herself to her feet, then headed for a particular pile of books at one end of a shelf near the door. She shuffled the pile around, moved another book or two, then pulled a thick one off the shelf. It still had its dust jacket, bright red with black lettering.

"Is it her?" she demanded, turning the back cover to face him.

The picture was, like most cover photos, years old and touched up to begin with, glamorized for the fans. But the heavy black hair, the dark eyes, the aristocratic bones of the face were the same. The airbrushed photo was familiar as the real woman had not been, but some echo had been called up in his memory, and he gave her the name he had heard me use for her—Jenny.

The book was *The Black Palace*, by Imogen Montague Vail.

"She only came those two times," said Vangie. "Both times she went upstairs with Mac. First time she stayed a couple of hours. Second time maybe fifteen, twenty minutes." She shook her head. "What was he doing, messing around with big shots? What could he have that such a woman wanted?"

"Did they seem friendly?" asked David. "Fond of each other? Arguing, maybe? Could you have heard them down here, if they had a spat?"

"Heard them? Honey, when he brought home pizza from Al-binetti's on Broadway I could smell the anchovies down here. When he caught a cold, I could hear him reach for a Kleenex. Believe me, they didn't fight. She was too much for him, that woman. Whatever she wanted he would have had to give." Vangie turned the pages of *The Black Palace* thoughtfully. "She hated the human race, this Queen of Spades," said the old woman. "Her people, they have no will, you see. They flounder around at the mercy of their glands. Even the good guys are bastards between the sheets. A profound anger. Not merely resentment of individuals, but the species in general. What is it, the line from Yeats?"

" 'An intellectual hatred is the worst.' " David supplied the line instinctively and Vangie smiled. "Did McKelvie have any other visitors? Anyone who came to see him, asked for him when he was out?"

"You mean Boots?" she said. "Brown leather boots, old, out of style—those pointed toes."

"Cowboy boots?"

"No. The cut was wrong. Boots like the Beatles. You remember, back in the Sixties? The London Look, it was hot stuff. Wide-bottomed pants to go over short, ankle-length boots. They were good leather, and always the pointed toes."

"So it was a man? This Boots?"

She hesitated. "Probably. Maybe. The pants, I can tell you, weren't wide enough at the bottoms. Jeans, and tight, rolled up to clear the tops of the boots. A good polish, though. Does a woman polish her shoes? In this house it was my Walter's job. Every Sunday night, out came the Esquire Boot Polish and the brushes. Every shoe in the place."

"Did Boots go upstairs?"

"No. McKelvie would come down, they would talk outside, lean against the parked cars sometimes. Even lousy weather, snow. Always outside."

"So you got a look at him, then?"

She shrugged. "Up to the hips, is that a look? It's stretching a point to call them hips. Narrow. Skinny legs. From down here, that's all I could see."

"Did Boots come often?"

"Like clockwork," she replied. "Twice a week, Tuesday and Saturday. From the day after Christmas till New Year's Eve. That was the last time, New Year's Eve. Since then, no Boots."

"If you saw them again, do you think you could recognize—"

Suddenly he broke off. The buzzer from the outer door growled angrily, then growled again. David flinched, and felt Vangie staring at him.

She looked at the speaker on her wall, but didn't move. This guy didn't seem like a killer, but how could you tell? Some of them, maybe, had nice manners and read a lot and had bottomless blue eyes to die for. The Geraldo stuff, obviously, was spur-of-the-moment malarky, the best he could do in a pinch. He had something at stake, and he was nervous as a cat in a roomful of rocking chairs, to quote Tennessee Ernie Ford.

Once again she heard Walt's voice in her ear: *"When tempted to trust, count ten and pick up a big stick."* Instead she picked up Walt's tire iron and made her way to the door. The buzzer was insistent.

"What?" she said into the speaker.

"Police," said a woman's voice. "Detective Sergeant Bryce. A man from your building has been found dead. We need to ask a few questions."

Vangie took a deep breath. "Murdered?" she said into the speaker.

"It's possible. Someone was seen in the area."

David tried to keep perfectly still, but the coffee cup rattled against the saucer in his hand. She glanced over at him, then turned back to the speaker.

"This someone was a woman?"

"No. We got a tip about a man, fairly tall, good-looking, late thirties-early forties, black hair." The sergeant sighed into the speaker with a hiss. "Could you just let us in, ma'am, please?"

Vangie took her hand off the speaker button and turned to David. Before she spoke, she studied his face for a moment, making her decision. After all, however the hell he came by them, he had brought her back the photographs. She could almost see Walt shaking his head.

"The bedroom's through there, honey," she told David. "Take that coffee cup with you so the cop-person won't ask who my company is. And don't break it, okay?"

He obeyed her, and in another minute there was a buzz as she opened the hall door for Sergeant Bryce. Then the sound of feet, two pairs, and the door closed behind the two cops. Vangie's heavy-footed cane thumped its way across the living room.

"I'm Sergeant Peggy Bryce. This is Detective Schrader," said the cop. David left the bedroom door open just far enough to get a look before he pushed it silently shut. Bryce was small, but quick and wiry, and she spoke slowly, with a trace of Southern accent.

Vangie saw the bedroom door close. *"My dear,"* implored the voice of Walt in the ear of her memory. *"To take a chance is one thing. To put your neck in the guillotine is something else."*

She drew Sergeant Bryce aside and spoke in a hoarse whisper. "The guy you want," she said. "He's in there, in my bedroom!"

Then she let go and sank heavily down on the green plush couch to watch, as Ed Schrader drew his gun and flattened himself against the wall beside the bedroom door. Peggy Bryce, her own gun still in her purse, did the honors, but she wasn't much like the cops in Vangie's books.

She knocked politely on the door. "Police," she said calmly. "Better come on out now, if you don't mind. Just a few things we gotta clear up, okay?" She waited a beat. "Come on out, please." Another beat. Then she nodded to Schrader. "Okay," she said.

He didn't kick the door down. He didn't even throw it open and dive inside with his gun drawn. He just reached over and turned the door knob, then shoved the door open with the toe of his oversized nonregulation sneaker. The two cops moved cautiously into the bedroom, guns in hand.

Vangie sat on the sofa, mouth gaping, both hands over her eyes. In a minute Peggy Bryce was back, sitting beside her.

"Mrs. Glickman," she said gently. "There's nobody in there, ma'am."

Vangie took her hands from her eyes and stared through the open door into the bedroom. Sergeant Bryce was right. The man who had brought back her precious photographs, the man with guilt written on his handsome face like a neon sign, was gone, and so was the next-to-the-last cup and saucer of Vangie Glickman's wedding china.

6

"The guy you want? He's in there, in my bedroom!"

Though the old woman spoke in a whisper, only three feet and a sagging door separated her from David, who had been trained by no less than the Royal Academy of Dramatic Art to listen for mumbled cues and pick them up from half a stage away. Once more he had to make a choice—get away or stay and answer questions, explain why he'd left McKelvie's body without calling a cop, why he'd been in the park, why he'd come looking for Vangie. Even if he gave a fake name, they were bound to find out who he really was eventually. He could almost see the front pages of the tabloids, faked-up shots of his face, all the skewed bits the plastic surgery had left behind exaggerated to make him seem bizarre, deranged and out of control.

And there would be Gemma's face, his four-year-old daughter, tear-stained and wailing. And the stunned face of Alex, his wife, perfect and pale and never betraying the secret damage of their too-public lives.

He had seen those photographs before, on all the front pages and the magazine covers. At the time of the slashing, he had almost lost Alex, and Gemma with her. He couldn't let it happen again. There was only one choice. He would have to get away and clear things up himself, forestall the publicity somehow.

There was a knock on the bedroom door. "Police," said Peggy Bryce's calm voice. "Better come out now if you don't mind."

David looked desperately round the small room. One window,

barred, opening onto a tiny passageway that separated this building from the one behind it, barely wide enough for a man to walk down. A fire escape from upstairs debouched into this narrow space, and the passageway led to a gated exit facing Eighty-seventh Street, a leftover from the days when coal was delivered into the basement chute. He had to get into that passageway somehow.

"Just a few things we gotta clear up, okay?" The sergeant's voice was too friendly and much too close.

Off the bedroom was a tiny bathroom. Not likely to have a window, thought David, but if there was one, it, too, would face that precious passageway. He prayed that the old boards wouldn't creak under his feet as he moved toward the bathroom door.

It was only as he did so that he realized he was still holding Vangie's delicate blue-and-white cup and saucer. He was about to put it down on the night table when he changed his mind. At the foot of the bed was a cracked plastic carrier bag stuffed with balls of blue and orange yarn and a piece of knitting still on needles. Hurriedly he dumped the knitting onto the bed, keeping the balls of bright yarn for protection, and nestled the cup and saucer securely among them.

There was a window in the bathroom, wire-reinforced and double-bolted, high up in the wall and too narrow for most crooks to crawl through—but not barred. Outside was the fire escape from the two upper floors, and the passageway. Hanging the carrier bag on a clothes rack within reach, David pulled a low bath stool underneath the window and climbed up. The bolts were rusted with moisture from years of steamy showers; his heart sank when his first effort failed to budge them. But he couldn't give up. He stood on tiptoes, putting all his force into his forearms, shoving the heel of his right hand against the head of the bolt. At last it jolted loose and slid free!

"Come on out, please," said Sergeant Bryce from the living room.

One more sharp push. The second bolt shot free and David forced the heavy old window, painted shut years ago, to open. The only way to get through was at an angle, first one arm and shoulder, grab onto the fire escape, then the head and the other arm, then hang and balance till the legs were through.

But the carrier bag had to come with him. He grabbed it and leaned out the window to set it precariously on the nearest iron step of the fire escape ladder. Then he pulled himself through, snatched the carrier bag, and was gone.

"Musta got out through here," said Ed Schrader. "You oughta get bars on that window, ma'am."

Vangie nodded. The mist was thickening outside and the cool damp air through the open bathroom window felt good against her hot face. *Shame,* she thought. *A lousy thing to do, Walt or no Walt.* She had regretted her betrayal of Mr. Photographs almost as soon as the words were out of her mouth. Those kids with the burning papers had made her nutsy. She had liked this guy David, even if his story didn't quite add up, and when you liked you took on a responsibility.

"Did he give you a name, Mrs. Glickman?" asked Peggy Bryce. "What made you let him in?"

The old woman was determined to make up for her lapse of faith. "He said he had a package for Mrs. Graybill, upstairs. I take her mail, her daughter comes once a week to take it to the rest home."

"When you opened the door and saw there wasn't a package, did he force his way in? Threaten you at all? Was he armed?"

Vangie shook her head. "Good manners," she said. "A polite fellow."

"What did he want?"

"Questions, questions! My head is flying into pieces here. Please!"

Ed Schrader was dusting the bedroom door, the bathroom door, and the window for fingerprints. Sergeant Bryce led Vangie into the living room and eased her onto the couch.

"I'm sorry, Mrs. Glickman. Just a few more questions. About his name. He didn't give you a name, last name, first name, anything?"

Vangie blinked, stalling. "Something Italian," she said at last. "Frank DePalma." This was the name of a distant cousin, dead some fifteen years. *Forgive me, Frank, but as a cousin you were nothing to write home about anyway. Maybe you'll be some good to Mr. Photographs.*

"And why did he go into your bedroom?"

The Sergeant's eyes were stone gray and empty. *She doesn't believe a word of this,* thought Vangie.

"He said he wanted to wash his hands, with all the infections today you couldn't be too careful. Should I have said no?"

Schrader came out of the bedroom with his fingerprint gear. "Prints all over the place," he said, "most of 'em smudgy as hell. Doors, everybody that goes through grabs hold, you got half a dozen layers of prints. The window sill, he wiped them out when he slid his butt across it."

Peggy Bryce frowned. "He had to work on those bolts, Ed. He had to push the window up, it must've taken some handling."

"Bolts are too small for prints," he told her. "And the window? Hell, you use your hand, the heel, not the fingers, for Christ's sake." He demonstrated. "Gotta put some arm under it, see?"

"I see," said the Sergeant mildly. "I also hear."

Ed Schrader looked worried. "Sorry, Sarge. I mean, Sergeant. Ma'am. The language, it's a habit."

Bryce smiled at Vangie. "He's hard to housebreak," she said, then turned back to her partner. "There's one place you might check," she told him. "He had to catch hold of that fire escape to pull himself out the window. Try outside."

"In the rain?" Schrader didn't sound happy.

"It's not rain yet," Peggy Bryce told him. "But if you don't get out there, you're going to think you're in a hurricane when we get back to the office."

Once her partner was gone, the sergeant turned back to Vangie.

"You do know who he is, don't you? No fairy tales, honey. I'm too old for Sleeping Beauty."

The old woman shook her head. "Know him? The truth? No. He came to my door. Honest Injun."

Peggy nodded. "And you liked him. What did you tell him?"

"What did I know? He asked about Mr. Mac."

"Did he tell you McKelvie had been murdered?"

"Dead. He said, dead. That was all. He asked a few questions. Did McKelvie work at home, did I pal around with him, give him coffee."

"And what did you say?"

"I never met the man, even. He was quiet, a decent neighbor. What else did I know?"

"Frank DePalma." Peggy Bryce couldn't help smiling. "You made that up?"

"More or less."

"Because you changed your mind. You figured maybe he wasn't the man we wanted?"

"He admitted he was there, he saw the dead body. He *is* the man. But, for you, the wrong man. Not a killer. I have had killers, Sergeant, killers pounding on my door. Their eyes, staring. I knew better all along, but at the last minute I got scared, I did a crappy thing to him."

"But Mrs. Glickman. He ran."

"So? He had reasons of the heart. Further complications."

Peggy Bryce got up, handing Vangie a card. "This is my number at work." She scribbled something on the back. "And this is my apartment. I'm not going to drag you to the station and make you look at pictures or talk to police artists. None of that. But you have to make me a promise, honey. If you're right about this guy, he'll be back. He'll get in touch again, and when he does, you call me. Understand? Just me, on my own. To talk. Is it a deal?"

Vangie hesitated. What choice did she have?

"A deal," she said.

"Mr. Photographs!" muttered Vangie Glickman as she shut the door behind Sergeant Peggy Bryce.

She dragged her bad legs painfully to the ancient sofa and lowered herself into her usual spot next to the lamp table. On it lay the pictures. Her daughter, Elizabeth, was now dead. Her husband, Walt, also dead. She herself, the slim, laughing young woman from the chorus of *Slap-Happy* who had splashed on that Florida beach with Walt— That woman, too, was dead. She lived only a photographic life, eating memories. Even the old brownstone was dead, its crumbling brick and creaking boards and leaky plumbing entrapped in a new universe, ruled by terrorists on many levels, official and unofficial, and populated in separate cells by freaks and hermits, holdouts from a former world—herself and Elva, Freddy Adler and his flute, Mrs. Graybill waiting in her antiseptic room on Staten Island for the human kingdom to make a comeback.

And Mr. Photographs.

He was one of them. That was, Vangie knew, what she had seen in his face. Not guilt, not fear, but exile. The bottomless blue eyes were on the outside looking in. What he had seen in McKelvie was what she, herself, had seen. An ally, a compatriot who spoke the language of a country that no longer existed except in the surviving mind. And they both wanted the same thing, too—to find McKelvie's killer.

Vangie fought off the indulgence of tears. She might have betrayed him once, but never again. She poured a generous tot of whiskey into the last of her blue-and-white cups and drank it down.

"My apologies, Mr. David Photographs," she said aloud. "If I tell the cops on you again, may I die and come back as a cockroach. With apologies, also, to Mr. Kafka."

It was late afternoon and her shift was almost over, but Peggy Bryce sat at her desk, thinking. Probably she should've brought the old girl in and pumped her for every detail, at least made her go through the mug books. That was procedure. As the only woman and the newest member of the division's Homicide Task Force, Peggy was under a lot of pressure. She was determined to succeed, but she was just as determined not to ignore her instincts in favor of a book of rules made up mostly by men playing men's games for men's reasons.

That was why she hadn't pressured Vangie Glickman. She was a tough old girl; the eyes behind those cornball pink plastic glasses worked like a lie detector. Instinct had told Peggy that if she pushed too hard, the old woman would grow a shell like an armadillo and they'd get nothing. Sometimes you had to give people choices, even risky ones.

Not that she'd taken much stock in that anonymous tip about the dark-haired guy at the scene, anyway. It had been left at the duty desk out front, typed on plain white paper, electronic typewriter, no fingerprints, and the description of the scene in the park was perfect —position of McKelvie's body, clothes, location of the gun in the grass, of the soggy wad of yellow paper. Almost too detailed, the choice of words precise as if it had been edited. Same thing with the description of the tall, dark guy who'd turned up later at Mrs. Glickman's. Better than a goddamn photograph and a helluva lot better than a police artist could've done.

She smiled, listening to the diction of her thoughts. She was starting to sound like Ed Schrader. Well, better him than the King of Smarm, Captain Gifford "Rat-Cheese" Colby. City Hall had insisted Colby head the Task Force when the number of homicides began to mount, as it always did, with the onslaught of spring weather. He had a lot of pals in Trump Tower and he putted with the big boys at all the right Long Island golf clubs. His tongue was glib and his talk was cool and he handed out orders like General Patton on D-Day, but everybody on the force knew that if you needed backup, Rat-Cheese would be in conference, and you'd better get Lincoln.

Peggy closed her file and glanced across the room at the rubber soles of a pair of brown loafers propped up on a desk. The soles were run over at the backs and the imitation-leather uppers were cracked and starting to peel. Inside the shoes were a pair of feet in white cotton socks tinged with grey from too many washings. The feet were attached to Lieutenant Abraham Jeremiah Lincoln. If Gifford Colby was the absentee landlord of the Homicide Task Force, Lincoln was its seasoned, reliable workhorse.

She tossed the leftovers of her day—a subway token, the last of her trusty BurgerMaster Quik-Eats coupons, and the gold hoop earrings that felt like cement overshoes when you'd had them on for eight hours—into her bag and slipped the strap over her shoulder. Then she picked up the file on McKelvie and went over to Lincoln's desk. He didn't look up at first and she had a chance to watch him unobserved. A quiet guy, a wide face with a narrow scar below the right eye, a tight boxy chest, muscles that stayed tensed by habit.

"Got anything?" he said, looking up at her.

"Guy in the park." Peggy tossed the file on his desk. "If you get a minute, take a look, okay? We got a tip, but it feels lousy to me. Who delivers an anonymous tip typewritten to the front desk?"

Lincoln raised his eyebrows and the bags under his washed-blue eyes disappeared for a moment. "Typed? Not phoned?"

"Right. Weird thing is, the guy he fingered turned up at the victim's building this afternoon, asking questions. Spotted us and took off."

"But you still don't like it."

Peggy shook her head. "Even less. The whole thing doesn't smell right."

"Setup?"

She shrugged. "You tell me, Linc." She fiddled with a photograph on his desk, a blond woman of Lincoln's age—the middle forties—and two teenaged boys. "So," said Peggy. "How's it going, splitting up the old community property?"

Lincoln stared grimly down at his big hands. On the third finger of the left a pale shadow lingered, the faded circle left by a ring worn there for years and now removed. "How do you take half of nothing?" he said.

She ventured to let the tips of her fingers brush his arm, the first time she had ever touched a fellow officer outside the line of duty. Somehow, it didn't seem so risky with Lincoln. He wasn't the type to take advantage. He didn't look up at her, but she saw his fingers cup slightly, then relax.

"I went through it three and a half years ago," she said. "So. Welcome to the club, okay?"

He smiled, briefly. "Losers Anonymous," he said, and opened the McKelvie file.

Once he was free of Vangie's apartment, David slipped down the narrow passage, his broad shoulders scraping the wet bricks of the buildings on both sides, the precious carrier bag with the china cup and saucer bumping dangerously. He could not have said what he meant to do with it, nor why it must not be broken nor even chipped. But as soon as he had passed the gate onto Eighty-seventh Street and made it safely up to Broadway, he stopped to check, rearrange the balls of yarn, wedge the china more securely into the bag.

The Broadway bus was just pulling out; he barely cleared the closing doors and rode it, lurching and swaying in the center aisle, ten blocks uptown, to Ninety-sixth Street. There he caught a crosstown bus and rode through the park, getting off at Lexington Avenue. Next he caught a third bus downtown, then another crosstown at Forty-second Street, to get off at last a few blocks from Times Square, in the heart of the theater district.

He passed by the Booth Theatre, where the marquee now announced a new star in *Night of the Iguana*, and went into a small drugstore, one of the few shops in the area where he wasn't known. He bought a package of plastic safety razors and a barber's scissors with long, sharp points; there was a display of bright folding umbrellas near the door, and he bought a yellow one, and an electric blue nylon raincoat that folded up to pocket size. With his purchases and Vangie's knitting bag neatly ensconced in a brand-new red-and-black plaid tote bag, he went out onto Forty-second Street again, turned onto Seventh Avenue, and headed downtown to Penn Station.

It was then almost six o'clock; cabs passed him, and one of them might have been ours as we headed for the Hornsby Empire a few blocks away. But David's careful, circuitous route was hardly meant to be noticed. He moved quietly through the rush hour crowds, a shabby man who needed a shave, the bottoms of his jeans mud-spattered, the shoulders of his old tweed jacket glistening with mist. Nobody noticed him except to move away an inch or two, toward someone who looked more prosperous, more as they imagined themselves to look.

Once at Penn Station, he put his new plaid tote bag into a locker, keeping out only what he would need—the razor, the barber's shears, and the blue nylon raincoat. The men's room was nearly empty, but he had to wait until the last man was gone before he wedged the heavy steel wastepaper bin against the door. With this guarantee of temporary privacy, he set to work.

First a shave. Not comfortable without soap, and those damn faucets only let out a teaspoonful of tepid water at a time before they shut off automatically. When he'd finished there were three nice nicks oozing blood, but the two-day growth of dark beard was more or less gone. He splashed himself with a stingy portion of cold water and studied his distorted image in the cheap mirror. Better, or at least different. It would have to do.

Next the hair. He'd ignored barbers since he left the show, and the dark fringe was creeping over his collar, crowding his ears, falling over his forehead. Gingerly, hoping he wouldn't regret it, he grasped the scissors and began to snip.

Somebody pounded on the door when he was half finished, but he ignored it and went on, gathering the clippings into a paper towel as he worked. He winced a little when he took a look at the finished product; much more and he could've doubled for Yul Brynner.

Finally he put on the blue nylon raincoat, threw the paper towel full of shorn hair into the trash can, then lugged the can as quietly as he could away from the door. With the shears in his jacket pocket, he left the men's room just as a pair of well-dressed but frustrated travelers arrived with a sullen janitor in tow. The two businessmen stared at David.

"Ain't nothin' a-matter with that," growled the janitor, opening the door wide.

"How the hell . . . ?" said one of the men.

David smiled. When he spoke, it was in his best English accent,

London standard, Olivier-inspired. "It did stick, actually, just a bit. Seems quite all right now, though."

"You catch that haircut, Ralph?" he heard one of the men say as he walked away. "Can't get a cut like that in this country. Class. Real British class."

Across the expanse of the station was a rank of phone booths, the only thing David cared about now. He folded his long legs inside one of them and dialed the number of his own apartment across town.

"Cromwell residence," said a middle-aged voice. It was Mrs. Jackson, the housekeeper, staying late that Thursday night to clear up before her usual Friday off.

"Hi, Mrs. Jack," he greeted her. "It's me. Is my lady wife around?"

"Oh! Oh, yes, she's here. Hold on, sir." There was a hint of relief in the housekeeper's voice and David realized with a jolt that he hadn't spoken to the poor woman in such a casual and friendly tone in weeks. Christ, what had he been like with Alex and the kid?

"David?"

Alexandra's voice was never loud, especially on the phone. Now it was almost a whisper and very close to the mouthpiece.

Fear, he thought. *I've made you afraid of me.*

"Alexandra," he said softly. He hadn't called her that for years. "Red."

She took a breath and he could hear it catch involuntarily. She had been crying. "Where the bloody hell are you?" she said. "Why aren't you here?"

"I'm at Penn Station, Red. Listen, and don't ask questions till I'm through, all right?" A cop walked by and he shifted the phone to his other ear, turning his face toward the wall. "I've been getting some strange phone calls for the last few weeks. I didn't want to take any chances with you and Gemma, so I didn't say anything."

"You've been nosing around on your own again? Damn it, D. Did you tell Winston?"

"I found out who was making the calls and traced the address.

I've been following him. Gilbert McKelvie. This morning he was killed in Central Park. The police are looking for me."

"Sweet Jesus," she breathed.

"They don't know who I am. At least I don't think they do. But I've got to lie low for a bit."

"Where will you go? Let me come with you! I can be at Penn Station in half an hour. Twenty minutes!"

"No. Gemma needs you." He paused. "I want you with me. I want you."

"Then wait for me, blast you! I can get a cab and—"

"No, Red. You have to find Winnie. Tell him what I've said. Tell him someone he knows is involved, a writer called Imogen Vail. Jenny Vail. She may be in danger, too, I don't know. But she knew McKelvie, she was with him this morning just before he was killed. If Winnie could talk to her—"

"Yes." She had stopped protesting and begun to calculate. "He'll be at the Hornsby by now, the Edgars. I'll find him. Have him paged. Something." A pause. "Where will you be?"

"I don't really know," he lied. "Somewhere where I can think."

"D., you've got to go to the police, you know. Go right now, before something absolutely stupid happens and they find out who you are and—and—"

"Not yet, my love," he said. "Another day, maybe two. I need time. If I go to them without the answer, I'm still a suspect. That means I'm front page news, and so are you. So is Gemma. Do you want that?"

She said nothing for a while and he could hear, somewhere beyond, the high, clear voice of his daughter singsonging a tuneless bedtime rhyme with Mrs. Jack.

"Are you all right, D.?" asked Alexandra at last.

"Yes."

"You've been so—"

"I know. I've left you alone."

"And there's nobody—else? I thought . . ."

"Christ," he said. "Christ, no."

Again there was silence between them. He knew she would not break it.

"I'm sorry," he told her. "Tell them I'm sorry."

"Bloody hell," she whispered, and hung up.

7

"Okay, Mr. Sherman. One more time. Why did you suddenly leave your own table and follow the victim?"

"If you recall, Captain, Jenny wasn't a victim then, she was a fellow writer and an old acquaintance, and I've already told you at least fifteen times. It wasn't sudden. I'd been thinking about it all evening. I knew I should go over and say hello. I was table-hopping, like everybody else. She said she wanted to speak to me, but we were interrupted. I went off to try and find her. By the time I did, she was already dead."

It had been a long night, and I was just about out of patience. Though more than half of the seven hundred guests had been "processed," as the cops called it, and released with no more fuss than the leaving of phone numbers where they could be reached, I was still the object of more attention than anybody my age enjoys at one-thirty in the morning. I was sleepy, my upholstered areas were petrified from two hours on a folding chair, and I was sweating like a stevedore.

I stalled for a minute and fished inside my sausage casing of a suit for my handkerchief. Though I hadn't had a chance to look at it yet, the program I'd swiped from Jenny's table was still safe. So long as I kept my jacket buttoned, a gnat couldn't have gotten out of there without my knowing it.

"What did Mrs. Vail want to talk about?"

The big cheese asking the questions was an aging preppie of the

Sheffield mold, with carefully disarranged sorrel-colored hair just graying at the temples and far too many teeth. In full fancy dress uniform complete with medals, he lounged behind his makeshift desk as if it were the best table at The Four Seasons. Captain Gifford Colby was obviously born to command—or so his mother had told him in the womb—and casual elegance was his middle name. I, on the other hand, was neither casual nor especially elegant, and he seemed to find something subversive about me from the word 'go.'

The *real* subversive in the room, however, was my old friend Lieutenant A.J. Lincoln, whom Merriman had managed to phone during the mass confusion that struck my colleagues once they realized Jenny's death wasn't fiction. Lincoln had been duty officer of the night at the Homicide Task Force and was the first cop on the scene, but hotel security had ideas of its own about the sort of rozzer it wanted hanging around the place and issuing statements to the press. Jenny was a VIP and the Hornsby Empire would be in the news for days, at least. They wanted a cop with the right image, and Lincoln's middle-aged spread and the white socks inside his K mart loafers disqualified him the minute he flashed his badge. Enter the photogenic Captain Colby, official figurehead of the Task Force, summoned by Medusa herself, formidable Loretta Hornsby, from the annual spring awards banquet of the Police Brotherhood, where he was about to get yet another of those scarlet ribbons for his chest.

Linc, obviously underwhelmed by the peacock plumage of his commanding officer, slouched gloomily in a folding chair at the back of a tiny interrogation area hastily screened off from the reception room, while Colby's aides orbited like moons around their leader, fetching and carrying coffee, note pads, telephones, pencils, files.

Colby picked up a pencil, stared at the point. It didn't seem suitable. He put it down, and one of the Moons instantly offered him another. "Mr. Sherman," he said, "I asked you a question. What did Imogen Vail want to talk to you about?"

I sighed, and tipped Lincoln a wink as Colby pretended to write something on his note pad. "You've asked it so often, Captain, I suppose I mistook it for background static. I don't know what Jenny wanted, how could I? She was killed before we got a chance to talk."

"Did you see her often? Did you get together and compare notes, say, about your publishers or editors? Writers do that sort of thing, don't they?"

"This one doesn't. I've never believed you could make the best-seller lists by hanging out at book fairs and baring your soul to the brethren. I prefer to stay home and do it on paper."

"But Mrs. Vail did attend a lot of conventions, didn't she? Book fairs, as you say, and writers' conferences. Made a number of speeches, public appearances. Well known to her peers. And her books were on the best-seller list almost as soon as they came out, weren't they? Whereas your own . . ."

"In case you've forgotten your Aristotle, Captain, you've just committed a classic post hoc fallacy. One fact doesn't necessarily depend upon the previous existence of the other. Jenny's books sold well from the beginning, when nobody had the slightest idea who she was or whether she was a good after-dinner speaker. And if you don't mind, we'll leave my absence on the best-seller list out of this."

"Oh, but I'm not sure we can, you see. You wanted what Jenny Vail had, didn't you, Sherman? You'd lost this Edgar Award to her how often—ten times, twelve?"

"Nine, but I don't see—"

"The old cart horse outclassed by the thoroughbred, publicly humiliated year after year. You *must've* wanted her out of the way."

"I may have wanted her books out of the way. Personally, they didn't appeal to me. But the woman and her books were two different things. Which, by the by, is another classic fallacy. I really would suggest a good course of syllogistic logic, perhaps a little night school—"

"So you had no resentment for the lady?"

"We were old friends."

"And yet you say she didn't call? She never communicated with you?"

I considered, just for a split second, telling him about the white roses and the bottle of champagne, but it was only a temporary lapse. I glanced at Lincoln, who hadn't missed a syllable I'd said, and decided to save my evidence for him.

"Jenny Vail and I knew each other years ago, when things in the mystery business were a lot less complicated," I told him. "Now it's all fan conventions, big-time public relations, lecture agents, award-committee politics, merchandising. We're not so much people, or even writers, as products."

Gifford Colby sat opposite me, nodding sagely now and then, himself no stranger to the art of packaging. He straightened the errant crease in his slacks and carefully draped one leg over the other like a B-girl in a Forties movie as I went on.

"Personally, as I've said, I don't cotton to being shrink-wrapped and price-coded, but Jenny made another kind of choice. It seems to have served her well enough," I admitted. "At least it made her a lot of money in the last few years. I'm not sure what else it left her with. Not very much, I suspect."

"But Mr. Sherman—Winston. May I call you Winston?"

Now we were in for the All-Chums-Together approach, followed, no doubt, by the Frontal Attack. Colby's technique had all the subtlety of a crosstown bus. He offered me more coffee and forged on.

"You see, Winston, it's this way. If you knew her well enough to suspect she was unfulfilled, you must've known her pretty well. A lot better than you're telling us. You get my point? You wouldn't be likely to just intuit that sort of thing, now would you, a fellow like you?"

I smiled and stood up, my suit creaking at the seams. "Captain," I said, "let me tell you a bit about fellows like me. We rarely buy our cuff links at Cartier. We do not have ourselves coiffed and styled by Sassoon. We are often forced to drink wine younger than we are. We abstain by religious scruple from any form of exercise for its own sake, we chat as seldom as possible about our serum cholesterol, and we spend more time with Shakespeare and Dorothy Sayers than we do committing to memory the ten commandments of the Westchester Instant Weight Loss Diet. But we—fellows like me—we do, just now and then, 'intuit' a thing or two. We old cart horses can tell in a minute when a woman is worried and afraid, and we damn well know when somebody in a uniform like an organ-grinder's monkey is running a cheap bluff on us." I pushed back my folding chair. "Either you take me down to headquarters and put ink on my thumbs, or I'm going home, Captain. You've let at least a dozen people waltz out of here who had better motives to kill Jenny than I did. The fact that I happened to find her body doesn't mean a thing, and you know it. Tough cheese, Colby old sweetheart, but it just won't wash."

I turned on my heel and was about to stalk out in as much dudgeon as I could muster, when one of the Moons whizzed past me with a file and handed it to the captain.

"Sherman!" Colby was practically yelling. It was the first time all night he'd sounded like a real cop. I stopped, but I wasn't about to give him the satisfaction of turning around. I kept my back to him. "What's your relationship with Gilbert McKelvie?"

I shrugged. "So far as I know, the only thing we have in common is that neither one of us knows the other from Adam's ox. Why? What's a Gilbert McKelvie when he's at home?"

"Dead, as a matter of fact." Colby actually did me the honor— such as it was—of unfolding himself from behind the table and stalking over to where I stood. "He was found dead this morning in Central Park, the Shakespeare Garden. You said you're a Shakespeare professor."

"That still doesn't give me much in common with the poor soul."

"It's a place you might choose to meet someone you knew. Isn't it?"

"I told you. I *don't* know him. Didn't know him."

"Then why was this found next to his body?"

He shoved a piece of yellow paper under my nose—or, more precisely, several pieces stapled at the corner. They had been crumpled and smoothed out again, and the mimeographed print had smeared in the rain and dried crazily. It was the seating chart for the Edgars dinner, the front cover folded back so that the first visible page was the one with the list of ticketed guests in alphabetical order, along with their table numbers. I scanned the columns, following Colby's moving forefinger until it landed on one particular name circled in black marking pen. The name was mine.

"This McKelvie," I said. "How was he killed exactly?"

"One bullet to the head." Colby's mouth was almost in my ear, and his voice was unnervingly soft. "We've got the weapon. It was ditched at the scene. One of the new plastic miniatures, airport-proof, pocket-size. Ballistics is checking it out now, but we're sure it's the gun."

"Fingerprints?"

"Only the victim's. McKelvie's prints on the program, too. One other set, not identified yet."

"And you think the two deaths are connected?"

"Until tonight, those programs were only available to a limited number of people, those involved in organizing things—hotel staff, steering committee members, typists. McKelvie could only have gotten it by knowing someone." He raised his perfectly curved sorrel eyebrows and cocked his head at me. "You tell me, Sherman. You find one body and your name is found on another, both on the same damn day. I'd call that a connection, wouldn't you?"

I gulped a bit of air, but I didn't budge. "What time this morning was McKelvie killed?"

"Between eight and eight-thirty A.M.," said Colby. "I suppose you're going to tell me you've got an alibi?"

I didn't feel much like smiling, but I forced myself to turn round and give him one of my best. "Matter of fact, I do. If you'll just step into the ballroom, that rather gorgeous lady in the bright red dress will be glad to tell you that I was in bed with her until almost nine this morning. In view of the late night we'd be having at the Edgars tonight, we decided to sleep in. Up in Ainsley, on the Hudson Heights, about an hour and ten minutes from here if the train's on time."

Now it was Colby's turn to gulp air. I caught a glimpse of Lincoln's broad face before he hid his grin behind a handkerchief and faked a coughing fit. I marched past the pair of them with my tail in the air and my whiskers twitching, and headed back to the ball-room.

Nearly three hundred of the guests were still waiting to be inter-viewed, lounging wearily at half-cleared tables and not really doing justice to the management's complimentary coffee and sandwiches. Eddie and Sarah had been cleared in one of the first waves but had refused to go back to the Battersea without me; I was just making for the Garner and Sloan table up front where I'd spotted them, when Lincoln caught up with me.

"Wish I had a fancy uniform like that," he said. "It's tough at the top."

"Maybe that's why they only let idiots up there," I growled. "Put his brand of logic together with too much power, and dumb can be dangerous."

"I don't know," said Linc as we wove our way through the empty tables. "Colby may not be all that dumb. He's right about one thing, anyway. You sure as hell know more than you're telling. Waiters were too busy to remember seeing anybody at the table where Jenny Vail was killed, but they *do* remember you, Doc. And that *was* your foster son we got the tip about in the McKelvie murder, wasn't it? Half the cops in Manhattan are looking for him right now."

My mouth fell open. "David? What tip? How?"

"Don't worry. Colby doesn't know who he is yet, I haven't spilled it. But the description was as good as a publicity still, if you know the guy as well as I do. Then, when I saw your name circled on that paper they found at the scene—"

"You seriously believe David's mixed up in McKelvie's death?" I shook my head. "That's ridiculous, Lincoln. You've been spending too much time with that jackass Colby. It couldn't have been a description of David."

He pulled a Xerox copy out of his coat pocket and unfolded it. "Read it yourself," he said.

He was right, of course. The description was minute, down to the minor inconsistencies of facial configuration left from the numerous plastic surgeries. I handed the paper back to him.

"I still don't believe it," I said.

"Oh, relax. Neither do I. I know he's just snooping around on one of your little Sherlock expeditions."

"Believe me, Linc, I've got nothing to do with this one. If Davy's involved in some sort of sleuthing, he's going it alone, confound him! Blast that uniformed chimpanzee, asking me idiot questions when the kiddo's out there on the run. I've got to get out of here and find him, Lincoln."

He frowned and shoved the paper back into his pocket. "Where you figure to start looking? He won't go home to his wife and kid. Whoever offed that guy in the park might be on his tail and David's smart enough to know it. He won't go near anybody he cares about, not without being damn sure he's clear."

"You think the person who sent you that anonymous tip, the description—"

He shrugged. "If we're all out there chasing David, the killer's got plenty of time to disappear. Or take out anybody he figures knows too much."

"Like Davy." My knees were beginning to get shaky again.

Lincoln put a heavy hand on my shoulder. "Your best chance of finding him is to let him find you. He knew you'd be here tonight, didn't he? Hang around awhile. He might try to reach you. He's a whiz at disguises, he makes his living with them. Who knows, maybe he's already contacted your—contacted his sister."

"If he had, Sarah would've been in there beating Colby off me with a stick so we could go rescue him. No, she hasn't heard any more than we have." I hesitated, bringing him up short. "Don't say anything to her yet, Linc. A favor, for old time's sake. Give me a chance to get to the bottom of this myself."

We were almost at the table. He looked over at Sarah, then back at me. "Deal," he said. "But anything you find is mine. When David gets in touch, you call me. Not Colby. Me." His pale eyes narrowed angrily. "The Task Force was my idea. While he plays golf with the mayor, I run it. It's mine, and I want it."

"Spoken like a true cart horse," I said.

"Just be careful, that's all. And don't lock horns with Colby once too often. He's more than just a pretty face, you know."

We had reached the table now and when she spotted us, Sarah jumped up and practically dragged me to the chair next to hers.

"For pity's sake, Win," she cried, "tell us what's going on! Whatever has that manicured ninny been doing to you in there all this time? It's been two hours!"

"And thirteen minutes," said Merriman.

He grabbed a bottle from the waterlogged ice bucket in the middle of the table and poured a grayish sort of liquid into one of the wineglasses still scattered here and there among the dirty coffee cups, the sticky plates of melted, mud-colored ice cream, the wilting bouquet of pink tulips, and the coy little wooden shoes.

"This was once intended to be champagne," Eddie announced, handing me a glass. "As in my own case, I'm afraid the fizz is gone but the intentions are still noble."

He looked as though he'd been sampling the stuff most of the evening. Though in forty-odd years of friendship I've never seen the man actually sozzled, Merriman does achieve a pleasant glow. With black tie dangling rakishly around his open collar and blue eyes gleaming with curiosity, he had lost even the echo of his winter's ill health. Whether it was the mystery of Jenny's death that had finally cured him or that bottle of cheap hotel champagne, he looked ready for anything, even at one-thirty in the morning, and it did me a power of good to see him.

Sarah, on the other hand, seemed to have wilted as Merriman built up steam. The glorious scarlet dress was a mass of wrinkles and her eyes were scrunched up at the corners as they always were from what she called a "demon headache."

"Are we free to leave?" she whispered, casting an eye at Lincoln.

"Just a bit longer," I fudged. I had to stay long enough to give David time to reach us, and with all those cops swarming around, it wouldn't be easy. "I just want to talk things over with our friend, here," I assured her, nodding at Linc.

"You didn't tell anything important to that vacuous poop with the medals, did you?" she said. "The roses, I mean, and that card?"

"Just because I'm reduced to appearing in public in this non-sensical suit," I grumbled, "it doesn't mean I've lost *all* my self-respect. Of course I didn't tell him."

"I knew you wouldn't," she said, and gave my arm a dangerous squeeze.

I gulped down the flat champagne, which tasted like flat champagne, then set about unfolding for our cop the long tale of Cliff's phone call, the white roses, and the message on the bottle of Dom Perignon. I left out that night in Minneapolis. I couldn't see what it had to do with what had happened to Jenny, and I certainly wasn't going to break it to Sarah here and now. She would have enough to handle when she heard about David's new career as Public Enemy Number One.

Lincoln asked very few questions during my recital, and was now writing away on his yellow note pad. He had kept his promise and said nothing in front of Sarah about the mysterious Gilbert McKelvie and David's involvement—whatever the hell it was. He hadn't even asked us to stay on, and I knew he'd given up any hope of David's contacting us here. But something held me anyway, as though that silly fraud of a room must somehow contain a truth to link the two disparate deaths, to explain what Davy had to do with them and why he hadn't come to me for help as I had so often gone to him.

The place was emptying fast now; the little porcelain statues of Poe, unpresented, stood in a forgotten row on the podium. I could've had one for the taking, I thought, and it might've brought me twenty bucks at the right sort of pawnshop. Hardly a thing to die for, and even less to live for. How had it come to seem so important to me? I have never believed myself subject to many of the delusions of my kind, but at that moment I felt I had been sleepwalking half my life.

I sat fiddling with a piece of paper under the wooden shoe at what had been my place at the table as I took a quick inventory of the remaining guests. Even they looked different to me now.

I didn't see Philip Vail or the kid Gregory. Hazel Hancock, too, must've left her phone number and taken off, but a subdued Jed Sloan was standing at the edge of the room talking intently to Lovely Rita Kovacs. Lydia Hallam, Jenny's editor, red-eyed and distracted, sat at a table just below the speaker's platform, with her the thin, pale El Greco woman who'd argued with Jenny. If it were possible, I'd have said she'd grown even thinner during that difficult evening. She looked shrunken and shocked, like an accident victim after the crash, hardly sure she was still alive.

"Who is she?" said Lincoln, following my gaze.

"Her name's Marina Vilnius."

The answer came from Tracy, my new editor, who had just joined us bearing a bottle of what looked like the true, the blushful Haig & Haig. She poured me a flowing beaker and set the bottle down at my elbow; I inhaled the stuff gratefully and patted the top of her pretty head. Van Twist or no Van Twist, the kiddo had certainly done her homework when she took over from old Cliff.

"Marina Vilnius?" Merriman was searching his memory bank, with a shot of Scotch to top up his champagne diet. Then he lit up with recognition. "Madame Natasha!" he cried. "Those horrid little books with the dripping daggers on all the covers. The peerless sleuth, Madame Natasha Something-or-otherov, is a deposed Russian princess exiled to a palatial apartment on Riverside Drive."

"Marina was Jenny Vail's crown princess," said Tracy. "Jenny practically bludgeoned Lydia into putting her on the Crocodile list."

"Is she that good?" asked Lincoln. He grinned. "I never read mysteries myself."

Tracy winced. "She's so-so, actually. If you ask me, Crocodile overbuys. They've just got a couple of biggies like Jenny up top and a few Jed Sloans slithering around the bottom. In the middle, a lot of tossaways they can dump when the cash flow is down. That's Marina. Disposable stuff. Not bad enough to qualify as pulp and sell to the sleaze market, not good enough to get decent reviews and climb up the list. At a more selective house, she'd be out like a shout."

"And with Jenny gone, she might be out at Crocodile before

long, too." I saw Lincoln's ears prick up, bless his heart, and was damn glad he was on our side—and David's. "She had every reason not to want the lady dead, apparently. Though it looked as if they were having a bit of a spat this evening."

"Why would Imogen Vail sponsor a mediocre writer? I mean," said Lincoln thoughtfully, "Vail was pretty hot stuff, wasn't she? Big reputation, all kinds of awards. Surely she could pick and choose who she wanted to pass her crown along to."

"The world and his wife wanted a cover quote from Jenny Vail," I said. "But she had a habit of sending all bound galleys back unread."

"Galleys?"

Tracy smiled. "Publishers send out proofed copies of new books, bound together in plain paper covers, to critics and famous writers and reviewers, hoping for quotes to put on the *real* covers. And Winston's right. Jenny was a bitch about it. She never recommended anybody—except Marina."

"Which leads the teeming brain to one distinct alternative," said Merriman.

"Blackmail?" Sarah shuddered. "Such a nasty word."

"But a good career move," said Tracy. "Marina wasn't just Jenny's heir apparent, you know. She was also her publicist, and a damn good one, too. In that position, it'd be easy to get the goods on a woman like Jenny Vail, and easy to find the right way to use it, too. Marina might've had something on her. Used it to get a recommendation to Lydia, a decent contract. It's done all the time in one form or another."

"And what if Jenny had enough and threatened to put her little blackmail on the front page?" asked Lincoln. "She could've pulled that off, couldn't she?"

"She could," I told him. "But was Marina Vilnius a big enough name to be hard copy?"

"Honey," said Tracy with a distinctly Scotch giggle, "if little Marina died and rose from the dead in Times Square at rush hour, she wouldn't be hard copy."

Lincoln crossed out something on his note pad. "Sounds like a fifty-fifty bet to me. Who else? How about the husband?"

"Philip Vail? Eminent man, intellectual, high standards. He and Jenny separated years ago," I told him.

He scowled and stared at his ringless third finger. "I suppose," he muttered, "she walked out on him."

Sarah shook her head. "Philip Vail couldn't possibly have killed Jenny, Lieutenant Lincoln. He was sitting right in front of us all the time, wasn't he, Eddie? Jenny walked straight past him when she left her table and he never moved a muscle."

"Yes, my dear," said Eddie. "But he did get up during the ceremony. He said a word to Miss Hallam, then went striding off somewhere. And I distinctly remember he wasn't in his seat when old Winchester Hyde, here, set the table on a roar with his announcement."

"Merriman's right," I said. "I looked for him specially, but he wasn't in residence. By the time I gave the mike back to old Landis to calm things down, suspend the awards and so on, Vail was in position again. Cool as a cucumber, too."

"Oh, yes," said Eddie. "Unflappable. Sign of real breeding, you know, that sort of sangfroid. Kept a stiff upper lip even through that scene with the beastly kid, earlier. Anyone know who *he* was?"

"Grandson," mumbled Tracy, more asleep than awake, her head leaning on my shoulder. "Gregory. Grandson."

"Gregory Vail?" said Lincoln.

Tracy gave in to the Scotch and the lack of sleep and only a quick bear hug from me stopped her sliding under the table. I propped her up and kept my arm around her while I answered Lincoln's question.

"It wouldn't be Vail. Jenny only had one daughter, a girl called Cynthia. Writer of some kind, too, no idea what. She died a couple of years back. It was in all the papers at the time. Mugged and beaten, brain-damaged. She lived longer than anyone expected."

"No wonder she looked that way," said Sarah softly. "Ruined. Your Jenny."

"And Gregory, too. The boy. Damage takes a lot of forms, doesn't it?" I pulled the dozing Tracy a little closer into the shelter of my arm and reached for Sarah with the other. We were both thinking not of Cynthia Vail but of our own David. How could I tell her he was somewhere in the belly of the city now, running from the cops and maybe from the real killer of Gilbert McKelvie?

"If you're lining up suspects, Lieutenant," said Merriman, "I suggest you consider that fellow Sloan. He pointed a fake gun at the lady early this evening, but from the look on her face I'm certain she thought it was real." I might've known good old Eddie wouldn't fail to notice Jenny's hasty escape. "Perhaps," he continued, "she had a reason to be afraid of him."

"She was certainly afraid of somebody," I said. "When I spoke to her, her purse was open. There was a gun inside. When I found her, the purse and the gun were both gone. She must've been expecting somebody armed and dangerous."

Lincoln shrugged. "In this city? A lot of women carry guns, and Jenny was wearing a small fortune in semiprecious stones."

"But whoever stole her purse didn't take her rings. Or did he?" Sarah pulled over an empty chair and put her feet up.

"No," the cop admitted. "According to our guys, nothing but the purse was missing. All the jewelry was still there—rings, earrings. She had on a diamond-and-amethyst pendant."

"What about those blessed amethysts, Winnie? Some sort of totem, were they, with your Jenny?" Merriman studied me, heavy-lidded.

"I can't remember her having worn jewelry of any kind, really," I said. "She had Philip's wedding ring, of course."

"Well, I still think she was *expecting* to be killed tonight," insisted Sarah. "The gun in her purse, combined with the note on that wine bottle—surely it's important. The poor woman seems to have been surrounded by people who envied her, used her, or resented her. Surely there was *somebody* who loved her."

"It certainly wasn't Rita Kovacs," I said, directing Lincoln's sharp eye toward the lean and hungry lady. "She's been campaigning against Jenny for president of this bunch of mystery-mongers, and it wasn't exactly a Sunday picnic. An angry young woman, got a reputation for it. Even taken a swipe or two at me."

"And we haven't yet mentioned the object of her famous lawsuit. Steven Stanway won't have to bother about stopping production on the Lieutenant Hilliard series now. The ratings will soar," said Sarah, curling her lip and reaching for the Scotch.

He wouldn't have to worry about buying the rights to my Winchester Hyde books, either, I thought with a sigh. But on the other hand, *I* wouldn't have to see that Mephistophelian profile in my dreams and wake up wondering if I'd sold my soul to the company store.

"I was hoping to beat Jenny out of an Edgar," I said. "Lydia Hallam couldn't have much enjoyed being her editor. Let's face it. Imogen Vail was an aggressive, difficult, highly successful lady and a lot of people didn't like her much. The fact that some of them were in plain sight when she was shot doesn't mean a whole lot when you realize you can drive over to Brooklyn and hire yourself an apprentice hit man for around two hundred bucks. We have to know a lot more about Jenny before we can begin to eliminate anybody."

I knew this was the time to bring that snatched program out of its hiding place in my jacket and lay it on the table. I was among friends; I knew Linc didn't seriously suspect me, anymore than he did Davy. But he was a cop, and even cops who now and then bend the chain of command to get at the truth are loath to break it entirely. However you dished it up, my friend Lincoln wasn't in charge. Gifford Colby was, and from what I'd seen of him he was too much like most of the people who'd had grudges against Jenny Vail —self-important, ambitious, smug, and absolutely ruthless where his own interests were at stake. I had no idea what was on the piece of paper Jenny had shoved into that program, but all my instincts told me I'd better find out before I made it community property. It might turn out to incriminate David in some way, and I had to dig a lot deeper before I could know for sure. I had, in fact, to find David and get the truth out of him. It was going on three A.M.; he'd be more likely now, I was sure, to try and reach us at the Battersea, where he knew we'd spend the night before heading back to Ainsley in the morning. It was time to make the move.

"Wake up, kiddo," I said, shaking the sleeping Tracy by the shoulder. "Time for these old bones to hit the hay."

But one final mystery was pricking at my thumbs. I reached for the piece of paper underneath that damn little wooden shoe.

Tracy relinquished my shoulder and sat up, then groaned and poured another Scotch. "I've been afraid all night you were going to open it," she said. "At least he's not here anymore to gloat."

"Who's not here?"

"Van Twist. Didn't you know? The little bald guy with the bushy eyebrows, down at the end of the table? That was Willem Van Twist."

The paper turned out to be a white envelope with the Garner and Sloan crest. I opened it, read it, and groaned, and as I handed it to Sarah I heard the telltale tearing sound I'd been bracing myself for all evening. They were the final exposures in what seemed an epidemic of unmasked humbugs, and if I still cherished any innate superiority to my hustling colleagues, I lost it in that crowning one-two punch.

My phony evening pants had split straight up the back seam, and the Flying Dutchman had sent me a bill for dinner.

8

It was almost four in the morning when the three of us finally stumbled out of an overpriced taxi at the unimposing entrance of the Battersea Hotel, our Manhattan GHQ. Though I had Merriman's overcoat draped urbanly round my shoulders to hide the rip in my pants, I didn't feel the least bit like Noel Coward; my feet were so heavy I might've been wearing a ball and chain as I trudged through the comfortable moth-eaten plush of the old familiar lobby. And David was nowhere in sight.

"Hey, Doc!"

Sarah and Eddie were already in the elevator holding the door open when Bert, the night desk clerk and resident pinochle shark, waylaid me. A groan issued from between Sarah's clenched teeth, and in another minute the elevator was headed for the seventh floor without me.

"Where the hell ya been all night?" Bert was his usual debonair self. "Some article! You're a lucky man, Doc. She's been parked here waiting for ya the whole damn night. I tried to get her in a cab, but no dice." He dug me in the ribs with a bony elbow. "Listen, ya got a little something on the side, Doc, you oughta let old Bert know, right? I coulda run interference."

"She?" A ray of hope had flickered momentarily across my weary old brain, but even David wasn't *that* good at disguises. I scowled at Bert and toddled doggedly toward the elevator. "Do I look like a man with a tootsie around every corner?"

In spite of the occasional temptation on her part or mine, and perhaps because of our lack of a marriage certificate to hang banefully over the bed, Sarah and I are the most profoundly wedded people I know. Whatever had happened between me and Jenny Vail—and there'd been precious little—had been years ago, a foolish dash at the middle-aged fences that were closing in on me. I had added the episode to that earlier gasp of expiring youth, my harebrained pursuit of Rachel Thurlow, a lady graduate student whose prim passion soon chilled me back to the reality and warmth of Sarah.

Bert cackled soundlessly. "Never woulda figured a fella like you to be a sucker for redheads."

"That's the second time today I've been mistaken for a Lothario," I told Bert, "and it's very flattering. To an old cart horse." I'd have curled my lip, but it was too tired. "Only I haven't got the foggiest notion what you're talking about. If some redheaded floozy—" I broke off. At last the light had begun to dawn. "You *did* say redheaded, Bert?"

He grinned. "They don't come any redder, Doc." He motioned me to follow him, then tiptoed through the clumsy overstuffed chairs and racks of newspapers to a sagging old couch half hidden by expiring pot plants. Bert held back a sickly palm frond to give me a look. "She showed up about ten o'clock," he said, gazing down at the young woman curled asleep on the couch.

I hadn't seen her for a month, not since the family Easter egg hunt, and lying there on the bulgy brown cushions she seemed smaller than I remembered, defenseless without the model's professional poise I'd found so annoying when David first brought her home from London. Her English bisque complexion looked pale and sallow in the Battersea's old-fashioned lamplight; no makeup disguised the strain at the corners of the wide-set eyes and the straight, full mouth, and sleep did not relax her. The famous mop of Fergie-red hair was pulled straight back into a rubber band, a few strands escaping to wander across her cheek. She was dressed in one of Davy's old raincoats about four sizes too big for her, and her hands were almost hidden by the sleeves. But it was Alex.

"Thanks, Bert," I told him. "Now take a hike, okay?"

The worry in my voice erased the grin from his raw-boned features. "Trouble?" he said, studying my face.

"Is there anything else?" I moved the potted palm aside and sat down opposite Alex, trying not to wake her too suddenly.

"Who is she?" whispered Bert.

As usual, I was stumped for the right label. Though Sarah and I raised him, David is not my son, but surely he is a great deal more than my friend. Alexandra isn't my daughter-in-law and little Gemma isn't my granddaughter, but what they are eludes all the glib categories invented by sociologists to snare the few of us still determined to escape the pin-and-label. Significant Other, Extended Family—such concocted froufrous were hardly good enough. A little less than kin and more than kind, I might've said, with apologies to old Will.

As it was, I just said, "Send a pot of black coffee up to the room, will you, Bert?" He nodded and disappeared.

"Kiddo." I put my hand on Alexandra's arm.

She jerked as if I'd hit her, then lay there staring up at me; from the look on her face, I might've been a total stranger. After a minute she sat up and pushed back the escaped locks of hair from her freckled face. There was no expression in her voice when she spoke, nor did she look at me. She just stared down at the grimy, mismatched tennis shoes on her feet.

"God, Winnie," she said at last. "It's happening again."

I took both her hands in mine and she grabbed them, pulling herself down off the couch and onto the floor at my feet, her head cradled against my knee.

"I've heard some of it from the cops, Alex," I said. "The dead man in the park. Lincoln told me as much as he knew. You tell me the rest."

She was still holding my hands, the nails digging into my palms.

"I thought he'd lost his mind," she said. "He doesn't sleep. He hardly talks to anybody." She glanced up at me. "You knew that."

I nodded. "Sarah and I both tried to talk to him when you were home last, but he wasn't having any."

"He goes out in the middle of the night and wanders about. Sometimes he disappears all day. For the last week, I've barely seen him. I thought he had a woman." She took a deep, painful breath. "I asked him, but he says not. And he wouldn't lie to me, not dead on. Would he?"

She loosened her hold and I stroked her hair clumsily. Such gestures of public affection do not come easily to me. The comforts of touch and embrace were never offered me as a child; I learnt them late, with intense relief, and all from Sarah. When I touch, even now, it is with the awkward trepidation of an amateur, a venture which, though casual for almost anyone else, is of considerable cost to me and precious beyond the spending when returned.

Alex leaned her head perceptibly against my hand, like a stray cat grateful to be temporarily less alone.

"These excursions of David's," I said. "How long have they been going on?"

"Almost ever since he left the show. At first it was just now and then. I knew he was nervy. He's always taken walks when his conscience is playing him up. He's never really gotten over seeing his mother killed, you know. He blamed himself. Should've dropped the disguise with her, should've stuck closer to her, should've forgiven her for running out on him as a kiddie. That's really it, you see. He still resents what she did, he can't help it. He can't let her go."

"How long since you've seen him, Alex? Since he phoned you?"

"He left this morning, early," she said. "He has done every day this week. He doesn't come in until late, when Gemma and I are both asleep. Doesn't usually phone, even. But tonight he did, around seven o'clock."

She got up to stand awkwardly in a puddle of dim light from a wall sconce, her hands stuffed in the deep pockets of David's coat.

"Are the police really looking for him? Do they think he killed that man?"

I stood up and put my arm through hers. "Did he know this man McKelvie? Was he a friend, a fellow actor?"

She shook her head. "D. said McKelvie had been phoning the

flat, anonymous phone calls. For weeks, he said. He never told me, damn him!'"

"So he launched a little private investigation of his own," I said.

"He found some way to trace the call. It's not very hard these days, you know, all the electronic toys. Anyway, he found out where McKelvie lived and began to watch him. He followed him to the park this morning. I don't know whether D. actually saw the man killed. But he did see someone else, a woman. He said I ought to tell you, in case she was in danger, too. I tried to find you at the Hornsby, but the police had everything roped off and I couldn't even get them to page you. They said someone had been killed at the dinner, and then, of course, I nearly went bonkers. I mean, you were all there—and if D. had decided to find you on his own . . ."

"Who was this woman David told you about? If she knew McKelvie, she may be able to clear up the whole thing, get the cops pointed in the right direction and away from David. Did he give you a description of her, anything that might tell us who she was?"

"Oh, he seemed absolutely certain who she was, Winston. He even said you knew her."

I had the same feeling I get in the doctor's office when the old boy trots out my latest X ray. Chilly, unknown fingers were creeping up my backbone.

"Alex," I said, "her name wasn't—"

She nodded. "I heard it on the late news down in the lobby. Imogen Vail, the woman who was killed at the Edgars. Jenny. Jenny Vail."

"He said he was sorry." Alex sat down on the edge of the bed in our room on the seventh floor and took a sip of Bert's muscular black coffee. "He asked me to tell you, too. Sorry." She glanced up at me. "I told him he had to go to the police, but he wouldn't. Not yet, he said. Another day, maybe two."

"How *dare* he!" Sarah's dark eyes burned with anger, and she gave the hotel armchair a good, sound kick.

Every sign of weariness had disappeared from her the minute she set eyes on Alex. I'd tried to soft-pedal the danger David was in, but it hadn't been much use.

"Where is he?" she demanded. "Is he all right?"

"He sounded awful," replied Alex. "Worn out. Running on pure nerve. But excited, somehow. That's what frightens me, you know. I almost think he's enjoying it."

"Perhaps he is, my dear," said Merriman. He stood in the open door of his adjoining room, thoughtfully buttoning and unbuttoning his old gray traveling cardigan. "For some people, risk is an addiction, like gambling or drugs. But in David's case, I'd say it's his way of retrenching, of dealing with the elemental things he might otherwise evade—as most of us do, after all. He didn't much like being a victim, naturally. Then this recent business with his mother. Shattering experience, drives all sorts of little bits and pieces into hiding. For some people, the hiding never ends. In the ordinary way of things, one scarcely notices anything missing. But in the kind of tricky situation David's gotten himself into during our recent forays into true-life crime, he's had to pull those dormant pieces back again and use them. Perhaps it gives him a kind of control."

"What rot!" cried Sarah. "That's just a lot of Hemingway nonsense. David's nothing like that. Nobody is."

"No?" I said. "Then tell me. Why did you make yourself go back to the concert circuit after that bout of stage fright you had? Remember what you told me? 'I have to take the risk.' "

"But I wasn't risking my *life*, I was only playing the damn piano! And David's already reclaimed his career. He hasn't got a thing to prove."

"Have you considered that while the kid was picking up those pieces Merriman was talking about, he may have found one or two he never knew were there? That sort of discovery changes all the rules. He's damn good at this sleuthing stuff, you know." I leaned back on the pillows and lit a Turkish Delight. "I'm not so bad at it myself, as a matter of fact. And I can tell you, it's no game and no macho test of manhood, either. It's a human responsibility, the kind you and I drummed into Davy all the while he was growing up. He's shouldered it the way we taught him to, that's all."

"*I* taught him to behave like a good citizen, not to run off mixing himself up in murders! Oh, damn you, Winston! I knew this was bound to happen."

I had never seen Sarah so angry, and in a way she was right. I had encouraged David's instinct for exploring the human enigma ever since the days when, with brimming mugs of cocoa and a plate of my best chocolate chip cookies, the kid and I would hide out in my Cave, reading aloud the best bits of *Hamlet* and *Macbeth* and *Great Expectations,* and ironing out the plot of my latest Winchester Hyde adventure. At some point, perhaps in the moment when he lay on the wet pavement outside his apartment building watching a madman with a knife close in on him, David had outgrown the sort of mystery he could unravel on a stage, and I, too, had found a peculiar satisfaction, as I fended off the inevitable downhill slide toward an old scholar's dusty death, in trading fiction for the real thing. Now, it seemed, we were both in over our heads.

But I also knew that we had both had some pretty deliberate help getting into this particular stewpot. David's anonymous phone calls, that bottle of wine with the card in Jenny's handwriting—to anyone who knew the pair of us, they were as good as an engraved invitation. We were becoming known among our friends and a fair number of our enemies for poking around in crimes and misdemeanors of the nastier sort, and the coincidences of that grim day and night were too glaring for me to ignore. Somebody had been manipulating the pair of us like a couple of marionettes, making sure we both looked as guilty as hell.

I stubbed out my smoke and stood up to face Sarah. "We taught David a lot of out-of-date stuff, like the value of individual life. Out of the Ark, all that, these days. None of us really worth much, all expendable at the convenience of whatever happens to be bigger and meaner than we are. And almost everything is, isn't it? I suppose we did him a disservice, after all. *We* taught him not to ditch anyone or anything he cared about without a fight. *We* taught him the truth was worth paying a helluva price for. Only thing about principles, though. They make you predictable, and pretty easy game for anyone who doesn't happen to suffer from too many of them himself. Somebody knows what David will do and what he won't, and is using that against him. But let's get one thing straight. *We* taught him, old girl. Sorry, but I'm not letting you out of your share of the bill."

Sarah said nothing, just got up and swished into the bathroom. In a minute the scarlet dress sailed out the door and landed on the carpet in a silken heap. "I surrender," she said, coming out at last in her old cords and a jersey. "But I don't give a hoot for anything except David. Where is he, that's what I want to know!"

Alex finished her coffee and stood up to gaze out the window at the wet street below. "He said he was calling from Penn Station. I offered to meet him somewhere, some hotel, wherever he wanted. But he wouldn't let me. He said he'd have to lie doggo for a bit, and I wasn't to look for him. He didn't want me involved." She laughed, her face against the grimy glass.

"He probably didn't want you to have to fib to the police, my dear, in case they came round asking where he was. Or, perhaps he thought they'd be following you, as well." Eddie had begun to fidget, pacing back and forth at the end of the bed.

I shook my head. "The cops are on his trail, but according to Lincoln, they don't know who David is. I'm sure Colby doesn't know, or he'd have said so when he was giving me the third degree about McKelvie. Linc promised not to tell them just yet, and I don't think he'll go back on it, not without a lot of pressure."

"He may not need to," said Eddie as he whizzed past. "There's a rerun of *Greyhawk* every evening at eleven, you know. If the description they have is exact enough, the good captain would only have to see the credits to recognize that face of David's."

"Why did he question *you* about McKelvie? Who is he? Did you know him?" Sarah sank down in a chair. "Damn it, Win. You never said a word about him back at the Hornsby. You're as bad as David. And don't give me any more ten-dollar sermonettes, thank you very much. What else aren't you telling us about?"

"This," I said, and dug inside my jacket for Jenny's program. I took out the piece of the seating chart she'd written on. It was still folded in half, as she'd left it. "Jenny was writing this just before she left her table," I explained. "She left it behind, and after she was killed I swiped it, just in case." I unfolded it and scanned the tiny, crabbed letters I knew were Jenny's. It wasn't addressed to me, that was for sure.

" 'Dearest Philip,' " I read aloud. " 'I wouldn't refuse you anything but this. Clear out before the acceptance speech and find Gregory. Keep him with you. Love, J.' "

"What on earth do you make of that, Win?" asked Sarah.

"He was trying to talk her out of doing something," said Alex. "Something dangerous."

"Or he wanted to restore the conjugal ties." Merriman took the page from me and studied it. "That beastly boy seems to have been rather precious to her, doesn't he? I mean, one observed Vail's tenderness, naturally. But Jenny seemed to be rather at odds with young Gregory."

"What acceptance speech? Did she assume she was going to win another Edgar?" Sarah sniffed. "Pretty arrogant, I'd say."

"Or was she talking about the presidency? Pretty hotly disputed race, Hazel Hancock tells me." I nabbed the paper from Eddie and stuffed it into my old flight bag, open on the end of the bed.

"And what was 'this'?" he inquired. " 'Anything but this.' "

"I don't know," I said, "but right now I'm much more interested in the whereabouts of one David Garrick Cromwell than in deciphering that note." I heaved myself up off the bed, heedless of my southern exposure, and began tossing razors and shirts and socks into the flight bag willy-nilly. "I don't know who McKelvie was, or what he had to do with Jenny Vail and her little conspiracy, but I'm betting David does, and he's going to tell me before this night is over."

"Technically, Winnie, the night was over almost five hours ago. It'll be light in another forty minutes." Merriman screeched to a halt and smiled. "I rather favor early morning sleuthing myself, and I'd follow you to the ends of the earth, Hyde, old thing. But where exactly do you think our desperado is? Where can you go on a train leaving from Penn Station? Princeton, Baltimore, Washington, D.C.?"

"Forget about Penn Station." I shrugged into my old houndstooth overcoat. "When a fox is running from dogs, he backs and circles and crosses his trail and makes them cross theirs till he's got them so confused they hardly notice when he breaks cover and runs. And when he does, he runs for hard country, where he's at home and they're not, where he knows every hole he can crawl into and every false trail he can lead them down. David knows Manhattan pretty well, I'll grant you. And he's played Baltimore and Washington a time or two. But there's one place he knows a damn sight better." I squashed my plaid touring cap down over my eyes and picked up the flight bag. "I think he's gone home. You lot can stay here and get some shut-eye if you want to. But I'm headed back to Ainsley, if I have to get there by cab!"

As it turned out, I did. The earliest train headed our way from Grand Central didn't leave for another three hours and none of us wanted to wait. At Alex's insistence—and, I might add, with her bankroll—we flagged a cab outside the Battersea and begged, bribed, and wheedled a cabbie named Francisco Reyes into driving us straight home. What with Frank's getting lost a time or two trying to find the turnoff onto the Palisades Parkway, and my dozing off when I should've been giving him directions around the Clinton campus and up onto our bluff, it was almost seven-thirty that morning when the cab pulled into our long front drive.

"Tres viejos locos y una mujer con piedras en la cabeza," Frank muttered with a weary grin as he drove off counting up Alex's two hundred and fifty mint-condition bucks, and I didn't need to speak Spanish to know what he meant.

During the night the fine rain had stopped at last; the sun was drying the grass-grown flagstones of the front walk, but otherwise the rambling old house looked exactly as we'd left it—no muddy footprints on the terrace steps, no front door mysteriously ajar. I ushered Alex and the others into the hall ahead of me, and just as I was about to join them, I heard that sound again.

It was the same metallic noise I'd heard the previous morning, just before the delivery of the roses and champagne—a sliding sound, like something heavy running on rails, then latching shut. I'd assumed it was a car door at the time, but now that I thought about it, it was more like the sliding door of a van, the kind that opens on the side instead of at the back. When I first heard it, from up in our bedroom, it had sounded close by, maybe even in our back drive under the portico outside the kitchen door. Now it was farther off.

I stepped out onto the terrace again and shut the door behind me. There was no sign of anything with wheels in our drive or on the street beyond, where our bit of woods ends and the redwood decks and cedar shakes of Erskine Estates begin. I could hear an engine far off, headed down the hill to town, but I couldn't see whether it was a van or just some commuter's import huffing off to the depot.

I was headed back inside, when I caught a jagged flash of color among the trees at the far edge of the garden, where a steep old path leads down through the undergrowth to the Hudson River. It was just a flicker of neon orange, like those unmissable hard hats the highway flagmen wear, and it disappeared almost before I could be sure I'd seen it. I rubbed my eyes and looked again, but there was only the midnight green of pines and the lush new foliage of hickories and maples, sprinkled here and there with starlike dogwood coming into bloom.

The familiar beauty of the old place and the clear light of the morning made my edginess seem as surreal as the events of the night before. The wing of a bird out in the trees, the noise of a car door closing—even if I hadn't invented them, they were hardly sinister.

I heard the phone ringing in the front hall, but nobody was answering it. I turned to go inside and had just made it up the steps when something hard and obviously human struck me in the midsection. He landed on top of me and, locked in a lunatic embrace, we toppled off the porch and hit the ground with a crash, then rolled a few more feet into the junipers along the walk. I heard a half-smothered sound, like an explosion somewhere very far away, then a sort of whine and the pop of splintering wood, as something cut through the morning air an inch from my nose and buried itself in the redwood box of pansies beside the steps.

I'd never been in a real guerrilla war before, but let me tell you, it doesn't take long to get the hang of it. I wasn't just in the neighborhood of those bullets. They were aimed straight at *me*. Me? It didn't make sense. If the killer was out to shoot anybody, it should've been David, not me. We certainly looked nothing alike. But I didn't hang around mulling it over.

Having landed flat on my belly, I thought I might be able to crawl into the punishing shelter of the junipers, but I soon found I couldn't move anything but my feet. The hard weight of the man's body still flattened down on top of me, crushing my chest against the wet grass. I couldn't get my breath, and there was a sharp pain in my right elbow when I tried to push him off.

"Keep still, damn it!" he whispered. "He can't see you, he's just firing blind."

I didn't have enough breath to make conversation. We lay there for another minute or two in silence, his face smashed against my back and his arms pinning mine. No more bullets pelted past us, and at last his weight rolled off me and I could breathe freely.

"Stay where you are," he said. He scrambled away crab fashion, on all fours, skirting the edge of the shrubbery. Then I heard his sneakers squeaking on the wet grass, to stop beside my aching elbow. "You can get up now," he said. "The shooter's gone."

I rolled over onto my back and lay there in the grass to get a good look at him. He wasn't much past thirty, long and thin and square all over—square jaw, square shoulders, square hands. His eyes, though, were round and pale brown and guileless, and his mouth, when he risked a smile, was firm and full-lipped. He reached me a fragile-looking hand.

I just stared at it. "I've got bruises in places I didn't know you could bruise. I've got what feels like a dislocated elbow. I think I've got a piece of this damn evergreen up my nose. And if you imagine you can get me up from here without heavy equipment and a crew of ten, you've got another think coming."

I moved my elbow and winced, and in a minute he was down beside me on the ground. He crouched there, his thin fingers exploring my arm above and below the joint, moving it gently. His touch was delicate, but not afraid of hurting me—which he did once or twice.

"Twiddle your fingers," he said at last.

"Twiddle?" I snarled, but I did it.

"Not bad twiddling," he said, "without rehearsal." He rocked back on his heels. "It's just a bruise. Ice and a nice shot of Haig & Haig ought to take care of it. Separate applications. I think you'll live."

"Thanks to you," I said. "And who the hell *are* you, by the way?"

"Julian Stockfish." He grinned, the angles of his lean face softened, even graceful. "Just call me Fish." He grabbed my good arm and hauled me easily to my feet.

"Well, you're certainly an *odd* fish," I said. "With a grip like that, you're either Beowulf or the Six Million Dollar Man. Tell me, do you hang around in my shrubbery like this every morning on the odd chance some outlaw's going to draw a bead on me from the woods? Or did you just stop by to tell me where you've hidden David out?"

9

"I don't have any more idea where David is right now than you do," said Julian Stockfish, digging into the platter of scrambled eggs I'd just plonked down in the middle of our kitchen table.

I'd managed to sneak inside and up the back stairs to wash and change before Sarah spotted the aftereffects of my little romp in the shrubbery. The tattered remains of my fake evening suit, grass-stained and rent from elbow to ankle in a dozen strategic spots, now occupied most of the trash can by the back door, and I was comfortably clad in a washed-out seersucker bathrobe with an attractive openwork pattern burned into the lapels by decades of drifting ash from my Turkish Delights. I lit one and was pleased to note no glare of health-crazed indignation from our guest as the sweet-smelling smoke gusted his way.

"David called me last night," Stockfish continued. "Told me he was on the lam." He shook his head and grinned. "I tell you, I've met a lot of hoods in my line of work, they'd auction off their grannies for a hot tip on a two-year-old. These slimy dudes are sitting home right now reading *The Art of the Deal* in the sauna, and who's on the run? Old Claudio, the straightest guy I ever met."

"What line of work are you in, exactly?" Sarah nibbled nervously at the corner of a piece of toast she'd cremated. "You're not some sort of spy, are you?" She was remembering our last escapade, playing hide-and-seek with a fair share of the Western intelligence community up at Lake Tamarack. "I'm not having anything more to do with spies. Ever."

The introductions had been a bit awkward, since I knew next to nothing about our guest myself beyond the fact that he'd saved my bacon in the bushes. I'd sworn him to secrecy about that and asked his help in keeping an eye on the others, at least until we'd found David and sorted things out a bit. When he had been cleared of suspicion, I could call Lloyd Agate, our friend on the Ainsley police force, and get a squadron of cops to surround the joint day and night. If I told Sarah I'd been shot at, she was sure to kick like a mule and insist we lay off and hand things over to New York's Finest. Which meant Gifford Colby, who, if I was any judge of official mentality, would go for the closest available suspects—David and Yours Truly. I wanted to keep my hands on the reins a little longer, so I hadn't mentioned that neon-orange marksman outside. I was itching to ask Stockfish about the van I was certain I'd heard, but it would have to wait. I helped myself to eggs and settled in for the seminar.

Alex, looking a bit more herself, laughed and helped me out with the introductions, "Don't worry, love," she assured Sarah. "Julian's an actor, not a spy. He met D. when they were in *Much Ado About Nothing* at Lincoln Center, the summer before Gemma was born."

"I remember that show, yes," I said. "Bit of a fiasco, as I recall. I always thought David should've played Benedick instead of that twit Claudio." I scoured my memory in vain for our square-jawed friend. "But I'm sorry to say I don't recall anyone fishy in that particular cast at all."

Stockfish laughed. "Hell, I was just the Messenger. 'He was not three leagues off when I left him'—that was my big line."

"But you can't say as much for David now, I take it? Three leagues off, that is? There's certainly no sign of him here."

Eddie, who hadn't bothered changing from his evening duds, sat tentatively on the edge of his chair, poking at his eggs with a fork. At last he pushed his plate aside, as though he hadn't enough energy left to talk and eat at the same time. The temporary euphoria induced by murder and cheap champagne had worn off hours ago. The hand that held the fork was less than steady and there were huge dark circles under his eyes, but the eyes themselves were bright with speculation. He had caught me earlier, digging the bullet out of that planter of pansies with my old Scout knife when I figured everybody was too busy inside to notice. Being Merriman, he just stood there peering at the object lying in the palm of my hand, told me I'd better make breakfast before Sarah decided I wasn't coming and created a waffle that would live in infamy, and then trotted blithely inside to make his own morning cup of Earl Grey. The explanations would come later, when we were alone.

Julian Stockfish slathered ketchup on his eggs and began his tale. "I tried to get some answers on the phone last night," he said, "but you know David when he dummies up. You'd get more skinny out of those party animals on Mount Rushmore. He did tell me the guy we were tailing had bought it early yesterday morning, in the Shakespeare Garden in the park. Asked me to keep an eye on you guys. I've been following your cab ever since you left the Battersea."

"Confound it, you might at least have saved us cab fare," I growled. "And what do you mean, 'we were tailing'?"

Stockfish dumped four spoons of sugar into his coffee, then topped it up with cream. "Actually, I do have another line of work besides acting. Last part I had was the Third Alligator in *Swamp Babies*. Big bucks in musicals, but it does weird things to a guy, thinking like a reptile, you know? Anyway, that's when I became a private eye. There was this girl I knew, her apartment kept getting broken into. Cops brushed her off, she couldn't afford private security, electronic jazz. I helped her out, staked out the place, finally caught the jerk." He shrugged. "Kind of liked it, right? Beats the hell out of an alligator suit." He dug into his pants pocket and flipped open a small leather case. "See?" he told us proudly. "Got a regular license and everything."

"So David hired you to help him watch McKelvie?"

"He came to see me about a week after the anonymous calls started. Wanted me to find out where they were coming from. I used to work for the phone company, too. Also Con Ed, and a major garbage collector or two. You'd be surprised what people throw in their garbage cans." He got a little pink around the ears. "See, I didn't really have to tap the line exactly. There's this call-screening gadget, works by microwave. You put it onto your answering machine and this digital gizmo tells you the number the call's being made from. Once we knew the number, I just called old Thelma at Directory Assistance, bought her dim sum, and took her to see *Les Miz.* She found us the address to match the phone number." He flashed his grin again. " 'Course, if the cops found out, I might not have that license much longer and Thelma'd be racking up unemployment."

Alex, anticipating my usual routine, had just raided Sarah's desk in Erskine's old study and come back with pencil and legal pad, which she shoved under my nose. There were some figures on the first lined sheet headed "Heating Contractor, Estimates." I took one look at the skyrocketing sums, gulped, and tore off the page.

"What was the address old Thelma gave you?" I asked Fish.

"Three forty-eight West Eighty-seventh," he said. "Apartment Two-A. It's an old brownstone—four, five tenants, mostly old-timers."

I wrote it all down. "Any information about McKelvie? Married, single, kids, job—anything?"

"Not much. I didn't spend a lot of time on it. David asked me to spell him once or twice, Easter weekend when he was up here with you, a couple of other times. Aside from old Thelma, that was all. But I got interested. Ran McKelvie's paper on my own time. Driver's licenses, birth certificates, marriage licenses, income tax returns, parking tickets, Social Security, unemployment. Everybody's got a paper life, right? It grows and grows and when you die it sometimes goes right on living for years after you're pushing daisies. I'm telling you, this guy's got nothing. According to what I could find out, he reads book manuscripts for publishers, one or two agents. Free-lance. No long-term employment records. No unemployment. He hasn't filed taxes in five years. Hasn't got a bank account logged in any of the regular computer systems I can tap into. No driver's license, no car, no wife, no paternity records, no medical. No birth certificate in New York State—which doesn't mean he hasn't got one somewhere else, of course. There's a Social Security number in his name, applied for two years ago. This guy is what—maybe forty-two, forty-three? Until two years ago he gets along without a Social Security card? Come on, right?"

"So you think," said Alex, "that until two years ago, Gilbert McKelvie was somebody else? He invented the name McKelvie and applied for a Social Security card to verify his new identity?"

Stockfish nodded. "I think he's underground. On the run, maybe. He's not Witness Protection; they're more thorough with the paper trail. I'd have found a dozen forms of computer ID for him if he was one of theirs. Nope, if he did a dive two years ago, he did it on his own. Or maybe with a little help. There's this woman. He met her in the park every morning. Not just now and then. Every morning. Yesterday, after the guy was shot, David found out who she was."

"Jenny Vail," I said. "The lady who was murdered last night."

"Yeah. I heard the news on the car radio. And just maybe," said Stockfish, "she's the lady who's been keeping old McKelvie under wraps for two years. Footing the bill, at least."

"Question is," I said, pondering, "why? When we know that, we may know why the pair of them were killed. And by whom."

"But why did the lady send Winnie, here, wine and roses yesterday morning, with a rather distinctive card attached?" Merriman looked at me expectantly.

I shook my head. "I don't know. I spoke to her last night just before she was shot, and I mentioned that card. Jenny didn't seem to know what I was talking about."

"But if *she* didn't send it, who did? You said it was her handwriting." Sarah pushed back her chair and began to stack the plates.

"Jenny Vail's been slapping her signature on the inside covers of books for twenty-five years," I replied. "Samples of her handwriting are pretty easy to come by. And any number of people might have learned to imitate her hand for the sake of professional convenience—agents, secretaries, housekeepers."

"Publicists," added Merriman. "Didn't like the look of that Vilnius woman, myself. Spidery sort of creature. Straight out of Charles Addams."

"Yes, and what about Philip Vail? He's even more likely," said Sarah. "You forge my signature all the time, Win, paying the gas bill or signing for Package Express deliveries when I'm out. You can hardly tell it from mine most of the time."

"That's easy. You write like a chicken making footprints in the snow and nobody can read it anyway," I grumbled. "Besides, we've got that note she wrote to Philip to compare it with. Any good handwriting analyst could tell for sure. Julian, what about these calls McKelvie made to Davy? Threats, were they?

Stockfish dug into his pocket and produced a tiny microcassette recorder. "I've been playing this sucker over and over for days. I played it all the way up here in the car, for all the good it did me. We taped every call on David's machine—except for the first two or three. Not that it mattered. They were all the same, really. They came every night after ten, sometimes eleven." He switched on the machine.

"Hello?" David's voice. "Look, I know it's you. Hello!"

"Mr. Cromwell. David."

The voice was an even baritone, almost completely unmodulated. It had no variance of pitch, no reedy highs or emotional basses. There was no perceptible foreign accent, but the words broke into even syllables, sounding as though they had been learned by rote. Mis-Ter Crom-Well Da-Vid. Whatever the rhythm of the speech, it didn't sound to me like English.

"Who are you?" David again. "What do you want from me?"

"Someone is going to die." Some-One Is Go-Ing To Die.

"Where are you? Let me meet you, let me talk to you face to face."

"Someone is going to die. You can stop it." You Can Stop It.

"Don't hang up! Christ, can't you tell me what—"

Then the sound of the connection being broken.

"Wind it back and play it again," I said.

"Win, what he said!" Sarah grabbed my hand.

"I know. Play it again, Julian. Listen to the background this time, not the words."

Stockfish looked from one of us to the other, but he asked no questions, just did as I asked. When the conversation ended, he switched the tiny machine off again. "Well?" he said. "What do you make of it?"

"Funny sound, that humming in the background," said Alex. "Like the humidifier we have in Gemma's room. Droning."

"But it has a regular rhythm, you know." Eddie frowned. "Approaches and recedes, more or less. Something moving. An oscillating fan, would you say?"

"Not in February," I objected. "Isn't that when you said the calls started, Alex?"

"Forget the background noises," Sarah insisted. "What about the words?"

I explained to Julian. " 'Someone is going to die. You can stop it.' Those were the exact words on the card attached to that bottle of champagne. Except for the signature. 'Best wishes, Jenny Vail.' "

Merriman was drawing circles with his forefinger on the plastic place mat, round and round, round and round again. His fingernail made a slight hiss on the grainy finish of the mat, a regular rhythm that came and went and came again, growing louder as the circle closed. Suddenly Eddie bounced up from his chair and made for the door that leads into his private apartment, the old servants' quarters at the foot of our back stairs.

"Key, key, key," he said, dancing on tiptoe to reach the nail just under the Delft platter in the center of the plate rail by his door. "Blast," he cried. "Damn and blast and bother! Key, key, key!" He searched his pockets, turned them inside out.

"Merriman, stop acting like an old maid with a bee in her knickers and pretend you've got good sense! What in the name of Ned's the matter with you?"

"My keys, you insufferable old rhinoceros! My keys! I left them on the nail under the Dutch plate, where I always leave them. I remember distinctly, because of the Flying Dutchman, and I hung them up just before we left for the train yesterday. Now they've gone!"

"Oh, applesauce," I told him. "Look in your other pants."

"These *are* my other pants, blast you!"

"Somebody's broken in again!" cried Sarah. "The same man who broke in yesterday with those awful roses and the champagne came back when we were gone and stole Eddie's keys!"

"Keys to what?" said Stockfish soberly. "What was on the key ring?"

"Back door, front door, door to my rooms," Eddie enumerated. "Spare key to Winston's office in the Arts and Letters building on campus. I'm retired, but I maintain squatter's rights, and I do like the view from that side of the campus. Light's especially good for watercolors. Keep a little easel up there and a few paints. I incline to watercolors, you know, oils being messy and too expensive for any ordinary—"

"Merriman!" I roared. "Put a sock in it!"

He bit his lower lip and smiled wanly. "Thank you, Winnie. I retract the rhinoceros." He turned to Julian and explained. "When excited, I do babble, rather. But it's that background noise on the tape, you see. I think I know what it must've been, only you all need to come into my parlor for a demonstration. Alexandra, my dear, be so kind as to get the spare key from Beethoven, will you please?"

We all waited in nervous silence while Alex charged through the swing door into the dining room and hefted up the bust of old Ludwig on the sideboard. In less than a minute she was back with the key and we all filed inside.

Eddie's small parlor—part library, part picture gallery, watched over by a scowling portrait of his late and none-too-loving wife, Gwen—was, as always, in perfect order. If anyone had been snooping around in here, he'd certainly been more careful than the bozo who'd gone through the papers in my Cave.

Merriman trotted over to the windows. Under them was an old oak library table, and on the table was an equally old record player, not components with woofers and tweeters and speakers that would've done the job at Jericho in half the time, but a square, lidded box with two heavy, smallish speakers attached by thick wires. He fiddled with the switches and turned it on, then stepped back.

In that small, quiet, tidy room, the sound was a threatening roar, as it must've been in David's ear each night on the telephone. A spinning, gathering sound, drawing in, then pulling back as the turntable revolved. Eddie was right. The background noise on the tape was almost certainly that of a record player turning and turning on the dead space at the center of a played-out album.

"Excuse me?" said a voice from the open door. "Excuse me profoundly, but the back door was unlocked."

We all turned and stared at him, and poor little Krishnan Ghandour, our English for Foreign Students man at Clinton, blinked and opened his mild brown eyes a little wider.

"So sorry to interrupt," he said. "But I really must speak in private. If you can be spared, sir? An imperative matter, imperative!"

He took me by the arm and propelled me out the door of Eddie's parlor, through the kitchen, and into the dining room, where he finally let me go.

"Krish," I said, "if Sheffield's sent you over here about that silly Professor of the Year Award—"

"Absolutely no." He looked at me reproachfully. "I have no patience with this man. I am determined he shall not have this award. I have suspicions as to his character!"

"Sheffield? Didn't know he had one."

"I cannot prove as yet, but I am not without resources."

"Krish, this is beginning to sound like a chapter out of *The Moonstone*. What the devil are you talking about?"

"The Floating Fund. I cannot say more at present. But I have resources."

"You mean that slush fund Sheffield's been hoarding to redecorate the Faculty Lounge? What about it?"

"I shall need your help, Winston. When I have the information."

"Are you trying to tell me that the famous Floating Fund—"

"I shall have to confront this Sheffield."

"—has floated out of sight?"

"Shhh." Krish put a finger to his lips. "We must be careful. Give no excuse for undue scrutiny until the right moment. So, in view of this, I must ask you, Winston, to be more careful with the lights."

"Lights? What lights?"

"In your office, Winston. Last night you left the light burning in your office. It was observed by this Sheffield. He has been mentioning it in the Faculty Lounge this morning. Most opprobrious, his remarks! Most. I was forced to play cribbage with him. I have no fondness for cribbage, a game of limited intellectual scope, but I wished to observe him, and—"

"I didn't leave those lights on, Krish. I didn't even go over to the campus yesterday! I don't have classes on Thursdays, you know that. I—"

I stopped short as an idea planted itself in the foggy acreage of my tired brain. All sorts of pieces seemed to be floating around in the atmosphere, and I was sure they must fit together somehow. My Cave searched. Eddie's keys gone. A mysterious light in my office at school. David in hiding. A man shooting at me from the woods.

I put my hand on Krish's shoulder. "Kiddo," I said, "has anybody been in my office since that light was spotted? Sheffield didn't get the passkey from maintenance and go snooping, did he?"

"He made no mention," he replied. "A lot of bother, threatening to send you a bill for the wasted electricity and so forth. Highly insensitive remarks regarding your advancing seniority."

"Did you happen to look up at my window from outside, Krish? Is that light still burning?"

"Certainly not. I took care to observe from the parking lot. I am convinced Sheffield has contrived the business merely in order to discredit you. The whole faculty is aware how much he wishes you to retire. I believe there was never a light at all!"

I slapped him on the back and began to prod him toward the front door. "Got your car outside, Krish? Fine, excellent! Let's go!"

"But sir, your bathrobe!"

"Casual attire, just the thing for a spring morning!" I grabbed my overcoat and swathed myself in its concealing folds. It seemed to be my week for trendsetting in the matter of dress.

Half expecting another bullet from the bushes, I ducked quickly into Krish's shark-finned Plymouth and locked the door behind me. He got in behind the wheel and the engine began to purr as he turned round and started down our drive. The longer I thought about it, the more at least a couple of those odd-shaped pieces seemed to stick together.

"Step on it, will you, kiddo?" I said. "I think there *was* a light in my office, all right. Only I didn't turn it on."

Krishnan turned his big brown eyes on me, looking pleased as punch. "An intruder? I should be glad to be of service, sir! Who do you think it might be?"

"Oh, a big-time desperado," I told him, "and I can use all the help I can get!"

10

After he had made two phone calls from the booth in Penn Station—
the one to his wife Alex, the other to his cohort Stockfish—David
checked his watch. It was seven-fifty P.M. A plan had been taking
shape in his mind, made of bits and pieces he'd learned from life-
long experts in evasion—my dead friend, John Falkner, for instance, and Cary Pasco, the spy. In ten minutes the Metroliner
would be pulling out as it did every hour until ten at night, bound
for Washington, D.C. Though it was headed in the wrong direction,
that train was going to take him home.

It was late for commuter traffic and the waiting line at the ticket
counter was short. "Cash?" asked the weary clerk hopefully.

The man in the bright blue nylon raincoat shook his head.
"Sorry," he told her, and handed over his MasterCard with "David
G. Cromwell" embossed on the front for all the world to see.

Then, armed with his automatic-carbon ticket and lugging the
snappy plaid carrier with Vangie's knitting bag inside, he followed
the other passengers down the stairs to the platform where the eight
o'clock train was already loading. He selected a car at random.
None of them was full at this hour and there were plenty of seats.
Standing in the aisle and ignoring the grumbles of other passengers
waiting to make their way forward, he carefully took off the blue
raincoat and folded it, laid it on the second aisle seat from the back
of the car, then took the yellow umbrella from the carrier bag and
laid it on top of the raincoat. Next he removed the bag of yarn

containing Vangie's cup and saucer from the plaid carrier and put the empty carrier up on the luggage rack over his seat. His last move was to slip the ticket stamped with his name and credit card number under the slot above the window where the conductor would look for it when he came by to check tickets and found no one in the aisle seat.

Minus the unmissable blue raincoat and the plaid bag, blending nicely into the scenery in his old tweed jacket and jeans, David moved through that car and the next and another after that, then swung off onto the platform and stood, plastic knitting bag in hand, waving at the face of an unknown woman in one of the windows. She watched him, puzzled, and at last waved back.

He stayed until the train pulled out, then loped up the stairs into the station again and out onto Thirty-fourth Street, where he hailed a cab for Grand Central. David G. Cromwell, his existence verified by credit card, was safely on his way to Washington, and the last commuter train for Ainsley left at eight forty-three. The unofficial David, funny haircut and all, intended to be on it.

But how? He was known on that train, he'd been riding it off and on ever since he was a kid, and even if none of the conductors who knew him happened to be on duty tonight, he certainly couldn't get off up at Ainsley without being spotted by Scrappy Gill, the night ticket agent.

Makeup was the order of the evening, a nice believable little bit part that would make him anonymous. But he didn't set out every morning to tail McKelvie with a selection of stage makeup in his back pocket; any shop that sold it would be locked up tight by now. He would have to improvise.

Once again he turned in at a drugstore, the open-all-night kind that stocks everything from pickles to playing cards. From a rack opposite the prescription counter David chose a pair of wire-rimmed reading glasses of a strength so slight they were almost window glass. Then he prowled the shelves until he found a display of spray cans containing a dry, comb-out shampoo, the kind intended for sick-room use. Mrs. Jack had used it on Gemma's hair when she came down with the megavirus of the year just before Christmas; the stuff went on like hair spray, but left a gray-white powder when it dried—perfect for instant aging.

What else? On a clearance table at the back, he found a checkered cap that almost fit him. Not quite enough. He squinted at the brightly-lighted shelves. Something to make him disappear . . .

At last he spotted it—munchies! Nothing like junk food to induce confidence. A lone man reading a book—risky. A lone man hiding behind a newspaper—dangerous. But who would be suspicious of a lone elderly passenger scanning the *Times* classifieds and munching taco chips? Besides, he hadn't eaten all day, unless you counted Vangie's bourbon.

As David transformed himself in the Grand Central washroom, he couldn't get his mind off her. In the plastic knitting bag the precious cup and saucer lay safe and unbroken. He made a sudden decision. Pulling the checkered cap snugly down over his grayed hair and adjusting the wire-rimmed specs, he made for the nearest phone booth once again.

Vangie was in the book—or Walter was. W. Glickman, 348 West Eighty-seventh, 555-9943. He fished in his pockets for change and punched the buttons.

"What?" She was thick-voiced. *The bourbon,* he thought. *A liquor store that delivers.*

For a moment he could think of nothing at all to say. They were two ends of a faulty connection, already broken once. If he let her go now, she would slip away for good, like Vernelle Maguire.

Do you think I could make it, if I opened the door again? Do you think I could turn back time?

The words he spoke into the telephone were not his own. They were a verse from one of the Auden poems he had read over and over since McKelvie's calls began. He gave them to her as McKelvie must have played his record, a coded message sent into the closing dark.

DREAMLAND

"O stand, stand at the window
As the tears scald and start;
You shall love your crooked neighbor
With all your crooked heart."

His voice was unsteady and almost out of control; it frightened him, another breach in the wall of discipline he had built all his life. But she recognized him.

"So," she said softly. For a moment he could hear her breath close to the mouthpiece. "So, my friend."

"Go softly, Vangie," he told her. "The cup and saucer are safe."

But she only hung up the phone.

Almost before Krish could finish jockeying his lumbering old Plymouth into a parking space in the faculty lot, I was out and toddling at a good clip in the direction of the side entrance to the Arts and Letters building. He bailed out and caught up with me at the steps.

"You see?" he said, pointing to my office on the third floor. "No lights currently."

He was right. The high window looking out over the Hudson was closed, as I'd left it, with the window shade at half-mast as usual; Sheffield's abominable cost-effective ceiling fixture was shedding none of its charnal glow. The green-shaded banker's lamp on my desk provided by the faculty as one of my annual retirement gifts hadn't shamed me into leaving, and I far preferred the mellow funnel of its archaic forty-watt bulb. I could just see the corner of the green glass shade if I craned my neck, and the color was dark, certainly unlighted.

There *was* a light in the room next door, though, the office belonging to Hilda Costello, resident feminist whip, doyenne of Film Studies, and Tommy Sheffield's only serious competition for Professor of the Year. There are a good many things I could tell you about our Hilda beyond her resemblance to Wallace Beery and her closet fondness for the occasional cheroot after a good cafeteria lunch of Wieners Au Gratin and Gelatin Jewels. But what was bothering me at that moment was her ears.

Now Hilda's are in most respects no different from the auricular appendages of any other adult female, but they seem capable of picking up gossip from the far solar systems. These twin satellite dishes were right now separated from the interior of my office only by a partition so thin that the smoke from my Turkish Delights frequently seeps through it, causing exaggerated attacks of instant bronchitis and anonymous No Smoking signs Scotch-taped onto my door. If, as I believed, Davy had let himself into our kitchen with his own key last night, swiped Merriman's set from its customary nail, and come here to knit up the raveled sleeve of care on my office floor, the last thing I wanted was Hilda in residence with her ear to the fiberboard during our reunion.

I knew of only one thing La Costello loved more than eavesdropping, and that was cribbage, the faculty sport. It was nearly the end of term and that meant tournament time.

"Krish," I said, "how would you feel about a little more cribbage in a good cause?"

The plan was simple enough. Krish would go up to Hilda's office and tempt her away from her duties with a game of cribbage down in the lounge. In order to avoid chatty colleagues who might find my unusual attire noteworthy, I would sneak into the building and hide out in the supply closet next to the mail room where I had a good view through the open door into the lounge. Once the game had begun and Hilda was out of earshot, I'd slink up to the third floor and into my office. I would snaffle David, sneak him out and into the back seat of Krish's car, then honk the unmistakable old horn, which sounded like the NBC television network identifying itself. Krish would leave Hilda crying "Fifteen-two!" to an empty stadium, drive us home, then return to take my afternoon mysteries class while I sorted things out.

DREAMLAND

At least that was the way it was supposed to work, except that I had failed to calculate the Comfort factor.

Our Faculty Lounge is on the second floor opposite the departmental offices where Sheffield has his cushy lair, defended to the death by a regiment of typists, Xerox machine hygienists and electric pencil-sharpener attendants. At their head, on her throne of state, sits Miss Hannah Comfort, who began her tenure not long after I signed on at Clinton back in the Fifties and endured, along with Merriman, Hugh (Tess-of-the-D'Urbervilles) Jonas and myself, *me.* the tyrannical dotage of old Dean Greymantle. When Sheffield took over in the Seventies, bringing with him a consignment of post-hippie pop-culture experts, elderly elitists like ~~myself~~ *me* were driven to the barricades to defend Shakespeare and Dickens from the inroads of Eskimo Lit. and Rock Lyrics. Merriman gave up his Milton and Chaucer for retirement, watercolor painting and the playing of his miserable clarinet, whilst I took to dickering, occasional blackmail and a part-time professorship of Mystery Fiction with the sop of a Shakespeare class whenever I manage to get Sheffield by the short hairs.

Miss Hannah, though, has suffered no such decline; indeed, her sun has risen and begun to shine as never before. When Sheffield is busy stroking the feathers of his well-connected wife, Diana, familiarly known as Lady Di, it is Hannah who sends out the grade rosters. When he goes off for his usual round of postprandial tennis to relieve executive stress, it is Hannah who approves the course list for the coming term. When Tommy's busy electioneering for some award or maneuvering himself into a better position with Lady Di's Daddy and the Board of Trustees, it's Hannah who interviews the candidates for vacant professorships, hears the pleas of failing football players, and adjudicates territorial wars over office space. When Tommy puts his foot in his mouth, Hannah pulls it out for him. So long as she continues to provide her dreaded pink punch on ceremonial occasions and keeps the fridge in the lounge well stocked with his favorite raspberry Perrier, he has no objections to this arrangement. Quite the contrary. Though I'm fairly certain she's

[handwritten in left margin: what about plain grammar; No mixture here—]

older than I am, Sheffield has never so much as hinted that Hannah should retire; the prospect, in fact, must haunt his dreams. Without her, he'd have to do his job himself.

But on that particular morning, I could've done without her nicely. Hannah's desk in the main office is just opposite the door where she can keep the telescopic sights of her gimlet eye trained on anyone who passes in the hall or rounds the bend of the staircase headed up to the third floor. I made it neatly up the stairs with only the usual number of student sniggers behind my back, and I had my hand on the supply room door when I heard a voice that could have called the cattle home across the sands of Dee.

"Winston! Dr. Sherman!"

I knew instantly who it was. Hannah's the only person who still remembers I have a perfectly legitimate Ph.D. I froze, as the martial squeak of her rubber soles approached across the tiled hall.

"He wants to see you, Dr. Sherman," she said. *"He's* been looking for you all morning."

"Are we talking about the Good Shepherd, Hannah?" I asked her, "or just Sheffield rampant?"

I turned to face her and found she was staring down at my feet, which happened to be wearing my favorite fire-engine-red quilted slippers. Hannah gulped and barely caught her harlequin spectacles as they slid off her bony nose. Her gaze moved up from my slippers to the black dress socks bunched round my ankles in accordion pleats. Above the socks she encountered the pale and hairless acreage of my lower limbs, disappearing at knee level beneath the horizon line of my overcoat.

"You're not wearing trousers!" she gasped, her lavender curls quivering.

"Oh, that," I said blithely. "Sporting my tennis togs, Hannah old sweetheart, decided to follow Sheffield's example and get in a bit of exercise before lunch. Rather fetching, these casual outfits, I can see why Thomas is so fond of them. Care to have a look?"

She turned decidedly pale, but before I actually had to open my overcoat, Sheffield rounded the corner from the mailroom, his hands full of computer printouts and something expensive-looking in buff parchment. I craned my neck to see the return address, but he shoved the thing into his jacket.

"Winston," he said, "just the man I want to see! I really have to have a word with you about—" Suddenly his mouth dropped open. "Winston," he said in a small, stunned voice. "Are those your *knees?*"

"No," I growled, "I take them on consignment, sale-or-return. What do you want, Sheffield? Spit it out. I've got things to do, you know."

Hannah remained frozen to the spot, eyes fixed on my red slippers. I ignored her, my own eyes on Krish and Hilda Costello, who were headed for the door to the lounge. Hilda took a look at me and exploded with a laugh that was probably heard in Nova Scotia, then went on inside. I could see her as she settled in at the cribbage board under the Presbyterian glare of Alvin, the stuffed moose. Hilda had a distinctly competitive gleam in her eye, and if Krish did things right, the game would last till lunch. I had every faith in him. Ordinarily the kindest and most ingenuous of men, he seemed to be relishing his venture into deception, to say nothing of his undercover investigation of Sheffield. The mystery bug, it appeared, had bitten him, too; he tipped me a wink as he passed, then joined La Costello.

I was getting impatient with Sheffield, still nattering on about the light he'd spotted in my office when he drove by late last night.

"What's the matter, Thomas?" I said. "Couldn't sleep? Something on your mind? Conscience got the midnight collywobbles?"

He moistened his lips and forged on. "Of course it's perfectly understandable, Winston," he whined, "at your age. We do become a bit forgetful. We lose track of practical details."

I caught a mild snort from Hannah. Even the spectacle of my bare knees wasn't enough to keep her here listening to that sort of piffle. She turned with a squeal of her rubber tires and flounced off into the sunset.

"Not that you don't command great respect from all of us,"

Tommy went on. "Immense respect. And *influence*. Your voice is heard by a great many of the faculty. If, for instance, you were to speak a word in season in support of a candidate for the Professor of the Year Award, his chances of being elected would be—"

"Enhanced?" The man was practically purring.

"Exactly. And if you were to speak such a word."

"In season."

"In season, yes. One might quite naturally overlook other—lapses." His eyes drifted once more to my knees and the bright plumage of my footwear. "Lights left burning, for instance. And other—"

"Quirks?"

He smiled. "You do understand?"

"Oh, perfectly," I replied. "And I can give you my answer on the spot. Remember the Floating Fund."

His eyebrows shot up to join his receding hair. "What—did you —say?"

"You heard me, Sheffield. The Floating Fund. Just keep it in mind, that's all."

And I headed for the third floor without a backward look.

"I don't suppose you actually killed this man McKelvie, did you?"

I found David stretched out in the far corner of my office, his head pillowed on the old stadium blanket I keep filed under "E" for emergencies. That is, he'd *been* stretched out until my key turned in the lock; by the time I opened the door, he was flattened against the wall behind me with my lucky horseshoe paperweight in his hand. I skewered him with a stare.

"You planning to lay me out with that thing? If so, just let me sit down first, will you? It's been a twenty-four-hour night and I won't have so far to fall."

He looked at the iron horseshoe raised above my head. It could've crushed my skull if he'd so much as relaxed his grip on it. His face was masked with a weeks-long exhaustion sleep no longer relieved; the dark eyes stared, incredulous. For an instant I wondered if Alex had been right in the first place. There was something alien in those eyes, something that was not the David I thought I knew. He put the horseshoe down on my desk and laughed, and the laugh, too, was remote and unnatural. The forced excitement of evasion and disguise had been dispelled by a night of half-sleep; he had combed the gray powder from his hair and the dark beard was growing back on his chin, but nothing had been resolved and the memory of that dead man in the park was, if anything, even clearer than before.

David had, I noticed, helped himself to Scotch from the antiregulations bottle of Highland elixer I keep in my filing cabinet—also under "E." And if anything qualified as an emergency, this did. I poured each of us a coffee mug of the stuff and asked the crucial question. I don't report to my credit that for a minute or two I wasn't altogether certain of his answer.

"Did you?" I repeated.

He sat down in the chair opposite mine, contemplating his Scotch, avoiding my eyes. "I'm sorry you have to ask," he said.

"Was that an answer?"

He looked me in the eye then, squarely, but only for an instant, then glanced quickly away again. His obliqueness pleased me; there was truth in it. Good liars never look away. Nor do madmen.

"If you mean, did I shoot him, no," he said. "Did I kill him? I don't know the answer to that. If I'd gone to the police instead of poking around on my own all these weeks, he might be alive now."

I sipped at the Scotch. "He might. Or you might both be dead. Or Alex. Or Gemma. Or me. What would the police have been able to do, exactly? I understand from your pal Stockfish that these calls of McKelvie's weren't openly threatening. Probably they'd have been classified as crank calls and handed over to the phone company. If they bothered to trace them, they might've charged the fellow with malicious mischief. It might've stopped the calls. But would it have saved his life?"

"Damn it, Winston. I should've done something. Something."

"The man played on his knowledge of you and led you into a

maze. Whatever he was up to finally destroyed him yesterday in the park. You couldn't have stopped that. Any more than you could've kept your mother from being killed."

His hands were unsteady. The whiskey sloshed out of his mug onto the floor. "I was acting. I was never honest with her, never for a minute."

I leaned back in my chair. "Most of the time, kiddo, honesty doesn't have very much to do with truth. What is it they say a man amounts to—about three bucks' worth of second-class metals? That's honest enough. But is it truth?" I shook my head. "Anyway, this isn't about dishonesty. It's about death. Isn't it?"

"I suppose it is," he said. He took a gulp of the Scotch. " 'That fell sergeant, death, is strict in his arrest . . .' "

"That he is. You shook hands with him a couple of years ago. Ever since, he keeps grinning at you from one corner or another. Even calls you on the phone. That's partly my fault."

"No."

"Honesty, remember? I've gotten you involved in risky business. Even this man McKelvie must have some connection to me, though what it is I couldn't guess."

"You mean because of Jenny Vail? I didn't recognize her until I saw her book, the jacket photo. I know it was Jenny he met in the park every day. Did Alex tell you?"

"She did." I wasn't looking forward to telling him the news.

"Did you talk to Jenny at the Edgars last night? Did she tell you anything?"

"Kiddo," I said gently. I set down my mug and got up from my chair and went to stand behind him, my hands on his shoulders. "She was murdered last night during the awards ceremony. I found her body."

I felt him tense, the broad shoulders straighten and the cords of the neck draw tight. He set down the mug and turned to look up at me. *"You* found her?"

"She'd sent me a message. Yesterday morning. She or somebody impersonating her. 'Someone is going to die . . .' "

" 'You can stop it.' "

"And I didn't. I never had the chance. But I'll tell you what I will do. I'll damn well find out who killed her, and when I do I'm betting we'll find the same person killed McKelvie, too. I owe Jenny the truth."

I stood looking out the window at the spring sun glistening on the pewter current of the dirty old Hudson. A slant-nosed white van was winding in and out of the aisles of parked cars in the lot, drops of rain from the night before glistening on its spotless surface. David came to stand beside me, and I took his arm as I went on.

"We can't beat that fell sergeant, Davy, none of us. On our own behalf or anybody else's. But we can damn well sink our teeth into the bugger. We can use what we're good at to do what we can. We can try not to inflict damage. Especially on ourselves."

"Winnie," he said softly. "I need your help."

I'd been waiting for months to hear him say it. I took a step in his direction and gave him one of my rare bear hugs, and I was damn glad I had, because a second later there was a crash of breaking glass and another of those blasted bullets whined past my cranium and plowed a neat furrow in Sheffield's crummy woodwork. Outside the driver of the white van hit the gas and took off with a roar.

David and I stood holding each other, too stunned to move.

"We'd better get you out of here before Tommy hears about that window and comes up here to hand me a bill for damages," I said at last. I fished in my desk drawer and found my Japanese sword letter opener. Its point was sharp enough to dig that bullet out of the door frame. In a minute I had the thing in my overcoat pocket. "What do you say we stop off at the cop station and see Lloyd Agate, kiddo?" I suggested. "Someone may be going to die, but I'd just as soon it wasn't me!"

11

Lloyd Agate didn't seem too surprised to see us when we walked into his tiny cubbyhole of an office at the Ainsley cop station—or too pleased, either. He lugged his size thirteen gunboats off the upside-down wastebasket and folded his simian arms across his paunch, looking us over. David's haircut rated a blink or two and my new spring outfit almost made one corner of his mouth lift, but not for long. Obviously, he'd been expecting us.

"Sit down," he ordered.

Krish, who'd performed his part of our plan with his usual conscientious efficiency, was still hovering nervously in the hall. He took one look at Agate's face and tugged at my sleeve.

"I shall wait," he said, his cocker spaniel eyes full of concern.

"Run along, Krish," I insisted. "We're among friends here."

He gave Lloyd another look. "I shall wait, nevertheless," he said, and as Agate shut the door I caught a glimpse of him, squeezing onto a bench between Big Red Yokanovich, bouncer at The Pussycat Club out on Highway 9, and Ms. Pumpkyn Pye—one of its most publicized pussycats.

"I said, sit down!" repeated Lloyd.

"Agate," I said cautiously, "I'd like to telephone Sarah, if you don't mind. I—"

"I'll have somebody call her. Sit down, goddammit!"

I risked another interruption. "I promised to call Lincoln in New York as soon as—"

"I just got off the phone with him. He's on his way up. What the hell do you guys think you're doing?"

I've known Lloyd ever since he was Sergeant Agate, a downtrodden forensic photographer sweating to get himself promoted to genuine crime and Detective Lieutenant. He turned up in my Remedial Comp. class, hoping to impress the brass with the impeccable prose of his written reports, and we've been in and out of a number of scrapes together since. It's only rarely that Agate flexes his official biceps, but he was certainly feeling his Cheerios now.

"I ought to put you in a cell, the pair of you, just to keep you out of trouble! I ought to charge you with—with—"

"Finding bodies? That's all either one of us is guilty of, and you know it," I said.

"I *don't* know it! You didn't damn well *tell* me, did you?"

"But Lloyd, be reasonable! We were out of your stomping grounds. I intended to call you as soon as I got a chance. We're a team, you and I and Merriman and David and—"

"Crap!" He slammed a fist on the desk; the photo of his wife and daughter did a nose dive and crashed. "You didn't intend to call anybody, not me, not Linc. You intended to keep right on piddling around in stuff you don't know a damn about, because you think this is some kind of game, the stiffs aren't real stiffs, and the bullets are just a bunch of fairy tales."

"Lloyd, you know better than that," I told him quietly. "You know me."

"The hell I do! Lincoln faxed me the files this morning. As far as I'm concerned, you're suspects like everybody else!"

"Okay, then. Let's take fingerprints. David," I said, "did you touch the gun that killed McKelvie?"

The kiddo had been sitting quietly, holding onto a flowered plastic carrier bag full of what looked like balls of knitting wool. I hadn't asked him about it, and so far he hadn't volunteered.

"I didn't touch anything," he said, facing Agate's frown. "There was a wadded-up piece of paper, and the gun. But the only thing I touched was McKelvie. He'd been shot once, straight through the forehead."

"You shouldn't have moved him, damn it! Nothing at a crime scene should be moved or touched." Lloyd bent to pick up the fragments of glass from the broken frame, then straightened up and squinted in David's direction. "Why *did* you move him?"

David hesitated, then propped the plastic carrier carefully against Lloyd's desk. He closed his eyes for a moment, changed his position slightly, then slumped forward from the hips, his long arms between his knees, his head dangling. For a split second I thought he'd passed out, but then he spoke, his voice muffled by the strange position.

"I left him sitting on that bench. I was a hundred and fifty, maybe two hundred yards away along the path when I heard the shot. When I got back to him, he was bent double," he said, "like this."

Lloyd took his own weapon from his middle desk drawer and went over to David. "The gun was here?" He placed it on the floor.

"No. Beside the left shoe. The butt toward my left hand, as if I'd been holding it."

Agate replaced the gun, then wadded up a sheet of paper. "Where was the paper?"

David took it from him and placed it carefully, just beyond his toes. "It was wrong, you see. It didn't make sense. She gave him that little gun, Jenny Vail did. Just before he was killed. She put it into his right hand, and he *was* right-handed. I'd watched him long enough to know that. So I knew he couldn't have shot himself with the gun in his left hand."

Lloyd took him by the shoulders and sat him up; David offered no resistance, just allowed himself to be manipulated like a stage prop.

"Okay, look," said Agate, his wide, gentle hands still resting on Davy's shoulders. "When you left the guy, he was sitting up more or less normally, right?" David nodded. "Okay. Point blank, close range, long range—wherever the bullet came from, the impact is gonna knock him backwards." He gave a shove with one huge paw and David slumped back, head dangling, mouth open, arms hanging at his sides. Agate sat him up again. "*Backwards*, not forwards."

"Which means someone moved the body *before* David got there?"

Lloyd nodded. "Somebody went through his pockets and dumped the stuff out, looking for something specific." He riffled through the mess of papers on his desk and yanked out a photocopied sheet. "This is the report Lincoln faxed me, and it lists McKelvie's effects. Besides the gun and the Edgars seating chart with your name circled, there was a wallet with a Social Security card and a couple of subway tokens, eleven dollars and forty-six cents cash, a roll of Tums, a wad of Kleenex. No credit cards. No keys. He didn't have a driver's license or a car, but he had an apartment, and there should've been keys."

"So you think whoever killed him went through his pockets looking for something, and when he didn't find it, stole his keys in order to take a look at his apartment?"

My brain was ticking off the list of guests at the Edgars dinner, most of them friends and acquaintances, people not unlike ~~myself~~ *me* in many ways. Which of them, I wondered dazedly, was capable of such cool, purposeful brutality? Which of them had been in that sweet-smelling garden, watching and listening, noting David's every move? And which of them had known us both, involved us both on purpose, and not turned a hair when he saw me that night at dinner, waiting his chance to kill again, to inflict more random damage upon an already desolated planet? Their bland faces, like publicity stills, clicked past the lens of my memory one by one, and I opened my eyes wide, trying to replace their sinister ordinariness with the grubby reality of the police station.

"If the murderer took McKelvie's keys, he'll go back to the brownstone," said David. "He'll go looking for whatever he didn't find."

"He took Jenny's purse, too," I said. "Probably for the same reason. But as I recall, she had a duplex in one of those high-security buildings just off Fifth Avenue, not far from the Frick Museum. Not easy to waltz in there and shake the place down, even if he *did* have her keys."

"Lincoln's got patrol cars covering both places." Agate tried to sound reassuring. He mumbled something about the manpower shortage and the budget crisis, but his collar seemed to be pinching and his ears were distinctly pink.

"But, Lloyd," David objected. "Anybody clever enough to do what this man has done could spot a patrol car in a minute, wait for it to pass, and walk straight in. That old brownstone is a long way from burglar-proof, and with McKelvie's keys . . ."

"What it needs," I grumbled, "is a stakeout."

"What it needs, is Fish," muttered Davy under his breath.

Lloyd didn't seem to hear us. "How long did it take you to get back to the bench from where you heard the shot?" he asked.

David frowned. "I'd have to time it to say for sure. The path was wet. It took me a minute to realize what the sound actually was. I was following Mrs. Vail, and when the shot came we both stopped. She turned around and saw me. She was as shocked as I was."

"But she didn't try to go back?"

"No. She went on. I turned around and ran. So, all in all, maybe three minutes, maybe four before I actually got back to McKelvie."

"And you didn't see anybody else, nobody in the Shakespeare Garden, nobody on any of the paths?"

"I didn't look, really. But there are trees. Statuary. Shrubs. Someone could've been there, I suppose, crouching down. I was only seeing McKelvie." He looked up at Lloyd, the dark blue eyes steady. Whatever hint of imbalance I had seen in them that morning was gone now, like some inaudible frequency on which he had suddenly tuned out. "I felt he was a friend," he told us. "Might've been a friend. His death seemed so—so casual. Impersonal. I— wanted him to matter. You see? I didn't like to leave him there, bent like that. He might've fallen. The rain . . ."

His voice drifted, then fell silent. This, I thought, was the madness Alex had feared, the imbalance I had seen in David's eyes. "I wanted him to matter." I looked over at Lloyd; he said nothing, but my look was returned with interest. "Why don't you begin at the beginning, David," he said at last, "and tell us everything you know."

And so, with a tape machine turning and a cup of terrible cop-house coffee in his hands, he gave us the whole confused tale of the anonymous calls, his private surveillance of McKelvie, his abortive afternoon visit to Vangie Glickman, and his evasion of New York's finest in the person of Peggy Bryce. I added what little I knew—Jenny's note to Vail, the wine and roses of the previous day. When we had finished, one burning question remained unanswered.

"But you never touched the murder weapon?" I repeated. "The little gun that was lying at McKelvie's feet, the one Jenny gave him. You never had your hands on it?"

"No."

"All right, then! According to that display dummy with the chestful of medals, there were two sets of prints on the gun when they found it, the dead man's and one other set they hadn't identified. Take David's prints and compare them with the unknown set and—"

"It's not unknown anymore." Lloyd had forgotten all about his official posture. "According to Linc, the extra set matched Jenny Vail's prints."

David nodded. "I told you, I saw her give him the gun and she wasn't wearing gloves or anything."

"But," said Agate, "it doesn't help, because the gun in the grass wasn't the gun that killed McKelvie. Linc just got the ballistics reports this morning. The gun Jenny gave him was a new model Rankin miniature thirty-eight, never fired. And the bullet the medical examiner dug out of his skull was seven millimeter, needle-nosed."

"Don't tell me," I said. "The same kind of bullet that killed Jenny?"

"And fired from the same gun. Fancy stuff, French-made, experimental." His broad, gentle face was lined with frustration. "But nobody's found that weapon yet."

I sighed. "So it might as well have been David as anybody else."

"They can't eliminate him, not with what they've got so far. And by the way, Colby had a police sketch made from that description on the anonymous tip and one of his boys happened to be reading the *Enquirer* in the checkout lane at Sloan's. Nice picture: 'Star Walks Out on Broadway Show.' Care to guess what tomorrow's headline's going to be?"

"For pity's sake, Lloyd, can't you give him a paraffin test? He's never fired anything but stage guns in his life!"

"Goddammit, David!" Agate got up and began to pace. "Why did you run? If you'd come to us right after the guy got killed, told us what you saw, the whole thing, we'd have done a paraffin and that would've been that. I know you didn't shoot the guy, but how are you going to prove that to a D.A. looking to make a name prosecuting a TV star? It's been a whole day, and a paraffin wouldn't prove a thing, not now. You should've come to us yesterday."

Us. We. Those all-powerful official pronouns were making me nervous. I began to grasp at straws. "What about a lie detector?"

David smiled. "Winnie. I'm an actor, remember? I lie for a living."

"But if the same gun killed both McKelvie and Jenny Vail—"

Suddenly I got an inspiration. In my overcoat pocket was the bullet I'd dug out of my office woodwork before we left the Arts and Letters Building. I fished it out and handed it to Agate.

"Take a look at that, will you? Funny-looking little article, isn't it? Would you call that needle-nosed?"

He squinted at it and then pulled a huge volume off the filing cabinet behind him, causing an avalanche of files and dumping over a plastic cup of prehistoric coffee. He heaved the book onto his desk and began to page through it, the wicked, pointed little bullet in his other hand, its nose barely dented by the collision with Sheffield's simulated oak-type door frame. Lloyd stopped at a page labeled "Terrorist Weapons."

I took one look at the words and choked. " 'Terrorist?' Tell me that doesn't say 'Terrorist Weapons!' "

He jammed his big thumb down on the page and ran it along a row of life-size photographs of bullets, stopping near the bottom of the page. He took the one I'd handed him and laid it on top of the photo. It fit exactly.

"We'd need lab tests to know if it came from the same gun. But it's sure as hell the same kind of bullet as the ones that killed McKelvie and Mrs. Vail. Where did you get it, Doc?"

"To be perfectly accurate," I told him, "*it* almost got *me*. It was fired through my office window just before we came over here, by somebody driving one of those fancy new vans, the kind with the slanting front end that looks like an aerodynamic cigar box. If you'd let me get a word in edgewise, I'd have told you before."

Lloyd snapped to attention. "What color?"

"White, and—"

"License?"

"No soap, kiddo. I was three stories up, you know, and I didn't have my specs on. But I'd give you odds it wasn't a New York plate. The numbers were lighter, sort of blue, maybe green, and the background was off-white."

"Think you could identify the make from some pictures?"

I shrugged. "I'm not much of a lad for mechanical toys, but I'll give it a try."

"What kind of van? Step-van, back-open, passenger, slide? Did it have a name on the side, any unusual paint, any customizing—fancy tires, little curtains? You know the kind of crap people load onto them. Anything like that?"

"It wasn't a commercial van," I said. "I couldn't say for certain, but I'd be willing to bet it has a sliding door on the side. I heard one of those doors slide shut yesterday, just before my study was searched, and again this morning, before the first of those bullets arrived."

"There was another?" Lloyd frowned. "What time this morning?"

"Landed in the pansy planter outside my front door just after we got back to the house this morning, missed my nose by an inch. If that little darling in your hand matches the bullets that killed our two friends, Lloyd, it means that the same jamoke who shot Jenny and this fellow McKelvie is after me," I said with a shiver. "And Davy, here, is off the hook."

"How so?" said Agate, a hopeful gleam in his eye.

I pushed my chair back and stood up. "Davy couldn't have been firing at me through the window, Lloyd, because he was standing right beside me in the office at the time. If he hadn't been there, I'd be splattered all over Sheffield's no-wax vinyl tile right now." I growled. "And *he'd* probably send me a bill for the disinfectant, posthumous and C.O.D."

Krish, delighted to escape the dubious company of Pumpkyn Pye, was eager to drive me home, but Lloyd insisted on providing a squad car. He kept David, pending the ballistics tests on my pet bullet, but aside from the paperwork, it looked as though the kiddo's short career as a desperado was over.

Julian Stockfish drove Alex down to the station in his tiny red Honda to wait it out with David—and presumably to set up a little private surveillance of McKelvie's brownstone, the kind the cops couldn't quite afford. What with Lloyd's patrol car on duty outside, it wasn't likely we'd be invaded by any more needle-nosed projectiles for a while, and I, for one, was ready for a few hours of shut-eye before Lincoln arrived. I trudged up the stairs and was about to fall down on the bed where Sarah was already napping, when I remembered that invitation to the Perfidy, Unlimited tea. Surely they'd postponed the thing, but having no wish to offend the Red-Headed League, I figured I'd better call Hazel, who knew everything about everything, and bow out. I lumbered back to the telephone in the hall and picked up the receiver.

But I didn't get a dial tone. What I did get was Merriman's voice on the downstairs extension, sounding nervous enough to explode. I'd have hung up instantly, of course; eavesdropping isn't my idea of playing by the rules. But then again, rules were made to be broken. Or at least bent a little now and then.

"You're absolutely certain, are you?" said Eddie. "I am, as you are aware, an antediluvian specimen and apt to prove unequal to sudden reverses. Three h-h-h-hundred thousand? After t-t-t-t-taxes?"

"Oh, quite." The voice on the other end was English, mildly

amused. "Three hundred thousand pounds, plus accrued interest since your uncle's demise. Around half a million at the current rate in dollars."

Merriman made a suffocating noise, like a garden hose with a kink in it. Then he cleared his throat and tried again.

"But Mr. Sweeting, about the other heirs. I mean to say, I'm quite sure Uncle Horace had two sons and a daughter. Surely one of them had issue, as you legal chaps put it. My claim seems pretty tenuous, doesn't it? I hardly knew the man, after all."

Sweeting was unshakeable. "I do assure you, Mr. Merriman, we have investigated the claims of several other distant heirs—great-nieces, adopted grandchildren, and so on. None of them legitimate, and all of them contrary to your uncle's final will, filed some two months before his death. He'd kept his eye on you, you see, for many years. Investigated your career, your way of life. Sir Horace was a most perspicacious old gentleman, to the very last. And, I may say, with a remarkable knack for turning a dollar." He coughed slightly. "There is, of course, the matter of the baronetcy to be considered. Your American citizenship naturally precludes—"

"Oh," said Eddie hastily, but with, I thought, a tinge of regret. "Oh, naturally."

"Unless you might wish to emigrate, take up residence at Fernleigh Court—"

I didn't wait to hear the reply. It was more than I could bear. I hung up the extension as quietly as possible and sank down on the telephone bench to get my land legs back. What with Jenny's death and David's adventures, I'd completely forgotten about that telegram Eddie had stuffed into his pocket the morning before. Or should I say, "Sir Eddie?" He hadn't been kidding about the inheritance and the stately home. Fernleigh Court, Sweeting had called the place. About seventy bedrooms, more than likely, and a skeleton crew of twenty-five, except during hunting season, when Her Majesty might stop by to pot a couple of hundred pheasants.

We were going to lose Eddie, I could feel it in my bones. With half a million bucks and a mansion in England, why on earth would he stick around here, freezing to death all winter in three rooms that used to belong to Erskine Cromwell's boozy housekeeper? He'd go, of course he would. Sir Eddie. Sir Edward Merriman. It had a ring to it, after all.

I was absolutely sure of it. I was going to lose the only man I'd ever known who could work the *Times* crossword faster than I can, and do it in ink; the man who taught me everything I know about steam trains, Chinese puzzle boxes, and first editions of Dickens; the only man who can knock me off my high horse and make me relish the fall. I'd almost lost him to pneumonia twice that winter, and terrible as that prospect had been, this, in its insidious way, was worse. Death was a thing we held in common; it posed no threat to our friendship. We were both, so to speak, on the same mailing list.

But money was different. It tilted the familiar world askew and through its lens people, even old friends, looked different, perhaps became different themselves in self-defense. It trivialized the significant and lent the trivial an aura far beyond its worth. When you had it—no matter how you came by it—a peculiar sort of credit was invested in you. You might appear the same as you always had, but somehow, in the sacred temples where the treasure of this earth is laid up, calculated, set out at interest compounded semiannually, and harvested at the current rate, the word got out. Money, the high priests would whisper, adjusting the knots of their power ties. He has money. When he speaks, money is his voice. When he falls ill, money is his medicine. If he runs a stop sign, drives with a few drinks under his belt and gets caught, money is his defense, money his jury, money the lawbook of his judge. Is he ignorant? Money buys wise men to put words in his mouth. Is he a fool? Money surrounds him with dunces to make him seem wise. When he weeps, his tears, too, are money, and when he comes at last to die, money is his priest, his mourner, and his everlasting life.

When I had first known her, Jenny Vail had not been rich. The multimillion dollar advances had come only in the last five years or so, since her books claimed a permanent place on the best-seller lists and Stanway's TV series hit the top ten. As the money grew, so had her isolation. Only those who wanted something—book jacket blurbs, personal appearances, photo opportunities—approached her. Old friends who wanted nothing saw the new suspicion in her eyes—or thought they did—and stayed away.

As I, myself, had stayed away. Our transitory subzero love affair might have relaxed into a long friendship, but I had not pursued it. Perhaps I envied her, resented those lost Edgars more than I thought. Or perhaps pride, always my besetting sin, had told me good fences made good neighbors and refused to let me so much as acknowledge the annual gift of her newest book. I hadn't even read Jenny's books, except for a few chapters of one of her early efforts. I'd worked hard at convincing myself they weren't quite the thing, too Freudian, too full of soap opera gimmicks. Now I began to wonder if the reason I hadn't read them was not so much that I wouldn't like them, as that I was afraid I might like them a bit too well. And what if the invariable yearly gift of an autograph copy had not been, as that dollar-sign-shaped lens had shown it to me, a cheap shot at a less spectacular colleague? What if it had been a token of unremarked friendship and silent understanding?

But I had not understood. Two years ago when her daughter Cynthia was killed, I'd meant to write a letter, once the uproar in the papers died away. There had been no funeral, not even a prayer service. I sent a check for twenty dollars to some sort of memorial for Cynthia, I wasn't sure exactly what. I even bought a card, handsome embossed thing, tasteful prepackaged sympathy. But I didn't send it. The annual gift of each year's book continued unbroken. No. I had never understood.

Robbed of all desire for sleep, I shambled into the Cave and slumped into my springless old chair. Jenny's white roses, brown and withered, still lay on the desk beside the unopened bottle of Dom Perignon. I reached instead for the Haig & Haig and poured a tumblerful, then lit one of my Turkish cigarettes and inhaled gratefully, heedless of mortality. Downstairs I heard the wobbly notes of Eddie's clarinet as he played his ten thousandth version of "Misty," and I have to admit I was getting a bit misty myself. I might've been a fool where Jenny Vail was concerned, but I was damned if I was going to let the same thing happen with Merriman. I might not be able to keep him from becoming Sir Eddie, but I was certain I could postpone the *bon voyage* party for a while, anyway. If anything could win him away from tea with Her Majesty, it was a good mystery, and two of them had just fallen in our laps.

Not to speak of a couple of needle-nosed bullets. Terrorist bullets. I shivered and hoisted the Haig & Haig again.

"Aren't you coming to bed at all, Win?" Sarah was standing in my doorway, hair cascading down her back, eyes scarcely open.

" 'Macbeth hath murdered sleep,' " I said.

"Are you thinking about her? About Jenny?"

I took a swallow of the Scotch. "Among other things."

"Were you in love with her?" She sat on the edge of my desk, her fingers fiddling with the dead petals. "Oh, not now, I don't mean. But once. Some time."

"I won't lie about it," I said. "You were off tickling the ivories in all the capitals of Europe at the time. I met Jenny at a writer's conference our publishers had set up. We were both bored, feeling like a couple of prize hogs at a county fair, ribbons around our necks and all. I was lonely. I think now that Jenny must've reminded me of you."

"*Looked* like me, you mean? Jenny Vail?" Sarah frowned. "Oh dear. Do you think so?" She lit one of my cigarettes. "Maybe if I did something different with my hair."

We were both silent, then, smoking and listening to Eddie's music. I figured the time was ripe to tell all.

"Sarah," I said, "somebody's been shooting at me. Outside this morning, Julian Stockfish saved my neck, and then—"

"I know." The rose crumbled in her hand. She walked to the row of high windows looking down into the garden. "Didn't you think I might wonder how you got grass stains all over that ridiculous stage suit? I dug it out of the trash can and had a look. Besides, the police car that brought you home hasn't left, it's still parked at the end of the drive. He's a very nice policeman, really. Terribly young, peach-fuzz beard. His name is Wade."

"And naturally he assured you nobody would be shooting at me while he was on the case."

"Mmmmm," she said.

"At least it served one purpose, my playing target. David's no longer Public Enemy Number One."

"He deserves to be paddled." She paused, considering. "All that about the bullets, what you told us when you got home? It was very confusing. I don't understand a thing about caliber and ballistics and blunt noses and needle noses. It's nice you're not dead, of course."

Sarah remained by the windows; in spite of the cop parked outside, it made me a bit nervous. That terrorist gun had a pretty long range, and if the van was the same one I'd heard in the drive when the roses were delivered, the shooter knew exactly where my Cave was. I went over to stand beside her and she, as I'd hoped, moved back to my desk again and out of danger.

"Aren't you going to tell me to stop snooping around before I get myself shot? Let the cops handle it?"

"Did you sleep with her?"

The words came quickly, in that precise Bette Davis diction which always becomes more pronounced whenever Sarah is angry or afraid. I could feel her eyes on me, but I didn't turn away from the windows.

"Yes," I said.

"Often?"

"Once."

"You never told me. You told me about Rachel Thurlow."

"And you never told me about you and Stefan Turbacz, not till I started poking into his death thirty years too late."

"Yes," she said, then was silent for a long space. At last I felt her beside me and she slipped her arm through mine. "I suppose you'll have to find out who killed her," she told me softly.

"Will I?"

She nodded. "Oh yes. Otherwise she'll always claim a bit of you."

"As Stefan did of you for all those years?"

"The picture of him, you see. Dead. You saw Jenny dead last night. She won't let you go. Like that man McKelvie and David. He'll have to go on, too, now. Till it's over."

"I'm glad you understand," I said.

"Understand?" she said. "I'm damned if I do. But I'm too tired to be brainy." She let me go and started for the door. "Come to bed," she said.

I didn't argue.

12

You probably know what it's like. You tell yourself you're going to take a little nap to make up for the sleep you lost during the night, and the minute you stretch out on the bed your eyelids grow little springs on them and refuse to stay shut. Covers that usually remain neatly tucked in instantly pull out and your toes get cold. The goosefeathers in your pillow have been switched for baseballs when you weren't looking. You try counting sheep and every one of the silly buggers looks back at you and snickers.

When a particularly vacuous animal with Sheffield's face jogged past my interior telescope carrying a briefcase and baaing something about the Floating Fund, I knew it was time to call it quits.

Dressed at last in more or less conventional garb—my favorite plaid sport shirt and a pair of putter pants I've had since Ike gave up golf—I went down the back stairs to see what sort of lunch I could scare up. Merriman, never much inclined to sleep even when he hasn't come into megabucks, was sitting at the kitchen table, smoking his favorite old tape-mended briar and fiddling with the legal pad on which I'd written my notes. We hadn't had a moment alone since he'd caught me digging the first of my bullets out of the pansy pot. He looked up at me and blinked.

"Smoking behind the woodshed?" I said. "Thought you'd decided to give it up after that pneumonia business last winter."

"In case you don't remember, Goopus," he said, puffing out a fragrant cloud of Mixture Seventy-Nine, "that was *viral* pneumonia, caused by crossing paths with the wrong sort of microbe. Nothing keeps the bugs away like a nice fire, and besides, it helps me think."

He fell silent and I began to forage in the refrigerator for leftovers. "I suppose your canny brain has the whole mess figured out by now, has it?" I said at last.

"I'm afraid not. It's a puzzling business. Contradictory."

"And it didn't just begin yesterday. I'd say it's been at least two years in the making."

I pulled out a tinfoil package and began to unwrap two pieces of leftover quiche lorraine. It seemed to be growing green fur. I pitched it into the trash and dived into the fridge again.

"Two years," Eddie echoed. "Of course, I see what you mean. McKelvie officially became McKelvie two years ago. Got his Social Security card, and so on."

"It's two years since he moved into that building on Eighty-seventh, according to Davy," I said. "The old girl in the downstairs apartment, Vangie Glickman, told him McKelvie had moved in two years ago."

"A nosey parker after my own heart, that lady. Sounds as though she's been sniffing after the poor fellow from the start." He chuckled. "What was your Jenny doing two years ago?"

"She wasn't *my* Jenny," I grumbled. "I forget, anyway, which title of hers came out that year. I think that was about the time her daughter was killed, but I'm not exactly sure. I'd have to check it in the *Times* microfilms at the library."

"By all means. Because if those dates coincide, Winnie—"

"Then McKelvie and Jenny were both killed because of Cynthia's death?" I found an acceptable chunk of cold meat loaf and began to slice it. "That's quite a leap of faith, Merriman. Anyway, whoever killed them is now trying to knock *me* off, and I never even *met* Cynthia Vail."

"Let me see," he said, swiping a slice of meat loaf. "What were we fiddling about with two years ago?"

"Digging into the Danson Foundation for the Arts," I replied.

"Computer embezzlement, cooking the books to line Andrew Danson's pockets. What the hell has that got to do with Jenny? She certainly didn't need to apply for any foundation grants."

Merriman wrote something down on the legal pad, then scratched it out again. "Blast! Everything seems to have *something* to do with money, though," he said. "Jenny had far too much, McKelvie apparently had none at all. The Vilnius woman coveted it, and so did Sloan and Miss Kovacs, who wanted her little bit of power, as well. Grandson Gregory may have been in line to inherit his granny's millions. Steven Stanway has it in sackfuls, and I believe Philip Vail's fairly oofy, too, wouldn't you say?"

"If that means rich," said a voice from the dining room doorway, "the answer's yes."

It was Lincoln, closely followed by Lloyd Agate. I could hear Alexandra's clear soprano resounding from the living room, along with David's baritone. Suddenly the house was full of activity and I still hadn't cornered Merriman about *his* new bankroll. I sighed and finished building my pyramid of meat loaf sandwiches.

We ate them in the living room, accompanied by crisp yellow apples and cups of my best fresh-ground coffee with homemade oatmeal cookies to dunk or not, as the spirit moved us. When Merriman, Lincoln and I carried the food in, we found Sarah huddled with David on the window seat, deep in sober conversation. Neither of them was smiling, nor was Alex, who sat on the piano bench looking like a little kid who's just been ticked off for not practicing.

It's been my experience that food, even leftovers, brings rest to many a perturbed spirit, and it seemed to hold true in this instance, as well. Sarah wasn't exactly perky, but she joined her brother and old Merriman on the sofa and settled in for our strategy meeting. Julian Stockfish, looking a bit pleased with himself at having a couple of cops for a captive audience, played the tape recording of David's anonymous call again; I trotted upstairs for that bottle of wine and the card that came with it, and handed round the interrupted note to Philip that Jenny had hidden in her program. Once we'd shared all the information we'd collected so far, we returned to the subject of Philip Vail.

"He's old money," I said, "I do know that much. The Vail family goes back to the days of the Astors, the Goulds, the Vanderbilts. Great-grandfather ran for president, I think. Couple of senators in the family, a Secretary of State. All Harvard men, most of them knocked around Europe, played whist with Henry James, roulette with Scott Fitzgerald, baccarat with Princess Grace. Back in the Twenties, Philip's uncle, Marcus Vail, was an editor at E.P. Alexander, where Philip works now. One of the great editors, old Marcus Vail, in a league with Maxwell Perkins—man who edited Thomas Wolfe, you know, Hemingway, Fitzgerald. Marcus Vail wasn't quite so lucky, or his taste didn't quite come up to Perkins's. But he built E.P. Alexander and Sons from a little textbook house to a real force in American publishing."

"And nephew Philip followed in his footsteps," said Eddie. "Had no taste for the political tradition of his forbears, I take it."

"Did he ever turn up at any of those famous literary soirees of your father's, Sarah?" I said. "Philip would've been barely out of college in those days, just getting started at Alexander's. You didn't seem to remember him at all when you saw him at the Edgars last night."

She shrugged. "I didn't. But that doesn't mean he wasn't there. I hated those ridiculous parties of Erskine's and I was usually playing the piano all night. I could go through some of the old scrapbooks in the file room. An old-line family, hereditary class. A young impressionable kid likely to become influential. Sounds just the sort Erskine would've been drooling to get his hooks into, the predatory old toady."

"Give it a try, why don't you," I said. "Never know what you may dig up. Linc, can you get some of Colby's handwriting experts to check out that note that arrived with the wine, see if it matches the letter Jenny was writing to Philip?"

He held the heavy, embossed notepaper up to the light, then brushed his fingers over the front, then the back of the sheet. Next he picked up the letter I'd swiped from Jenny's table and gave it the same treatment.

"The writing *looks* genuine," he said. "But the impression is a lot heavier on the notepaper than on the letter. That's just cheap copy paper, and a normal handwriting should make a deeper impression on it than on this heavy card stock, but it's the other way around."

Stockfish took the card from him and studied it. "They've typed the message with an electronic machine," he said. "Almost no impression on the back and perfectly even on the front. Hard to trace, but not impossible. Then there's a gap before the closing and the signature, more blank space than you'd usually leave. If somebody faked the signature—"

"Traced it, say, from a book she'd autographed." David was smiling, the first real smile I'd seen since he surfaced.

" 'Best wishes, Jenny Vail,' " I said. "That was the way she autographed every book she signed."

I should know, I thought guiltily. All those unread volumes she'd sent me over the years carried the identical message.

"I got suspicious the minute I saw the thing," I said. "Who trots to the typewriter and raps out a card to send with a bottle of champagne? It's a sentimental gesture. You write it by hand and sign it by hand. I thought the thing looked phony, figured it was part of some elaborate publicity stunt cooked up by that publicist of hers."

"The Vilnius woman!" cried Eddie. "Did you see her after Jenny's death was announced? Instant hysterics, a perfect Niagara Falls of foul crocodile tears."

"As I recall," said Sarah drily, "hysterics were pretty much the order of the evening. Even the chilly Ms. Kovacs was sniffling, and I'd hardly have taken *her* for a weeper."

"We'll run the two samples through the lab, but I'll bet you a Greek dinner Jenny Vail never sent that bottle of bubbly," Lincoln said. He frowned in my direction. "Too late to check the note for fingerprints, though."

"Shall I dance a bit further out on the present limb," asked Eddie, "and suggest that if Jenny had nothing to do with the message on that bottle, she very likely had nothing to do with those anonymous calls, either?"

"The message was the same, so probably the calls were made by the person who sent the wine and flowers," said Lloyd. "McKelvie met Jenny every day. David traced those calls to McKelvie."

"And, induced by the forged card, it would be natural to assume she was a party to the calls." Merriman sat paring his apple with his pearl-handled pocket knife.

"I think McKelvie knew I'd find him," David said. "He made it easy for me to follow him. He stuck to the same route every day. He even waited for me when I didn't keep up with him. He led me straight to Jenny every day." He got up and began to pace back and forth in front of the French windows. "What if someone else put him up to those phone calls? Someone who knew both Winnie and me. Someone who wanted him to lead me to Jenny Vail."

"Somebody whose voice you'd have recognized. The tape you played for us?" Lloyd reached for another sandwich. "The flat tone, the way the words break into syllables? Sounds like a synthesizer to me."

"I thought a synthesizer was some kind of Japanese musical instrument," I growled. "Like an electric violin."

Sarah shuddered. "Or those abominable little plastic things they blithely refer to as keyboards. Electronic music is a contradiction in terms. Phooey!"

Stockfish laughed. "He means a machine that can simulate a human voice, come out with one that's completely anonymous. But even the computer has to start someplace, right? I mean, they start with a real voice and alter it?"

"Sometimes." Lincoln made a note and fished in his pocket for a small plastic bag. He dropped the minicassette into it and methodically wrote a label for the evidence bag. "If this isn't completely electronically produced, the lab ought to be able to uncover at least a form of the real voice, the one it used as a base. Then we can play it for you, see if David's right and it's somebody you recognize."

"But if Jenny didn't finagle McKelvie into making those phone calls," said Sarah, "then who did? Surely not the old lady downstairs?"

"There was Boots," said Davy. "The pair of ankle boots she saw through the window. Whoever it was came to see McKelvie regularly between Christmas and New Year's, and was always careful not to go up to his apartment."

"So as not to leave any fingerprints," put in Alexandra.

"Skinny, with tight jeans, and boots you haven't been able to buy since 1969? It hardly sounds like Philip Vail, does it?" I returned to where we had begun.

"Win," said Sarah, "when you were talking about Philip's uncle Marcus, before, I remembered something. At least, I think I did. Wasn't Marcus Vail a partner in E.P. Alexander at one time? You know more about publishing houses than I do, but I distinctly remember having handled books with Alexander and Vail on the title pages. Don't I?"

I shrugged. "If you do, the partnership didn't last long. It's been E.P. Alexander and Sons as long as I can remember. Be interesting to find out, though, if there was a falling-out between them, or money troubles."

"Seems to me," said Merriman, "that I've been reading in the financial columns about Alexander and Sons just recently. Subterranean rumblings about shaky stock and probable corporate restructuring. Always the knell of doom."

"The Dow Jones your pillow-book these days, is it, Merriman?" I snarled. "For your information, every publisher in New York's in financial trouble. The era of the book is coming to an end. Half the best-sellers on the list are nothing but printed sound-bites, with two-inch margins and a forty-five minute reading time, tops. It's only a matter of time till some Flying Dutchman buys us all up and recycles us. But so far as I know, Alexander hasn't had to sell yet. Hazel would know, though. I'll run it past her."

Which reminded me, I'd never gotten round to calling her about that lapsed invitation to tea.

"What kind of society does Vail move in?" asked Lincoln. "You know, lunch at Trump Tower, jetting off to Malcolm Forbes's birthday party in the afternoon—that stuff?"

"Life-styles of the rich and shameless? Hardly Philip's thing, no. You won't see his name in the society columns, and Jenny didn't have much use for it either. The jet set aren't exactly trendsetters down at B. Dalton's, not until they get their autobiographies ghost-written." I studied Lincoln's face, puzzled. "Why? Does it matter how Vail gets his jollies?"

"It might." Lloyd Agate took the reins. "It's that gun, Doc. The one that killed Jenny and McKelvie, the one that's been shooting at you? See, it's experimental, like I told you this morning."

"For which, read 'illegal,' " said Julian.

"Right. But that doesn't mean you can't get your hands on one. It's not that hard, only you need two things."

"Don't tell me," I grumbled. "Money."

"And the right connections," supplied David.

"The gun's plastic," Lincoln explained. "Well, most of it is. Lightweight, you can take it anywhere and it won't weigh you down like a conventional gun. Besides that, you can walk through any metal detector in any airport in the world and it won't raise a beep. It's got a removable infrared telescopic sight and an adjustable barrel so it can be used at either long or short range."

"Also a silencer," added Lloyd. "And it fires those nasty little seven-millimeter bullets, pointed as hell. You can pinpoint a target and those babies will make a hole so precise that until the victim falls down, nobody will even notice he's been shot."

"An assassination gun," said David quietly.

Lincoln nodded. "The inventor, this French guy in Marseilles, offered the production rights to our government, but they turned him down. So he sold them on the open market. They're made in a cute little factory in Libya, marketed through big-time international arms dealers who set up sales demonstrations on neutral islands, some-times on their own yachts. Places where anything they want to sell is perfectly legal. Not all that many assassins mind if they can't get a gun permit, right?"

"How much, exactly," asked Eddie, "would a weapon like that cost when it's on sale? Including money-back coupons and so on."

Lloyd picked up the shards of his oatmeal cookie and laughed. "Better start saving up, Mr. M. Would you believe twenty thousand bucks, cash on the line?"

"Let's hope it comes with instructions for easy assembly," I said. "That way not many of the things will ever see the light of day."

"The point is, of course, that only somebody rolling in ducats could afford one," said Eddie, "and only somebody likely to know somebody who knows a major arms merchant would know where to find one."

"But do the jet set actually buy all that many experimental assassination weapons?" said Alex. "It seems so incredible."

"It *seems* like a lot of hooey!" announced Sarah. She'd been quiet for a while, nibbling away at a sandwich that was still only half eaten. "Of course arms dealers have a lot of money and a good many of them love to throw it around. That man Akkoseoglu, with his pink mansion in Beverly Hills and his yacht the size of the Queen Mary. You read about them all the time. But you wouldn't actually have to *know* a man like that socially. All you'd have to do is hire someone who knew how to make contact. I'll bet Julian, here, could do it, couldn't you?"

Stockfish grinned. "Well, actually, there's this guy I know, Bonaparte Shanks. He knows this guy who runs a laundromat uptown who can get you anything. That's the word. Anything you want. He used to supply the Haitians during that crack war with the Colombians, he sent a big shipment over to the IRA right after Saint Patrick's Day last year."

"Could you take this laundromat king to lunch, Julian?" I asked him. "Ask for a test run of our favorite murder weapon and see what turns up?"

"But don't you see?" Sarah protested. "It doesn't make any sense! These murders—they could both have been done with perfectly ordinary guns, couldn't they, Lieutenant Lincoln? Why did the murderer need the kind of gun you'd use to shoot the President when he throws out the first ball at the World Series, for pity's sake?"

I saw exactly what she meant, and it had been troubling me like sand under a fingernail all during our discussion.

"Was McKelvie shot at close range?" I asked Lincoln. "David described the wound as small and almost perfectly round. Now, according to my sketchy knowledge of bullet holes, a wound at point-blank range wouldn't be perfectly round. It would be feathered out a bit at the edges, and there'd be powder burns."

"Ordinarily, yes," he replied. "But not with a needle-nose bullet. It makes a clean wound and gives an almost instant kill. Ballistics did some tests. The guy was shot from around a foot away, maybe a little more but not much. The bullet didn't splinter the skull and come out, as it would have at either point-blank or long range; it lodged in the heavy bone at the back of his head and stayed there."

"So whoever shot him couldn't have been hiding in the shrubbery," said David. "He must've been standing right in front of that bench."

"In which case, McKelvie knew him. Or her." Alex shivered and gulped her coffee.

"Mrs. Vail was shot from behind, almost point-blank," said Lincoln.

"Which indicates," Merriman piped up, "that *her* killer couldn't afford to let her see him, and McKelvie's had no fear of raising a hue and cry if he showed himself."

Sarah put down her plate. "Jenny knew she was going to die. I told you that. She had that gun in her purse to protect herself. Maybe the killer had seen it, knew she'd be able to defend herself."

"McKelvie had a gun, too, Jenny gave him one," I objected.

"She could've used it," said David. "She handled the gun as if she were used to it, she was comfortable with it."

Lincoln wasn't surprised. "Know what the most popular new sport for women is, according to *Manhattan Today?* Target practice."

"But McKelvie hated it. When she put that gun into his hand, he just stared at it. Then he shoved it into his pocket as though it were burning him. He couldn't possibly have used it, not on the spur of the moment. Anyway, he had no confidence in himself. 'I wasn't any use to her.' That's what he said. 'I wasn't any use to her. I'm none to you, either.' "

"Her? In the past tense? Could that refer to Cynthia Vail?"

"I don't know," David replied. "Jenny wanted him to do something. 'If you mean what you say, you have to do it now.' " He looked around the room, from one of us to another. "I'm an actor, you all know that. I've spent most of my life learning how to read character, how to think like other people. Some of them are pretty mixed up, psychotic even. Edwin Booth used to go to the madhouses and spend nights there, learning to think like the madmen, what made them laugh, what made them afraid. I followed McKelvie for a long time. I watched him. He wasn't mad, but he *was* afraid. It sounds to me as though he was caught between Jenny Vail's demands and somebody else, somebody who got him to make those phone calls to me. To set me up, if that's what you want to call it. Whoever it was, Boots or somebody else, that's who killed McKelvie and Jenny."

He sat down on the piano bench next to Alex. I'd caught her, off and on all through our makeshift meal, studying his strained, weary face. Now she stood up.

"Right then," she said briskly. She backed up inch by inch until she was about a foot from David. "You're McKelvie. You're sitting there on your park bench, you're nervous with that silly little gun in your pocket. You're feeling trapped, scared. I suddenly appear in front of you with a gun aimed at you. What do you do?"

"I don't run, that's for sure," I said. "McKelvie was exactly where Davy left him, except for his position."

"But you *know* me," she said. "If D. is right, you know me quite well. I may be a close friend, or even a member of your family. We don't even know who this man was, you see. D. knows him from the inside, but we need the rest. Facts. If he cared for this killer, even if the killer seemed to have gone a bit bonkers for the moment, he wouldn't pull out a gun and shoot. He'd try to talk them out of it, wouldn't he?"

"And the killer would know that, how McKelvie was likely to react. Just as he—or she—knew Jenny would be likely to take out her gun and shoot."

"Well, Alex is certainly right about one thing," I said with a sigh. "We have to find some facts to hang our suppositions on."

"And may I remind you that nobody has yet answered Sarah's excellent question," insisted Merriman. "If both these people were shot in a perfectly ordinary way, why wouldn't a perfectly ordinary gun with a silencer have sufficed? The fellow's only used the long-range capabilities of the weapon when he fired at Goopus, here, and you may have noticed that on both occasions, he has missed. Since the gun is noted for its pinpoint accuracy, we must either assume that the assassin is blind as a bat, telescopic sight and all, or that he never intended to shoot Winnie in the first place and was only giving a bit of a demonstration. Am I right?"

"Let's hope so," said Lloyd. "But I'm keeping a man on you anyway, with a description of that white Aerostar you spotted at the school this morning."

"And don't forget that splash of neon orange I saw in the trees," I said. "It looked like a hard hat."

Fish shook his head. "Gloves. Hunter's gloves. I saw his hands move as he raised the barrel to aim. Then I spotted you at the front door and—well, you know the rest."

I rubbed the bruise on my elbow. "Indeed I do. So, this scary terrorist gun is just a fancy red herring, intended to send us off looking for phantom arms dealers and fellows who play footsy with the IRA?" I shook my head. "It had to be somebody who knew that kind of a weapon existed in the first place. That's pretty arcane information, you know, not the sort of thing you find in *Reader's Digest*. And the gun still had to be paid for, which brings us back to the same old tune. Twenty thousand bucks is a lot of spondoolix."

The phone in the hall began to ring and David loped off to answer it, while we began to discuss how to divide the job of gathering information.

"I'll start with the files on Cynthia Vail's mugging," I said. "If the dates coincide with McKelvie's magical birth on Eighty-seventh Street, it'll be a beginning. Maybe David could go and talk to Mrs. Glickman again. I mean, I assume he's free to help us, isn't he, Lincoln?" I chuckled. "I'd have given my autographed Mickey Mantle baseball cap to see Colby's face when he found out the kiddo was off the hook!"

Lincoln grinned and cleared his throat. "As a matter of fact, I haven't been able to reach old Rat-Cheese— That is, Captain Colby. Seems he had to be in Washington, D.C. this morning, took the first Trump Shuttle down when he got the word that a certain party used his credit card to buy a ticket on the Metroliner last night."

"So he's still down there, Johnny-on-the-spot for when the D.C. cops collar the perp," said Lloyd.

"Heigh-ho the derry-o, the cheese stands alone. He's probably having his hair done for the photo session even as we speak." Merriman cackled and reached for an oatmeal cookie.

"Wait a minute," I said. "If Rat-Cheese is out of town, who's in command of the Task Force?"

Lincoln nodded, eyes closed in delicious enjoyment of his triumph. "Me," he purred. "And as a matter of fact, I was going to ask David about going back to that brownstone with Sergeant Bryce tomorrow. She—"

"It's for you, Winnie," said David, returning with long strides to his place beside Alex. "It's Hazel Hancock. Sounds upset."

"Oh my hat!" I said. "I forgot all about the Red-Headed League! If I'm not careful, they'll be buying terrorist weapons next, and believe me, *they* won't miss!"

I toddled off to the phone at a fast clip, my mouth still half full of apple, and grabbed the receiver. Not without, I might add, making sure I was out of the line of fire through the glass in the front door.

"Haze," I said, "my sincerest apologies. I meant to call you earlier, but something came up. About that invitation to tea this afternoon, maybe you could pour a little oil on the troubled waters if I've offended Perfidy, Unlimited."

"Hell, Winnie, we've postponed the crapola until after Jenny's funeral. All the officers are holed up at the Hornsby; the management's so worried about the bad publicity they even cut the price of the rooms. Most of us are hanging around. Listen, Winnie—"

I caught a tinge of something in her voice—not sadness or even a case of nerves, exactly. But the old Hazel seemed to be missing, the energy drained. I figured a little shoptalk would perk her up.

"They never got to the Best Novel award," I said. "Never got to the installation of the new president, either. Rita Kovacs should have a walkover now. Are they going to hold the rest of the ceremony?"

"Listen, Winnie, I—"

"Or will there be another vote on the presidency?"

"Winnie, will you cut the goddamn cackle! I called you because Philip wants to see you as soon as you can get into town."

"Philip? Philip Vail wants to see me? What on earth for?"

"Everybody knows you've turned into the Miss Marple of New York State. He probably wants you to help him out of this."

"Hazel, have you been at the booze again? Make sense, can't you! Help him out of what?"

"Sweet Jesus and Mary, Winnie," she said. "Philip's in jail. The damn fool confessed to Jenny's murder an hour ago."

13

I didn't believe it. Philip Vail might've been capable of a lot of things. He had the brains, the self-control, the cool composure to be an excellent crook, perhaps of the Moriarty kind—a manipulator, a master planner of dirty jobs. But to pull off the dirty jobs himself? To blackmail or coerce McKelvie into making those anonymous calls? To hide in the bushes with a gun? Worst of all, to sneak through a hotel kitchen, put a gun to the back of his wife's head, and pull the trigger? Never mind the morality of the thing; I had no idea of Philip's morals. What I did know a bit about was his taste, and aesthetically it would've been beyond him. There was a delicacy about the man, even in the brief scene we'd witnessed between Jenny, Gregory, and himself, a sensibility that bordered on the neurasthenic and set definite limits on his capabilities. He might've planned the murders, he might even have paid for them, but he could never have carried them out alone.

Yet he was, according to Hazel, stubbornly trying to take the whole rap himself. The reason—I had to agree with Merriman—must have something to do with the cataclysmic death of his daughter Cynthia, and before I saw him I wanted to find out everything I could about what had happened on that Manhattan street two years ago.

Which is why, while Krish showed my no-doubt-dozing Mystery Fiction class my favorite video of Basil Rathbone in *The Hound of the Baskervilles* that Friday afternoon, I did them one better and hit the sack for a good four hours myself.

When I woke, it was to Merriman shaking me by the shoulder. " 'Methought I heard a voice cry, "Sleep no more!" ' You can snooze later, Hyde," he said, hauling on my arm. "The seven o'clock news is on, and I don't think you ought to miss it!"

"Go away," I mumbled. "Go to sleep. At least hang from a rafter for an hour or two. But go away and let me alone."

He was excited again, fairly dancing. "Come on, confound you!" he cried, and proceeded to keelhaul me out of bed and across the hall to the guest room where we hide the TV set. My tongue seemed to have grown unaccountably while I slept; it kept pushing my mouth open and hanging out between my teeth like a slice of baloney sliding out of a sandwich. My knees felt like tapioca and I flopped down in the easy chair as Eddie turned up the sound. A honey blonde with carnivorous blue eyes was interviewing my old pal, Rat-Cheese Colby.

"Captain Colby," she said, "the Homicide Task Force under your command has moved with remarkable speed. Does the arrest and confession of Philip Vail mean that both baffling cases are about to be closed? I refer, of course, to the bizarre death of Gilbert McKelvie yesterday morning in Central Park, and that of novelist Imogen Vail at last night's Edgar Awards banquet. Are you satisfied with Vail's confession to both crimes, Captain?"

Colby turned slightly, offering the famous profile to the camera. He wasn't in his dress uniform and medals today, and his idea of plain clothes was a charcoal suit of supple fabric and impeccable cut, a perfectly knotted silk tie of gleaming gray brocade, and a pale cream-colored silk shirt.

"He'll look good on the back of a bus," I said. "The perfect outfit for a campaign poster. There smirks a candidate for mayor if ever I saw one."

"Shhhh," hissed Eddie.

Colby flashed his pearly whites at the blonde barracuda. "Actually, Tanya," he said, "we're still checking and double-checking. I've been coordinating the investigation most of the day from Washington, but now that I'm back, I'd estimate we'll have both cases wrapped up within twenty-four hours." He faced the camera and tilted his chin back a bit, determination in every fibre. "I intend to make the sidewalks of New York safe," he said, just the slightest hint of tremolo in his gutsy delivery. "Safe for us and for our children. Safe for—for democracy."

A flicker of smothered amusement passed over Tanya's carefully painted features. "Could you tell us a little about Mr. Vail's confession, Captain?" she said. "Did he give a reason for his alleged commission of the two murders?"

Rat-Cheese hesitated, not sure his public image was worth prejudicing a jury if he gave the press a bit too much too soon. He hedged, fiddling with his manicure, then made up his mind. The public image won. "It seems to have been," he said, "a marital dispute of some sort. Contested divorce, I believe. Mrs. Vail seems to have been—involved—with McKelvie. She continued to refuse her husband a divorce although they'd been separated for some time. A stressful situation that simply exploded, Tanya, would be my estimate."

"Eyewash!" I roared. "Jenny Vail slipping over to Eighty-seventh and Amsterdam to warm the sheets with McKelvie while she keeps old Philip dangling on the hook? You can listen to that gibbering idiot if you want to, Merriman, but I'm going back to bed and get some—"

"Be still!" he commanded. "Look."

It was Philip Vail. They had taken his tie and his shirt collar was open, the cords of the long neck tensed. His gold eyeglasses were missing and the ice blue eyes, fixed like a blind man's, had dark smudges under them. A lock of soft, fine gray hair, usually combed carefully back from his face, fell across his forehead like a shadow. The long, graceful hands were cuffed in front of him and a cop walked on either side, steering him helplessly down an anonymous corridor painted an insipid, narcotic green. He walked sightlessly, looking at nothing.

At the door to an interrogation room, Tanya, microphone in hand, remote camera balanced behind her on the shoulder of a hirsute young flunky, was waiting. "Mr. Vail," she said, "is it true that you've confessed to the murders of Imogen Vail and Gilbert McKelvie? Do you have any comment to make, Mr. Vail?"

The cuffed hands came up in the timeless gesture of prisoners, a shield to preserve such fragments of personhood as may remain beneath the shameless stare of public justice. I expected Philip to slip away, then, through the door into the small, bare interrogation room, his hands still shielding his face. But he did not. He stood for only a brief moment, the trapped hands brushing his eyes. Then he lowered them, and for the first time the pale gaze seemed to come into focus. He refused the inhuman eye of the camera shoved at him by the flunky and looked instead at Tanya. For an instant, so fleeting that no one in the cutting room had noticed and excised it, the roles were reversed by Philip Vail's assessing eye. Tanya, the prepackaged display merchandise through which his own complex reality was absurdly destined to be funneled, was suddenly on trial herself, and the tall, weedy, aging figure with the manacled wrists was her implacable judge. I could almost hear his soft, discreet voice pronouncing sentence. Fool, it said, and not unkindly. You are a fool, my dear.

"I have nothing to say," he told her, an unsteady smile playing round his mobile mouth. "Thank you." And he walked into the interrogation room and was gone.

Eddie switched the set off. "Hell," he said.

We were both silent for a moment, then. I could hear Sarah downstairs at her piano, pounding away at the crashing chords of something too passionate to be anything but one of those Russians I always confuse with each other—Prokofiev, Rachmaninoff. She only resorted to them when she needed something to pound, and I felt like pounding something just then myself. Merriman put it into words for both of us.

"I *like* the man, Winnie," he said. "I refuse to believe he murdered those two. Behind those eyes is a subtle mind, and something old. Not aged, I don't mean. Something of the old world, before plastic and television and artificial bloody intelligence. Did you see the look he bestowed upon that archtwit Tanya?"

"I did." I hoisted myself out of the chair. "But the fact that he doesn't cotton to Barbie dolls doesn't mean he couldn't commit murder. Obviously he's given Colby and the press a motive they can understand. A phony love triangle, a little smarmy sex."

"I agree entirely. Perfect for the gutter press, they'll try him on the front pages."

"The whole story's right out of one of those books of Jenny's," I agreed. "Or at least the cover copy. Philip's made it up."

"He seems to *want* to be convicted. Or at least arraigned. It only takes one look into those transparent eyes to know that if he'd really done it, the motive would've been something much more complex than a love triangle." Merriman joined me and we made our way downstairs. "But why," he asked, "would Philip Vail make an entirely false confession? He's the sort of man who abhors fuss, you could see that with the beastly kid last night."

"He must've had a damn good reason," I agreed, shrugging into my overcoat in the downstairs hall. "He may be shielding somebody. He may be playing for time. If he's read enough Agatha Christie and he really did do it, he may even want to be tried and acquitted so he can never be tried again. Remember *The Mysterious Affair at Styles?*" I pulled on my cap and headed for the door.

The crashing Russian chords from the living room came to a sudden halt. "Where are you going, Win?" called Sarah.

"Library." I stuck my head through the open double doors. "Want to do a bit of digging into the death of Cynthia Vail."

"But what about the sniper? He might still be out there, waiting for you. Can't you get the files from Lieutenant Lincoln? Can't you just stay here and—"

"Hide out?"

She scowled at the piano music. "I suppose you *could* ride in the police car."

"I could."

"That *ought* to be safe enough."

"Ought to be."

Her hands were poised over the keyboard. "Well, go on then,

why don't you? But I refuse to worry about you, and if you're not home by eleven I shall lock the doors and push furniture in front of them and you'll have to *sleep* in that damn police car." She played a thunderous chord and the piano trembled. "I love you," she said, tossing her long braid over her shoulder. "I thought I'd remind you, in case you're dead by the time you get back. But don't let it go to your head."

It was still light outside but getting chilly, and the mist of the previous day was drawing in again. The patrol car still hovered halfway down our drive, though young Wade had been exchanged for a mournful specimen called Carlo. Lincoln had taken off, of course, as soon as he heard about Vail's confession, and Alex and David had hitched a ride back to town with Stockfish—she to relieve the long-suffering Mrs. Jack, and the two young men to coordinate their private watch on Vangie Glickman. I saw no cars—nor any white vans, either—lurking in the street as I closed the front door behind me.

Merriman was lurking, though, lying in wait for me on the terrace, a striped muffler wound around his throat against the damp. Snipers, it seemed, held no terrors for him. I toddled around to the horse's-head hitching post where I keep my old bike tethered, and Eddie followed.

"I just remembered something, Winnie," he said. "Those dates we were talking about earlier—where were you two years ago, and all that? It's two years since you took over that talk show of John's, isn't it? I suppose it was dear Tanya, bless her shallow little heart, who made me think of it, with that ridiculous interviewing style of hers."

I unlocked the bike and wheeled it onto the drive. "You may have something there," I admitted. "When Cliff called, he said Jenny had asked him for my number at WNYT, and the name of my producer. I'd better give Myra Fish a ring when I get to town tomorrow, find out if Jenny ever got hold of her." I sighed. "This is the most frustrating business we've gotten into yet, old friend. A dozen suspects, none of whom we seem to be able to eliminate. Everybody looks guilty, including Davy and me. And as if we didn't have enough confusion, Philip Vail muddies the waters even more with this fake confession."

"Then we'll just have to unmuddy them," he said. "We cannot sit idly by and let a man like Philip Vail destroy himself, no matter what his reasons. I'm absolutely sure he didn't murder anybody, and we'll just have to prove it."

"We?" I said. "You're still in on this, are you?"

"Of course I'm in on it, you addlepated old behemoth, why wouldn't I be? If you are intimating that I'm too advanced in years to employ my little gray cells—"

"Don't have kittens, Merriman, for pity's sake! I just thought you might have—other plans."

"Plans? What plans?"

"Oh, bit of travel. Little light shopping. In London, say, or—"

He cocked his head on one side and looked at me as though he'd just spotted antlers sprouting between my ears. "Archimedes!" he cried.

"Cowabunga!" I countered, and heaved myself onto my bike.

"No, don't you see, Hyde," he said. "This case. There's something missing. Not just the facts about any individual, I don't mean. It's the X factor. The lever that will shift the whole thing into place! All this confounded muddle of disinformation, that elephantine list of suspects—something we aren't yet able to isolate must tie them all together. They have something in common, blast them, that points to the real murderer. If we can only find it . . ."

"Okay, Archimedes," I said. "But if you haven't solved it by the time I get back from the library, I may have a few pedestrian facts to add. And for the love of Pete, Merriman, get some sleep."

I put my feet on the pedals and rolled a ways down the drive. From the squad car, Carlo's woebegone face, like a middle-aged Italian basset hound, peered out at me.

"Need a lift, Dr. Sherman?" he intoned. "I'm not supposed to let you go anywhere on your own. Orders."

"Yes, Winnie," Merriman chimed in. "Do behave yourself. You have quite enough holes in your head already."

I rolled up even with the squad car. "Carlo," I said, "I'm riding my bike over to the campus. If that Johnny with the fancy squirrel gun wants to take another pop at me, so be it. I need exercise and I need to think, and some of my best work has been done on this bike. Follow me if you have to, but I'd rather you stayed here and kept an eye on things. I've got a notion that crawling into a hole and pulling it in after me is exactly what that buzzard wants me to do, and I'm damned if I'm going to cooperate."

As I labored down the long drive, I looked over my shoulder and saw Carlo talking into his radio mike. By the time I turned onto the curving road that winds along above the Hudson toward the campus, I could hear an engine behind me. I looked around. Sure enough. Carlo was creeping along at the snail's pace of my bike, as I pedaled meditatively up and down the hills. We met another squad car—no doubt the relief he had radioed for—headed for the house, but aside from that the drive was quiet enough.

In time, though, we collected quite a nice number of cars, all too nervous to pass a cop car on a hilly curve, and by the time we reached the campus gates I was heading a bumper-to-bumper parade almost three blocks long. Kids on skateboards hooted and waved, tomcats on early evening patrols fuzzed up and made for the nearest trees, and the surly old bulldog on Walnut Street who always goes for my ankles was so taken aback by my entourage he completely forgot to bark. I rode at the head of my troops like Julius Caesar entering Gaul, and any snipers in the neighborhood must've been laughing too hard to take decent aim, telescopic sights or not.

It was almost eight o'clock, the clear darkness of early spring just beginning to win its battle with Daylight Savings Time, as I found myself a quiet table in the reference section of Clinton College Library and began to do what I was trained for, when computerized cross-referencing and microfiche were just a twinkle in their father's eye. There is still one thing the human brain—even an elderly one like mine that's only had four hours of sleep—can do that the Information Revolution has so far found no way to duplicate. It can do more than ferret out facts; it can imagine them.

From the microfilmed issues of the *Times* I squinted at, the facts

—though in some ways revealing—seemed clear enough. On a Tuesday morning, the ninth day of April, Cynthia Vail Canfield, thirty-nine, had been out jogging, following her regular early morning path through Central Park, across North Meadow to exit at Ninety-sixth Street, then uptown along Central Park West to 110th Street and on to Broadway, where she met her son Gregory, a freshman at Columbia, for breakfast three or four mornings a week. Ms. Canfield was divorced, a single working mother, a free-lance journalist with credits from half a dozen of the slick news weeklies.

The attack on her had been sudden and unusual, both in its ferocity and its openness. It had happened in broad daylight—early, but not early enough to avoid witnesses. Eight people had seen the beating, delivered by a shabbily dressed man—some said black, some said white, some said Hispanic, some said woman—wielding an iron pipe. Eight people had watched him grab Cynthia, watched her drag herself toward the Russian Orthodox Cathedral on the corner of Ninety-seventh Street, watched the length of lead pipe crash down on her again and again. Eight people had crouched in doorways, between parked cars, behind garbage cans, watching the mugger run away into the park and disappear, watching the woman's battered body and hoping it would somehow revive, be whole again and jog on down the street, hoping the tiny vital bit of the nature of things that had lurched out of control would be restored and life go on as before. Eight people, their names withheld, established a memorial to be placed by concerned citizens in the Shakespeare Garden of Central Park, which Cynthia had loved.

It was all they could have done. They were ordinary people, and afraid, unwilling to grapple with a stranger's death. If they had defended her, they might themselves have died, and nobody blamed them for surviving. Had the mugger been wearing a Nazi uniform or driving a Russian tank, it might've been different. Courage came easier against such ideological terrors. Against random maniacs, the best defense was a healthy and universal fear.

According to my research, no arrest in the mugging-murder of Cynthia Vail Canfield had ever been made. Police spokesmen classified it as "casual crime," random, spur-of-the-moment, and almost impossible to punish or prevent. In a copy of *Today* magazine from the week of Cynthia's death, I found a photograph of her, a striking slender woman with her mother's dark hair and Philip's transparent blue eyes. She did not smile at the camera, but fixed it with a sober, suspicious stare, her head tilted back defiantly, her slim throat arched. In the hollow of her neck lay the same diamond and amethyst pendant Jenny had been wearing when she died.

I piled up the back issues of magazines and began to reroll the microfilm in the reader, my imagination racing. The Orthodox Cathedral, the Shakespeare Garden, the ritual wearing of amethysts. Whoever McKelvie was, he must've been involved in Cynthia's death somehow. Was he the divorced husband, Canfield, of whom no mention was made in any of the news stories? Was he one of the eight witnesses to the beating? Had Jenny, perhaps, been doing exactly what I was doing now, had she found some scrap of information that made her believe her daughter's death was anything but a casual crime?

There were only two people I could think of who might be able to tell me—Philip Vail and his grandson Gregory, but before I tried talking to either of them, I needed a real night's sleep. I loaded up the research materials and toddled between the bookstacks in the direction of the checkout desk when I heard a stage whisper behind me.

"Over here!" a voice said. "Over here, please!"

Beginning to feel like Saul on the road to Damascus, I pushed aside a two-volume set of *Sartor Resartus* to find Krish. He was standing on tiptoe, his black-rimmed glasses sliding down his nose. At a table behind him, one of those popular tables the students usually commandeer for surreptitious games of slap-and-tickle because they're hidden like forest glades among the towering stacks of fusty volumes, sat none other than Miss Hannah Comfort, a manila file folder clutched against her bony bosom.

"Please join us," whispered Krish. "You will find it of interest, I promise."

I groaned inwardly and succumbed; I owed the kiddo for helping me out that morning, and I knew how serious he was about his anti-Sheffield crusade. Just as I got to the table, I thought I heard a sound from somewhere in the stacks, a stifled sneeze, maybe, or a sniffle. Terrible weather, though, and lots of runny noses on campus, so I thought no more of it.

"All right, Hannah. What's the poop?" I said.

She glanced over her shoulder. "I'm not sure I ought to tell you."

Krish offered a testimonial. "Dr. Sherman? I assure you, the soul of discretion! No trouble will arise. Please, repeat the information."

"Well," she said, lowering her voice even further. "It's the Floating Fund. I've checked all the books. It was supposed to have been placed in a certificate of deposit at the Equity National nine months ago. It ought to come due in three days, but it's not there! I've gone through every record a dozen times, I've had the bank do a search, and there's simply no sign of that money anywhere."

"Exactly how much money are we talking about, Hannah?" I asked. "I mean, it doesn't run into the millions or anything, surely? Sheffield hasn't cut *that* much out of my salary!"

Hannah checked a column of figures in her folder. "Nine hundred sixty-seven dollars and thirty-five cents. Without adding the interest." She shook her head and the lavender curls quivered. "I simply can't find it, Dr. Sherman. It's disappeared."

"I beg your pardon," said Krish. There was a gleam in his big brown eyes I didn't quite like. He was beginning to have a lean and hungry look. "I beg your pardon. This nine hundred sixty-seven dollars and thirty-five cents has not disappeared. It has been stolen! Embezzlement of faculty funds. Misappropriation. And the culprit? This fellow Sheffield!"

"Krish," I said, "I know you're hot on the trail, but don't get carried away. Thomas may have the gray matter of an underdeveloped armadillo and the ego of a Chinese emperor, but do you really think he's a common thief?"

" 'Choo!'"

My sneezy friend was playing a return engagement behind the bookstacks. I craned my neck, but all I saw was a brownish blur as footsteps retreated to the far end of the aisle.

"Anyway," I went on. "The fact that the money's missing doesn't mean Sheffield's got it. He hasn't got a dime that isn't Diana's, you know, and Lady Di isn't exactly liberal with the purse strings. He hasn't been buying any yachts, has he, hasn't been tooling around town in a new Ferrari?"

"Campaign funds," said Krish.

Hannah nodded. "He's right."

"He has invited every member of Arts and Letters to dinner at the Hudson Oaks Country Club."

"Nonsense! He hasn't invited me," I objected. Krish just smiled and went on.

"Twenty-five dinners at forty dollars per dinner, almost a thousand dollars! It is known that Mrs. Sheffield does not approve of this campaigning for the Professor of the Year Award. Her father does not approve. She would never have provided the money for these dinners."

I heard another sneeze from the center aisle and looked around just in time to catch a glimpse of Thomas Van Doren Sheffield's brown-checked shoulders skulking out of sight.

"The money *is* missing," said Hannah. "And he *is* very determined to win that award. 'No matter what it costs,' he told me." She adjusted the harlequin glasses on her beak. " 'No matter what it costs.' "

"Ergo, Sheffield padded his coffers with the Floating Fund?"

Krishnan beamed. "You know my methods, Watson. Apply them!"

I frowned. For all Sheffield's pomposity, I couldn't let Krish's newfound passion for crime-solving railroad him. I'd have to get to the bottom of it somehow, before the Faculty Awards dinner on commencement eve. With a sigh that came from my shoe soles, I trudged towards the parking lot where Carlo, the Knight of the Doleful Countenance, was still waiting beside my bike. Two days ago, I thought gloomily, I'd have called you a liar if you dared to suggest it, but the last thing on earth I wanted at the moment was another crime to solve.

14

It was night again, and Vangie was afraid.

There was a brand-new iron grille across the bathroom window and a heavy new safety bar wedged against the front door, but fear paid no attention. It slipped between the crumbling bricks with the pulsing roar of a boombox out on the sidewalk and the triumphant shouts of questing boys, it breathed through the heat pipes with the pilot-light nausea of some unknown, unburnt gas.

It was the time change that got you. In winter, dark was dark. In summer, light was light. But in the spring, when the hotshots began to play around with time, a gigantic jet lag set in. So some knothead could get in an extra daylight round of golf on Long Island, the entire solar system had to get rearranged; suddenly there was an extra hour of waking life, a false hour in which shadows refused to lengthen and the shapes of furniture turned sinister and strange. It was a nervous reaction of the spheres, Elva Ziegler told her, the universe registering an official protest against this puny fiddling with its timeclock in favor of street fairs and sidewalk sales. In the false twilight of that purloined hour, the wild gangs of kids prowled the half-dark like excited cats, hunting, playing with death like a mouse. Muggers used the gift of unreal light to mark their victims, set up traps they could spring when true night at last arrived. Danger grew with the extra hour, and fear arrived with the dark.

As she did every night when too little light remained to read without a lamp burning, Vangie made her rounds. Though the doors and windows had not been opened all day, she went from one to the other, Walt's tire iron in her right hand, leaning on her splay-footed steel cane with her left. She shook the door and checked the three deadbolt locks and the chain, rattled the iron wedge to be certain it was tightly set. Then she got an old spaghetti pot, filled it with water and put it beside the door, just in case the crackheads came back again with their burning spills of paper.

She checked the bedroom, peered under the bed and opened the closet, rattled the iron grille on the window; when she had tried the bathroom window and looked behind the shower curtain, she returned to the kitchen. She switched on the countertop radio, hoping to hear the news. There was a big TV set in one corner of the living room, but it didn't work; she would've thrown it out except that Walt, who bought it, had set great store by the cabinet work, the double doors that closed to hide the screen. On the radio, the news was better anyway, and you didn't have to look at dancing hamburgers and little blue men waterskiing in the toilet bowl.

Vangie fiddled with the radio dial, trying to find the local news. All day she had kept the phone beside her as she read, mended, made honey-and-lemon cough syrup for Freddy Adler's bronchitis. But he hadn't called again, her Mr. Photographs. The News at Noon had said nothing, except about the murder of that Jenny Vail, the bitch, the Queen of Spades. McKelvie had faded into the background in these stories now, he was just wallpaper; even death, obviously, had its pecking order. The two crimes were supposed to be connected, the same killer for both.

The death of the Queen of Spades had not, somehow, come as a surprise to Vangie. For whatever reason—her dislike of the woman's cool arrogance, her mild jealousy of Jenny's intimacy with McKelvie —the old lady found herself able to deal calmly with this brutal murder so far removed from her life. It was like a story in one of the novels on her shelves, a case for Poirot and Captain Hastings or Albert Campion and Mr. Lugg—the few coveted awards that could make and break careers, all those writers (most hopeful, many ambitious, some ruthless, one murderous) and the few glittering celebrities, like the Queen of Spades, balancing on the pinnacles of their careers. She got her copy of *The Black Palace,* Jenny Vail's last novel, down from the shelf again and pored over it, hunting for clues. Something had prepared her for the woman's death; maybe it was in the book, and whatever it was, maybe it would clear Mr. Photographs—and clear Vangie, herself, as well.

Because, she thought, the shadows of her worn old furniture looming huge across the kitchen floor. Because what if he *did* kill her, and Mr. Mac, too? What if he came here and I told him who she was and he went out my bathroom window and hunted her down and shot her dead? Mr. Photographs, the murderer.

Her breath left her for an instant with the thought and the possibility of mortal guilt assailed her in the voice of Walt: *"To play into the hands of knaves and swindlers is one thing, my dear, a crime against the pocketbook. To be the dupe of brutes and barbarians—a sin against life. You might as well dance a waltz with Adolf or play checkers with Uncle Joe Stalin."*

Vangie shook herself free and put her doubts on hold. The Nightly News was coming on.

"The Metropolitan Homicide Task Force announced late this afternoon that publisher Philip G. Vail, sixty-three, estranged husband of millionaire mystery novelist Imogen Montague Vail, slain at last night's Mystery Writers of America dinner, today confessed to the killing of his wife and to that of Gilbert McKelvie, whose body was found yesterday morning in Central Park. Captain Gifford Colby, coordinator of—"

Philip Vail, sixty-three? Confessed? Vangie didn't know a lot about this David Photographs, but the handsome guy—you could bank on it—was not sixty-three. Someone else had confessed to the murders, and David was okay! Free, at least, no cops breathing down his sweet neck. Relief warmed Vangie and the shadows retreated. She twirled the dial until there was music, some of the classic stuff Mr. Mac had liked. Then she remembered that in her excitement she had forgotten to check the kitchen windows.

They were high, hard to reach above the sink. She pulled a metal step stool over and labored up one step, then another, balancing with her cane on the counter top. She rattled the grille across one window and was about to check the second, when she saw the boots.

They were exactly as she had remembered them. A dark purplish brown, darker at the ends of the pointed toes, where the color graded into off-black. The shine was permanent and obsessive, maintained with care for many years. They were worn soft, molded to the shape of the small feet. *If we're talking men,* thought Vangie, *a size six, maybe, and narrow, but with a high instep, the hardest kind of foot to fit.* No wonder the guy had been wearing those boots since the Beatles broke up. With such a foot, you paid plenty for shoes; as in the clothing racket, people of odd configurations were considered fair game, you had them over a barrel. A pair of good leather boots—Chelsea boots, they'd called them—would've cost, tops, fifty bucks in the Sixties. Now you'd pay two hundred, maybe more, for a special fit.

Boots hesitated on the sidewalk near the front door, and the kids lounging by the garbage cans turned up the boombox, issuing a challenge. Was Boots afraid, would he walk by them stone cool, would he take the risk, tell them to bug off? The feet turned, and Vangie thought they had faked him out, but in another second he stopped. As before, he was wearing the tight, faded blue jeans, not the fancy acid-wash crap but genuine old jeans, faded from washing and wearing a long time. The legs were slim and straight, the steps primed with energy or anger, as he turned again and headed for the doorway.

Vangie took another step up on the stool until her feet were on the linoleum-covered countertop; she craned her neck, trying to see as much as she could of Boots before he left her line of sight. But all she saw was a figure, slight, athletic, purposeful, in a light tan windbreaker and a tan golfing cap, the bill pulled down over his face.

It was getting too dark to see any more, and Boots had turned off the sidewalk now, headed for the entry door. He had never come inside when McKelvie was alive, but now that his death had been publicized all over the city, Boots wanted in.

Vangie lowered herself carefully to sit on the countertop, legs hanging stiff, then climbed gingerly down. The outer door was locked, as usual; Mr. Boots would be standing in the stinking entry now, deciding which tenant to ring, just like David Photographs had done. Elva, Freddy, or herself—they were the last holdouts; he didn't have much choice.

She positioned herself at her door, tire iron in hand, waiting for the ring on her buzzer.

There was none. The key turned in the front door lock and the slight man in the tan windbreaker came inside, his boots clunk-clunking in the hall. Vangie opened her door a crack. Whatever he wanted, it must be upstairs in Mr. Mac's apartment, still sealed by the police tapes. Obviously he had the keys. She might be able to get a look at his face when he turned to go up the stairs.

Angling her body and pushing her cheek against the door frame, she peered through the slightly open door. The booted footsteps paused, checking the mailboxes in the hall. Then they made the turn and the man she had called Boots came into full view. Vangie could see only his profile—a broad, straight nose and high cheekbones, reddish-brown hair straggling out of the golfing cap, wide-set eyes whose color she couldn't see, and an ear with a small gold stud in it.

It was only a glimpse. A minute later Boots had reached McKelvie's floor, and she could hear his keys jingle. She closed her own door soundlessly, shot the three locks and set the chain, then stood listening, the unnatural evening closing around her. Upstairs his feet were moving, things were being tossed around.

Vangie's mind was spinning. A man had confessed to the murder, this man Vail. Her friend Mr. Photographs was cleared, and now this guy Boots was up there searching the dead man's room. It didn't make sense. But whoever he was, he had no right up there, messing around with things, pawing through the debris of a ruined life. What should she do?

Vangie scrounged in the cupboard drawer where she kept important papers, then reached for the telephone to call Peggy Bryce.

* * *

"What is it, man?" Tyrone DeCordova was dancing, as usual, loose limbs jittering, shoulders waggling. Julian Stockfish grinned at David and slapped his best stakeout man on the back.

"Anything shakin', Ty?" he said.

"I am due, man, for a large and strengthening repast. Hey, Fish, man, you bring my Twinkie?"

Julian handed him the cellophane-wrapped survival rations, and Tyrone zipped off the wrapper with practiced ease. In another second the gooey stuff had vanished.

"There isn't a light in her apartment," said David. "She never goes out of the building. There ought to be a light."

On the third floor, Elva Ziegler's place showed a flickering light, and the second-floor flat—McKelvie's—was in darkness.

Tyrone talked through the creme-whipped filling. "Dude went in 'bout ten ticks back, had keys. Walk right in, no fuss, no muss."

Now it was David who had the jitters. "But, dammit, the killer has McKelvie's keys, Fish! That's exactly—"

"Don't like go into overload, my friend." Tyrone began licking his fingers fastidiously, one after the other. "There's another guy resident in this palatial dwelling, right? One Frederick Adler?"

"Maybe it was him." Vangie hadn't described Freddy, so there was no way of telling. "But I don't like it. I'm going in there," said David.

"Hold it, Claudio." Stockfish grabbed his arm. "Ty, what did the dude look like? Was he carrying?"

"Could be. Funny little dude, blue jeans, pair of them cowboy boots—"

"Holy shit," murmured Julian Stockfish, and took off running to catch up with David, who was already in the entryway pounding his fist relentlessly on Vangie's buzzer.

Peggy Bryce had put in an eighteen-hour day. Her arches felt like she'd been tortured by the Inquisition and the taco she'd had nearly eight hours ago had long since disappeared, leaving only heartburn behind. Still, she considered waiting around for Lincoln, asking him out for dinner and a drink. The guy needed R and R.

Rat-Cheese was on Lincoln's case tonight, they'd been going at it in the captain's office for more than an hour. It was what she hated most about being a cop—the power games. Guys like Colby spent years stroking, reading the smoke signals from the higher-ups, sucking up to anybody with rank, and when they got it themselves, they were ruthless; Colby had canceled all old debts, picked out the office slimebag and kept him oiled for anything he could use against his staff, any kind of personal weakness that would bring pressure. Rat-Cheese had been worried about A.J. Lincoln from the start; he wanted him out, off the Task Force. Lincoln was smart, and he had the guts to let the brass—Colby's own bosses—see it. Not good politics, but he didn't care about that, just good police work. And he wasn't buying this confession of Vail's. He was ordering lab work and handwriting analysis, pushing for the Hair and Fiber report. Colby wanted the thing over. He had his confession, a nice arrest, an arraignment so he could ring up a sale at the dinner for party hopefuls next Saturday night. Councilman, maybe even mayor— politics was Colby's dream, and he wasn't going to let this double murder case queer it for him. He wanted a quick arrest, and Lincoln was standing in his way, threatening to make him look like a monkey.

But Lincoln's mind was on that damn divorce, too, and Colby knew it. He was making noises about throwing A.J. off the case.

Peggy jumped, jarred out of her thoughts as the phone on her desk began to ring. "Homicide Task Force, Sergeant Bryce," she said wearily.

"It's me," whispered Vangie. "Mrs. Glickman."

"Oh honey." Peggy sighed. Another flake of her humanity that had gotten away when she wasn't looking. She had meant to call the old girl and tell her not to worry, that her mystery man had been cleared by the attack on Linc's friend, that old snooper up in Ainsley this morning. "Vangie, honey, there's nothing to worry—"

"He's upstairs." The old woman's voice was thick with fear. "He had the keys!"

"Who is, honey?" Peggy Bryce sighed. "Who's upstairs?"

"Boots. He used to meet McKelvie, from Christmas to New Year's. Then he didn't come. Now he's upstairs in Mr. Mac's place, throwing things around!"

That meant he had broken the police seal and tampered with possible evidence, and no friend of Lincoln's would do a thing like that.

"Stay where you are, Vangie," ordered Peggy Bryce. She grabbed her purse and looked around the office. Nobody for backup. She could radio for a squad car to meet her; Linc had one on hourly patrol. "Stay right where you are and keep your door locked!"

"The buzzer! They keep pushing my door buzzer. What shall I dooooo?" The voice was a rising wail.

"For God's sake, honey, don't open that door!" commanded Peggy. "Don't let in the Angel Gabriel till I get there!"

"She's not answering!" David turned to Stockfish. "We've got to get in there. Can't you shoot the lock or something?"

"You been watchin' too many old movies, man." Tyrone was behind them, behind him three of the kids who'd been jiving to the boombox out by the entry. They squeezed into the tiny cubbyhole.

"Shoot the lock, man!" A tall white blond with a snake tattooed on his cheek shook with silent laughter. "Call the posse and like round up the strays."

His two friends stared with glazed, vacant eyes and dug each other in the ribs. "Posse," they repeated. "Posse, man."

Stockfish bent to examine the lock. "It's been busted before. Ty?"

Tyrone dug into the pockets of his baggy pants and came up with a tiny, hooked steel rod. He was about to insert it into the lock when Whitey tapped him on the shoulder.

"Allow me," he said. Elbowing David, Fish, and Tyrone out of the way, he grabbed the door handle, twisted it hard to the right and held it while he landed a hefty kick on the bottom panel. The door shivered. Whitey turned the handle again and opened it wide. "Your personal like security system," he said. He stepped across the door and blocked it. "Fifty bucks, man."

The two hollow-eyed kids were suddenly alert. For fifty bucks, you could get a foil of crack; when you split it, you were in business for yourself.

"Tyrone?" Stockfish flattened himself against one wall of the tiny vestibule, opposite David, who was smashed against the other by the two crackheads.

Tyrone nodded. Then suddenly he bent his head and crouched, spun on his heel like a figure skater on a single blade, and sprang. Whitey went down like a ton of bricks and David pushed past him, Stockfish close behind.

Vangie's door was still closed tight and no light showed underneath it. David pounded on it with both fists.

"Are you in there, Vangie? Are you all right?" He listened, but there was too much noise from the dancing lessons Tyrone was giving the crackheads out by the front door. "Vangie, it's me, it's David. You don't have to open the door, just tell me if you're all right!" Still she didn't answer.

"We better break it down," said Fish.

"Wait. Vangie. 'No man is an island, entire of itself. Every man is a piece of the continent, a part of the main.' "

At last there came the sound of the three deadbolts shooting free and the door creaked open. The pink glasses gleamed in the grubby light from the hall.

"I'm okay," she whispered. "Upstairs! It's Boots!"

Stockfish was already halfway up the steps. David reached through the chained opening to put a hand on Vangie's arm. "Stay inside," he told her. "Lock the door and stay put."

The tussling in the entryway had moved out to the street and in the distance David could hear a siren as he followed Julian Stockfish upstairs. The door of McKelvie's apartment stood open. Fish went in first, got his back against a wall, then beckoned David in. They checked out the closets, the bathroom, even the broom cupboard in the kitchenette, David with a heavy lamp in his hand, Fish with his usual weapon, a dog chain.

"Fire escape?" said David, experienced in such matters.

They peered out the window and down into the tiny crawlspace, but there was no sign of anyone. They looked at one another, eyebrows raised.

"There's only one room," said Stockfish. "Wouldn't take long to toss."

He was right. Aside from the bathroom and one sizable closet, the flat was one long, narrow room, a kitchenette near the entry door. In the rest of the room, there was almost no furniture. Bookshelves had been built onto the walls by some former tenant; they contained many volumes, but none of them had been shelved. They were piled neatly, as though by some unknown filing system, and the man Vangie called Boots had not bothered to disturb them. The records beside the portable stereo, too, seemed untouched. Across one end of the room, under the window that overlooked the street, lay a mattress—no bed frame, just a bare mattress with one pillow and a few old, threadbare blankets. The blankets had been pulled away and the mattress slit, the pillow cut open. Tufts of fiber filling littered the bare tile floor, blowing like tumbleweeds in the draft from the open hall door. On one wall there was a small desk and the drawers had been pulled out and dumped on the floor—a writing tablet, some pens and pencils, Scotch tape, paper clips.

"You think he got out of the building?" asked David.

"Past old Tyrone?" Stockfish shook his head, grinning. "Not a prayer. What's upstairs?"

"One tenant, middle-aged woman, astrology nut. One empty apartment."

Fish nodded, and slipped quietly out the door, David beside him.

* * *

Downstairs, Vangie waited, listening, the tire iron in her hand. She could hear the two pairs of feet in McKelvie's room upstairs, but no one—not even Mr. Boots—had come down yet. Outside, the squad car Peggy Bryce had called was nosed in at the curb, two husky cops shaking down the crackheads and the hapless Tyrone. Vangie could see their feet shuffling, jittering, the feet of the cops braced and steady. In the dark of her apartment, the revolving red lights of the squad car threw eerie, extraterrestrial patterns on the walls, made the old furniture look huge and cold and hard as monuments.

Up there was Mr. Boots, maybe a creep who had wiped out a couple of lives, now trotting around like he owned the joint. Freddy Adler was at work tonight, bronchitis and all, but upstairs was Elva Ziegler, turning over her Tarot cards, reading the stars, not suspecting death was out in the stairwell hanging around.

"Baloney," muttered Vangie to herself. Feeling her way along the walls, she found the light switch and turned it on. Suddenly the place belonged to her again. Leaning on her cane, she labored into her bedroom, turned on another light, and began to pull open dresser drawers, looking for something. In a place this small, how do you lose things? *"A system, my dear,"* Walt would've said. *"A system for everything."*

It was quiet upstairs, she didn't like the sound of it. Maybe Boots had been waiting for David and his friend, maybe they were laid out up there, getting cold. Still no booted footsteps had come down the stairs. Sometime the guy would have to come down, and she would be ready.

In the bottom drawer of her dresser, Vangie found her Polaroid. The film had been in it for a while, but the flash was okay and it was fast. She couldn't stop Boots with a flying tackle when he made his getaway, but she could take a photograph.

With her tire iron at the ready and a taste like burnt flesh in her mouth, Vangie pulled a chair to the doorway, opened the bolts and undid the chain. She sat down to wait.

* * *

Only two doors opened off the third-floor landing. From beyond one of them, the two friends could hear a soft voice, an incantation: "When Mars rules Scorpio and the moon is in Libra, Aquarius and Saturn indicate relocation to Florida and mutual attraction with a traveler in Gemini near your Sun. . . ."

David beckoned Stockfish to the opposite door. Julian approached it on tiptoe, dog chain in hand, swinging slightly; he bent to examine the lock, then gave David the nod. Davy had just got his hand on the knob when the door flew back, catching him head on and sending him flying, rebounding with a crash against Elva Ziegler's door. He lay stunned, only half conscious, as a lithe figure in jeans and windbreaker tore past, headed for the stairs. Of the face he saw nothing, but on the small hands were neon orange hunter's gloves.

Julian swung the dog chain; the air whirred and hummed as it inscribed great circles above his head. He let it go and it must've struck Boots across the backs of his legs. There was a high, strange cry and the sound of his compact body falling a few steps, down to the second-floor landing. Julian was after him, down the stairs in less than a second, but Boots was waiting. The chain caught Stockfish full in the face and he fell, crashing through the stair rail and landing in the first-floor hall, his leg bent crazily under him.

Vangie, still at her station, Polaroid in hand, heard the booted feet, unimpeded, come clattering down the stairs. She peered out through the crack of her open door, waiting, sighting the viewfinder at the bottom of the steps. From upstairs she heard Elva's angry voice and David's groggy one. Her finger hovered over the shutter button.

Clunk, clunk, clunk-clunk. Boots was coming faster now. There was a turn in the steps after the landing, six steps, then turn, then four more to the bottom. She had counted them often enough when she dragged herself up each night to Mr. Mac's place with a photograph to shove under his door.

Three steps to the turn. Two. One. TURN. Now four, three. Two. One.

DOWN!

Vangie stepped out into the hallway and snapped the shutter. The camera whirred, clicked. The photograph emerged. Boots spun round, staring, her eyes meeting Mrs. Glickman's.

A woman, thought Vangie. *Bones do not lie. A woman's bones. A face I have seen somewhere, somewhere in a photograph.*

And then the gun appeared.

It seemed to come from nowhere, to appear in Boots's hand by magic. It was smaller than Vangie thought a gun would be, and less frightening. There were more steps—David's—on the stairs, hurtling down three or four at a time, half falling. Boots raised the gun, aimed. Vangie stood frozen, unable to duck back inside her door. Boots glanced toward the stairs, considering. Then she turned and ran.

"Honey, you got anyplace else to stay?" asked Peggy Bryce. She'd just been getting out of her car when the guy with the orange gloves came charging out the front door. She followed procedure—gave chase, shouted the warning, fired a couple of times over the guy's head—but so far they only wanted him for questioning, there was no probable cause to wing him. It would've gone to the Shootings Team, the guys they called the Thumbscrews, and it wouldn't have been ruled a righteous shoot, you could bet on that.

So the guy, the best lead they had, had gotten away. The old girl was telling her now that it wasn't a guy at all, it was a woman, but you couldn't see anything from that Polaroid she'd taken. Must've had the film in that thing for about ten years, from the looks of it. Grainy as hell and blurred. Peggy sighed. Maybe the lab could do something with it.

"You shouldn't have taken a risk like that, Vangie."

This was the guy they'd spent a day and a night chasing from here to D.C., David Cromwell. Peggy considered him. An actor, naturally she'd heard the name, though she never had time for TV and who could afford show tickets? Good-looking, but where did he get that haircut? Well, what the hell, maybe the guy could be some help. Peggy had nothing against show biz. Most of the cops she knew weren't such bad actors themselves.

"I thought I told you to stay in here and keep the door locked," he said. "You could've been killed."

Vangie shrugged and got up to make more coffee. For the first time in years, maybe since Walt died, she felt something like happiness. When she faced the open barrel of that gun in Boots's hand, fear had frozen her to the floor. If the woman had fired, old Vangie would've been a sitting duck, a martyr to her fear. Now her apartment was bright and warm, fragrant with coffee and toast and the strawberry jam her sister sent from Oregon. The place was full of people—David Photographs with his goofy new hairstyle, Peggy Bryce. Elva Ziegler, too, was here, and Freddy Adler, just back from work, still wearing his blue coveralls from the hospital laundry where he washed and spun dry till eleven three nights a week. Elva sailed around the room in her midnight robe with the Mylar stars on the back, her purple turban a little askew, laughing, asking everybody's sign.

Life, thought the old woman as she fished her odds and ends of cups out of the cupboard. *Suddenly, life is playing a return engagement.*

"He's right, Vange," said Freddy. He was pale from too much time with the Clorox, and bald except for a lock of dirty-blond hair arranged carefully across his forehead. "You shouldn't take chances."

Vangie scoffed. "Am I the one riding in an ambulance to St. Elizabeth's with a broken ankle?" They had taken a furious Julian Stockfish away less than a half hour earlier. "Besides, I had the tire iron."

"Well, anyway, honey," said Peggy Bryce. "I don't think you ought to stay here alone."

"She's coming home with me," announced David. He'd phoned Alex just after the ambulance left with Fish.

But Vangie shook her head. "If Elva stays, if Freddy stays, I stay."

"They didn't get a look at him. You did."

"Not him. Her. I know. A woman's bones. Something familiar around the eyes. I need to think."

"Okay, her. She could come back for you."

"Nope. If Elva stays and Freddy stays—"

David grinned. "Vangie, you're an old curmudgeon. I think I know a place where you'll be in perfect company. All of you. And it's the best place in the world to think."

So it was agreed. They would stay the night, catch-as-catch-can, at David and Alex's flat, then he would drive them up to Ainsley in the morning, flute, turban, crystal ball, tire iron, and all. Leaving a squad car outside for guard duty and transportation, Sergeant Bryce went off to rescue Tyrone, who'd been rounded up with the crackheads. It took a while for everybody to get packed and ready, but it was still before midnight when they gathered in the downstairs hall to leave. There was an odd feeling among them, almost festive, like schoolchildren off on a field trip. Freddy, shy and awkward, clutched his flute case and fell into line beside Elva Ziegler, short and hefty and looking like a turbaned tea cozy in her black cape. David led the way, with Vangie on his arm.

"Tell me one thing," she said, pausing in the lighted doorway. "My teacup that you swiped when you went on the lam? What did you—"

There was a strange sound, a smothered crack, like the sound of fireworks set off in a barrel. Vangie stopped, her hand clutching hard at David's forearm. She slumped over against him, heavy and limp, and he caught her and fell with her, dragged her into the shadows.

"Get down!" he shouted to the others. "Get into the dark!"

There were no more shots. No more were needed. Vangie Glickman was dead.

15

"But Haze," I told her, "what are you worried about? The bullet that killed Mrs. Glickman last night was fired from the same gun as the one that killed McKelvie and Jenny. Philip was still in the gentle arms of the law at nine P.M., waiting for bail. He's cleared, confession or not. Unless they can prove conspiracy—that he hired the gunman or connived with the killer—the best they could do now is obstruction of justice. If I've got him figured right, Colby will count himself lucky and look for a better pigeon. Philip's in the clear."

I expected her to light up with that familiar grin and slap me on the back, but Hazel Hancock's sober mood didn't seem to change at all with the knowledge of Vail's vindication. The most I got was a half-smile that faded when the waiter arrived with our coffee.

I had returned from my Friday night library expedition to the news of Vangie's murder, and after David's phone call my hoped-for night's sleep had been, to say the least, fitful. My Saturday had begun with a dull headache lurking at the corners of my eyes; my mouth was dry as sandpaper, my ears were ringing, and my mind kept wandering from the subject of Vail's confession to the picture of that old woman I had never seen except in my mind's eye— Vangie Glickman. Again and again since David's call I had heard the distant, muffled shot, the same sound that had come from our woods that bright early morning; again and again I saw Vangie, surrounded by friends, at last venturing a step into the battleground of the world; again and again I saw her slump and fall, saw Davy pull her down too late into the safe dark.

It might've been David, I thought—as I had been thinking all night. The police believed the killer had made his escape, then circled back, perhaps during the confused few minutes when the ambulance arrived to collect Julian Stockfish. The murderer had climbed a fire escape on one of the buildings across the street and settled down to wait, undeterred by the squad car on guard outside. He had no idea they would take the old woman and the others away for the night, but like a good soldier, he was prepared to wait all night in the mist. When the police had gone, he would return, rid himself of the threat Vangie posed, perhaps collect whatever he'd been looking for in McKelvie's apartment when David and Stockfish interrupted him, and then disappear for good.

It might've been David who was shot. But it wasn't. It might've been me that morning on the terrace. But it wasn't. Instead, it had been Vangie. My fuddled brain could think of only one reason.

"She saw that killer and she knew who it was," I said out loud.

Hazel stared. "Who? Who saw? Jenny?"

"No. Jenny was shot from behind. I meant Mrs. Glickman, the old lady who was killed last night. She got a good look at the murderer when he came down the stairs, even took a photograph. Smart old body, great presence of mind. She swore up and down it was a woman, not a man. The cops don't take much stock in that, and the photograph turned out to be a blur. But I'm not so sure." I shook my head. "I think she may have been right. I think she recognized that face she saw in the hallway. Oh, not consciously, and not right away. She didn't have a name to hand to the cops when they finally showed up. But in time, she would've dredged it up from somewhere, figured out how she knew it was a woman, why she was so sure. Just the way she figured out who Jenny Vail was after she'd seen her go up the stairs with McKelvie. I think she recognized the killer and the killer knew it, saw it in her face."

"And had to get rid of her before she figured it out and put a name to him. Her? You really think it was a woman?"

Hazel frowned. She couldn't have had much more sleep than I had had, but she always ran in some sort of emotional overdrive; though she sat perched uncomfortably on the hard maple chair of the Hornsby's coffee shop, her lithe, muscular body seemed still in motion, only hovering momentarily between destinations. It was stuffy in our small corner of the shop, and Hazel's short brownish hair stuck to her forehead with sweat. What makeup she wore—a bit of pencil on her brows, a nearly invisible swipe of pinkish lipstick—disappeared as she grabbed a paper napkin from the dispenser on the table and mopped her face with it. Robbed of even those few touches of camouflage, she emerged stoical and pale, except for two fever-blooms of color on her high Indian cheekbones. For a moment I saw the face of her Lakota Sioux great-grandmother, as Hazel's clear green eyes gazed out the coffee shop window, past me, past the street, past the buttes and bluffs of lifeless concrete, past the dirty river and out to sea and past the sea itself, mapping the sky.

"Homesick, Haze?" I said gently.

Her hand stirred her coffee absently, moving with a will of its own. Hazel was elsewhere. Then, with visible effort, she dragged herself back. The honking cackle resounded.

"Hell, Winnie," she said. "I'm beat. This place is like a sorority house at night; half the women members of Perfidy, Unlimited are on my floor and somebody's pounding on the door every five minutes, wanting to know when they're giving out that final Edgar for Best Novel."

I gritted my teeth, determined not to fall into the old delusion again, as Hazel went on.

"You and old Rita and the rest of the superstars may have quite a wait before the other shoe drops. They're talking about holding another Edgars dinner in the fall in Jenny's memory, maybe even changing the venue to L.A. or San Francisco. The West Coast members need pacifying. Should've heard them this morning at the PU business meeting." She glanced around the coffee shop, sharp-eyed and intent. "Look around you, Toots," she advised me. "They're all out of their cages now. If you want someone whose mind runs to murder, dis is de place."

She was right. Rita Kovacs was huddled with her vice-chairman,

Jed Sloan, who looked a bit hung over after the events of the past two days. Harlan Landis sat sipping coffee with Marina Vilnius, again dressed in funereal black, a dramatic black hat framing her long, pale El Greco face. Even Rabbi Perlmutter was there, leaned over a table talking intently to a hefty blonde with hair like a dishmop, and a prim sixtyish little person in a pouffy pink hat who had the unmistakeable air of being SOMEBODY.

"Who's the Queen Mum, the one with the hat?" I asked Hazel.

"The name eludes me."

"Which name? Sapphira Holmes? Madge Rutherford? Constance Lowell? Then there's her hard-boileds; she does those as Kirk Kane." Hazel took a sip of coffee and made a face. "It's Mary Louise Kirk, actually, national secretary. She's older than God and we can't find anybody who hates her, so we all thought she ought to give a little eulogy for Jenny when we have the tea. Could hardly let the Godmother do it, not after the way she went for Jenny's jugular."

Lovely Rita bent low over her coffee cup, her big hoop earrings glittering, her froggy eyes scanning the other tables. They stopped at ours and she looked away quickly.

Hazel snorted. "Bitch," she said. "You want a female suspect, honey, my money's right there. Know what she's been doing since Jenny got killed? She's been camped out in the lobby of the Waldorf, doing her number on Steven Stanway. He's set up over there like General Patton on D-Day, making conference calls to California, London, Toronto, hanging around for Jenny's funeral, that's what the word is. Actually, he's show-shopping, and if old Rita's got anything to say about it, he's going to replace Jenny's series with The Dusty Dvorak Show, head writer Rita Kovacs."

"Why bother to replace it at all? Anything connected with Jenny will be hot after all this publicity," I said. "The lawsuit's in limbo now that she's dead. Unless Philip—"

Hazel shook her head. "Philip's not Jenny's heir. He told me yesterday when I saw him in the lockup."

She shuddered involuntarily, the tense muscles rebelling again. A negative electrical charge seemed to come from her, suppressed anger at the image of Vail as I'd seen him on TV—manacled, worn down, helplessly manipulated by intelligences less than half his own. Hazel, as usual, figured something ought to be done, and if you wanted a thing done, you'd damn well better do it yourself. I'd heard her say it a hundred times, though I'd never seen her in action before. This was the fighting editor, the Hazel Hancock who lived on black coffee and Camels for days at a time during the protest marches of the Sixties, sleeping in the back of her ancient van and pounding along the highways west of everywhere to a place she'd got wind of, the place to be, where something was going down, blowing up, coming apart before her eyes.

I hadn't known her then; our acquaintance came later, when the protests were all wrapped in cotton wool and laid away like quaint episodes from some long-canceled TV show. Hazel had married, divorced, and settled down in Sioux Falls to run a respectable regional daily, branching out to mystery novels in her middle age. I suppose she reminded me of my own Iowa boyhood and youth, and her outspoken middle western common sense made her a frequent and welcome visitor up at our place any time she happened to be breezing through on a book tour. The ghost of her fighting days seemed to have disappeared for good, and I had often wondered about it. Looking now at the intense little woman sitting opposite me in faded jeans and turtleneck, the glint of gold from her earrings warming her face, I missed that old Hazel I had never known, and I had a sneaking hunch that she did, too.

But her mind was on Philip Vail. "He's a damn fool, Winnie," she said. "Are you still going to see him? He's over at Jenny's place, hiding out. Tending the shrine, is more like it."

"He never stopped loving her, did he?" I said.

I knew the answer. I had seen it in his face when Jenny touched his arm that night. Not passion. They had left that behind long ago, if it had ever been there at all. Not the love of fools and children, straining to bend itself to impossible perfections, easily had, easily broken. Theirs was an inexorable coupling, tough as the fusion of metals, one hard core drawn relentlessly to the other and impossible to break free no matter what the daily torments, the punishments and damages. From such a loving there was no escape, maybe not even by death.

Or murder, I thought. Had Philip wanted to be free of his difficult wife badly enough to hire her death, absolving himself by means of another murder committed while he himself was in custody? To use the old woman on Eighty-seventh Street, to play her and sacrifice her like a chess piece—it sounded more like Jenny's sort of game than his, but perhaps he had learned from her, toughened himself in the furnace of her will.

Or perhaps there was someone else, someone who loved him enough to free him of Jenny, whether he wanted to be free or not. Someone who hated her, saw how she used him.

"You use me." The words of the boy Gregory came back to me. *"You fucking use the world."* Might Vangie Glickman have mistaken a young man of nineteen or twenty for a woman?

"Philip loves the whole goddamn world," said Hazel, bringing me out of my thoughts with a crash. "He doesn't see any of the crap, Winnie. He was brought up in this ivory tower. Books, music, art museums, the grand tour of Europe with his grandmamma when he was six. Everybody's a work of art to old Philip, every sleeze-bucket's got a soul you can scrape the shit off of." She reached for her huge bag and wolfed down three aspirins with the dregs of her coffee, then signaled the waiter for a refill. "Maybe you can talk some sense into him," she said. "He deserves better than he's getting."

"You mean Jenny's will?" I stirred something the packet said was 'Non-Dairy Creamer' into my coffee; it looked like sawdust. I closed my eyes and swallowed. "If she didn't leave her rights in the books to Philip, who's the heir? The grandson, that kid Gregory?"

"Why do you think Philip confessed?" she said.

"You mean, he thought—he thinks the kid did it?"

Hazel nodded. "To tell you the truth, I'm not so sure he's not right. A screwed-up little bastard, especially after what happened to Cynthia."

I considered her. "I never realized you knew the Vails so well, Haze."

She smiled. "Research, Toots. Old Hazel's got a nose for news."

There was more to it than that and we both knew it. I found Vail interesting, complex, a subtle, perceptive mind. Merriman was convinced he was innocent and couldn't bear, as usual, to see anything of value going to deliberate waste. But Hazel's involvement with Philip Vail was more than just the interest of a reporter in a good story, or even of an author in a valued editor.

"But you and Philip, Hazel," I said. "Bit more than friends?"

Again the familiar honk of her laughter exploded in the quiet coffee shop, making the knots of buzzing partisans look our way. "Me and Philip? Winnie, you slay me, honest to God! Were you born yesterday, or just this morning? Philip Vail's been sleeping with Lydia Hallam for the last ten years, ever since he and Jenny separated."

"With—with Jenny's editor at Crocodile? She's his—"

"She'd probably prefer something shitty-cute, like bed partner. Philip's old-fashioned, and sophisticated enough not to be afraid of the real word. Mistress."

She crossed her legs and winced slightly. Age, I thought. In spite of her youthful figure, Hazel was not young. Like mine and Philip Vail's and Jenny's, her mind had been fully furnished when the world was otherwise, before the debacle of Vietnam and the orgies of overcompensation that succeeded it. Wave after wave had washed over us, eroding substance and replacing it with packaging, deflating the value of work and investing everything in the juggler's art called marketing. Having been taught our insignificance in a million ways, we hardly noticed the universal trivialization to which we were subject, hardly protested when the great mythic ceremonies ceased to matter; marriage, conception, birth, coming of age—even death mattered less than it ought. Wars were videotaped and replayed like parlor games, over potato chips and beer.

To this shrunken world and its priorities, some of us adapted. Like Jenny, we settled for making money and buying what currently passed for a life with it. Some of us persisted, as I had done, in swimming upstream; though money eluded us, we had learned the survival techniques of square pegs in round holes since time began. Though I'd only met her at a couple of official publishing functions, Lydia Hallam had always struck me as a kindred spirit, singularly uncomfortable around the new crop of permanently perky post-adolescent editors like Tracy Valentine who ruled the roost at most of the big publishing houses these days.

"I'd have figured Lydia for a loner," I said. "But I must say, Vail's no coward, playing footsie with his wife's editor."

"It's the best-known little triangle in publishing," replied Hazel. "I'm surprised Cliff Munsen didn't tell you." The waiter, figuring we'd taken up space long enough, presented me with the bill, and Hazel grabbed it. "Winnie," she said, "you're still coming to the PU tea party, aren't you? I think old Rita-babe's got something up her sleeve, but I haven't been able to find out what. I'll keep my ear to the—oops! Look out. Here she comes."

Rita Kovacs had left her huddle and was headed our way. Hazel fished some money for the coffee out of her bag and slapped it on the table.

"You're on your own, Winnie," she muttered. "If she gets me in a corner, I'll be here all day."

I'd been about to ask Hazel what she knew about the financial affairs of Philip Vail's company, E.P. Alexander and Sons, but she took off and I was joined too quickly for comfort by the Lovely Rita, who managed a smile in my honor as she sat down.

"We haven't met," she announced. It wasn't so much a statement as a challenge. "I'm Rita Kovacs." Her eyes bored into me, looking for something to resent.

"Of course," I said. "You write those dust books, don't you? What was the last one called—*Dust Bunnies?*"

She inscribed this on her mental charge-sheet and glared at me from miles aloft. "Did you get the invitation? The Perfidy, Unlimited tea? We're dedicating it to Jenny's memory. We—the Central Committee—thought you might like to say a few words."

"Being an experienced male elitist and oppressor myself, you mean?" I nodded. "Glad to. Just let me know the time and place."

"We're not sure where we can get a room," she said, still observing me from the ionosphere. "We lost our reservation when we had to postpone, and we operate on a shoestring, everything volunteer. We're talking to a couple of people, but we haven't found the right place yet."

"Well, I'm sure you'll manage to network something. Maybe Hazel can help."

She scoffed. "She's been avoiding me for six months, man. I don't think she's likely to cozy up now. This project of hers keeps her pretty occupied; getting half a dozen big publishing houses by the balls isn't exactly a short-term deal, I know. Still."

"Project? What kind of project? Hazel didn't mention anything."

"What she wants, what we all want, is an honest-to-God, functioning Writers' Union, one that can get our royalty statements out of these bastards in the comptrollers' offices, establish a minimum basic contract and make them stick to it, get the loopholes and the goddamn lead out. You know how long it took before I got the advance check on my last book? Five months after I signed the fucking contract, man! Before that, I waited nine months while some little jerk with pimples down in the legal office taught himself contract law by correspondence so he could write my new contract. I lost my apartment and had to move in with my mother. The finance company repossessed my car. All this time my editor's having a major crisis because I haven't handed in my next book, they've taken my back list out of print until I knuckle under. Hell, what do I care, I'll be too old to eat before I see a royalty anyway." She paused and glared at me. "I don't suppose it bothers you, any of this crap, does it? I don't suppose anybody fucks with you, after all these years? Why should you care?"

I couldn't say I liked the Lovely Rita, even yet, but I understood at least a part of her simmering anger. I could've compared notes, told her about my own mythical contract with the Flying Dutchman.

But at the moment another sort of battle was at the top of my list of priorities.

"So Hazel's trying to set up a Writer's Union?" I said. "Getting the goods on the publishers so as to present the nastier facts to the brethren and get the workers to unite, is that the idea?"

Rita nodded. "She's been tied up with it for weeks. Jenny Vail was dead-set against a union, handed out a lot of crap about surrendering creative rights, all that shit. Hell, who's got creative rights anyway. These days you write what sells. I used to write poetry, can you believe it? Published in half a dozen little magazines. I used the contributor's copies for t-paper and started writing hard-boileds. Anyway, I figured, if I could grab the presidency from Jenny, I'd be in a position to work with Hazel. I wanted to talk to her. But she wouldn't see me in big old Sioux Falls, and I called her room four times yesterday. No answer."

I ignored the No Smoking placard on the tabletop and lit a Turkish Delight. A chorus of subtle coughing immediately rose from the other tables. I puffed faster and blew a couple of my famous smoke rings.

"Let me get this straight, Miss Kovacs," I said. "You didn't see Hazel when you were in Sioux Falls?"

"Shit," she said. "No way. I was beating the bushes out in the boonies, right? For the presidency? I figure I got Chicago in the bag, but there's all these little Agatha Christie clones out on the prairies, right? Iowa, Kansas, Dakota. Crapola, but they've got influence in the business. Bookstores love that garbage. So I figure Hazel's been on the Executive Committee, she knows everybody in the business, I'll swing over to Sioux Falls and take her to lunch."

"But she refused your invitation?"

Rita Kovacs shrugged. "Out of town, that's what her flunky at the paper told me. Long trip."

"No steaks and Coors? You never had lunch?"

"Read my lips," she said. "No fuckin' lunch."

"And yesterday. The phone calls you made to her room? What time, can you remember?"

She fixed me with her froggy glare. I blew a few more smoke rings and brushed the ashes off my tie into her coffee mug. "You're on to something, man," she said. "You got a lead?"

"What time did you call her? She was probably with Philip Vail, trying to talk him out of that phony confession."

"I called her twice in the morning. Pretty early, once about seven, then again around ten. Tried her again last night, eight-thirty or nine." She paused. "No shit, man, you think Hazel's got something to do with the Vail murder?"

"Don't be ridiculous," I said. "I've known Hazel for twenty years, and she could no more commit murder than you could learn to knit."

"You don't like me, do you?" Lovely Rita fired from the hip, I had to give her that.

"Did you want me to?"

"Not much. I don't like your books. They've got no street smarts, they're full of this stylistic shit, words flying around. Wit. Cute stuff. Twee, you know."

"Is that a street-smart word?"

"Maybe. It's the way people talk."

I nodded. "Only God can make a twee. I don't like your books, either. They've got no guts, just balls. No brains, just pricks."

"In case you hadn't noticed, my detective is a woman."

"In case _you_ hadn't noticed, I hadn't noticed."

She hovered for a minute, uncertain. "Okay," she said. "I can live with that."

" 'Fraid you'll have to," I said. "Truce?" I offered her a paw.

She took my hand in a grip like rusty pliers. "Truce," she said. She stood up to leave, then turned back. "Listen, about that piece? The one that iced Queen Jenny?"

"What about it?"

"I heard it was a seven-milli, French-Libyan, sniper stuff. Right?"

"Where did you hear that?"

"Sources," she said. "Were they righteous?"

"Maybe. Why?"

"Read the competition, man," she said. "Marina Vilnius? She used a gun just like that in her last piece of shit."

Lovely Rita walked away and I caught a glimpse of Marina, her black, half-closed Slavic eyes fixed on me from underneath the brim of the stylish hat. She looked battered, smashed, and fixed together again with screws and wires that didn't quite fit. The sight of her momentarily erased all the nagging misgivings about Hazel from my mind. On the night of Jenny's death, Marina herself had looked like a victim.

She had looked, I thought soberly, exactly like death.

16

When I left the coffee shop, I found Merriman waiting for me in the cavernous Hornsby lobby. He and Sarah had come in with me on the train, hovering like a pair of bodyguards in case our friend the sniper decided to turn his attention to me. Sarah had gone on to David and Alex's apartment, and Eddie, choosing not to sit in on my confab with Hazel Hancock, had refused to tell me what he had in mind for himself. I figured it had something to do with his newfound bankroll, but I should've known better. He was merely doing what Eddie does best—puttering around and sniffing the prevailing wind. Just now he was standing by a brass rack of assorted designer luggage, talking in subdued tones to a tall, thin white-haired gent in a blue-and-gold hotel uniform. I remembered him; he was the doorman at whom Jed Sloan had aimed his fake gun on Edgars night.

"Winnie," said Merriman, "this is Brendan Francis Michael Clancy, known to his brethren as Clancy the Push. He possesses, so he tells me, the record for having escorted more squiffed citizens off the premises than any other hotel doorman this side of Times Square. He is also possessed of remarkable literary acumen, and is a devoted fan of yours."

The tall Irishman beamed, his cheeks pink and glowing. "Ah, the best of the lot was *Death of a Jester!* That devil kept me reading till I missed the train for Brooklyn, did I not, and didn't I have to sleep the night in Johnny McManigle's bathtub, and when I phoned up the missus to say where was I and what was I doin', did she credit a word of it? She did not! So I gave her the book, which I'd finished durin' the night, McManigle's tub bein' less than the crown of comfort, and what does she do? She can't put it down and she misses the bus from her mother's place and has to spend the night herself!" He whipped a copy of my latest, *Death of a Double Agent*, out of his back pocket. "A fine bit of work, this, too," he said, opening it to the title page. "Would you ever put down your John Henry for me, sir? Or should I be sayin' your John Henrietta?"

Clancy had a giggle and I dug in my vest pocket for my book-signing pen. "You were on duty the night of the Edgars, weren't you?" I said. "When the man in the trench coat shot you with that phony gun? Must've scared the daylights out of you."

He smiled, his pink cheeks dented with dimples. "Scared, sir? Not a bit of it, now. With two portraits of Andy Jackson tucked away in my pocket, my only fear was spendin' the proceeds all in one place."

"You mean Sloan had set it up with you in advance?" asked Merriman. "Paid you forty dollars to help him make an ass of himself, did he?"

Clancy nodded. "All planned out, careful and correct, and a secret between himself and myself, so as to create a sensation."

"Most effective," agreed Eddie. "Certainly made him the cynosure of all eyes."

The pair of eyes I had in mind were Jenny Vail's. They had been full of fear. "Mrs. Vail wasn't in on the trick, was she, Clancy?"

"Not as I know, sir. It was the ladies made up the whole thing, suggested it to young Mr. Sloan not three days before the dinner." He grinned proudly. "And wasn't it myself fired the blanks during the meal and the ceremony, too, all according to plan?" His grin faded and he seemed to age before our eyes. Suddenly the stage Irishman was replaced by a sorry old man. "I went off duty at seven, just before the dinner started. They said the gunshots were a joke, d'you see, all the mystery writers there, it would make an occasion of it. 'Living theater,' that's what they called it."

"Who did?"

"The ladies, sir. The lady mystery writers. A committee, that's what they said. Three ladies."

"Could you describe them, Clancy?" Merriman fished out his little red leather notebook and a pen. "What did these three weird sisters look like?"

"One of them was tallish, sir, skinny. Eyes like the wolf in Red Riding Hood. One was gray-haired, wearing a pale blue hat with feathers. One was short, brown hair, blue jeans, and a sweater."

"Rita Kovacs," I said. "Eyes like a crocodile, that woman." I shivered. "The hat with the feathers would be the Queen Mum, their national secretary."

"And the third weird sister?" Eddie frowned. "Sounds like our Hazel."

"What of it?" I snapped. "She belongs to the Red-Headed League. She's on half a dozen committees for the Edgars every year. It doesn't mean anything."

Merriman skewered me with a sober gaze. "What's coming to a boil in that stewpot brain of yours, Hyde? I didn't attack the woman, you know, I merely—"

"Forget it," I said. "Go on, Clancy. Go on about the fake gun-shots."

"Not much else to say, sir," he said. "They gave me a time schedule, when the shots should be fired. Gave me a gun full of blanks, inspected by the boys in hotel security. They wanted the dinner not to be dull, that's what they said." He stared at his shiny black shoes. "Dull it was not, sir. Dull it was surely not."

"When did you fire the last shot, Clancy?" I said. "What was the schedule?"

"I let off the first during the reception, when they blinked the lights to call everyone inside to dinner."

"The shot that gave Sarah the whim-whams," said Merriman, scribbling a note.

"The second was in the ballroom, when the fella was giving the welcome to start the awards." Clancy took the smoke I offered him and stowed it away in his jacket. "And the last was just before the prize for the best novel."

"Which came after Jenny was dead," I said. "But Clancy, there was another shot, while Landis was giving the history of mystery novels. Just as he got to Charles Dickens and *Our Mutual Friend,* there was a shot."

"Not fired by myself, sir. Knowing there was eight or nine awards before the best novel when I was to let off the last gunshot, I stepped into the serving pantry at the back for a bite of something. Terrible racket in there, clattering and clanging of crockery and trays and that. I didn't hear any other shot."

"I did," said Eddie. "Mr. Landis is in no danger of being lured away from writing to the lecture circuit. The whole audience was nodding off, but I heard him getting to Dickens and being a loyal Dickensian myself I pricked up my big ears. There was the shot, but now that I think of it, it hadn't quite the same sound as Clancy's blanks. Hollower, more muffled."

"A silencer," I said. "That was the shot that killed Jenny. It must've happened while I was working my way through the ballroom trying to spot her."

"Which means that if she was there already, sitting at that table waiting for somebody to come and kill her, she must've known exactly where she was headed, gone there straightaway from the Crocodile Books table up front. There wasn't enough time for her to have wandered."

"And *that* probably means," I added, hitching onto his train of thought, "that the meeting was prearranged. She wasn't waiting around for *me* to find her. It was a trap the murderer had set ahead of time."

"Which Jenny, afraid as she was, walked into. The bait must've been powerful. Irresistible. Something she cared for more than she cared for life. Clancy," said Merriman, patting the doorman's pocket. "You haven't forgotten our little bargain? The *locus in quo?*"

"I have not, sir," replied Clancy the Push. "If you'll just follow me, and try, if you don't mind, to look like a pair of misplaced refrigerator salesmen."

He sailed off through the lobby and Merriman fell in behind him, fairly glittering with delight; I, as usual, brought up the rear.

"I don't suppose you'd give me a flight plan, would you?" I said, steaming up behind them. "Where the hell are we headed? Refrigerator salesmen?"

Merriman ducked past a pair of Japanese gents wearing matching electric blue blazers; ahead of us, Clancy shimmered toward the elevator marked "Ballroom." Eddie turned to me and smiled, one of those long-suffering ones that make me want to tap-dance on his little pointed head with hobnailed boots.

"The scene of the crime, Hyde," he said patiently. "Clancy has agreed to arrange for us to get into the ballroom. It's currently hosting a sales meeting for purveyors of energy-saving refrigeration units."

"A roomful of ice-box salesmen!" I groaned. "Oh, my fur and whiskers!"

A couple in matching red blazers got onto the elevator ahead of us, then a pair of female sergeant-majors in navy blue. Everybody had a little badge and a plastic portfolio of some kind. Clancy spoke a word to the tiny, ancient elevator man who held the door for us.

"Archie, here, will look after you," the Irishman said with a wink. "If he topples, just lean him in the corner till the elevator stops."

"*Rrrrrrrr!*" growled the old fellow.

Another couple, this time two hefty men with German accents wearing matching park-bench green, pushed their way onto the car just ahead of Merriman and me, and we barely made it as the doors closed.

"Archie?" I muttered to Merriman. "More like Noah, judging by his age and the look of his passengers. All these animals seem to travel two by two."

The elevator slammed to a halt with the pointer over the door at the ballroom level.

"Out!" yelled the old man. He slipped with a jolt off his tottering stool next to the controls and began to shoo the many-colored passengers on their way. Merriman was about to follow orders and decamp, but I had other plans.

"Noah," I said. "Er, that is, Archie. Do you ever work nights around here?"

He snorted. "Nights, weekends, rainy days, hot days. Any time these damn kids feel like a day off or a night on the town. Got me over a barrel, haven't they? If Archie says no, we'll just send him to the glue factory. *Rrrrrrr!*"

"Were you on duty the night before last?" said Merriman. "Busy night round here, with the mystery writers' dinner and all, I expect they'd need experienced help."

The old man nodded. "They need me, all right. Damn kids can't count past ten, somebody asks for the fifteenth floor they take him to ten and let him walk from there. Of course I was on duty. A Thursday night? Of course I was."

"Just after the dinner began, did you take a boy downstairs?" I said. "Kid about nineteen, brownish hair shaved on the sides, one gold earring?"

"The brat?" Archie nodded. "I took him down all right, and gave him a piece of my mind, too. I may be old, but I'm not stupid. 'Stupid old bugger,' that's what he called me. Tried to work my buttons himself. Nobody works my buttons. *Rrrrrrr!*"

"Did you ever bring him back up?"

"Nope. Wouldn't let him back on my elevator. No sir."

"Is there another way to the ballroom level?"

"Fire stairs. Kitchen elevators, where they bring the food up to the serving pantry for the ballroom. Have to have a key for them, though. Fire doors are locked unless the alarm goes off. Then the sprinklers go on, the locks open automatically. Electronic. Hate electronics. Push buttons. Self-service elevators. *Rrrrrrr!*"

"So the beastly kid couldn't have gotten back to the ballroom level unless he rode your elevator?" asked Eddie.

"And he left long before Jenny was killed. Surely Philip Vail knew that. He's spent enough time around this hotel to homestead in the lobby. He knew Gregory was gone and in the clear."

"What about a woman?" Merriman piped up. "Did you take any of the ladies down in the elevator? It would've been fairly late in the evening, around nine-thirty, when the awards were well along. A woman alone?"

Old Archie shook his head. "Nobody went down after the brat, not until the police started letting people go. They already asked me, that overstuffed booby with the fancy uniform asked me fifteen times. Nobody. Nobody at all."

Merriman handed him a picture of Alexander Hamilton to be going on with, and trotted after me toward the main ballroom. I eyed the wad of bills he was stuffing back into his pants pocket. "You don't have to flash your bankroll, you know, even if you are Ainsley's answer to J. Paul Getty—"

"Tickets, please?"

We had reached Checkpoint Charlie, the folding table set up at the entrance to the ballroom. A double harness of paunchy sad-eyed salesmen in brown blazers stood at the ready with clipboards.

"Doesn't have a name tag," said Tweedledum.

"Name tag, nope," echoed Tweedledee.

"Doesn't have a notebook."

"Notebook, nope."

"Doesn't have a ticket." Tweedledum eyed me sadly; he looked like the Maytag repairman on New Year's Eve. "Ticket?"

I shook my head. "Sorry, kiddo. No tickets."

"No tickets," he informed Tweedledee.

"No tickets, nope."

"We're the inspectors," I said.

"Inspectors, yes," echoed Merriman.

"Don't need tickets. Inspecting the serving pantry today."

"Serving pantry, yes."

Tweedledum shook his head. "Not serving. Not today."

"Naturally," I said. "Can't serve while we're inspecting."

"Have to be inspected," said Merriman firmly, "before they can serve at all."

Tweedledum looked at Tweedledee. "Give them name tags?" he said.

"Name tags, right," chorused Tweedledee.

Tweedledum's pen was poised over two small plastic badges with pins on the backs. "Names?" he said, with a look that contained the sorrows of every energy-inefficient icebox known to man. "Have to have names."

"Stanley," I told him. I turned to Merriman. "Dr. Livingstone, I presume?"

He nodded. "Livingstone, yes."

Truth in packaging notwithstanding, our new labels got us where we wanted to go. The ballroom was hung with flags the colors of all those matching blazers we'd met in Archie's elevator, and the tables had been arranged in semicircles cupped around a central platform where two green-jacketed women were demonstrating something on a chalkboard. The serving pantry, which I'd taken for a real kitchen on the night of the Edgars, was empty, the swing doors shut, and the corner where I'd found Jenny's body had been vacuumed clean as a whistle. Even the bloodstained carpeting and the wallpaper soaked with her blood had been cut away and replaced with temporary sheeting, as though the hotel were merely redecorating. Whatever we had hoped to find, it certainly wasn't likely to be here now.

On the platform the two icebox salesladies rattled on about twenty-first-century coolants and ecology-conscious insulating foam. I hardly noticed them; I could see nothing in that room but the memory of Jenny. The wooziness of that moment flooded over me again and I looked around for a chair.

I didn't see one, but I did see Merriman. He'd gone through the swing doors into the serving pantry and was poking around at another door that latched from the pantry side with a slide bolt. When my knees stiffened up enough to toddle, I joined him.

"Look here, Winnie," he said, slipping the steel bolt aside. "Seems to be a passageway of some sort. Obviously only open when they're serving from the pantry, here. Wonder where it leads."

The door opened with a click, and when you pushed it back against the wall a blocking device on the hinge kept it open. Beyond the doorway was a small sink and a set of shelves full of water glasses and pitchers. The thing seemed to be a sort of additional serving hatch; in the main serving area were the warming ovens and refrigerators, but this was the only running water. Waiters supplying the tables with before-dinner ice water could do so from here without getting in the way of food being handled in the pantry itself.

Beyond the sink and the shelves of glassware, the passage turned a square corner and ended suddenly at yet another bolted door.

"Stay here," I said.

"Where are you going, Winnie?"

"Just stay here, confound you!"

I trotted back through the passageway, past the sink, through the pantry and into the ballroom again, then made my way past Tweedledum and Tweedledee at the check-in table. Now I was in the reception room, Louis the Fourteenth's throne room with the fake murals and the phony marble columns.

I stood in the middle of the room, getting my bearings. The serving pantry was on the left, the ballroom elevators dead ahead, the fire stairs off to the right. At the far left was the bar, and just beyond it the rest rooms. But at the opposite end of the bar, hidden behind a column and wallpapered with one of the murals so as to be invisible when it was closed, was a door.

I made my way to it and hammered with my fist. "Merriman! You still in there?"

The bolt on the other side slid free and the door creaked open. It was the same passageway all right, but there was no sign of Eddie. I closed the heavy door behind me and made my way toward the pantry again.

"Merriman," I hollered. "It leads to the bar. Perfectly logical, some sort of beverage service hatch. Oh my hat, what now?"

Eddie was on his hands and knees, crawling along the gray institutional carpet just beyond the sharp turn in the passageway. "Got it!" he crowed, and grabbed my hand to pull himself up. "Let's go into the pantry, where the light's better."

I followed him. We stood under one of the big fluorescent fixtures as he unclenched his fist. On the palm of Merriman's hand lay three small pearls, all the same size and color, a sort of pinkish cream.

"Fake, of course," he said. "See, this one's peeling a bit round the drill hole. Cheap fakes, at that."

"But what were they doing there?" I said.

He shrugged. "Someone obviously lost them. A broken string of pearls is common enough, specially when they're old—as these are —and cheaply strung in the beginning."

"Merriman," I said, exasperated, "this passageway is used by waiters! There weren't any women waiting table that night. If somebody's pearls went bust in this hallway, it was either a secret cross-dresser, or a woman where she didn't damn well belong!"

He frowned. "That dress of Jenny Vail's, Winnie. Were there pearls with the amethysts?"

I shook my head. "Of that I'm positive. Just the amethysts and some sort of silvery stuff for trimming."

The frown stayed on my friend's face and his bright blue eyes met mine for a brief instant, then looked away. "Winnie," he said, "it's a logical problem. You've always been a knothead, but you don't refuse a logical argument."

I scowled at him. "If you're insinuating that I'm turning a blind eye—"

"Of course not. But the mind has many rooms and some have dark corners that don't look well in the light of reason."

"Get to the point."

"Right," he said. He tore off a page from his red leather notebook and leaned on the countertop to draw a diagram. "Here's the ballroom," he said, boxing off a large area. "Main doors there. Swing doors to the serving pantry here." He marked them off. "Up front the platform, our table, Jenny's, Philip Vail's, and so on. Back here by the swing doors the table where you found the body." He looked up.

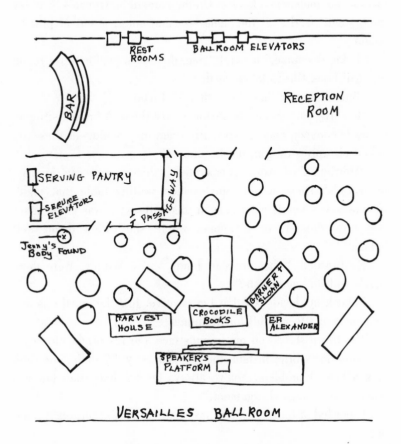

"And beyond the swing doors the passageway that led out to the
bar and the reception room. So what?"

"The murderer was a woman. We have Mrs. Glickman's word for
that, and the evidence of the lost pearls. The killer had made an
appointment with Jenny to meet her here, at this table in the back.
She was already at the dinner. Nobody got in without a ticket. The
security was even tighter that night than it was this morning. A
female murderer wearing cheap pearls came out of the serving pan-

try without being noticed by any of the waiters. Lieutenant Lincoln told us as much that night. But nobody much would've been using the little hatch in that passageway from which water and beverages were served. The champagne was already at the tables by then and the water-glass service ended when the ceremony began."

"So the murderer—murderess, that is—hid out in the passageway and then came out waving a great brute of a gun and shot Jenny? Without a waiter seeing her? Applesauce, Merriman. Unadulterated applesauce!"

"Suppose the murderess wasn't lying in wait. Suppose she was out in the reception area, perhaps in the ladies' room. The doors between the bar and the pantry were locked open. She only had to wait until the barman was otherwise engaged, then duck through and wait around that right-angle turn until nobody was in sight. She'd have come out of those double swing doors right behind Jenny's head as she sat waiting at the table."

"But the gun! Any waiter would've noticed a woman waving a gun around."

"Perhaps she didn't wave it. She must've had it in a handbag, concealed somehow, as Jenny had her own little gun."

"The gun we're looking for is no miniature, Merriman, as you blasted well know! It's got a long thin barrel to handle those miserable little bullets, and with a silencer—which she must've used—it would be even longer. All the women I saw that night had tiny little fussy purses like Jenny's and Tracy Valentine's, like that little beaded jet thing of Sarah's. Evening bags. They'd have no more held a—"

Eddie fixed me with a sober stare. "All but one, Winnie. There was one woman who didn't have an evening bag. She had a pocketbook. Hard leather, no bulges would show in it. She was in costume and might've removed her wig, even put on a jacket of some sort in that passageway to be less noticeable. Perhaps she even managed to get hold of one of those blue Hornsby jackets the waiters were all wearing. The waiters would hardly have paid much attention to one more woman table-hopping, anyway. Everybody was doing it." He paused. "And the woman I have in mind was wearing pearls as I recall."

"If you mean—"

"You know exactly what I mean. I mean that you must consider the possibility that dear, kind, forthright Hazel Hancock killed Jenny Vail."

I closed my eyes for a moment. He had only put into words the thoughts that had been gathering force in my mind since my talk with Rita Kovacs. But I hated him for the words. He was my oldest friend, but I turned on him, furious.

"Hazel Hancock wouldn't kill anybody, and you know that as well as I do. You might as well suggest that *I'd* commit three murders!" I studied his face. "You would, wouldn't you? You and your rich uncle and your three hundred thousand pounds sterling, you think I don't know about that? Money's changing you already, Merriman, it's cutting away all your loyalties. You're capable of—of—"

"Cold logic?" Eddie put his notebook away. "I suppose I am, yes. If the facts supported it, I'd have to consider the possibility that you killed three people, just as I consider it with Hazel." He laid a hand on my arm. "I didn't say she *did* it, Winnie. I'm fond of her myself. But you can get killed by ignoring the facts, and this killer has been taking pot shots at you, as well." He blinked. "Shouldn't like to lose you, you know, even though you are an old rhinoceros."

"Hazel wouldn't," I said. "Take pot shots at me, I mean. And what has she got against this McKelvie fellow? I could understand her disliking Jenny, envying her even. Half the women in Perfidy, Unlimited did that. But it's too much." I shook my head. "I don't believe it."

Eddie nodded. "That is, of course, your right. But you do consider it?"

I hesitated, seeing again the open doors to the reception room as I'd seen them that night, just before I found Jenny's body.

"Merriman," I said softly. "I saw Haze just before I found Jenny at the table. Saw her through the main doors. She was at the end of the line for the ladies' room. She could've ducked back through that damn passageway and gotten into line—"

"Close your eyes, Winnie," he said. "Try to get a picture. Was she wearing the pearls when you saw her?"

I shut my eyes and tried to summon the sight of her. Perhaps it was the darkness of that small, warm room in my mind where I stored away such friends as Merriman and Hazel. I could see the dowdy little figure of Mrs. Mapleton, the gray nylon wig, the flared skirt, the sensible shoes—even the pocketbook. But beyond that I could not—or would not—go.

I opened my eyes to see Merriman's fixed on me. "Of course she was," I lied. "Of course Hazel was wearing the pearls when I saw her."

"I see," said Eddie sadly, then turned and walked off through the roomful of refrigerator salesmen.

I followed slowly, unwilling to face him again. He knew, as I did, that Hazel had not been wearing Mrs. Mapleton's pearls.

17

"She read everything," said David. "Fitzgerald, John Donne, Housman. And every mystery novel written this century. Look at them."

As I followed his glance across the muddled shelves and the overflowing heaps of books in Evangeline Glickman's small, dimly-lighted flat, I recognized title after title I myself had read and enjoyed—Dickens, Chekhov, Simenon, Sayers, Allingham. A dozen of my own titles were there, too, some long out of print; I spotted four of Hazel's Mrs. Mapleton books, one of Rita Kovacs, and two or three the dripping-dagger specials by Marina Vilnius. There were also, of course, Jenny's best-sellers—not all of them, but a selective few, spaced over a number of years and ending with the copy of *The Black Palace*, which lay open on the moth-eaten old divan in the middle of the living room, just as Vangie had left it.

Eddie and I had barely joined the others at David's place a few blocks away when there was a phone call from Sergeant Peggy Bryce. Would we meet her and A. J. Lincoln at Mrs. Glickman's building in half an hour to go over the evidence? She sounded angry and a little stunned; naturally we all agreed, and David phoned Stockfish, his broken ankle now neatly encased in a plaster cast, to meet us there.

It was an opportunity I hadn't expected, especially considering that Colby was now back on the job and officially in charge of the case. It was against all the rules and procedures of cop-house bureaucracy, and I knew something big must be in the wind if Lincoln and his lady cohort were willing to take the chance. Once Alex had seen Gemma off to her Saturday morning play group, the five of us set off—David and Alex, Merriman, Sarah, and Yours Truly.

We decided to walk uptown, following the same route David had taken on his nightly vigils, past the security mansions of Central Park West, then into the narrow canyon of Eighty-seventh Street. A few restored brownstones were scattered like sandblasted islands among the stained and crumbling brick structures that had not been "gentrified." In these ancient catacombs untouched by Reaganomics and yuppification dwelt the holdouts, leftovers from systems of living, of value, that had ceased to function years, even decades ago. Here were old communists who remembered the Spanish Civil War and the days when the upper West Side had been a haven where shattered idealists could gather, play chess, sip wine, argue the fates of vanished nations; here were the old aristocrats, children of princes whose thrones had been burnt from under them, traded for missiles, oil wells, megacorporations; here lived the frail old women of small means and long memory, who spoke many languages and understood one another perfectly without words, reading the fine web of memory around the eyes, the stoop of aching shoulders, the arthritis-knotted fingers, the fear lines that pulled the mouths tight.

Sometimes, as we passed Columbus Avenue and headed up to Amsterdam, I caught a glimpse of a face at a window, eyes wide, hands pressed flat against the glass, and I wondered if I had seen the same face years ago when Sarah and I were young and explored the city hand in hand as though it were a private kingdom we had just inherited.

At the end of Vangie's block some kids lounged, brought out by the Saturday sunshine, their eyes blank and vacant. They barely spoke, just poked each other and sneered at the five of us as we marched past. From a third-floor window in a building down the street a big white sheet fluttered, a message written on it in bright red paint. "PUSHERS AND JUNKIES," it said. "BE WARNED. WE WILL CALL COPS."

Well, I thought, Vangie had called the cops, but cops were human, fallible, outnumbered, outflanked by fancy weapons like that terrorist gun. They were a tiny militia—imperfect, eroded, and brutalized by constant fear, led in part by manipulative fools like Colby with personal power schedules whose importance outweighed the demands of their jobs. Vangie had called the cops and found Peggy Bryce weary and without backup and Lincoln tied up in Colby's office, being scolded for doing his job too well.

Now Vangie was dead. Jenny Vail's death, even McKelvie's, might've been explicable according to some motive we had not yet discovered, but this old woman's was not. She had been in the way, that was all; she had seen too much, been expendable and easily dealt with. I glanced again across the titles on her shelves: a mind stocked with the best of an ancient civilization now under siege and falling from its own weight. A generous mind without vanity or the cheap pomposities of those ill-educated in the finest schools. A mind blown casually off the face of the earth.

I began to understand more fully David's preoccupation with death. It seemed to look at me from the eyes of those lounging boys, to hover in the dust on Vangie's bookshelves. I had known Jenny Vail and I had never met Vangie Glickman, but this last death, which could've had no motive but the killer's fear of discovery, stirred something in me I could only call rage, and I knew that Merriman was right. Premeditated murder is a logical game, and so long as the killer sticks to the rules it remains manageable; civilization still has rules of its own to deal with it. But Vangie's death had been as impulsive and as casually brutal as the beating and death of Cynthia Vail. It cheapened life and it stepped beyond all codes ever invented to manage the unmanageable. So long as it remained unpunished, it tinged all of us with guilt and made us trivial and shabby.

Worse still, there was no end to it. It needed no provocation, and once that boundary had been passed, the killing could go on and on, eliminating one after another as the killer imagined them to be a threat. There were no exceptions. I couldn't afford to close my eyes and look away from the truth. Whoever had done this would have to be stopped and stopped now—even if it *was* Hazel.

I had no idea how long I'd been standing there thinking until Sarah came quietly up beside me and slipped her arm through mine. "Win," she said, "come and sit down. Lieutenant Lincoln doesn't want to start without you."

I nodded and joined the others gathered on the worn furniture in the middle of the room. Lincoln was there, of course, and Peggy Bryce, her gray eyes hard and angry. Julian Stockfish had met us in the hallway, leaning on a crutch, and Vangie's neighbors were there, too—Freddy Adler, pale and moist-eyed; and Elva, turbanless, her lank gray hair falling out of a few hairpins, her broad nose red and her big blue-green eyes rimmed with pink.

David had brought that same plastic carrier bag he'd had with him on the Friday morning when I found him hiding in my office. Now he put it down on the kitchen counter and carefully lifted out several balls of bright-colored knitting wool, then a delicate blue-and-white china cup and a matching saucer. He set them down beside another of the same pattern the old woman had left out on the counter.

"She told me not to break it," he said dully. "I thought, if I could keep it whole . . . It might mean something, if I brought it back to her. I never got the chance."

Merriman sat in Vangie's straight chair, her trusty tire iron across his lap. "Naturally she couldn't wield this properly when Boots came down the stairs, her hands being occupied with the camera. Shame the photo didn't come out well."

Lincoln dug inside his jacket and pulled out a cupped Polaroid picture. "That's why I called you guys here, as a matter of fact," he said. "I—We. Sergeant Bryce and myself." He stared at the floor. "We're off the case."

"Oh, my Sunday hat," I said, "don't tell me! Colby's on the rampage?"

Peggy Bryce stood up and began to pace the floor with quick, light steps, back and forth between the heavy old pieces of furniture. "He's going after Philip Vail. He's got that fake confession, and Vail's got no alibi, or if he has he isn't talking about it. Nobody seems to be able to place him during the few minutes when his wife must've been shot."

"But," cried Merriman, nearly beside himself, "Mrs. Glickman was shot with the same gun! Vail was locked away at the time! It's—"

"The gun hasn't been found," said Lincoln. "Colby's going for conspiracy with person or persons unknown."

"A hired gun?" said Stockfish. "That's crap."

"You know it and I know it, Fish," said Lincoln. "But Colby doesn't want to mess up his record with an unsolved celebrity murder. He wants a quick arraignment and a nice reward from his politico pals upstate."

Stockfish hefted his cast onto a pillow. "About the gun, Linc? I had a little talk with my gun guy, Bonaparte Shanks, you remember him? Piece like that isn't exactly a Saturday night special, you know. Gun freaks like Bony, they groove on this technological stuff, they'll remember it in a minute if they hear of a deal going down anywhere in town. Might take a day or two on the jungle telegraph to get results, but I'm betting we'll finger the guy. Or was it a woman, like the old lady said?"

Lincoln handed me the fuzzy photo. "All you can see is a blur. She must've moved the camera when she pushed the shutter. Leaning on her cane and all, she was off balance. Do me a favor, Doc? If I send this through our lab guys, Rat-Cheese'll have me up on charges. Take it to Lloyd Agate. Ask him to see what he can do with it. Polaroids are tough to work from, but we ought to give it a try."

"Sure thing," I said, studying the photo. The figure of Boots had been captured just at the bottom of the stairs, half turned toward the hallway, a short-waisted torso in a light jacket and a blurred profile topped by a light-colored flat-billed golfing cap. Almost nothing was visible of the face, except for a lock of hair across the ear and part of the temple. "Lloyd might make something of it," I said, with more bravado than conviction. "Agate might drop ashtrays and mow down folding chairs like dominoes, but where evidence is concerned he's as good as a surgeon."

"I pulled the old file on Cynthia Vail Canfield's mugging," said Peggy Bryce. "Nothing there to indicate it was anything more. In fact, when I ran it through the computer, there were two or three other muggings in the area of the Orthodox Cathedral, spaced a month or two before and after Cynthia's. Same MO, people out jogging or walking dogs in the morning, beaten with a piece of pipe and robbed. The others survived, and their descriptions of the guy match the ones the witnesses in the Canfield case gave. Cynthia was just unlucky," she said softly. "Maybe she didn't have enough money with her. Maybe he was crapped out of stuff and wired. Maybe the weather was lousy and he took it out on her."

"What about Vangie?"

The voice was Elva Ziegler's. When she spoke she stood up suddenly, like a child in an old-fashioned schoolroom, her short, rubbery arms extended at her sides, looking for something to grab onto, something that would not give way.

"What about Vangie?" she said again. The red-rimmed eyes stared first at one of us, then the other. Suddenly she sat down. "I don't understand," she said softly.

Freddy Adler reached over and patted Elva's hand shyly. "It doesn't seem like they care much," he said. "That's what she means. The big shots. This other woman you were talking about? Now Vangie. It's like she just died in some accident. An act of God, like they say."

"Phooey," said Sarah, her chin tilted back defiantly. "God may act out of the storm and the whirlwind, but I very much doubt He requires telescopic sights and terrorist bullets. And as for that inane jackass Colby, he's exactly like my late and unlamented father. He doesn't care much for anything but himself and his puny ambitions, and he could find a way to turn the Second Coming to his personal advantage, providing he got the papers there to cover it in time." She got up, marched over to Vangie's tiny kitchen, and began to poke around among the pots and pans. "I need coffee. We shall just have to ignore the ignoramus and get on with it, that's all, but I can't possibly do it without a cup of coffee, so there!"

David and Alex helped her sort out enough mugs and cups for coffee all round, and Elva found a bag of middle-aged raisin bagels which she sliced and began to toast. I wandered back to the bookshelf and pulled down one of Hazel's paperbacks. Inside was her usual photo, years old. The high Sioux cheekbones, though, were the same, and the wide-eyed, distant look I'd seen that morning as she gazed out the window of the Hornsby coffee shop.

"Of course she *wasn't* wearing the pearls when you saw her," said Merriman's voice beside me. The aroma of his pipe tobacco took me back through all the years of office conferences, faculty meetings, late-night philosophizings in my Cave. The man had wormed his way inside my head over the years, and it was too late to throw him out now, even if I wanted to.

"No," I told him. "No pearls. But there may be a perfectly simple explanation."

"By all means. Those pearls may very well be up in her hotel room this minute."

"Absolutely." I shot him a sidewise look. "And if those damn Chelsea boots *are* Hazel's, they could be in that hotel room, too."

"Possibly. Don't keep a good pair of boots more than twenty years and then throw them away lightly." He frowned. "Can't recall having seen Hazel wearing boots up at our place, can you, Winnie?"

"I can't, but I wasn't looking. Anyway, you have to wear boots in South Dakota. It comes with the territory. I wouldn't necessarily have noticed the kind they were, even if she had them."

"There's one way to find out," he said. There was a touch of the old gleam in his eye. "I haven't burgled anything in donkey's years."

"Hotel rooms aren't easy. Electronic locks and guards everywhere. We'd need a specialist."

He nodded. "Our friend Julian seems a resourceful fellow, full of surprising nooks and crannies, all sorts of talents stored away."

Eddie trotted off and in a minute I saw him settle down beside Stockfish. When we'd all been provided with bagels and coffee, Lincoln cleared his throat nervously.

"Okay," he said. "I've never done anything like this before. I play by the book, always have. Orders are just like laws. But this guy Colby—"

Peggy Bryce broke in. "We don't think you'll take advantage, that's what A.J.'s trying to say. You won't go out of bounds if we ask for a little help."

"Vail didn't do it," said Lincoln. "I think the old lady was right. I think it was a woman, one who had something to do with both this guy McKelvie and Jenny Vail. If I had enough time and manpower, I could prove it. But not if I'm off the case and working on something halfway across town. What do you say?"

It was Alex who spoke up first, quietly and without fanfare, her careful British accent poignantly clear in that room still heavy with the absence of Vangie. She reached for David's hand.

"I think we must," she said. "Somebody simply must."

Elva nodded, the tears rolling down her round cheeks, and Freddy Adler, paler than ever, raised his fist like Rocky, counting himself in. We were, it appeared, a team.

"Okay," said Lincoln. "I'll give you what we've got. First, the white Aerostar was found last night, ditched over in Jersey, just outside Belleville. No license plates, interior doused with gas and torched, burned clean. Ash analysis looks like she burned up all the clothes, too."

I sighed and exchanged frustrated glances with Merriman. "So much for those confounded boots," I said.

"No prints on the outside of the van," Lincoln continued.

"Those damn orange gloves," I growled.

Peggy Bryce took up the recital. "Hair and fiber team got nothing of any interest from either McKelvie's body or Jenny Vail's. We never had time to get that tape of the anonymous phone call to the lab for a voice reconstruction, and I don't suppose the lab up in Ainsley . . ."

"No such coconuts," I told her with some regret. "Nothing fancy in the budget up in our neck of the woods."

"Well," said Lincoln, "at least we found Jenny Vail's gun. It turned up at a pawnshop in the West Village, registration number and all. No prints, brought in by an old guy in his seventies, lives in the neighborhood. No connection to McKelvie or Mrs. Vail. Says he found the gun in a trash can outside his building and figured it was worth a buck."

"Some bag lady's probably keeping her tinfoil collection in that fancy beaded purse of Jenny's right now," I said with a sigh.

"Our friend Boots probably thought the bag contained something incriminating," said Merriman. "Or, she might've been laying down a false scent. Fancy footwork, that sort of thing."

"More likely just an impulse," said Peggy Bryce. "A kind of reflex, when it was over. Killers do it sometimes, pick up something from their victim's house—a magazine, a scarf. We find things stuffed in their pockets and they don't even realize they've got them, where they came from."

"And then, naturally, we get accused of engineering a plant so we can frame them," said Lincoln. "Next item. We managed to get a report on those two notes—the one on the wine and the anonymous tip that was handed in to the Task Force? Electronic machines are tough to track, but there are some new methods—impression, type of print wheel. The lab says they were typed on the same machine, and it looks like it was a Murayama. Recharges like a lap-top but you can print out right on the spot. They're pretty common, so it probably won't be much help. The handwriting, that signature of Mrs. Vail's? It was traced, just like we figured."

"A classic red herring," said Merriman. "All that fiddling about with David and Winnie just after the deaths delayed things long enough for Boots to dig herself in."

"And naturally," said Sarah, "those two notes and the anonymous calls got the pair of them mixed up in it. But why sign Jenny's name to the note and send the white roses as though they were from her?"

"To make it look as though the whole thing revolved around Jenny and McKelvie, those meetings of theirs," said David. "I never got close enough to hear any more than fragments, as I've already told you. Whatever it was, I think I was being led down a blind alley. Red herring, as Eddie says."

"There was nothing in McKelvie's apartment," said Lincoln. "Our guys went over it with a tooth comb last night; they found zip."

"The man had no personality," I complained. "Nothing to hang your hat on."

"He worked on the fringe of publishing," said Merriman, "and Mrs. Vail was involved in publishing all her life. Married an editor, from an old publishing family. Stands to reason our killer is involved in publishing, too."

"McKelvie stopped every morning at the Orthodox Cathedral, where Cynthia was mugged. He and Jenny met in the Shakespeare Garden, where there's a memorial to Cynthia." I leaned back on the ratty couch and lit a Turkish Delight, the disparate pieces of the puzzle whirling in my head.

" 'I wasn't any use to her.' " David sat fiddling with *The Black Palace,* running an impatient thumbnail along its spine. "That's what he said to Jenny. He must've meant Cynthia. Whatever it was, whatever brought them together, it has something to do with Cynthia's death. McKelvie lived like a penitent. You ought to see that room upstairs. He had nothing, seemed to want nothing."

"You think he was responsible for Cynthia's death?" asked Alex.

"I think he thought so. Maybe he'd been taught to think so, by Jenny or by the killer. Boots came to see him, too, between Christmas and New Year's. She forced him into making those phone calls. Vangie said he made them right after he played that record. He'd receive a phone call himself at nine, then play the record, then phone me."

"Record?" Now we were in Sarah's bailiwick. "What sort of record?"

"Classical," said Freddy Adler. "A mass, I think. Earlier than

Beethoven. Maybe Haydn. Not Handel. Not Brahms. Definitely not Bach."

"Can you hum it?" she said.

"I can do better than that. Hold on," he said, and dashed out of the apartment. In a minute the sound of his flute echoed down the stairwell, clear and piercing.

"Mozart," said Sarah. "The *Missa Lacrimosa*. Lovely." She closed her eyes. "He's very good. Mr. Adler, I mean."

"Lincoln, can we get into that apartment of McKelvie's?" I had an idea, and it was just worth taking a look-see.

He fished out the keys—obviously having come prepared—and we all trooped upstairs, to be joined by Freddy Adler, flute in hand.

The apartment was just as David had described it, barren and monastic except for the many books stacked with methodical precision, and the heavily laden cabinet of records. On a cheap pine table was an old-fashioned portable record player not unlike Merriman's, next to it a small touch-tone telephone.

Sarah was already on her knees searching through the record albums when Eddie switched on the stereo, turned up the dial to Loud, then took the phone off the hook.

"He'd just finished playing the Mozart mass, you see, and this machine has no automatic shutoff. Perhaps the music nerved him for the telephone calls, who knows? At any rate, he picked up the telephone and simply didn't lift the needle off when the record ended. David, is that the sound you heard in the background?"

Davy nodded. "But what about that doctored tape he played into the phone? You think Boots had time to find it and destroy it?"

"If there was a tape," said Elva Ziegler from the doorway, "there must've been a tape recorder." She sank down on what was left of the slashed mattress and tucked her feet under her, fingers pressing her temples, eyes squeezed shut. "Nobody make a sound," she said. "The aura is reddish-brown, and very angry."

We looked at each other and blinked. Sarah, ever the Doubting Thomas, pulled an album from the record cabinet triumphantly. *"Missa Lacrimosa!"* she cried.

"Sshhhh! I'm losing the aura!" ordered Elva. Freddy only smiled and shook his head.

Sarah pulled the record, still in its white paper sleeve, out of the cover. She reached inside the sleeve for the album, then took the thing by the corners and shook its contents onto her lap. Half a dozen folded sheets of computer paper fell out, along with three pieces of heavy bond, cream-colored and embossed with a dark blue logo.

"Doesn't look much like Mozart," I said, peering at the bond sheets and handing them over to Merriman. "E. P. Alexander's letterhead, Philip Vail's signature."

"And addressed to Jenny's producer," chimed in Merriman. "The Grand Panjandrum with the Little Knob on Top—Steven Stanway."

"The other two letters are the same, Philip to Stanway, on Alexander letterhead," said Sarah. "But they don't make any sense."

Merriman frowned. "David, have a look, why don't you? Read them out loud."

"Brown!" cried Elva, and unfolding from her guru posture she began to sweep the room like a small, tubby mine detector, while David read Philip Vail's letters.

" 'Dear Mr. Stanway. Your offer of March twenty-fifth, 1986 has been received and noted and is being discussed by the parties concerned. Transfer of funds would have to take place before the close of business on April tenth. Will advise.' " David looked up from the expensive paper. "A deal was going down. Maybe Stanway wanted to buy TV rights to some book on the Alexander list. Would he have dealt directly with Philip Vail?"

I shook my head. "Subsidiary rights don't go through Editorial, they go into a separate bin altogether. 'Transfer of funds?' That means big money, and quick. A major deal closed and paid for in just over two weeks. Sounds like Alexander needed money and Stanway was offering to provide it. Read the next one."

" 'Your offer has been accepted, with provisos as previously stated.'" He unfolded the third letter. "'Your payment has been received.'"

"All terribly vague," said Alex.

"Purposely so," Merriman agreed. "More of Philip's well-known discretion."

"What about the computer printouts?" Sarah scowled at the things and handed them to me.

"Don't look in this direction," I grumbled, and handed them over to Julian Stockfish. He pulled a pair of Ben Franklin specs from his pocket and studied the washed-out type.

"They're sales figures from Crocodile Books on Jenny Vail's novels," he said. *"Unsuitable Evidence, What Dark Beast, The Mourning Bride."*

"What Dark Beast?" I said. "That was her first best-seller, hit the list the day after it hit the stores."

Julian nodded. "Looks like it. Right off the chart. Same with the next one, *The Mourning Bride.* The other one, though, *Unsuitable Evidence,* the one before *Dark Beast?* Nothing fancy, just respectable. That must've been one helluva beast. It put her right up there with P. D. James and that woman with the three names."

"Brown, brown, reddish brown," muttered Screwy Elva, now working her way along McKelvie's obsessively neat bookshelves.

"Was *What Dark Beast* really that remarkable?" asked David. "Why did it shoot onto the best-seller list that way?"

"I can't answer that," I said. "Maybe our killer could, though. And maybe Philip Vail and Mr. Stanway can, too. I'm seeing Philip this afternoon at Jenny's place. With a little inducement of the right kind, Stanway might just consent to join us."

"Inducement? You mean blackmail."

David was smiling for the first time that morning. After his weeks of nervous strain, we'd all been afraid Vangie Glickman's death would knock him off the edge, but the opposite seemed to be the case. He was, of course, sorry—as we all were. But there was a new sense of control, an almost professional calm about him as we discussed and deliberated. He was waiting for the right time to make his move, exactly as he'd been trained to wait for the proper cue.

"Brown!" Elva Ziegler exploded, jumping up and down and whirling like a dervish in the middle of the room, clutching something small and metallic to her considerable bosom. "It was right there, under the brown spot where the water pipes dripped through the ceiling! A brown aura, just like I said, rusty brown! Hung on a nail right behind the radiator!"

It was a small tape player, the cheap kind you buy in discount stores, with a plastic carrying strap attached to a lanyard hook on one corner. The building had heat registers from a central gas furnace in the usual place along the baseboards, but the old, aluminum-painted steam radiators had been left in place, though obviously disused. Vangie's had held a straggly pot of Boston ivy and McKelvie had used his for an auxiliary bookshelf. Nobody but Elva had thought to look behind it! Proud as punch, she handed the recorder to Peggy Bryce and then parked herself stolidly on the mattress again, arms folded like The Genie in the Jug. As for the rest of us, we could only gape.

Sergeant Bryce looked at Lincoln and frowned; whichever weary cop had searched this place and missed what Elva's aura had homed in on was in for it now, and no mistake. She switched on the tape.

"Mr. Cromwell?" said the mechanical voice. *"David? Someone is going to die. You can stop it. Someone is going to die. You can stop it. You."*

Peggy was about to switch it off, but I shook my head. "Let it play," I said. We all stood listening, and for a long time there was nothing but the slight hum of the empty tape and our own tense breathing. Then suddenly there came another sort of sound; though it seemed to mean nothing to any of the others, I knew it instantly, and so did Eddie.

It was the raucous honk of Hazel Hancock's laughter.

18

We returned to David and Alex's apartment for lunch, and while the others were finishing up with coffee and brandy in the living room, I found time at last to phone Myra Fish, my producer at WNYT.

"I left a message on your machine, Doc," she said. "Damn, I hate those things. Nobody ever answers their messages anyway."

"Naturally," I said, "what do you think they want the machine for? It's such a comfort having something mechanical to ignore. Listen, Myra—"

As usual, she plunged past me. "If I didn't hear it from Peter Jennings, I wouldn't have believed it, Doc. Jenny Vail! Because she called me Thursday morning. Actually! Thursday morning, and Thursday night you find her with two holes in her head! I tried to call you right after she hung up, but your machine wasn't on and nobody was answering."

I groaned silently. The phone call I'd assumed was from Sheffield had been Myra, relaying Jenny's message. "I was trying on my tux," I told her. "What did Jenny want?"

"She said she'd been elected president of your mystery writers bunch, whatever the hell you call it, for next year, and she'd be making her acceptance speech at the Edgars that night. In the speech, she was going to announce something 'of great concern to all writers and book lovers.' Her exact words, Doc. And could she get you to interview her on *Bookends* the day after, so she could elaborate."

"Sounds like a publicity stunt."

"That's what I thought, but I called her publicist, that Vilnius broad? She didn't like the idea one bit, tried to get me to reject Jenny out of hand." Myra sniggered. "Me, reject Queen Jenny? One interview with her, we could get three grants out of the National Endowment. I told her I'd get back to them after I'd talked to you, and Jenny was supposed to contact you at the Edgars. You know more about the rest than I do."

"She didn't give you a clue to what it was all about?"

"Zilch," said Myra. "Sorry. What can I tell you, Doc? You gotta answer your telephone better."

I hung up and was about to join the others in the living room when I decided Myra might be right. I'd never used the thing, but when we caved in to necessity and bought the abominable answering machine that takes up space in our front hall, it came with something called a remote beeper. Out of habit, like some primitive tribesman who refuses to go out without his bear-claw necklace, I stuck the beeper in my pants pocket every time we left town. Now I fished it out and dialed our number back in Ainsley. Personally, I was a lot more comfortable with Elva Ziegler and her multicolored auras, but I let the magic of electronics do its stuff for once.

The first message turned out to be from Hilda Costello. Even before she gave tongue, I recognized the glottal click of her adenoids kicking in.

"Winnie," she said, "what the hell's Krish got on Tommy? Something's in the wind and I want to know about it, but the little toot won't tell me. Clue me in, Winnie, and once I've won the award, I'll see what I can do for you."

The frequency of the next voice always seems to convey itself to me by some mystic means, in the manner of dog whistles. I heard it, I could've sworn, even before the next message began. The voice, naturally, was Sheffield's.

"Winston," he whimpered. He was practically whispering, which meant he was calling from home, where Lady Di or one of their two matching daughters, Frick and Frack, might overhear him.

"Winston, I must talk to you. Urgently. At your earliest convenience. Ppppppppp-prison is involved. Ch-ch-ch-charges and sssssssss-serious allegations, and—Ooooooooh, God." He gulped a time or two and sniffled. "We'll forget about that broken window in your office, Winston," he said. "Forget about everything. Pleeeeease."

"Oh, for pity's sake, Sheffield," I said, forgetting for a moment that he was only a tape recording. "If you're going in for a life of crime, pull up your socks and stop sniveling."

But by that time another message had begun. It was my new editor, Tracy Valentine.

"Sorry to call you, Henrietta," she said. "I don't usually work on Saturdays myself. But I got a phone call from Steven Stanway's personal assistant last night. He wants to buy your Winchester Hyde books for a TV series. I told him to contact Emily Brownson. I hope that's okay. Also, the legal office called me yesterday. Your contract is ready and they're sending it out by Federal Express. You'll have it on Monday." She paused. "Funny thing. They're sending the advance check with it. They almost never send the money until at least three months after the contract is received. Cash flow. Anyway, congratulations."

I hung up feeling dazed. After so many months of stalling, the Dutchman had at last decided to give me not only my contract but my advance! And in the same breath Stanway had made a bid for the rights to my books!

It was too much of a coincidence. Something was going on in the citadels of power and I seemed to be smack in the middle of it—thanks, I had to believe, to Jenny Vail, Hazel, or whoever had involved David and me in this bloody mystery. I paged through the phone book until I found the number of the Waldorf. Steven Stanway's personal assistant answered.

"Yes, Miss Slocum," he said. "Thanks for getting back to us. Mr. Stanway's in a meeting at the moment. Can you hold?"

"Sherman," I said. "The name is Winston Sherman."

"Surely not," he insisted. "Henrietta Slocum, the Winchester Hyde books?"

"Winston?"

The voice was softer than when I'd heard him call Jenny's name across the Versailles Ballroom, but the timbre was the same, that carefully casual inflection of the man trying to wear his power lightly—but not so lightly that it doesn't show. I could almost see Steven Stanway grab the phone and push his confused young assistant out of the way.

"Winston," he repeated. "Glad you got my message. Always been a fan, you know. Can we do lunch, say, two, two-thirty? The Algonquin?"

"Tell you what," I said, calling his bluff. "Let's have a little chalk talk instead. Say, two-thirty, Jenny Vail's apartment. I expect you know where it is."

In my mind's eye, I saw the piggy eyes narrow and the tanned fingers stroke the forked Mephistopheles beard.

"Two-thirty," he said, and hung up without a quibble.

Sarah and Eddie were headed back to Ainsley in Alex's commodious black Oldsmobile, a napping Gemma in the back seat, by the time David and I got to Jenny Vail's apartment, just after two o'clock that Saturday afternoon. The building was old, one of the great houses built during the boom years of the early twentieth century by the kings of industries then rising, now mostly fallen to the Arabs, the Japanese, the West Germans. Oilmen, steel barons, publishing moguls had poured their money into these square stone palaces; built in an era of ostentation no subtler than our own, they had at least expressed their materialism in far better and more enduring taste.

Jenny Vail's apartment was on the third and fourth floors of an old mansion, now divided into four large duplex dwellings. It overlooked the park, today burnt free of mist by a bright April sun, its newly leafing trees more gold than green in the afternoon light. David and I were shown into a huge living room with forest green walls and mahogany wainscoting; a great carved mahogany mantel rose halfway to the beamed ceiling, and before the cold hearth, his long, elegant body perched upon an insufficient needlepoint-covered bench, sat Philip Vail.

He rose when we entered and came to meet us in the middle of the thick Aubusson carpet that formed the focus of the room. Vail seemed comfortable here despite his years of separation from his wife, and I couldn't help thinking that it seemed more his sort of place than Jenny's.

"Thank you, Winston, for coming," he said. "I know Hazel dragged you into this. She's been very kind, but really, it's no good."

He motioned to a handsome camelbacked divan and David sat down on it, while I chose a sturdy modern armchair opposite Vail's bench. He didn't sit for a moment or two; he stood like a figure in a relief, his pale skin and gray hair caught by the light through the four high windows overlooking the park. The darkness of the rich woods, the deep color of the walls, the shelved volumes in their aged leather covers made the room converge upon him, the lonely focus of its mystery.

"This was my uncle's house at one time," he said. He sat down gracefully on the bench, took the ivory cigarette holder from the pocket of his jacket, put a cigarette in it, and stuck it into the corner of his mouth without lighting it. The ice blue eyes swept over me, then over David, then back again, like searchlights in the dark room. "Uncle Marcus got a bit above himself, you know, so much fame, and when he inherited the Vail fortune back in the mid-Twenties, he bought old E. P. Alexander's mansion—this place. The old man was quite batty by that time, poor soul, and I always thought Uncle Marcus rather took advantage. Bought a piece of the firm, too, at a bargain price, but of course he lost that in the Crash of '29. He managed to keep the house, though, right through the Depression and the Second World War. Amazing."

"When was it made into flats?" David asked.

Vail looked over at Davy as though he'd just materialized there. We were present only in some remote corner of his mind where the routine necessities of living still survived untended, in spite of him.

"When? Oh, well, old Marcus died in the Fifties, you see.

House was part of his estate. Family couldn't agree to sell it. There were four heirs—my father, his two sisters, and an uncle. Couldn't stand one another, couldn't possibly have lived in the one house all together. So they had it made into the four apartments. And then, of course, one by one they simply—died. I'm the last. No sons. Strangers in the other flats now." The quiet, steady voice drifted.

"So this apartment of Jenny's is really yours?"

"Legally, yes," he said. "I have a little place of my own, now, over on East Seventy-ninth."

"You must've resented it a bit," I said. "Family home and all, having to surrender it to her when you split up."

"Oh," he replied softly. "Oh, no. She loved it so. Suited her, you know. Felt protected, old things around her. Fortress. I can live anywhere. One doesn't need much."

I took a deep breath and plunged in. "You didn't kill Jenny."

"Oh," he said. "No."

"But you've made the police believe you did. Unless we can find the real killer, they're going to charge you, you know that."

Vail's face was impassive, but the pale eyes flickered.

"He thought he was protecting me," said a woman's voice from the far end of the room. The door to what must've been Jenny's study was open, and in it stood Lydia Hallam, Philip's lover and his wife's longtime editor. She was tall, graying, her hair brushed back from her high forehead in a simple pageboy style. She wore spectacles with thin black wire rims and stepped with the unsteadiness of dim vision as she crossed the rich carpet to join us. "Philip thought I might have killed Jenny, you see," she said.

"That isn't true, Lydia," he insisted. We all rose when she joined us, but Vail didn't sit again. He stood behind his lover, who took his place on the fireside bench. "You couldn't kill anyone, most especially Jenny."

"I would've liked to," she said. It was perfectly matter-of-fact, no drama about it. "Sometimes, I would've liked to. She was so many people, Jenny. So many levels and layers and complications. The Iron Lung, that's what I used to call her. We couldn't quite breathe without her, but she was a sort of benevolent prison for us, too. She used everybody, discarded anybody who wasn't of use, but when she loved anyone, she never let go. She claimed the soul."

"Even your soul?" I said.

Lydia Hallam smiled. "Oh yes. Even mine. A year ago she talked about switching to another publisher and I fought for her. I didn't want to lose her. Not just for the sake of my career, either. I have other successful authors. She was—Jenny."

"She used people. That's what your grandson Gregory accused her of at the Edgars that night, Philip. 'You used me,' he told her. Did you believe your grandson might have murdered McKelvie and Jenny?"

Philip Vail fumbled in a Chinese lacquer box on a table under the window, found a match, and lighted his cigarette at last. "Gregory has been undergoing counseling ever since his mother's death," he said. "My daughter, Cynthia. After she was killed, he dropped out of college, came here to live with Jenny. It wasn't the best thing for either of them. The boy was convinced his mother was deliberately murdered, you see. Began to see plots everywhere, aimed at himself, his grandmother, me. Paranoia of the classic kind, that was the diagnosis."

David got up and moved over to where Vail was standing. "Was the counseling any use?" he said. "Was there any improvement?"

"At times. Antidepressive medications—you know the sort of thing. They don't erase the problem. 'The centre cannot hold.' " Vail's blue eyes closed and he inhaled deeply, then breathed out a cloud of smoke that hung in the dimness of the room like fog. "There are no solutions, these days, are there?" he said, his hand resting gently on Lydia's shoulder. "We continue, that's all."

"Philip," I said, "I'm a plain man. I'll speak plainly. What the hell did Jenny have to do with this man McKelvie? We know it's a fake name he took two years ago, the same year your daughter was killed. We know Jenny's been seeing him, making plans about something. We know she was afraid of somebody. We know your confession was a fake, meant to protect somebody or something, or

just to stall for time. Tell us what you know, right from the beginning."

Vail drew a breath and tossed the cigarette into the cold fireplace. "No," he whispered.

"Philip . . ." said Lydia Hallam.

Suddenly David turned and grasped Vail by the arms. They
stood locked together, eyes fixed on one another's faces. David's
slender fingers bit into the soft material of Philip's coat and I knew
he must be causing pain, wanted to cause it.

"Listen to me," David said. His voice was soft, the anger too
intense for noise to relieve it, but his words were very precise, the
consonants stinging and sharp. "Listen to me, Philip. Your wife and
McKelvie had their secret and it killed them. Perhaps they deserved
it, perhaps not. But it was their secret, their lives they risked. An
old woman is dead now. She died last night, because of them and
their plans. *She* read Yeats, too, Philip. *She* lost a daughter, too.
That old woman died last night, suddenly, in the dark. I held her. I
had to wash her blood off me before I could sleep. It's on you now,
Philip. Look closely. Turn on a bright light and strip naked and look
at what it's cost, this game of Jenny's. This game of yours."

He released Vail's arms and the older man took a step backward, reeling slightly, as though he might fall. He didn't, merely
moved to the couch where David had been sitting and motioned for
Lydia to join him. They sat with hands clenched together as Philip
Vail began his story.

"Believe me. It was never a game. Not to Jenny. Not to me. But
you were right about Gilbert McKelvie," he said. "His name was
really Lewis Canfield. He was my daughter's husband, Gregory's
father. They were divorced, oh, only a year or so after the boy was
born. Canfield wanted to write—well, everyone thinks he can write,
don't you find? Every professor with a first chapter in the back of
the filing cabinet. Every newspaper hack with an idea for the Great
American Novel. It's part of the myth, I suppose. Every little boy
can be President. Every little girl with blonde curls can be a movie
star. Every fool who can type out his name on a title page can write

the Great American Novel. Canfield could write, but he couldn't write *fiction*. Excellent observer, great critical sense, real love of books, but a born journalist, not a novelist, not in a million years, poor thing. He battered at it for years, supported himself as he could, had jobs at half a dozen papers and magazines around town, good jobs. But he lost them all, eventually. Couldn't surrender the delusion of himself as the new Scott Fitzgerald, you see." He paused, drew a breath, as though he had reached a decision. Then he went on. "In the end I gave him a billet at Alexander's, reading the slush pile. We still do read unsolicited stuff, you know."

"You say your daughter divorced him after only a couple of years of his literary obsessions. But you didn't. Divorce him, I mean. You seem to have followed his ups and downs rather closely, under the circumstances. You let him stay at Alexander's?"

Vail blinked, surprised. "Let him? Of course. I told you, he was a good judge of a book. Of course he stayed." He lighted another cigarette. "He wasn't strong. But I liked the man."

Just then the doorbell rang and the housekeeper who had let us in admitted Steven Stanway. In the dark elegance of the huge room his California tan looked sallow and his expensive casual clothes looked cheap and coy; he stood in the middle of the antique carpet like a kid who's gotten himself up in some outlandish outfit and presented himself at his mother's bridge party, hoping to be noticed.

"I asked Mr. Stanway to join us," I told Vail. "I thought he might be able to contribute something."

Vail merely nodded and Stanway took the bench by the fireplace. Philip Vail continued his story.

"About five years ago," he said, "Alexander began to be pressured to sell. We're a small house, you know, family business, and old-fashioned. No horror fiction, no romances, no brutality of the modern sort. People being flayed alive, necrophilia—that sort of thing. Tasteful mysteries in the Agatha Christie vein, gardening books, cookbooks, the odd bit of self-help. Biography, history. Literary fiction when irresistible and when the budget permitted. Well, naturally, we couldn't compete. Began to hear the drumbeats in the distance. A buy-out by that amazing oaf of a Dutchman who's just bought out your friends at Garner and Sloan—that was the threat. We had a choice, of course."

"A merger? That's the usual alternative, isn't it?" I asked. "Two or three smaller houses band together to resist the invader?"

"Mmm," he said. "Taking on one another's debts, inevitably being forced to drop a large number of valued authors, becoming embroiled in constant bickering about policy—what to publish, how much, how often. The administration grows out of all control, the old experienced hands are forced out or leave in disgust, the place fills up with well-meaning, undereducated, completely undisciplined children. Nobody knows what's going on anywhere. I couldn't let that happen."

"So you had to find the money somewhere else."

He nodded. "I put in everything I could, all the Vail money that wasn't in trust accounts and so forth. Sold most of the famous amethysts."

"Yes," said David, "what about the amethysts? Why did Jenny wear them?"

"Sorry," said Philip, "I thought you knew. The Vail family made its fortune back in the nineteenth century from the importation and wholesaling of semiprecious stones. Quite a fad just then among the genteel sort of woman for garnet necklaces and earrings, amethyst brooches. It was mainly through India in the beginning, but then the old man took on partners in Africa, South America. Supplied Tiffany with most of his stones at one time. Some of the settings were worth a fortune, simply as historical artifacts. As to the amethysts, my great-grandmother had a passion for them, had every really exceptional stone set by Louis Tiffany, some done by Fabergé. They became a sort of trust fund for the family. A lot of them went during the Depression, of course. But what was left passed on to the heirs. That dress Jenny was wearing had been my grandmother's, made by Worth. Jenny had it modernized a bit, neckline and so forth. It was my wedding gift to her. She wore it as a gesture—sentimental, sometimes, and sometimes hoping to plague me."

"Which was it on the night she died?" I asked.

Vail shook his head. "Bit of both. Usually was."

"And the pendant she was wearing? It was Cynthia's, wasn't it?" I remembered seeing it in the news photograph I'd looked up.

"My mother left a number of her pieces to Cynthia," replied Philip Vail. "Felt they'd give her a sort of insurance policy, in case Canfield couldn't support her. Cynthia managed quite well on her own, as it turned out. But when she was killed, those pieces went to Jenny. The rings, the pendant, some earrings. She wore them obsessively, ever since Cynthia died."

"She felt guilty," said Lydia Hallam suddenly. "She never really got along with Cynthia, Philip, and you know it. That's why she couldn't accept—"

He laid a gentle hand on her arm. "I'll finish about the money, first, shall I?" he said. "As I say, I was determined to prevent Van Twist's takeover, and I sold all the stones I could lay my hands on, except for Jenny's, of course. The real estate, as well. But not this house. Couldn't sell that. But it wasn't enough to stave him off." He stood up again and began to pace. "I wanted things to stay the same, you see," he said, stopping in front of my chair. "These changes, they're wrong. Not just aesthetically, though cluttering up the world with muck is bad enough in itself. The damage to the communal mind and so on. But the marketplace they've created is false, don't you see? The junk revolution. It's a false front that can't sustain weight, and in time it will die of its own idiocy. If we stake everything on it, none of us will survive."

"So when Mr. Stanway, here, offered to bail you out, you accepted," I said.

Steven Stanway barely batted an eye, just shifted his weight a bit on the needlepoint bench and brushed a speck of invisible dust off his knee. Vail looked at me, then at Stanway. Then he went on.

"You've found the papers?" he asked. I nodded. "I might've known you would. Jenny managed to get hold of them somehow. No idea how." At last he sat down again beside Lydia Hallam. "I didn't seem to have a choice."

"It was perfectly legal." Stanway found his voice at last. "It's been done often enough in my business. We simply arranged things to everybody's satisfaction."

"You decided to buy Jenny's Lieutenant Hilliard books for a series, about the time she published *Unsuitable Evidence,*" I said. "But you didn't just want a series. You wanted a hit. Her books sold well, but they weren't instant best-sellers yet. So you concocted a little plan."

"There was precedent for it," he protested. "Plenty of precedent."

"Oh, I believe you," I agreed. "On the other hand, the reading public, the viewing public, might've felt they'd been played for suckers if they'd found out that you pushed Jenny's next novel onto the lists yourself. When *What Rough Beast* was printed, you made a little deal with Philip, here, didn't you? You offered him the money to hold out against the Van Twist buy-out if he would do—what? Turn the book into a runaway best-seller, make it hit the *Times* list the day after it reached the stores?" I shook my head. "But as I understand it, that list is made up from the nominations of a selected number of bookstores scattered across the country, kept very hush-hush, even at the *Times,* and changed at random intervals, so nobody can fiddle with it and it can never be fixed. Unless . . ."

Lydia Hallam shoved her glasses up on her nose. "Unless you get hold of the list of bookstores ahead of time." She looked at Philip, a trace of a smile on her face. It was the end of something, an end she had waited out for far too many years.

Vail saw it coming too. We'd gone too far to turn back now. "The arrangement was that I would secure the information, the precious list of bookstores to be polled for the week the book appeared. Steven, here, would provide the money. Lydia would distribute it through the Crocodile sales representatives in various parts of the country."

"And it worked like a charm," I said.

Philip nodded. "*What Rough Beast* hit the best-seller list the day after it appeared. We agreed to a percentage of the show's profits for the first year and a flat fee, enough to fend off the buy-out. Steven, here, paid the money to a liaison chosen by myself, the same man who had secured the list of bookstores from the *Times* offices when I asked him. He was a newspaperman looking for a job; he'd worked for the *Times* before. He still had friends there. He was a likeable man, a good judge of a book, and the book editor was swamped."

"So you found yourself a ferret and sent him down the hole and he brought you back the list of polled bookstores," I said. And this, I thought miserably, was such stuff as dreams were made on.

"A ferret," said Vail. "A mole, if you like. He also, as I said, received the agreed-upon payment from Mr. Stanway. He then passed the check into a slush account and eventually into the E. P. Alexander finance office."

"To preserve the reputation of an old and honored firm," said David. "In effect, you fixed the list through espionage and then laundered the money."

"You can't launder clean money," Steven Stanway insisted with a smile. "Nothing was ever proven. Even the *Times* couldn't get together enough evidence against our man to press charges. They were suspicious, of course, and they fired him four days after the best-seller list came out. But there were no charges. Nothing in the papers. It was a perfectly ordinary business deal."

"That," I growled, "depends on the business. The mole, the man who infiltrated the *Times* for you? The man who funneled that money into the Alexander account? The man who was a born journalist and had worked off and on at half a dozen papers around town? The man who was an excellent judge of books? It was your former son-in-law, wasn't it, Philip," I said. "It was Gilbert McKelvie, of course."

"Lewis Canfield, yes." Vail's cool blue eyes looked across at Stanway but seemed to see nothing. He was walking again down that long hall, hands cuffed and helpless. "I used him," he said softly.

"What happened when Jenny found out exactly how she suddenly became a best-selling author?" I said.

Stanway laughed. It wasn't the sort of laugh you'd care to hear just before you settled down for a night's sleep.

"Your naïveté is a real delight, Winston," he said. " 'When Jenny found out?' The whole plan was Jenny's *idea*. She engineered it from the beginning, with the help of that publicist woman of hers. And I must say she played it beautifully afterward, as though her great success came as a huge surprise. Just the right amount of modesty. A marvelous performance."

I ignored him and turned to Philip. "Jenny knew?" I'd figured this was the information she'd planned to announce to the world in her acceptance speech and elaborate later on my *Bookends* program. I could picture Jenny doing an exposé. But a confession? "She knew about McKelvie's involvement? Canfield's, that is."

Vail didn't look at me. "For three years after our little arrangement, there was no trouble. Jenny's place as a best-selling author was established, the television series did well. Then Cynthia somehow got wind of it. Perhaps Lewis told her, I don't know. My daughter felt strongly about the politics of power in this country. She wrote about it often." There was pride in Philip Vail's soft voice. "Something of a crusader," he said. "Disapproved of her mother's manipulations and so on. Apparently she intended exposing our arrangement in one of her articles. Then she was killed."

He paused, drew a breath. Lydia Hallam took his hands in hers, drew them to her, let them go. His long fingers brushed across her cheek, slipped to her shoulder, lay still. The simplicity, the open affection between them was, I thought, a thing nobody—not even Philip Vail—could've had with Jenny.

"I told you about Gregory," said Philip. "From the beginning, no matter that there wasn't a shred of evidence to support it, he believed his mother's death was planned. In time, Jenny came to believe it, too. I think she had to. She couldn't accept the—the casual—the random—"

He stood for no particular reason, his hands in front of him, fingers spread against a wall invisible to the rest of us.

"She was a writer. She made a plot of it," he said dully. "She convinced poor Lewis he was in danger, too, and he went into hiding. I saw to it he still got work, paid the rent on that little flat of his uptown. I tried to talk to him. But he was a ruin long before that, and then after Cynthia died, he simply withdrew. He listened only to Jenny."

"She'd decided I engineered the whole thing, you see, Winnie," said Stanway. "Not the deal, but Cynthia's death."

I fixed him with a look. "And did you?"

"Why should I? Because of that story of Cynthia's? Who do you think would've printed it? We were an immense success by that time. Nothing we did was any more than intelligent business practice, the sort of thing a hundred companies do a hundred times a day in one form or another. And let's say the worst happened and the story was run. Let's say the great American public decided it had been foxed. You think they'd have turned off the TV set when good old Lieutenant Hilliard came on next Friday night? You think they'd have stopped buying Jenny's books because they'd been had? Hell, man, the sales would've gone sky high! Nothing delights John Q. Public more than a wheeler-dealer. Look at Trump. Look at Iacocca. Look at Murdoch. That article would've been damn good publicity, it might've given our ratings a shot in the arm. We could always settle out of court."

"All right," I said. "Let me put this in plain English. Jenny couldn't accept the stupid brutality of her daughter's death, and out of her guilt, her pain, her disgust with the sort of world she saw around her and put into her books, the world she knew she was helping to create, she constructed a rationale for Cynthia's murder."

"She needed to punish herself, you see," said Vail softly. "She needed to believe she was somehow responsible. It was she who concocted our bargain in the first place, she who profited most obviously from it."

"She had to be the center of the world." Lydia Hallam's voice cracked as she spoke, the words carved into the soft dark of the handsome room. "She couldn't bear it, not being in control."

"And she dragged poor Lewis along with her," said Vail. "He was simply—insufficient. If Cynthia hadn't died . . . ." He squatted on the hearth to pick up a match, then turned on his heel, crouching there in the shadows, his light eyes wide with despair. "He killed the lot of us, Winston. The monster. The thing out of the dark that came for Cynthia. Knowledge, talent, taste, beauty, youth—it's all at his mercy. He's still out there, you know. That's what the police tell me. Waiting. Resting. Gathering strength. That's what Jenny couldn't accept."

"So she invented a way to deal with it. And you confessed to her murder. I still don't quite fathom why. To protect the boy, Gregory? Surely you know he loves you. Anyone could see that when you were together that night at dinner. Losing you might very well destroy him. Was it Miss Hallam, here, you thought you were protecting? The police haven't involved her in the conspiracy charge. Surely she had an alibi."

"She does," said Stanway. "Lydia and I were talking over Jenny's attempt to break her contract for the series. I tried to nab Jenny, but as you know she wouldn't speak to me, she broke away and disappeared. I cornered Lydia and the Vilnius woman, hoping to find a way to calm Jenny down. We were together from the time you and Jenny left me until you stepped up to the podium to announce her death."

"And Gregory had gone home," said Lydia Hallam. "He came straight back here when he left the Edgars. Philip slipped out during the early part of the ceremony and phoned Miss Redmond, the housekeeper. Tell them, Philip."

"Yes," he said. "The boy stormed in here shortly after eight-fifteen and went to his room. I found him there when I came to tell him about—his grand-mother's death."

"In spite of what he said at the Edgars, he must've loved her very much," I suggested. "Having lived here with her, depending on her since his mother was killed."

Vail glanced at me sharply. "Shall I tell you what he said when I told him she was dead? He said, 'Will I get the money now?' "

"Gregory was angry because Jenny wanted to drop the TV show," said Lydia. "She'd earmarked the money for him, told him he could have it when he turned twenty-one next year. Then she suddenly decided to give it all up, writing, everything. She only wanted the presidency of the mystery writers group as a last soap-box."

I nodded. "And my show for another one, to unmask the sup-posed murderer of her daughter. But, Philip, you were as much involved in that deal as Stanway. Surely Jenny didn't think you'd connived to kill Cynthia, too?"

"Hell, Winston," cried Stanway, "she thought what she wanted to think! Don't you get it, even now? She had no idea what she was doing. She didn't need to make sense. She wasn't—responsible!"

I studied Philip Vail's aristocratic face. "So you confessed to protect—"

"Jenny," he whispered. "Oh. Yes."

19

The next day was Sunday, warm and bright and feeling like a real spring morning once the young sun had burnt the lingering night-time mist away again. We all slept late, making up for lost time, and I had just toddled downstairs, headed for the kitchen to scare up a makeshift brunch, when the phone rang. I wanted like the dickens to ignore the thing. I wanted a quiet Sunday without murderers in the bushes, without suspicions, and most of all, without Sheffield.

But if I'd answered Myra Fish's phone call on the morning of the Edgars, a couple of people who were dead might still be alive. I sighed and picked up the receiver.

"Winnie?" It was Hilda Costello, operating, no doubt, on the theory that the early bird gets the Professor of the Year Award. "Winnie," she said, "I want to know why Krish is pussyfooting around after Tommy Sheffield like the Red Shadow. Every time I turn around I find Hannah quivering and Krish looking like the Prophet Mohammed with a nail in his shoe. What's up? What kind of crap is Sheffield trying to pull now?"

"Don't get your knickers in a twist, Hilda," I said. "Krish has been reading too much Wilkie Collins, that's all. Nothing to get excited about. Just think about something soothing and it'll go away. Listen to the birdies. Read the funny papers."

"If I win that award, Winnie," she said, "I'm going to be chairperson of the curriculum committee next fall. That's automatic, you know. I've got this idea for a multidepartmental class—film, theater, English. Shakespeare and the Media. You haven't had a Shakespeare class in a long time. I could fix that."

"Possibly." But would she? Even if I sold Sheffield up the river, La Costello might very well forget her campaign promises after she got what she wanted. Besides—confound the man—Tommy had his good points in spite of everything. Department chairmen had been made and unmade with the winning and losing of that ridiculous award—and I wasn't so sure I could blackmail Hilda! "I've got other problems at the moment, Hilda old thing," I told her. "No idea what Krish is up to."

"Crapola. You've got your finger on every nerve from here to Biloxi, you old fake. By the way, who bumped off Jenny Vail anyway?"

"I'm still taking the pulse of that one, Hilda."

"Okay. Keep the lip zipped if you want to. But I happen to know what Tommy has you scheduled to teach in the fall. Care to hear?"

"Don't tell me. Back to Freshman Remedial Composition?" A dire possibility occurred to me and I gasped for breath like a guppy. "Not Remedial Vocabulary? All those lists of Latin derivations . . . ?" It was the KP duty of the English department. I might as well be giving spelling tests!

Hilda only laughed. "It's written on the wind, partner," she said. "Unless I get the goods on the big poop, you'd better start brushing up your Latin. Let me know if you change your mind."

She hung up and I paused for a minute, considering. Then I dialed Sheffield's home number.

"Yes?" said a sleepy female voice. "Who is it?"

"Ah, Diana," I replied, pouring on the old oil by the gallons. "So long since we've spoken. Hope you had a good night. Beautiful morning, spring breeze, birds whooping it up all over the place. Is Thomas available?"

"Available? He's been tossing around all night like Orca the Killer Whale. I don't think he got to sleep until after five. I certainly didn't."

"Well, just tell him I called, ask him—"

"Don't hang up!" she commanded. "I'll wake him up. I'll be delighted to wake him up!"

I could hear her in the distance, quick-marching away, no doubt to dump a bucket of ice water on the poor sap. It was another two minutes, maybe three, before Tommy picked up the phone. His voice was muffled.

"Winston? Are you still there, Winston?"

"Oh good grief, Sheffield, turn the phone over. You're talking into the wrong end."

"Oh. Oh, I *am* sorry. Winston, I can't really—"

"I know. Can't talk with Lady Di—that is, Diana—likely to overhear. You just let me do the talking. I had a call just now from that old ward heeler, Hilda. She wants your backside in a sling, Sheffield. She wants you hung out to dry and twisting in a northeast gale. She wants—"

"I knoooooooooow," he moaned.

"She wants me to tell her what I know about you and the Floating Fund."

"Please, Winston, no! If Diana finds out—"

"Finds out what?" barked a voice in the background.

"Nothing, darling," wheedled Tommy, ever the master in his own home. "Finds out that Winston's keeping me on the phone so long on a Sunday morning. That's all."

"Tchah!" said Lady Di, and I heard her hooves clack off into the distance.

"Is she gone?" I asked him.

"There's the extension," he replied doubtfully.

"All right, Sheffield. I'll meet you in your office this afternoon, three o'clock. Do whatever you have to. Slip Diana a Mickey and lock the girls in the broom closet. Just be there. And don't be late, or I'll feed you to the fish!"

After a leisurely lunch, a nap on the sagging couch in my Cave, and a little one-on-one Wiffle ball with old Gemma in the back yard, I climbed on my bike and headed for the Ainsley cop station to meet Lloyd Agate, Vangie's blurred Polaroid tucked carefully into my back pocket. Today there was no Carlo tailing me in a squad car as I labored up and down the hills; after Vangie's death I'd managed to convince Lloyd that I was just being bullied, not seriously threatened, and since Lloyd didn't have the manpower to spare, he'd reluctantly agreed to let me fly solo. Still, it was the first time I'd been out entirely alone since before the Edgars and I caught myself jumping every time a kid yelled, "What's up, Doc?"

I found Lloyd in the photo lab, deserted on this Sunday afternoon. He was swathed in a king-sized black rubber apron, mixing some foul-smelling stuff in a developing tray. I lowered my bulk onto a stool built for a leprechaun and handed him the Polaroid. He turned on a bright overhead bulb and squinted at it.

"Think you can do anything with it?" I asked him.

"Don't know yet. Polaroids are tough. Have to backtrack. Make a negative from this, then blow it up, see what we can get." He reached up and pulled down a powerful magnifying glass on a swing-arm, the sort draftsmen use. "She said this was a woman, right?" he asked. "The old lady who got killed?"

"Would've sworn to it," I replied, "if she'd had time. I think she may even have recognized our friend Boots, just couldn't put a name to her. See anything?"

"Profile." Lloyd used a fine steel pin for a pointer under the glass, tracing the line of Boots's cheek, the temple, the bit of brownish hair that showed under the flat golfing cap she wore, the ear. It was all blurry, and even the outline of the face was impossible to judge. He shook his head ruefully. "It's a tough sucker. But let's give it a try anyhow." He switched off the bright overhead and an eerie red developing light came on. I thought Lloyd was going straight to work, but he sat down instead, on another leprechaun stool opposite mine. "Truth or consequences, Doc?" he said.

"Shoot, my friend," I told him. Then I winced. "Bad choice of words."

"Any more bullets?"

"Not in my neighborhood, no."

"That guy McKelvie? After what Stockfish told us, Lincoln ran the guy's prints. Guess what?"

"His real name was Lewis Canfield and he was Jenny Vail's former son-in-law," I said. "Philip told us about him yesterday. Apparently she had Canfield convinced that they were likely to be murder victims themselves, wanted him to come on my TV show with her and expose the man she thought murdered her daughter. She must've tried to talk him into coming to the Edgars that night and cornering me after she made her big play from the podium. That's why she gave him the seating chart with my name circled on it."

"But somebody offed him before he got a chance. Vail didn't do it?"

"Absolutely not. As for the confession, quite frankly I don't think he gives a damn whether he lives or dies himself. Doesn't care who finds out about his deal with Stanway. And as for the mighty producer, he's positively proud of it. I think he'd actually have liked Cynthia to publish her story. But Vail? Whatever life he had has slipped away from him an inch at a time. He loves Lydia Hallam, of course, though she won't be able to hold him long. But murder? Not a chance. He didn't do it."

"Neither did the Hallam woman. Neither did Stanway. Neither did the kid, Gregory."

"All got alibis?"

"Lincoln smuggled me his latest files yesterday afternoon and I checked out a few of the others. Jed Sloan spent the evening drooling over some woman from California he wants a movie contract from."

"And Stanway says Marina Vilnius was with him and Lydia."

"Rita Kovacs hasn't got an alibi, not after Stanway left her. Nobody remembers seeing her. She says she was table-hopping, but Colby's boys couldn't get a fix on her."

I swallowed hard and asked the question I had hoped I wouldn't have to ask. "What about Hazel? Hazel Hancock."

Lloyd frowned, his broad face masklike in the red light. "I don't know," he confessed. "Don't remember anything specific about her." He studied my face for a moment. "Did she do it?" he said at last.

"I hope not," I breathed.

Then it all spilled out, every contradiction, every coincidence that had made me suspect her, even the hoot of her laughter at the end of the tape in McKelvie's apartment. I hadn't intended to tell him, but Lloyd's clumsy gentleness and his invariable cool head were too much for me. When I'd finished, he tapped a huge finger on the countertop.

"I see what you mean, Doc," he said quietly. "But none of it's real evidence. Even if it convinces you, no prosecutor in the world would be fool enough to file on it."

"It *doesn't* convince me!" I said. "I know Hazel, she's an older friend of mine than even you are, Lloyd. I firmly believe this is all a huge mare's nest, the pearls and what not. Rita Kovacs is a far more likely suspect in every way. But I have to know."

He nodded, a big paw on my shoulder. "I'll work on that Polaroid, Doc," he said.

"Work hard, old friend," I told him. "Work fast."

By the time I pedaled up to the Arts and Letters Building on campus, Sheffield was already in his antique-filled private office, known to the ranks as The Old Curiosity Shop. Every time I ventured into the place, Diana had added some new trophy or adornment. The walls were hung with horse collars, ice tongs, washboards, daguerreotypes of unknown patriarchs in ormolu frames. Handwoven baskets overflowed with Tommy's paper clips and office memos; his filing cabinet was topped by a stone crock full of dry weeds of nameless species; his floor was littered with faded little rugs probably hooked by Benedict Arnold's mother in the long winter evenings. I stubbed my toe on a wooden washtub-cum-wastebasket as I came in, wished the thing to perdition, and sat down with a telltale crunch in a cane-seated rocker beside the desk. Or should I say a once-cane-seated rocker?

In the years since he took the helm of our Arts and Letters faculty, Thomas Van Doren Sheffield has undergone many changes. When first he gleamed upon our sight he was pure Yalie—sweaters tied by the sleeves round his shoulders, Top-Siders in fighting trim, convictions undiluted by such mundane details as the fact that seven out of ten of our freshmen read and wrote at what was sixth grade level before they started diddling the achievement tests. Determined to correct our archaic perceptions, he rearranged the seating in classroom and faculty meeting into a circle, indicating that we were all now equal not merely in the political but in the intellectual sense, as well—though he, of course, remained just a tad more equal than the rest of us.

After a few seasons among us, he married Lady Di, heiress apparent of the Board of Trustees, but in time Thomas grew restless. Now and again his delicate foot slipped in one direction or another —I recall to those familiar with these narratives his fling with our then-professor of Women's Studies, Ms. Alison Barnes-McGee, and his ill-advised sporting of a cut-price hairpiece made of Taiwanese goat fur. Dreaming of recaptured youth, he has settled for lording it over aging diehards like myself. Seeking power, he has entrenched himself in the routine enforcement of humdrum and insignificant tyrannies nobody really notices any longer. Imbued with personal ambition, he has sought to rise from the ashes of our disemboweled curriculum to higher idiocies, and in the main he has succeeded. Things are not what they were at Clinton, and Tommy is mostly responsible for that.

But the one thing Sheffield wants most, the reason for all his strivings, continues to elude him. Tommy Sheffield, you see, wants to be loved, and the most he's ever managed is a sort of bemused toleration.

Which is why he determined to prove himself by garnering the Professor of the Year Award this year, even though he had about as much chance of winning it as I did of walking home with that statue of Edgar Allan Poe.

When I entered The Old Curiosity Shop he was slumped over

his bird's-eye maple desk, his head on his arms like a kindergar-
tener down for his nap.

"Heads up, Thomas," I said, leaning back in the rocker. "Let's
get this over with."

He picked up his noggin and moaned slightly, then put it back
again.

"So," I said, "you've lost the Floating Fund, have you?"

"Mmmmmmmm." It was halfway between a mumble and a groan
and I took it for assent.

"Nine hundred and some dollars?"

"Mmmmmmmmm."

"You spent it wining and dining the faculty, did you?"

His head popped up. "No! Of course not! I'd never do a thing
like that, Winston. Surely you don't believe I'm a—a—"

"Thief? No, just a ninny. Well, if you didn't spend it on your
campaign, what the devil *did* you do with it? Nine hundred bucks
doesn't just dissolve, you know."

"It does if you invest it in the Western Unity Savings and Loan
of Montauk. Nine hundred sixty-seven dollars and thirty-five cents."

"But Hannah said—"

"I know. I was *supposed* to put it into the regular college account
at the Equity National. But there was this advertisement in the
Financial Times. Almost three times the interest. I thought with the
fund invested at that kind of rate there'd be enough to redecorate
the Faculty Lounge right away, and everyone would be so—so—"

"Impressed with your acumen and your colossal devotion that
they'd reward you with the Professor of the Year Award?"

"Something like that. Except—except—"

"Except the president of the Western Unity Savings and Loan of
Montauk did a bunk with the Floating Fund and a few million other
bucks and is now living in penurious exile in his condo in the
Cayman Islands."

"You read about it?"

I nodded. "Next time you find yourself tempted to think, Sheffield, bite the bullet. Resist the urge. You gambled with the faculty

funds. You cut salaries, mine included, to scrape together enough money to tart up the lounge with buckets of dry cornstalks, I suppose, and chairs made out of old grapevines. So you could show off, my heating system went to pot in the middle of winter and I couldn't even afford—" I stopped, realizing I was beating a dead horse. "You messed up, Thomas. Call a faculty meeting. Confess your sins and be publicly shriven. Replace the money from your own pocket. It's the only way."

"Of course," he cried, "don't you think I would? I'd do it in a minute. But it's a *joint account!* If I take nine hundred sixty-seven dollars and thirty-five cents out of it, Diana will want to know what it's for. 'What did you buy now, Tommy? Where is it, Tommy?' If she finds out I lost that money, Winston, I'll—I'll—I'll have to disappear, that's all. I'll have to find some cheap little place in the country and disappear."

He was right, of course. If Diana found out he'd actually been pie-eyed enough to put money into that glory hole in Montauk, Tommy's status in the home—already that of a sixth-rate power— would sink right out of sight. I got up and began to potter round the collection of piffle on the marble-topped washstand by his door.

"Where do you keep it?" I said.

"Keep what?" he mumbled, his head in his hands again.

"The brew, the bodybuilder, the stuff you knock back when Diana's daddy reads you off in front of the Board of Trustees. The booze, Sheffield. You can't face a thing like this on raspberry-flavored Perrier."

I moved a moldy-looking teddy bear and opened a door of the washstand. Inside it was a label that said, "Made in the Phillipines." I took out a bottle of vodka and a stemmed glass and poured him a healthy shot, which he put away without a blink. "Now listen to me, Thomas," I said. "You've got to face this. I may not be able to finesse you out of it."

" '*May* not?' " A faint imitation of a smile played around his drooping mouth. "Does that mean you'll try?"

"There are conditions."

"Anything!"

"No more salary cuts."

He gulped. "Agreed," he said at last.

"And no Remedial Vocabulary," I snarled, my nose bumping his designer eyeware. "No Latin roots. No spelling tests."

"Whatever you say, Winston! Only please, hurry. There's only a week and a half before the Faculty Dinner. I'll have to present the end-of-term accounts! If I can't replace that money—"

"Then you'd better drink up, Sheffield," I said, "and start shopping for hideouts in some country where there's no extradition treaty."

"Ooooooooh!" he groaned, and poured another glass.

On my way home I stopped by to see Krish at Blanche Megrim's place, where Merriman used to rent a room until the Widow Megrim's avid attentions and her five hundred recipes for despoiling innocent tuna fish drove him to take refuge with us. Krish is too busy thinking about the bride he hopes to import from his native Pakistan to pay much attention to Blanche's nonstop Perry Como records and he actually seems to like her Tuna Surprise. The pair of them were sitting in the spring sunshine on La Megrim's front porch, Krish's hands enmeshed in a tangled hank of purple wool.

"Why, hello there, Dr. Sherman!" cried Blanche, peering over my shoulder as she wound the yarn into a ball. "Edward isn't with you?"

Edward, having endured pots of Blanche's patented watery chicken soup, calf's-foot jelly by the gallon, more bunches of grapes than the spies brought back from the Promised Land, and a perky get-well card at least twice a week during his winter's illness, would be hanged before he'd stroll in here on Sunday afternoon of his own free will.

"No," I told her, "he's busy. Working on a new picture. Always painting."

"Oh! I'll have to come over and take a peek," she simpered. "He's soooo talented, I always tell him. Soooooo talented!"

She freed Krish from yarn bondage and went off to get me a cup of her dreaded caffeine-free witches' brew. I parked beside my friend on the steps.

"Krish," I said, "about this Sheffield business. The Floating Fund?"

"Have you made a discovery?" He lowered his voice and moved closer.

"I just had a talk with the nitwit," I told him. "He didn't steal that money, Krish. He lost it, that's all. Invested it in a bank that folded before he could get the bucks out. He's in a real bind."

Krish sat thinking, his round brown eyes half hidden by long lashes. At last he opened them wide and looked squarely at me.

"I have been precipitate," he said. "I have acted in a nitwit manner, also."

"Well, I wouldn't say that."

"Oh, yes. I should have confronted this ninny Sheffield directly, as you did. I was bored, you see. Mrs. Megrim, an admirable cook, an excellent lady. But little conversation. During the winter, I read many mystery novels. Your own and others. They seemed to invest the world with—"

"A certain significance?"

"Exactly. Ordinary events took on a meaning, shaped themselves into a pattern. I was deceived."

"It's not a crime, Krish," I told him. "We're all allowed a few delusions. Where would we be without them?"

"But I might have done him great harm!" he cried. "If his wife should find out! Or Mrs. Costello! An appetite for mischief, that lady. She writes down everything in a small book. I have seen it." He shook his head sadly.

"We've got to help Tommy find a way to put that money back, Krish, without letting his wife and Hilda know where it's actually going. If he could pay it to you, say, for something specific, something you didn't much want? Then you could take it to the Equity National and squirrel it away in the department's name the way Tommy was supposed to have done in the first place. He could tell Lady Di he'd bought your—say your old Plymouth."

"My car? No. Absolutely not! I would not sell him my car. A valuable asset, an antique automobile? Under no circumstances."

"All right, all right. Something else, then. Think about it."

He nodded. "I shall consider."

"Let me know if you come up with anything," I said. "We have to put the poor goof out of his misery before he blows a fuse. And Krish? Lay off the Agatha Christie at least till the Fourth of July, okay?"

That evening I trudged up to my Cave to do a bit of preparation for my Monday afternoon mystery class on *The Third Man*. Sarah was down in the living room with a heap of Erskine's old scrapbooks of clippings spread all over the place, looking for some trace of Philip Vail even though I assured her we'd eliminated him as a suspect. Alex had put Gemma to bed in the old nursery and then turned in early herself, looking uneasily, as she passed the study door, at David, who'd spent most of the afternoon and evening with Jenny Vail's *The Black Palace*. As for Merriman, he'd disappeared into his rooms off the kitchen right after dinner and that was the last I'd seen of him.

I'd pitched the bouquet of withered roses, naturally, but the bottle of Dom Perignon still sat on my desk, a reminder of the baffling puzzle that pushed everything else—including *The Third Man*—to the back burner of my brain. Jenny Vail and Krish had made the same mistake; they had tried to impose sense on the senseless. Maybe, I thought, that was what I was doing too, expecting to see a pattern, some indication of motive where there was only the desire to destroy life.

But those lives had not been chosen at random on a street corner as Cynthia Vail's had been. They had been connected by the man McKelvie—Lewis Canfield, as we now knew him. Though his own son, Gregory, had barely known him according to Philip Vail, Jenny had certainly known Canfield, and Vangie had known him. The killer, Boots, had known him well enough to turn him to her use instead of Jenny's. Canfield had been a reader at Alexander's not long after he and Cynthia were married. Gregory was around twenty. Twenty years ago, Rita Kovacs wasn't even out of college, but Hazel Hancock had just gotten her start as a mystery writer. Beginners were often assigned to underlings rather than senior people. Hazel had had many publishers over the years. Which had been her first? Might she have known Lewis Canfield?

I went to the shelves that house my mystery collection and squinted at the bright spines lined up before me. Hazel's early covers had all been done in stop-sign yellow, I remembered. I spotted a patch of them and lugged half a dozen back to my desk.

The earliest date, the book introducing Mrs. Mapleton, had been printed in 1972, by Acorn Books, the paperback arm of—you guessed it—E.P. Alexander and Sons.

Of course that still didn't prove Hazel had ever known Canfield. He was dead, and though it might be possible to find somebody who'd worked at Alexander's with him twenty years ago, it would need time. The killer had already taken three lives and gotten away with it. From now on, killing would come easy. I didn't have any time to spare.

There was one way I could find out in a hurry whether Hazel had known Lewis Canfield. I could ask her.

I went out to the phone in the hall and dialed the number of the Hornsby Empire in Manhattan, asking for Hazel's room. I almost dreaded hearing her voice, but when she answered it was perfectly natural.

" 'lo?" she said. I could hear the TV set in her room gabbling in the background.

"Haze?" I said. "It's me. Listen, when you were at Alexander's back before they sacked Carthage, did you ever bump up against a guy named Canfield? Lewis, I think his first name was. Maybe Lew. Reader. Lower-echelon editor."

She didn't answer for a minute. The television show was a sitcom, canned laughter rising in waves and dissipating. Still Hazel didn't speak. Then suddenly she said, "Hold on, Winnie." The TV noise was silenced and I heard her inhale, then exhale, lighting a cigarette. "Okay, now. What was this joker's name?" she said.

"Lewis Canfield," I repeated. "Lew Canfield."

"And you say he was an editor at Alexander's?"

"Editor. Reader. Worked there off and on for years. It's not a very big firm. I thought you might remember him."

She blew out the smoke, inhaled again. "Can't say I do."

"You always get to know the staff, Haze, wherever you're publishing. You make a million contacts and you remember everybody."

"Damn right," she said. "I was published by Alexander's for ten years, Winnie. I got to know every editor in the place before I was finished." The raucous laugh exploded into the receiver. "They passed me around from one to the other like a goddamn football!" Suddenly the laugh died. "Nobody named Lewis Canfield ever worked at Alexander's in my time, Winnie."

I gulped. "Okay, then. Thanks, Haze."

She hung up—a bit too quickly, I thought—and I went back to my desk and poured myself a Haig & Haig.

"Pour another one of those, Winnie." David stood in my doorway, *The Black Palace* still in his hand. "May I come in?" he asked.

"Got the password?" I demanded, according to ancient custom.

" 'Darkness and devils,' " he said as he came in and parked in my creaky old typing chair. He put the book on my desk.

"Is that a critical judgement?" I asked, opening the cover and paging through.

"More or less. I understand what Vangie meant. 'An intellectual hatred,' that's what she said. It was more than bitterness or sorrow or anger. Those are normal enough. This book? It tastes like death. She wanted it, Winnie. She wanted to die and take the rest of the world down with her."

"Hazel said Jenny was finished, when we saw her at the reception," I told him. "Maybe that was what she meant. That edge of madness. The downward spiral. So easy, in a position like hers, to lose your balance."

He smiled ruefully and took a sip of Scotch. "I ought to know, is that what you mean?"

"You're not Jenny Vail, kiddo, not yet. She spent almost three decades plotting and calculating and using. She alienated her own daughter, she lost her husband to a woman who wasn't burdened with her obsessions. She threw away every loyalty, she schemed like a Borgia, and for what? The opportunity to put words on paper? Hell, she didn't even much like writing, she told me that once, a long time ago. The money? Philip had plenty of that for both of them. The fame? She enjoyed that, surely, but in time she was isolated by it, just as you are yourself every now and then. She loved the *game,* but she carried it one step too far and it ate her alive. And somebody else killed her for the dirty tricks she played. Rita Kovacs, maybe. Maybe—somebody else."

"It's a brutal game, Winnie." He reached into his pocket and dug out his wallet, then pulled from it a tiny newspaper clipping and handed it across the desk to me.

" 'Services are pending at Rasmussen Memorial Chapel for Vernelle C. Maguire, thirty-eight. Mrs. Maguire was found dead of carbon monoxide poisoning in the garage of her home at Twelve-thirty-three Rosebud Street in Rapid City last Tuesday.' " I looked up at David. "Did you know her, kiddo? A woman in Rapid City?"

"She wrote to me. A wannabee. You know the kind, you get plenty of them yourself. Phone calls, letters. She wanted to be a writer and she thought I might help her." He put the clipping back into his wallet. "Obviously I didn't."

"Vernelle Maguire?" There was something familiar about the name. "Wanted to be a screenwriter, playwright—what?"

"I don't think she cared. Most of them don't. Some of them can barely put a sentence together. It's the idea of the thing. The dream."

"What was the date on that clipping?"

"I don't know, exactly. I got it in the mail just before Christmas."

Boots had begun visiting McKelvie just after Christmas. "Who sent the clipping?" I said. Wheels were beginning to turn in my head, cogs slipping into line.

"It wasn't signed," he said, "just postmarked from South Dakota."

"Where in South Dakota?" I began to toss papers and books off my desk. I knew it was there somewhere, just as Boots had known when he searched my Cave. "What city?"

"Rapid City. Must've been Rapid City."

"Couldn't have been Sioux Falls?"

He hesitated. "I suppose so. I suppose it could. I didn't save the envelope. What the hell are you looking for, Winnie?"

"This," I said, pulling a brown mailing envelope from under a heap of student term papers. "It must've got mixed in with the rest of the clutter in here and I forgot all about it."

"What is it?"

I opened the flap and pulled out the manuscript inside, then read him the title page. *"Black Hills Death,* by Vernelle C. Maguire."

20

I spent that Sunday night reading the manuscript of *Black Hills Death*, Vernelle Maguire's mystery novel. She'd mailed it to me, according to the postmark, some time early in the fall, about the time her letters to David had begun. Like most first novels, it was unpublishable without a lot more work than most first novelists want to invest. The plot was lifted from Tony Hillerman, the style was pure newspaper shorthand. I don't think there was an adjective or an adverb in the entire book. The characters were mostly cardboard cutouts and none of them seemed to think about anything but sex.

Still, there was something. The spark was frail and any critic with too heavy a hand could've put it out for good. But it was there, a tiny germ, capable of better things. She had no idea of editing herself; she cut out everything that might have given the story life and left in the miserable copycat stuff. But now and then when she wasn't looking a phrase survived, a character caught breath and lived for an instant on its own. With work, I thought as I turned over the last page, with time and encouragement, Vernelle Maguire might just have made a writer.

But she had given herself no time. She had walked into her garage, closed and locked the doors behind her, switched on the engine of her car, and smashed the time clock once and for all.

Of course I knew she was somehow connected to Hazel. The South Dakota setting, the fact that Vernelle had written to both David and me—the coincidences were piling up. Had she sent one of her manuscripts to Jenny Vail, as well, or to Rita Kovacs and the other members of Perfidy, Unlimited? Had she been Hazel's protégée, perhaps, as Marina Vilnius was Jenny's? I still had a lot of questions before I confronted Haze, and a lot of the answers were out in Sioux Falls, South Dakota.

I placed a long-distance call to the editorial offices of the *Plainsman,* Hazel's newspaper back home.

"Yeah?" said a harrassed-sounding male voice.

"Winston Sherman, here," I said. "Sorry to bother you, but I need a little information about your boss, Hazel Hancock."

The voice relaxed. "You a friend of Hazel's?" he said. "You heard from her? Nobody here's heard from her since she took off."

"Oh, sure," I said. "She's back here in New York, doing fine. But you know Haze, keeps everything to herself. I think she seems troubled about something, hoped you guys might be able to fill me in, maybe I could engineer a little loan. We're old friends, Hazel and I, go back to the Flood. Money problems, has she?"

"Hell, money's the least of her worries," he said. "By the way, I'm Alvin Hooper. I used to work for Hazel."

"Used to?"

"Till she sold out, sure. Put the paper up for sale right after Vernelle died. Helluva thing, suicide. Hazel took it pretty hard, of course, you know her. The roots go deep. She just up and sold the paper to this West Coast syndicate and took off."

"When was that, Al?"

"Like I say, right after the girl died, her daughter."

"Vernelle Maguire was Hazel's—"

"Sure. Sure. You didn't know?"

Hazel had married a rancher named Pete Hancock and divorced him after a couple of years of mutual warfare. Pete had got drunk one night and driven his pickup across the median of the Dakota Interstate, into the path of a semi. But nothing Hazel had ever said had given me the idea they had had a daughter.

"Hazel went out to Rapid for the funeral," Al Hooper continued, "and then came back here and called up this guy in Portland who'd been pestering her for years to sell. She's got no money problems.

Hell, he paid her almost a million and a half for the *Plainsman.*"
Hooper paused and muttered something to somebody in the background. "Listen, Mr.—um—"

"Sherman."

"I gotta go, here, the goddamn computer's down again. But you
tell Hazel we're all on her side, okay?"

"Al? Don't hang up. A couple of quick questions. Does Hazel
wear boots?"

He snickered. "Hell, pal, everybody out here wears boots, otherwise when you guys from the East Coast come tooling through, you
get all down in the mouth till you get to Colorado. Out there they
issue the boots and Stetsons in the maternity wards." His voice
became serious again. "Sure, Hazel wears 'em sometimes. So do I."

He was right, of course. It didn't prove much; I forged on. "Does
she have one of those little lap-top computers? The kind you can
print out on wherever you happen to be?"

"A Murayama, you mean? Sure, sure. We gave it to her, guys on
the paper, little going-away present. She left here right before
Christmas. Hated like hell to see her go. Hazel belongs out here,
y'know? Oh, I know she spent a lotta years back East when she was
a kid, learning the ropes on the big papers. Boston *Globe*, Washington *Post*, New York *Times*. She's got drinkin' buddies on every famous paper in the—"

"Whoa, Al!" I almost yelled in his ear. "The *Times?* Hazel used
to work at *The New York Times?*"

He chuckled. "Surprises you, does it? Small-town editor, used
to work for the finest paper in the country? Hell, yes. Coupla years,
right before she moved out here. Like I told you, Hazel's got connections. But she belongs out here. You tell her that. Tell her to get
her tail back home."

"When she took off, Al," I said, my heart pounding, "what did
she take off *in?*"

"Oh, she didn't fly," he said with a chuckle. "Haze hates like
hell to fly. She drove, drives everyplace, knows every back road
from here to Bozeman."

"Did she take her van?"

"Van? Hazel drives a Jeep, buddy. Jeep wagon."

"Al, the car Hazel's daughter died in? The one she left running in the closed garage? You wouldn't happen to know what kind of car *that* was, would you?"

For a minute he didn't speak. "I'm not real sure," he said. "Listen, what's this about, buddy? Why're you pumping the hell outa me?"

"Hazel's in a little trouble, Al," I said. "Maybe I can clear it up."

He took another minute to make up his mind. "Vernelle drove an old Toyota," he said at last. "But there *was* a van. Hazel worried about Vernie driving that old heap. She bought her a used van, was gonna drive it out to Rapid for Christmas and surprise her."

"What was the make?"

"An Aerostar," he said. "Nice white Aerostar, only a couple years old."

It wasn't difficult to set things up. When I phoned Rita Kovacs, she sounded a bit surprised, but happy. The Red-Headed League still hadn't found a place to have its tea-cum-memorial meeting in honor of Jenny, and the members still in New York were getting a little nervous, watching their hotel bills pile up while they waited around for the funeral. When I told Lovely Rita that Philip Vail intended to follow the instructions in Jenny's will and have no formal services, she jumped at the chance to get the Perfidy, Unlimited meeting over with quickly and at no more expense than the train fare up to Ainsley. I even offered to provide the refreshments myself, and Erskine's enormous living room had certainly held bigger and rowdier parties in its time than the remnant of the Red-Headed League at high tea. The membership was to converge at our place next day, Tuesday, at four o'clock.

"And one more thing, Ms. Kovacs," I said as we prepared to hang up. "Ask around among your members, will you? Get your networks ticking. Find out if anybody got a manuscript from a woman named Vernelle Maguire. *Black Hills Death,* that was the title. Mailed from Rapid City, South Dakota."

"Oh, Jesus," said Rita Kovacs. "That turkey? God, I hate wannabees, I never know what to do with them. You say, 'Put in twenty years or so and you might make a book out of this thing.' Then two years later some editor buys it and you're sitting beside the poor schmuck on Edgars night."

"Vernelle Maguire sent you her manuscript?"

"Yeah, like I said. Listen, what's it got to do with—"

"I'm not sure yet," I told her. "I've got an idea, that's all. Can you check your sources, see if Jenny Vail ever got one of those manuscripts?"

"I can try," she said. "You're on to something hot, right?"

I ignored her. "Ask anybody you can think of. Except Hazel Hancock. I know you don't communicate too well with her. I'll talk to her myself."

"Okay," she said reluctantly. "But if you get anything, I want the story. I might be able to use it. True-life crime."

That afternoon I stumbled through my class on *The Third Man,* caring not a tinker's damn whether Harry Lime wound up in the sewers of Vienna or not. Out of habit I stopped for my mail after class and found Krish at the limping old Xerox machine in the corner of the mailroom, making a copy of some sort of official-looking document.

"Tax man on your case, Krish?"

He looked up and smiled. "A bill of sale. For a certain article this nitwit Sheffield is about to purchase from me."

"For nine hundred and sixty-seven dollars?"

"And thirty-five cents. Correct. An extremely valuable Buddha, very old. His wife will find it delightful."

"Now, Krish," I said, "I don't think you ought to, if it's really valuable. Surely there's some little . . ."

He motioned me closer and spoke in an undertone. "The Buddha? A gift from Mrs. Megrim, purchased by mail order from, I believe, Wisconsin. Brass-plated aluminum, turning already somewhat green. It takes up a great deal of space in my room, though of course a kind thought. She meant it to remind me of home."

"But doesn't the religion frown on selling such—"

He blinked. "I am not a Buddhist, sir. There are, of course, many Buddhists in my homeland. An admirable philosophy. But I, myself, am a Presbyterian."

"And Tommy's a lucky stiff," I said, patting the little fellow on the back.

"Shall I tell him now?"

"Oh, what the dickens, kiddo," I told him. "Let him twist in the wind a little longer."

With Tommy's tiny troubles more or less out of the way, the trap I'd just begun to set for one of my oldest friends took on even greater importance in my mind. If I was right about Hazel—and all the bits and pieces of evidence had me convinced that I was—then she had been caught in that same downward spiral that had pulled Jenny into the dark. She had killed madly, with mindless ease, and it would be easy for her to kill again and again. Our living room would be full of people. I heard over and over the sound of that muffled shot, the clunk of the needle-nosed bullet driving itself deep into the wood of my desk.

I'd called Lloyd, and he would be there with as many men as he could muster, stationed in the house and the yard, the woods on the bluff out back. It was Peggy Bryce's day off and she would be among the guests. Lincoln, tied up by Colby's ridiculous efforts to prove conspiracy against Philip Vail, wasn't sure he could make it, but was determined to try; of course we would have Julian Stockfish, whose pal Tyrone would play houseman for the afternoon. It would have to be enough.

Still, as I plodded up the three flights of stairs to my office I found myself wondering if I might be the demented one, creating plots where there were only circumstances, coincidental bits and pieces with which I was condemning a woman I had always thought of as a friend. It's a rare thing, real friendship between a man and a woman, a bond uncluttered with sex and its politics. Hazel and I had sat for long hours up in my Cave on her visits, smoking and talking. I was an Iowa boy myself and I thought I knew her, saw beneath the persona she presented to the ranks of East Coast power, the face she wore to hide her boredom with the cocktail circuit chitchat and the petty put-downs she was supposed to be too unsophisticated to register.

Elsie the Hick, she called this mythical self she gave them—the head-on manner, the no-nonsense haircut, the loud honk of laughter, the insistence on calling a spade a spade although she could've called it a spade in at least four other languages that I knew of. Elsie, she'd told me once, had been born at Radcliffe, where Hazel's Grandmother Springer was educated before she moved west with the country and settled in Dakota. Radcliffe was as much a family tradition as the Lakota Sun Dance she went to religiously, and Hazel obeyed it. The 'Cliffies didn't know what to do with this bright, tough new citizen, sophisticated in matters more ancient and far deeper than the use of the proper fork or the etiquette of football weekends. They could deal much more easily with Elsie the Hick, so Elsie was what she gave them; with old Elsie, their guards went down instantly, their superiority clouded their judgment, and Hazel could take them by surprise and manage them like so many jibbering monkeys in a high-class zoo.

Was that, I wondered, what she had counted on with me? Had she expected Elsie the Hick—the Mrs. Mapleton she had put into her books—to make me drop my guard and ignore any evidence that pointed in her direction? If it hadn't been for Merriman, I thought, I might've done exactly that.

I was surprised to find him at his easel in the far corner of my narrow office when I unlocked the door. The bullet-shattered windowpane had been removed and boarded up, and the only light came from the green-shaded lamp on my desk—much too dim for painting. But then, Eddie wasn't painting anyway, just sitting there smoking his pipe and staring at an empty piece of watercolor paper with a grayish blob on it, his brushes and colors still neatly stored away, not even a pencil in his hand.

"What does that look like to you?" He squinted at the pale gray area in the middle of the white paper.

I put my books and a file of student papers down on the desk and went to stand behind him for a better look. "Somebody's cafeteria lunch?"

"Rather like a rabbit, just there. Ears and so on," he said.

"Methinks 'tis very like a whale, my lord." I sat down and lighted a Turkish Delight. "The point being, of course, that we may be jumping at shadows in this business?"

"The point?" He shrugged and turned away from the easel to face me. "Not sure there is a point. Just a blob of paint on a piece of paper. It happened at random, actually. I set the pickle jar in which I wash my brushes on this clean sheet of paper, and it so happened there was a hairline crack in the bottom of the jar. To the eye, the jar looked perfectly sound. But this was the result. A bit of minor damage. Entirely random, impelled by no deep-seated motives, guided by no philosophy. A concatenation of circumstances. A hairline crack in the universal dream of perfection. Drat! Why Hazel?"

"Give her a chance," I said—though without much conviction. "Maybe we're completely off base. Maybe—"

He nodded. "I shall continue to hope it's that Morticia Addams woman, the publicist with the crocodile tears. Disliked her intensely and entirely unreasonably. Still."

"Merriman," I said, with some trepidation, "about what I said the other day, that inheritance of yours?"

He smiled and tapped out his pipe on the palm of his hand. "Oh, that," he said. "There seems to be a spot of bother about it. I'm too old to get rich now, anyway. Probably go on a spree and expire of a surfeit of something disgusting in some entirely unsuitable location."

"You mean you're not getting the money? But I heard you on the phone with that man Sweeting!"

"I know you did. I heard the click when you hung up the extension." He grinned and refilled his pipe. "Fernleigh Court, half a million doubloons, Sir Edward the Fair—all that. Of course, it *may* still come to pass. But it seems my old Uncle Horace was a bit of a lad. Ladies on every continent. All of whom are now staking posthumous claims for support and compensation."

"You don't mean palimony?"

He nodded. "I could, of course, continue to support them in the manner to which they are accustomed—take them on myself. But frankly, I wonder if I'm up to it? Besides, Mrs. Megrim might fly into a jealous fit, and then where would I be?"

"You don't seem very upset," I said. I felt at least ten years younger from the sheer relief of it. I might be about to lose one friend, but at least it didn't look as though I'd be losing Merriman. "That's a lot of money. Power. A whole new station in life."

"My nose isn't really long enough to look down, anyway, Winnie, not to do the thing properly," he said with a smile. "Though I won't object if the ladies leave me a bit of working capital to be going on with." He sobered. "Winston," he said, after a long pause. "I didn't stop up here to spill water on a piece of paper, you know. There was a phone call before I left home. Thought I'd better come and tell you."

"Lloyd?"

"No," he said. "Young Julian Stockfish. On the matter of that nasty gun our friend's been using."

"Has he found out who bought it?"

"He got no name, just a description. A man. Tall, thin, late forties, slump-shouldered, receding brown hair going a bit gray. Brown corduroy jacket."

"That sounds like—"

"McKelvie? It does indeed. In fact, Stockfish, being the clever lad he is, had taken a photograph or two of the man when he and David were following him round the West Side. The arms merchant identified it absolutely. That gun was bought by Gilbert McKelvie, alias Lewis Canfield."

"Who obviously never used it. He bought it for Boots. That's what she needed him for."

"And after he'd bought it, he became a liability and she had to get rid of him."

"Before she used the gun to get rid of her real target. Jenny."

"Then, when she broke into his flat looking for that tape she'd gotten him to play for David, Mrs. Glickman got a look at her and she had to be eliminated, too."

"She would've grabbed that Polaroid she knew Vangie took of her, but there was no time. Peggy Bryce was pulling up outside and David was coming down the stairs. She had a choice between getting the picture and killing the both of them or getting away."

"Yes," said Eddie, "and if that's true, she'd have had plenty of time to get away that night after she shot Mrs. Glickman! She could've been out of the country before any of us had a chance to stop her, long gone and scot-free! Don't you see, Winnie? Hazel didn't run! She stayed exactly where she was, going about her business! Surely that means—"

"Merriman," I said, "I told her that Polaroid didn't turn out. I told her on Saturday morning when we had coffee at the Hornsby. She didn't think she *had* to run."

We looked at each other for a moment. "Winnie," he said, reading my mind. "Don't be an idiot."

"We have to smoke her out," I said. "I'll have plenty of protection. I'm a devout coward, Merriman, and I can't say I'm delighted by the prospect of being a target. But it's the quickest way to get this over with. Boots could still be one of the other women in that Red-Headed League of Hazel's. It could even be some kind of conspiracy—Lord knows they seem to thrive on that kind of stuff, with all those networks of theirs." I was beginning to sound like Rat-Cheese Colby and I knew it. I picked up the telephone and dialed.

"Kovacs," barked Lovely Rita, when I was connected with her room.

"Ms. Kovacs," I said, "me again, Winston Sherman. Forgot to ask you one last favor. Pass the word among your members, will you? Hazel, too, in case I can't reach her myself. I've been doing some nosing around and there's new conclusive evidence. I know who killed Jenny Vail."

21

The chill and mist of the previous week returned and Tuesday dawned gray and enigmatic.

I spent the morning making wimpy little sandwiches and baking my special German chocolate brownies, partly because I'd promised to provide refreshments and partly in order to keep my mind off the fact that I'd set myself up as a target for a lady with a very nasty talent for death.

I'd considered keeping that delightful aspect of my plan from Sarah, but in the end I thought better of it. While we were cutting the crusts off those sandwiches I told her everything, all my suspicions, the bits and pieces that had me convinced but would never convict anybody of murder no matter how you put them together. Our murderer had to convict herself in front of witnesses, I argued, and what better witnesses than the Red-Headed League? When I'd finished, I laid down my knife and stood waiting for the explosion. She just kept working, cutting off each edge with absolute precision.

"Are you angry?" I said.

She whacked off another crust. "Not a bit. I'm getting used to it. I live in constant expectation of seeing you or David struck down by homicidal maniacs. If I let it bother me, I'd be living on Valium by this time."

"Would it help if I said I was sorry?"

"Absolutely not." *Whack*, went the knife, and another crust flew into the bag earmarked for the bluejays. "Win?"

"Madam?"

"About Hazel? I'm sorry."

But she was right. Being sorry didn't help a bit.

Sarah was already at her piano playing soothing non-Russian stuff when the partisans began to arrive in small bands by train and car at about half past three. The Queen Mum, Mary Louise Kirk, in pale blue chiffon and egret-plumed hat, arrived by taxi—the closest she could get, I figured, to a coach and four. Rita Kovacs showed up with Jed Sloan and the dish-mop-haired blonde from the Hornsby coffee shop, and Marina Vilnius appeared in splendid black crepe isolation. Nestor Perlmutter, looking as bereft as the prophet Jeremiah, hiked up the hill from the station, and Harlan Landis tooled up in his shiny BMW. By the time my own special guests, Philip Vail and Lydia Hallam, rang the front doorbell, the cliques had formed up nicely—the California crew in a knot by the fireplace, the Manhattan mafia on the window seat, the Chicago mob with Lovely Rita in the dining room, the Southern faction in a huddle in the sun room. When I peeked in to check things out, I spotted Sergeant Peggy Bryce cozying up to old Landis and Charlie LaCroix, and Alex trying with doubtful success to make conversation with Marina Vilnius. Merriman did his best to charm Vail and Lydia, who both looked weary and ill-at-ease among the battalion of curious, mildly hostile authors. I'd told them only that the meeting was a sort of memorial to Jenny and I'd like them to come. I knew Vail's sense of decorum wouldn't let him stay away, but judging from the looks on their faces, they both knew something was in the wind.

"The guest of honor is not yet like in attendance," said Tyrone, whizzing through the swing door into my kitchen. He was looking spiffy in a white waiter's jacket; his talent for not standing still was exactly what we needed, at the rate our suspects were packing away my food! He set down an empty plate and stowed away a couple of brownies himself, while I filled the plate with sandwiches. "The lady likes to make an entrance."

"Maybe she took off," said David. He was still studying that book of Jenny's, *The Black Palace*, and though I didn't know exactly what he had in mind, he'd asked if he could say a few words to the League before I began. "Maybe your bait was enough to scare her off."

"Brrrrrrr!"

A buzzer went off about a foot from my ear and I almost dropped the pot of coffee I was handing to my old pal, Carlo, stationed by Lloyd Agate to help us keep things in line.

"Brrrrrr!"

"That's Julian," said David. "We rigged it up this morning. Hazel's on her way up the drive."

Merriman poked his head through the kitchen door. He gave me a sober look. "Blast it all," he said, "the game's afoot. She's here."

Hazel was dressed, as usual, in pants and a sweater. Pants, I thought, would hide the welts Julian's dog chain must've left across the backs of her legs that night at Vangie's. If there *were* welts. If it *was* Hazel.

She had a big orange nylon bag with her, stuffed full of leaflets of some kind which she started passing out to the PU members the minute she hit the living room.

"Want a copy, Winnie?" she said.

I squinted at the mimeographed page. " 'Writers Unite—You Have Nothing to Lose But Your Overdrafts!' I heard you were set to become the Joe Hill of American publishing," I told her. "I have to admit I've about had it with that high-handed Dutchman myself. Nonexistent royalty statements, delayed contracts, fancy footwork in the fine print. But do you think it'll ever work, a real writers' union?"

Her cool eyes scanned the room. "Not like this, that's for damn sure. Look at them! A union? Hell, they don't trust each other any farther than you could throw the World Trade Center! They snipe and whisper and backbite like a lot of high school brats and when one of them makes it big they all claim half the credit. Then they trot out that goddamn little self-promotion bible of theirs and figure out whether to kiss ass first or just stick the knife in right away."

"But Hazel," I said, "you're *one* of them. You're one of the officers, aren't you? That book on self-promotion you were talking about? You helped Harlan write it, didn't you? You *organized* the networks."

"I thought we could change things. We're so much meat to guys like Van Twist, Winnie. You ought to know that. We had so much in common, so much to gain. I thought they might grow up. But look at them. Just look."

The mumbling knots of members had not drawn together, though it was clear that the afternoon's program was about to begin. Occasionally a look passed between one group and the other, but no smiles were exchanged, no friendly words. There was suspicion in the eyes, and anger; even among the members of the separate groups there seemed to be no comradeship, only the sort of mutual interest that ends the minute opportunity knocks.

I shrugged. "Looks pretty normal to me," I said. "Lock three writers in a room for fifteen minutes and two of them will have ganged up on the third guy. We've always had more differences than similarities, it's part of our charm. We've always tried to hustle the bucks and stiff the competition. Read Aristophanes." I studied her face. "You don't care much for them, do you, Haze? This Red-Headed League of yours."

"Care for them?" she said. She looked around from one of the huddles to the other, her green eyes distant and aloof. "I love them like a goddamn sister," she said. She laughed, the familiar raucous cackle hard as forged steel. "I love them to death."

"If we could begin, now," said Rita Kovacs. She stood in front of the huge stone fireplace that filled one end of the living room, before her the antique Italian lectern that had once been the heart of another mystery in Erskine's old house. On it David had placed his annotated copy of *The Black Palace*. The muttering groups of guests fell silent and Hazel took a place on the window seat near the French doors to the garden. Lloyd was somewhere out there, I knew, and if we were lucky Lincoln had joined him by now. Once things had settled down, Rita continued.

"As you all know, last Thursday night at the Edgars we lost a lady who gave us a whole library of memorable mystery novels, and we in Perfidy, Unlimited have decided to dedicate our yearly tea to her memory, to hear a few words from her friends, listen to some of her own words, and think about what's been taken from us so abruptly. With us are Jenny's editor from Crocodile Books, Lydia Hallam, and Philip Vail, Jenny's husband. Maybe you'd like to say a word or two, Philip?"

I hadn't expected that, and neither had Philip Vail. He and Lydia were standing at the back of the room, near the doors that opened into the entry hall. Everybody in the room turned to look at them. Lydia's arm was locked into Philip's, half depending on him, half supporting him, or so it seemed to me. Now he gently unlocked her fingers and slipped away from her to make his way toward the lectern where Rita stood waiting. Lydia followed him at a distance, pausing halfway across the room.

My glance returned to Hazel. She was directly opposite Philip as he stood at the lectern and her clear green eyes never left him. He braced his long, thin hands against the carved edge of the lectern and I thought for a split second he would topple. His weedy frame seemed skeletal, every bone perceptible under the fine cloth of his black suit. He looked around the room and I was certain the ice blue eyes rested for a long moment on Hazel, where she sat by the garden doors.

"Thank you," he said simply. "Such things should be marked. So much has gone, so many friends, and— Thank you."

Then he turned swiftly and strode off through the crowded living room, back to Lydia. She was about to go straight on out into the hall, then to Vail's waiting car. But he laid a hand on her arm and they found places on the piano bench Sarah had vacated, not far from where Hazel was sitting. Such things should be marked, Philip had said, and I knew he understood what was about to happen. It wasn't over, not yet.

Rita Kovacs had relinquished the lectern to David now. He was turning the pages of the book, hunting for a particular passage. Then he looked up. Tyrone was passing a plate of cookies and Carlo was busy refilling the teacups, as David began.

"I want to read to you a paragraph or two from Jenny Vail's last novel," he said. *"The Black Palace.* For those of you who haven't read the book, the Black Palace is the nickname of a huge office building on Fifth Avenue, the home of a multinational publishing company. In that building works a minor editor, a young woman of strong convictions, who discovers a profitable fraud being perpetrated by her bosses. She's about to reveal it to the public when she's killed. Her mother, a mystery novelist, goes about proving that the faceless powers in the Executive Suite of the Black Palace have had her daughter murdered."

"Sounds like a miniseries starring Joan Collins," I heard Dishmop mutter to Landis, and Landis smiled, as Davy began to read.

If I'd read the book, I thought with regret, when Jenny sent it to me, if my writer's jealousy hadn't made me shove it on the shelf with all the others, I might've saved us all a lot of time. I might even have saved Lewis Canfield's life, and that of Vangie Glickman.

" 'I think it is the fate of women always to be strangers,' " read David, and I saw him glance at Alex, then look away again. " 'In the ranks of their generations they stand isolate one from another, cut off by the kindly prisons of love and protection, the unshared ambitions that fall like leaves from aging trees and are replaced by others just as fleeting, just as foolish. My mother did not know me. The prospect frightened her, as though, coming too near, she might find in me some seed she never planted, from which strange, unrighteous fruit might come. I did not know my daughter. I, too, was afraid, and she abetted me, she hid away in silent places, thinking secret thoughts. Each on her solitary crag we spin our circles out, piercing the night with wild, suspicious eyes, alike in nothing save our solitude and our whirling self-sufficient dance, our hands that reach and never, never catch, lest we might be betrayed by some false dream, or some false friend. My daughter is dead, who was not my friend. My daughter is dead, whom I loved as I love the dark and the endless dance. Dead."

Hazel's face showed nothing, not the slightest flicker of emotion. I was about to get up and begin my own bit of the ceremony, but David wasn't finished.

"I have a letter here from another writer. Most of you probably haven't heard of her. She wrote me this note just before Christmas, from South Dakota. Her name was Vernelle Maguire, and she wanted to be a writer."

Rita Kovacs's pop eyes opened even wider and she looked in my direction and raised an eyebrow. One or two of the other women nodded.

"How many of you got letters from Mrs. Maguire?" said David. "Will you raise your hands, please?"

A few members shrugged, three or four raised their hands. Rita Kovacs was among these and so were Marina Vilnius and Rabbi Perlmutter. Hazel shifted the orange bag on her knee but continued to betray no emotion. In his corner by the fireplace I saw Merriman start at her slight movement and I knew what he was thinking. That orange bag was big enough to hold an assassin's gun.

David opened the letter and began to read.

" 'Dear Mr. Cromwell. I hope you won't mind if I call you David. Your talent has been greatly appreciated here in South Dakota. I have been writing mystery stories for several years now and have thought of several plots that would be good for your television series, *Greyhawk*.' "

"That's canceled, for God's sake," muttered somebody. David continued.

" 'Would you mind if I sent you my novel to read? Maybe I could change it and sell it to the movies. Do you think, if I got a good agent, it might help? Do you think I should move to New York? I have a husband. He thinks I'm crazy to keep writing. Do you think, if I left him and came to New York? Please let me know what you think. Sincerely yours, Vernelle.' "

"You didn't know, did you, Hazel?" I stood up to face her. "You had no idea your daughter was writing those letters, sending her manuscripts to the bunch of us. Where did she get the addresses? That PU handbook, the networks you set up?"

Hazel laughed. "I don't know what the hell you're talking about, Winnie."

"Jenny had the truth of it," I went on. "Mothers and daughters often don't communicate, do they? Fathers and daughters, either, for that matter. But then the fathers have to know that the daughters exist. You never told Philip, did you? You two were engaged back in the Fifties, after you graduated from college. It came out in the papers after one of the parties in this house. But the Vails didn't approve, did they? They were old mainline East Coast money, and they didn't cotton to nobodies from South Dakota."

"They behaved like pigs." Philip Vail's soft voice carried easily across the room. "Well-bred, aristocratic pigs. My mother. My famous Uncle Marcus. We fought them off for almost two years."

"And then Hazel had had enough and she went back to Dakota and married Pete Hancock. Didn't you ever wonder why a woman with a Radcliffe degree in journalism and political science would marry a high-school dropout who drank himself silly every night of the week? She needed a husband, any husband. It was the Fifties. Children without legal fathers were frowned on in those days. Taken away from their mothers."

I saw Sarah wince. It was the reason we hadn't had children of our own, and for a while our lack of a wedding license had made it quite a trick to keep David.

"I never had a daughter," said Hazel, her voice echoing in the silent room.

"I phoned Al Hooper at the paper, Haze," I told her. Again she shifted the orange bag on her lap. I stepped over to David. "Get out of here, kiddo," I told him in an undertone. "It's my party."

"Like hell," he said, and stayed put.

Philip Vail upstaged the pair of us. With long, uncertain steps he moved through the knots of thunderstruck members to stand in front of Hazel.

"Is Winston right?" he said. "The girl?"

"I never had a daughter," she repeated dully.

Vail knew a lie when he heard it. "Oh," he said. "Oh, my dear."

"When Vernelle died, you went to Rapid City and helped her husband go through her things," I said. "You found something. Something you believed had made her go into that garage and start the engine of her car behind the closed doors and . . ."

Philip Vail's hands were clenched into fists at his sides. "Enough!" he said.

I wanted to stop. I have never in my life wanted anything so much as I wanted to stop.

"You found a letter from Jenny Vail," I went on. "A brutal, cynical, destructive letter. A criticism of Vernie's manuscript so ruthless that it ate away everything, all the years of hopeless, helpless floundering, of trial and error. An angry letter that denied everything. Not just the value of the book she'd written, but the value of living, of hoping. Jenny never answered when unknown writers approached her, but she answered Vernie. Did she know, Hazel, did she find out whose daughter Vernie was? Or was it just the South Dakota postmark, the coincidence of place that unleashed her jealousy of you? Philip loved you first, before Jenny, before Lydia. She was out of control, she didn't need to know. Maybe she thought you'd put Vernelle up to it and that was enough. She poured out all her anger on that beginner's manuscript."

"Vernie could never have been a writer," said Hazel half to herself. "She didn't have the discipline. She wanted it too fast, too easy."

"And you told her that, too, didn't you? You tried to get her to see reality, but she didn't want reality. She wanted to keep dreaming. It's an old dream, Haze. We conquered a continent for it."

"She never asked me for help after that," she whispered. "She never talked to me about it again."

"No. She wanted to prove herself to you, didn't she? So she wrote to us, instead. She didn't mention that she was your daughter, you'd taught her to be proud. But she used your networks, the list of contacts in the handbook, and she wrote to all of us. Your colleagues, your friends. To me, to David, to Rita here, and Mary Louise, and Nestor, and Marina. To Jenny. But we were busy. We were lazy. We were human. Some of us pushed her manuscript under a pile of mail and forgot it. That's what I did, and that's why you came to search my study the morning of the Edgars, isn't it? You figured I might still find Vernie's book and put two and two together. But you didn't have enough time, and nobody can find anything in that study but me."

"Jenny didn't have to—to—" Hazel looked up at Philip, the green eyes tearless and very bright. "It was like being whipped. It wasn't just punishment. It was shame. Like your mother, when we—" She stood up, her hand inside the orange bag, her voice shattering with every syllable. "I wanted her dead. The bitch deserved to be dead!"

Philip Vail took a step toward her and a low sound came from Hazel, her whole body shaking.

"I loved you," she said, "for years and years and years, and you're nothing. Sweet Christ, you're nothing at all."

David strode forward and gently moved Vail aside. He was face to face with Hazel. "I was the last," he said, "wasn't I? She wrote to me last, one final chance after that mad letter of Jenny's. And I didn't answer. Then she died, and I had to be involved in the guilt. That was why you got McKelvie—Lewis Canfield—to make those anonymous calls. You made sure I was there, in the park, when you killed him."

"With the gun you talked him into buying for you," I said. "You'd sold your newspaper to a syndicate, you had plenty of money. You'd read about that gun in Miss Vilnius's last book, and she was guilty, too, wasn't she? She'd ignored Vernie's letter, too, like the rest of us. Besides, she was Jenny's publicist, her friend, her protégée. You bought a gun that would lead us as far from you as possible and point us toward her. Or toward Rita Kovacs. What was the source you mentioned, Rita? Who told you what kind of a gun killed Jenny? Was it a newspaperman? You kept in touch with your old gin buddies at the *Times*, didn't you, Haze?"

"Holy shit," whispered Rita Kovacs. "She fed me that stuff, she planted it?"

"It was her pals at the *Times* who passed on the skinny about

Lewis Canfield, the rumors about his having helped somebody fix the best-seller list before he got the sack from the book review desk. But, of course, Hazel knew Canfield anyway, didn't she, Philip? He was the first reader at Alexander's who recommended publishing her Mrs. Mapleton books years ago. They were old friends, and when Jenny became obsessed with this plot surrounding her daughter's death, and started pestering poor Canfield, he went underground to hide from her, didn't he, but she found him anyway, probably hired detectives. She could've afforded that. Philip helped him financially, but he couldn't talk Jenny out of her delusion, couldn't get her to seek help. She began to carry a gun, believed that her producer, Steven Stanway, would come after her. She tried to give Canfield a gun, too, that morning in the park, but he didn't want the thing. He just wanted to be free, didn't he, Hazel? He wanted to be free of Jenny Vail and then to disappear. He probably read about the research you were doing into the shady side of publishing in aid of that union of yours. Did he call you in Dakota, volunteer what he knew in exchange for your help?"

"None of this is evidence," said Hazel. "You talk a helluva game, Winnie, but that's all it is."

"You got Canfield to buy that gun for you so you wouldn't be recognized. What did you tell him it was for, research for a book? A collection? He trusted you, you must've been damn convincing," I said. "But then you always were. Elsie the Hick, she's a genuine original, one of the great roles. He thought you could expose Jenny's imbalance, didn't he? A newspaper story? A book? He trusted you and he knew you and before you could kill Jenny you had to get rid of him. Afterward he would've figured it out and disappeared before you could get at him, so it had to be before. And you had David there to take the rap, you got Canfield to lure him, keep him interested. You knew his imagination would do the rest. And you involved me for the same reason, with those roses and the wine signed with Jenny's name. We were old rivals, everybody knew that. You knew I wouldn't be able to resist, and I was guilty of Vernie's death, too, wasn't I? I didn't write any scathing letters, but I didn't help. I was your friend and I didn't help."

She laughed again, then, the sudden harsh cackle I'd heard on that doctored tape in McKelvie's apartment, the tape her midwestern frugality had forced her to use again. She'd forgotten to erase what had been taped on it before—some editorial meeting, a family dinner, a chapter of one of her books—and the electronically altered lines of the anonymous call hadn't covered the whole of the old tape. Her strength had become her weakness. It was that laugh that had given her away.

"You old jackass, Winnie," she said. "You're running a goddamn bluff and I'm calling it. Evidence."

"It's no bluff, Haze." I pushed David aside. "You had the gun in that big pocketbook of Mrs. Mapleton's. You left the dinner table and went out to the ladies' room, then you ducked back through the passage between the bar and the serving pantry and came out the service doors just where you'd arranged to meet Jenny. What did you tell her, that you had conclusive evidence of Stanway's guilt, that you wanted to help her? You came through those doors, you took out the gun, you shot her and propped her body up so it wouldn't be noticed until you had time to get back through the passageway again and into the line for the rest room, where I spotted you. You'd organized those phony gunshots all through the evening to cover the real shot you knew you were going to fire. It was a brilliant plan, everything worked out to the last detail. Only one thing. As you were going through the dark passageway back to the reception room, your pearls—Mrs. Mapleton's cheap dime-store pearls—broke. You caught the end before they all slipped off, but one or two got lost. They rolled up against the edge of the carpet where nobody saw them."

"Except me," said Merriman, and Hazel jumped, her hand diving deeper into the orange bag. Eddie took his fist out of his pocket and handed me a pearl and I held it up for Hazel to see.

"Anybody can buy a string of goddamn pearls," she said. Her eyes never left mine now, they held me like steel bands.

"You took a couple of potshots at me and missed on purpose," I said. "You wanted to make me nervous, make me turn to my friends for help. *You* were my friend, and I spilled everything to you, didn't

I? Just about everything. Except the photograph Vangie Glickman took of you before you shot her. You didn't have time to grab it before you cleared out, but I told you it was badly blurred and you didn't worry about it. What I didn't tell you was that I gave it to a friend of mine on the Ainsley police force." I was bluffing like crazy, of course; Lloyd had gotten nothing from that photograph at all, just a lot of smoke and mist. I kept pushing. "He's a wizard with a developing tank. He made a negative, then blew up that photograph a section at a time. It's the earrings, Hazel. They were on the photograph, plain as day. A small gold stud in the earlobe, not just a simple stud, when you saw the blowup. They were *your* earrings, Haze. I've never seen you without them. Two tiny leaves, one white gold, the other red. Black Hills gold, Hazel. Evidence. You burned up the van, the clothes, the boots. But you forgot the earrings."

I hardly saw her hand move but suddenly the gun was in it, not so large as I'd expected, a dull grayish color, a long thin barrel. Mary Louise Kirk, seated nearby, stood up and screamed; Hazel turned the gun at her and in that instant would've fired, but Merriman grabbed a poker from the hearth at his feet and tossed it to David. He landed a blow on Hazel's arm but she didn't drop the gun.

"All right," said Peggy Bryce from across the room, her own gun in her hand. "Everybody take it easy. Just put the gun down, honey. Just put it down right there on the floor."

Hazel spun on her heel and Tyrone made a dive for her, followed by Carlo. Peggy tried to get to them through the crowded room of frightened authors, but it was no use. She jumped up on the coffee table, hoping to get a clear shot at Hazel, but Mary Louise Kirk was in the way, egret feathers and all. In another blink, Hazel was gone, out the garden doors into the thickening mist.

David wasn't more than a yard behind her, running, slipping on the wet grass. She didn't turn, didn't fire, didn't speak, just ran, wildly, blindly, down the yard and into the woods. David's eyes were stinging with mist. He could barely see, and though his legs were longer he was not driven by the same despair. The small figure ahead of him cared for nothing, now. It ignored the old path that led down to the Hudson and went crashing through the hickories and the wiry scrubs of pine, down, down, to where the pewter-colored water gleamed, the sound of the moving river already audible. David followed the path, which was dangerous enough in the wet, early-gathering evening. It sloped down precipitously and he fell, slid, clambered up and ran again.

Behind him he heard faint voices—Lloyd Agate's, Julian's, A.J. Lincoln's, Tyrone's and Peggy's, mine. Philip Vail moved in silence through the trees, seeming to know his way by some newly discovered instinct. We were closing in on her, but that didn't matter to David. He must not let her go, must not lose sight of that dark, flying shape among the trees. She belonged to him now, as McKelvie had, and Jenny, and Vangie; she was a perverse trust he must keep for them all.

She had reached the bankside now. He could see the shape of her through the light new leaves of the hawthornes and dogwoods along the river's edge. She turned and saw him and he saw the shape of the gun, too, the same color as the Hudson, gray and dull and ancient as the first death. She turned back and looked out over the water, her small body arched like a dancer's.

He saw the flare from the long barrel before he heard the shot. The curve of her body buckled and hunched together and crashed and was gone into the dark of the underbrush.

When the rest of us reached them, Philip Vail was sitting cross-legged beside Hazel's body, his hand on her thick cap of hair. David knelt in the wet sand of the bank and took her hand, then gently let it go.

"Go softly," he said into the mist and the rising dark. "Go well."

22

It was Edgars night again, and that delayed award for Best Novel was about to be given out. Rita Kovacs was at the podium this time, a stogie clenched in her teeth, blowing smoke rings as she read off the names of the hopefuls.

"Nominees for best novel are: George Paul Donovan, *Ghost Dancer;* Margery Beekman-West, *Mr. Bones;* Rita Kovacs, *Dusty Death;* Imogen Vail, *The Black Palace;* Henrietta Slocum, *Death of a Double Agent.* And the winner is . . ."

I took a sip of the Dom Perignon provided by the Flying Dutchman and refilled Tracy's glass and that of my new agent, Emily Brownson, both of them dressed to kill in black velvet gowns. Sarah was wearing her red dress and I was clad in a brand-new, perfectly tailored evening suit of pure silk with black satin lapels purchased for me by Merriman, who'd finally come into his inheritance. He'd left his coronet at home, but was looking bright-eyed and bushy-tailed in his own new suit.

"The winner is—" Rita's face fell. "Henrietta Slocum," she said, and I thought I detected a little gnashing of teeth. *"Death of a Double Agent."*

The whole place burst into applause and Sarah planted a kiss on my cheek. I got up for the long walk to the podium where the cheesy little statue of a mildly inebriated-looking Edgar Allan Poe stood waiting for me. Elva Ziegler, in a silver turban set with amethysts, was applauding like crazy and Freddy Adler was playing "The Road to Mandalay" on his flute. As I rounded the table and passed old Eddie, I bent and gave him the best news of the evening.

"Merriman, don't look now, but your pants are split straight up the back."

I sailed on and mounted the podium, where Lovely Rita was waiting with my Edgar clutched in her bony claws.

"Ladies and gentlemen," she said with a snarl. "Henrietta Slocum. He's not street-smart, but he's damn well twee."

I pulled the microphone toward me, thinking what to say. The statue of Poe stood on the podium in front of me, trying to look as though it hadn't caused more trouble than it could possibly be worth.

"Well, take it," growled Lovely Rita in my ear. "You've got what you wanted. Take it and go!"

I looked out over the glittering, expectant audience and made my decision. "Thanks," I mumbled into the microphone. "But no thanks."

"Winston, for pity's sake, wake up!" It was Sarah's voice and she was shaking me awake. "They're about to give the award!"

I must've dozed off during Sheffield's State of the Faculty speech. We were gathered in the auditorium of Gould Theatre on the Clinton campus for the annual Faculty Awards Dinner. There were no little statues, just a printed certificate in a K Mart frame, the name inscribed by Hannah Comfort in her best Gothic calligraphy. But whose name? Who would win the Professor of the Year Award and rule the Curriculum Committee for the next year? Who would decide whether Yours Truly got a much-needed taste of his beloved Shakespeare or spent the semester boning up on Latin roots?

I didn't trust Sheffield to keep his bargain now that Krish and I had bailed him out of that kettle of soup with the Floating Fund. Oh, he'd been delighted when I told him the plan. It was the sight of that Buddha of Krish's that almost queered the deal.

"This?" whined Tommy when we hauled the old boy out of the trunk of Krish's Plymouth in the Sheffield driveway. "Do you know what Diana will say when I tell her I've spent nine hundred dollars of our joint account on a tin idol?"

"I beg your pardon," said Krish. "I have omitted to invite Mrs. Costello this evening. Perhaps I should call her now? Perhaps I should suggest she bring with her the little book in which she records information of interest to the Board of Trustees? Winston, have you Mrs. Costello's telephone number? She would no doubt appreciate this fine Buddha. We must give her a chance to see it. Now!"

"Never mind!" said Sheffield quickly, writing out the check. "It's a wonderful Buddha, really. I do appreciate . . . But what am I going to tell Diana? She'll never let me bring it into the house."

I shrugged. "Tell her you bought it for the Faculty Lounge. You're redoing the whole thing in an Oriental motif. Little incense burners, stone lanterns, potted palms. Place'll look just like the Raffles Bar in Singapore." I considered our brass-plated aluminum friend. Buddha was wearing a crooked sort of grin and he had one eye shut in a knowing wink, as though he knew a good inside joke. Obviously, I thought, he'd run into Sheffield in one of his former incarnations. "He'll make a nice stablemate for Alvin the Moose," I told Tommy. "Anyway, think how he'll look at Christmas with a little mistletoe tucked in his tummy, a nice red bow. Why, he's already green."

Sheffield had just moaned and handed over the check, which was now neatly stashed away in the Equity National where it belonged. Up on the stage old Howard Halverson of Classics was about to present the Professor of the Year Award. As he fumbled with the envelope, I took stock of the nominees.

There was Tommy, of course, with Diana holding his reins and the two offspring, Tessa and Vanessa—alias Frick and Frack—nipping at his heels. He was trying to look calm as he nibbled a nonchalant walnut, but his ears were pink and he was wearing that miserable Taiwanese toupee again. He figured he had the award in the bag and was all ready for the photo session afterward.

Hilda Costello, too, was looking smug and self-assured in a

sweeping tropical-print number that made her look like Chairman Mao at a luau. Dr. Skip Winthrop, professor of Sci-Fi and Horror Fiction, was the popular favorite among the students, who had packed in uninvited at the back to applaud in case he won.

Old Halverson had the envelope open now, and he began to read. "The nominees are: Hilda Costello, Thomas Sheffield, Silvester Winthrop—"

"Silvester? I always thought it was Skip!" whispered Sarah.

"It was," I muttered, "but from now on it's Silvester, believe me."

"And Winston Sherman."

"Me? What's the matter with old Howard, can't he read? I'm not on that list! I haven't bought anybody lunch. I haven't listened at any keyholes. I don't even have a little notebook!"

Eddie was grinning from ear to ear. "Krishnan told me about it some time ago, Winnie. He and Tess Jonas nominated you, and your stock has risen nicely, so he tells me, thanks to the dirty politics of Hilda's campaign and Sheffield's general—general—"

"Gormlessness?" I suggested. Old Halverson was about to read the name of the popular favorite, but I knew it wouldn't be me. After all—

"The winner is—*Winston Marlowe Sherman!*"

I was stunned. If Sarah hadn't landed a sharp kick on my shin, I might not have been conscious enough to stagger up to the stage and accept the certificate. As it was, I was waylaid by little Krish, who'd squired Blanche Megrim to dinner in penance for selling her precious Buddha. He squeezed my arm and his big brown eyes were lit with mischief.

"Now that you have the award," he said, "they expect you will retire gracefully. Personally, I know better. But perhaps you should enlighten them?"

I smiled down at him from my lofty new height of power. "Enlightenment is right up my alley, Krish," I said. "We're alike in that, Buddha and myself. We may turn a little green from the ravages of time, but we've got staying power!"

* * *

We had a little celebration that night. Lloyd Agate stopped by after his night shift ended and we phoned David to tell him my good news.

"Can you imagine it, Davy?" I said with great glee. "Me, head of the Curriculum Committee? I can undo some of the nonsense Sheffield's wreaked over the last few years, I can teach Shakespeare again! I've got a whole new lease on life."

"Me, too," he said. "I'm going to be a detective."

"You're *what?*"

"Julian Stockfish was going broke with that detection business of his, so I bought a partnership."

"You're not giving up acting?"

"Of course not. It's a sleeping partnership, really."

"Except when you happen to wake it up for a particularly interesting bit of snooping?"

He laughed. "You don't need a license to invest money, and I'm not ready to give up acting." His voice turned serious now. "But I need this, Winnie. It's important to me."

"You can't save the world, kiddo," I warned him. "Not even *with* a detective license."

"I know that. But you can give it a damn good run for its money."

When I hung up, I joined the others in the kitchen for coffee and the only dish Sarah knows how to prepare—sardine sandwiches. Merriman came trotting down the back stairs with that bottle of Dom Perignon Hazel had left in my Cave on Edgars morning.

"There's no use letting this go to waste," he said. "Besides, I thought—"

Lloyd Agate had shipped Hazel's body back to Dakota that morning, in the company of a silent and ravaged Philip Vail; in spite of our present festivities, she hadn't left any of our minds since that misty evening on the riverbank, and it would be a long time before I forgot the look in Philip's pale blue eyes.

"I thought," Eddie continued, "a little wake in her memory. As we knew her in the days before confusion."

He was about to open the bottle when Lloyd clamped a big paw down on it. "I don't think I'd do that, Doc," he said.

I looked up, surprised. "But Lloyd—"

"Why did she send the wine?" he asked me. "She could've put the note on those white roses. After she shot at you, we were worried about bullets, not wine."

"That's a lot of oatmeal, Lloyd!" I said. "You don't really think—"

"Let me take it down and get the lab to test it," he insisted.

I shuddered. "Take it, Lloyd. Get rid of it. If you test it, don't tell me. I don't want to know."

Merriman trotted into his parlor and returned with a geriatric bottle of sherry. "I've been saving this for best," he said, "and I have a little announcement of my own to make. Sarah, my dear, will you pour out?"

When we all had our glasses, he cleared his throat and began.

"As Winnie, here, knows and has probably by this time trumpeted to the four winds, I have been made the heir of my Uncle Horace's fortune. There was a bit of talk for a time about moats and messuages and stately homes and so on, and that would've been intriguing, of course, but hardly practical. So tiring, riding to hounds. Anyway, what with one thing and another—death duties, personal obligations the old boy incurred—"

"You mean the mistresses and those palimony suits," I said.

"Ahem. Yes. Any road, there wasn't a princely sum left over. I'm richer than I *was*, certainly. And I propose to devote the money to putting that new furnace in this place. Two furnaces, as I understand. Plenty of oof for that in old Horace's coffers, and I want no arguments. I'm of age, of sound mind—more or less—and I've made my decision. In the morning, Harvey Bettendorf will be here to begin tearing out the old furnace, so there'll be no sleeping in."

"One furnace, Merriman," I said. "I'll buy the other."

"When?" said Sarah. "Once Stanway found out he didn't need

to blackmail you to keep your mouth shut about his deal with Vail, he decided he didn't need to buy your books for television, either."

"And good riddance, say I!" cried Merriman. "Old Hyde's much too good for him!"

"Damn right," said Lloyd. "Guy turns out real crap, Doc. You see that cop show of his? Any real cop that came to work in a silk suit would get laughed off the force."

"Except maybe Rat-Cheese Colby," I muttered.

"And your new contract seems to have returned to the realm of myth again." Sarah sighed. "I don't see how we can refuse Eddie's offer."

He smiled and refilled my glass with sherry. "Certainly, Winnie," he said. "Bow to the will of the rich and mighty. Just consider it Dutch treat."

When Lloyd had gone, while Sarah was taking her last shower of the day, I retreated to my Cave for a final Turkish Delight. On my desk lay the heap of mail I'd meant to open for the last week and kept avoiding. There was a bill from the dentist, a promotion from a pizza parlor, and a letter in a pale green envelope. The handwriting was a woman's, a youngish, sprawling hand; it was postmarked Torrington, Wyoming. There was only one sheet, a garland of flowers across the top.

"Dear Winston," it said. "I've been reading your books since I was a kid, and they gave me the idea I might like to be a writer, too. I have been working on a mystery novel. Do you think, if I sent it to you, you could help me get it published? Do you think, if I found a good agent? Do you think I should come to New York? Do you think I could make it, if I tried?"